I0749274

Where Oceans Hide Their Dead

Where Oceans Hide Their Dead

A Novel

John Yunker

Where Oceans Hide Their Dead: A Novel

By John Yunker

Published by Ashland Creek Press

www.ashlandcreekpress.com

ISBN 978-1-61822-082-0

Library of Congress Control Number: 2018910845

This is a work of fiction. All characters and scenarios appearing in this work are fictitious. Any resemblance to real persons, living or dead, is purely coincidental.

Cover design by Rolf Busch.

To Bobbie, in memory

The earth shall soon dissolve like snow,
The sun forbear to shine;
But God, who call'd me here below,
Will be forever mine.

—John Newton

As long as there are slaughterhouses,
there will always be battlefields.

—Leo Tolstoy

Part I

Robert

1.

The killing begins at dawn.

Men and barely men spill out of the backs of rusted pickup trucks. Some are dressed for the job, wearing green rubber boots and bloodstained white overalls; others are in torn jeans, barefoot, shirtless. They carry axe handles or bats or pieces of rebar.

They take their time, yawning themselves awake, slowly cresting the craggy hill, pausing to take in the windblown waves in the shallow distance, then divide themselves as they approach their victims diagonally, picking up the pace, then swinging with purpose.

The victims, seals no more than a year old, scatter, clouds of sand and dirt rising. When one squirts through the tightening gyre, a man gives chase, cutting it off before it reaches the safety of water. He batters the creature into stillness, sticks a knife into its belly.

It takes a deep-seated desperation to do this sort of work, but in this part of Africa desperation is more abundant than jobs. That's what Noa had told him. She told him of the sands spotted black with blood, the mother seals, separated from their pups, helpless bystanders to the slaughter, heads swaying, sepulchral, their guttural voices calling out to lifeless bodies. And, as the men piled the bodies like sacks of soil onto the backs of pickups, the mothers made their sad retreat to the ocean, some with fatal injuries of their own.

The seals suffer this carnage every year, and still they return to these same sandy, rock-strewn shores. Robert suggested the seals were stupid, but Noa disagreed. *They have run out of desolate beaches*, she told him. This has been their home for thousands of years; they will not go down without a fight. *The seals*, she told him, *are the mirrors of our sins.*

Noa told him all of this more than five years ago, when they shared a ship's cabin and she was a hardened activist, he a seasick wannabe. They were passengers on a ship that placed itself with regularity between whales and whalers. Hull against hull, smoke bombs and stray bullets and shrapnel. Dangerous work by any standard.

But this was never good enough for Noa. She was impatient to do more, risk more. When the world awakened to their battle on the water and the cameras outnumbered the crew, she said, she would move on to those animals the world still ignored. There were so many species without sponsors, without any hope of attention.

The Cape fur seals brought her to tears. She swore that she would come down here one day and place her body between the seals and those spiked wooden clubs.

Robert had sworn to join her. He swore it the last night they spent together, both of them squeezed into a one-man cot in their vessel in the far North Atlantic. He swore to follow her wherever she went, and he intended to make good on his promise.

But he was an FBI agent, working undercover, sworn to a higher power, so any promise he'd made—and he'd made many—had been, in the end, a lie.

2.

In the dark of early morning, Robert pulls off the dirt road, behind a strand of dust-covered bushes. On the horizon he sees the moon reflected off the waves. This was supposed to be the road to Dunkel Beach, but without any signs he has been going on word of mouth.

A week before, he'd begun his Namibian odyssey 500 miles up north, at the Cape Cross Seal Reserve. There, Robert had comfortably played the part of tourist on holiday, with so many others around to blend in with. Slow-roaming herds of travelers discharged from tinted-windowed buses. Shoulder to shoulder with aimless, younger, round-the-world types with backpacks and beards.

He had been to Namibia years before, back when he was fresh out of the FBI Academy and eager for passport stamps. He spent two weeks on the trail of arms traffickers on their way south from Angola. So he was already familiar with the country's slower pace, crooked cops, and crumbling infrastructure. The money, in U.S. denominations, was the only thing that kept this part of the world running—though judging by the number of Chinese tourists he'd seen crowding the viewing area, he suspected *yuan* might be equally effective these days.

Robert gazed over the dusty beach, undulating with the motion of thousands of brown fur seals, crowded together like the humans who were watching them. It was the first hot day that week, and many of the larger seals stood high on their black flippers, noses vertical, as if posing. Others lay prostrate, pups at their sides, nursing. And amid these motionless bodies, seals commuted to and from the water, pausing every so often to bark at a competitor or howl at nothing in particular—or at least nothing Robert could discern. Even with wind blowing hard out to sea, the chorus of yelps and grunts was loud enough to drown out the sounds of the tourists and their beeping cameras. Robert wondered if the tourists knew that this beach was often the scene of great violence.

His eyes swept the beach, then turned to study the faces of the crowd.

She was not there.

He got back in his rental car and headed south, meandering from one increasingly desolate port town to another, where the number of travelers dwindled along with his hopes of finding her. The locals weren't of much help. Any time he asked someone about seal culling, he got that familiar, off-putting look—as if he were one of *them*. An activist. One of those outsiders bent on telling Namibians how to live their lives.

Just last night, in the harbor town of Lüderitz, he asked the clerk at his motel, a heavyset woman transfixed by a *Real Housewives* rerun, where he could find seals. She shook her head and handed him the same faded brochure from the Cape Cross Seal Reserve he'd been given a dozen times before. In fading light, Robert walked two blocks from the motel to the rocks bordering the shallow and mostly vacant port. A few lonely sailboats kept rhythm off to one side. At the end of a pier were two rusted fishing trawlers, the remnants of a once-thriving industry.

Robert's mind began entertaining thoughts of getting in his car, returning to Windhoek, completing the round-trip journey back to Washington. Gordon, his former boss, would surely take him back. Gordon had always said that it took a decade to create a reliable federal agent, and at thirty-five Robert was more than a decade into his tenure. Agents quit all the time in fits of madness or frustration, only to return a few days or weeks later. This little detour would qualify as madness. Searching for a woman he once believed dead, a woman who wanted nothing to do with him. A history he was now hoping to rewrite even though a part of him had grown comfortable with the current narrative. There was a comfort of sorts in assuming that, if alive, she would not take him back anyway. Perhaps he was not as scared of failure as he was of success—to find her and learn, finally, whether there could be a future on the other side of all those memories.

Robert stepped into a small bar named Kappy's and sat next to a man named George to watch a rugby match. George was chatty, and Robert's instincts told him that the man was worth listening to. George had been in town a week waiting for a road construction job to begin, drinking through the paycheck he hadn't yet earned. He talked about the jobs he had worked, meandering his way up the coast from South Africa. Fisherman. "I spent more time bent over the rail than catching anything," he said. Furniture mover. "Wrenched my *bladdy* back hoisting a fridge into the truck."

But there were worse jobs out there, he told Robert, pure *kak* jobs. "You ever seen them harvest seals?" George asked. Robert shook his head and bought him another round. "Check here, my friend. It ain't like plucking grapes." And that's when George told him about Dunkel Beach.

And now, with Dunkel Beach ahead of him somewhere in the darkness, Robert gets out of the car and turns his back to the biting wind. He should have packed a jacket. Even though the days feel like Southern California, the nights and mornings feel more like Northern Ontario. He continues down the road, and after about hundred yards hears the surf over the wind. Then the smell, foul and fishy. He stops and tilts his head and hears the yelps and grunts of a seal colony.

Noa had said that the sealers arrived before daybreak and were long gone before any tourists showed. The killing device of choice was not a gun. Guns were rare and bullets expensive. But wooden clubs were plentiful. The leaders usually carried the official killing tool—the hakapik, which looked like something mountain climbers use, a sharp ice pick at the end of a long handle with a flat hammerhead on the other side. The dull end was used for crushing the skull, the sharp end for dragging the body. From a distance, Noa said, the men could almost be mistaken for farmers sowing the land.

For so much of his adult life, the early hours of the day were the least enjoyable, not just because he was often hungover or sleeping in a third-world hotel room but because he always associated dawn with death. Years ago, while in training at the Academy, the early hours were used to test them. In the pre-dawn hours they were shouted at for yawning, for not reciting the correct phrase at the correct moment, ever reminded that they may be called upon to protect a life or take a life before the rest of the world was awake. Robert was excited back then, in his early twenties and aimless and eager to be a part of this new workforce, one that operated outside of business hours.

Robert hears movement to his left, swivels to make eye contact with a large cat. A jaguar, he thinks, but smaller. A broad, curious face, eyes catching the moon, then turning and sliding into the bushes. A sighting so brief Robert begins to wonder if he saw it at all.

Robert gets back in his car and checks his watch. It's only 4:45. On the horizon he sees a tiny light, most likely a fishing trawler. Most likely illegal. He watches the light move slowly across the windshield and thinks back to that night in his hotel, high above LAX, watching the lights of planes approaching the runway, wondering if he would succeed in his first solo undercover assignment.

His name was Jake for that role, and he was in LA for the Rights for Animals Conference. Playing the part of animal rights activist, he dressed in old jeans, a faded black T-shirt, Converse sneakers, and a wristband with the word PEACE imprinted on it.

He spent the first day downstairs wandering the sessions, from *Activism Against Vivisection* to *In Defense of Predators*. As an FBI agent, he was there to meet Neil Patrick Cameron, known as Aeneas, the infamous founder of the anti-whaling organization Cetacean Defense Alliance. As Jake, he was there because he was committed to the cause, eager to join the next boat sailing out to do battle with whaling ships.

When he met Aeneas at the CDA booth, Jake told him of his desire to join the crew. Aeneas told him the boat was full and to try again next year.

But Jake wouldn't be around next year; Robert and the FBI

didn't have the luxury of time. They were pursuing a domestic terrorist known as Darwin who had been torching mink farms in Idaho and releasing the animals. Darwin had caused millions of dollars in damage, which didn't include lost revenue for the farms. No one knew what Darwin looked like, and Robert suspected that it was Aeneas himself. What he did know was that Darwin was a member of the CDA and would be on that next boat out.

How could an outsider become an insider in less than a day? Robert was asking himself this as he exited a session and stepped straight into a woman in a long madras skirt and a white KISS ME, I'M VEGAN tank top. She grabbed his arms for balance, and he grabbed her waist. After an awkward moment, a moment that lasted a half second too long, a half second he would replay forever, she pulled back. Or he released his hands. When their eyes met, he smiled, and she wrinkled her brow. Then she began to walk away.

"Do you get many takers?" he asked.

She stopped and turned around.

"Your shirt," he said.

She eyed him suspiciously, studying him from head to toe. "You're vegan?"

"Of course," he said.

"Then how do you explain that?" She pointed at his wristband, the wristband that he suddenly realized was made of leather.

He smiled sheepishly. "I don't eat it; I just wear it."

"Perhaps you should visit the orientation session. Room 105. And take notes." She shook her head, and he watched her walk away. She had seen right through his disguise, though not far enough.

A car door slams, and Robert is jolted awake, eyes blinking into the dawn. He reaches up and grabs the steering wheel, pulls himself upright. The sun is still low, his car's shadow outstretched toward the water, and he notices a vehicle parked a hundred yards ahead of him.

It is an old commercial van made less so with bumper stickers wallpapered across its olive-green exterior. A roof rack carries large plastic bins of various sizes and colors. On another continent Robert would dismiss this heap as a bunch of surfers getting a head start on the waves. But not here, not now. These people are getting a head start, all right—but not on the surf.

Four people emerge, three men and one woman, a blonde with a ponytail. One of the men carries a video camera. The others carry signs. The woman is wearing sunglasses, and Robert can't tell if she's Noa, not from this far back. Noa's hair was dark when he was with her, twisted into dreadlocks. He curses himself for not packing binoculars.

He climbs out of the car and carefully approaches, keeping his distance. He watches them pause at the top of the hill before descending out of view.

What will Robert say if it is Noa? *Funny meeting you here? I just happened to be in the neighborhood? Took a wrong turn at Windhoek?*

And what if it's not her? What will he say then? The sightseeing line won't hold up, not at this hour, this far south. The truth is tempting but too risky. These people will be on guard as it is, and he'd only be perceived as another threat, particularly if he asked the whereabouts of one of their own.

But if he can't play the activist or the tourist, what role is left for him to play?

He notices his right hand behind his back, checking on a phantom gun. It is a strange feeling to be entering a situation, like so many others in which conflict appears inevitable, and not to be carrying a weapon. Though he had spent the previous twelve years silently resenting the weight of it, the perpetual pressure against his lower back, now that he is without it he feels unbalanced and vulnerable. His mind must adjust to a life of avoiding conflict rather than abetting it. From now on, evasion, not engagement, will be his life.

When he crests the hill he surveys the chaos unfolding on the shore below him. Spread across a sloping beach the size of a football field are hundreds of seals, yelping, heads waving, pups scattered about like schoolyard backpacks. Among them are a dozen men in two groups on opposite sides of the beach, swinging clubs at flapping, squirming pups.

Parked on the sand are two old pickup trucks, one towing an empty utility trailer. How did these trucks not wake him, he wonders, then notices the tracks extending along the sand for another half mile; they'd arrived by a different route.

Two of the activists stand far away, at the waterline, urging seals to escape, holding their pointless signs. The woman is screaming at one of the groups of men, bumping into them sideways to slow them down. This could be Noa—she'd always been the first to jump into the action—but this woman's body is leaner than Robert remembers.

Far off to the right is the activist with the video camera, a man in his twenties with shaggy brown hair and a beard to match, approaching another gang of sealers. His fellow activists, signs held high, form a backdrop. Two of the sealers are gesturing at the camera.

Robert picks up his pace until he is jogging down the hill, still unsure of what he is going to do or say. He needs to be closer to be sure, to see her eyes, but this is hardly the right time. He should wait, stay up on the hill. Yet something propels him toward the fight. Years of habit? Or maybe the simple fact that he wants the seals' crying to stop.

He gets closer, until he is standing behind one of the sealers, a kid maybe sixteen or seventeen years old, with no shoes and no shirt, oblivious to Robert's presence. As the kid raises high a rough-hewn wooden bat, Robert grabs it and pulls him around, and the kid's eyes widen with surprise.

The kid pulls back on the tool until Robert lets him have it. The end that Robert was holding is stained dark red, as are his hands.

"Beach closed," the kid says.

"So what are you doing here?"

The kid swings the bat at Robert, who ducks, then lunges into the kid's abdomen, knocking him to the ground. He grabs the bat again and turns to follow the woman's voice. Still standing, still screaming. He continues across the sand toward the cameraman.

The seals are kicking up clouds of sand and dust, and he now understands the meaning of the bandannas across mouths. The process, if there is one, entails men circling the seals, scaring them into one another, and, eventually, one of the men landing a lethal blow. But so few of the blows are lethal. The seals keep changing direction, the objects of some primeval game of baseball.

A young man is stabbing a seal in the eyes with a Bowie knife. The throaty sounds of crying fill the air, and pups scurry about with milk leaking from their mouths. And now, drips and pools of red in brown-and-white gull guano on rock are mixed together, a grisly Pollock.

The cameraman is surrounded. The boy that Robert disarmed shouts at him, then slaps him hard enough for his camera to fall to the ground. A man in prison-orange pants comes forward and strikes the cameraman with a club, knocking him to the ground.

Robert comes up behind the man with the orange pants, grabs his long hair, and pulls him hard onto his knees. Then he pushes him onto his back and steps on his windpipe. He uses the bat to wave off the other men as they gather around.

"You all right?" Robert asks the cameraman, who is sitting up.

"Yeah, mate. Thanks."

A handful of sand hits Robert in the face. The kid stands a few feet away, improvising. More men have joined the semicircular fray, with Robert and the activist in the middle like renegade seals.

"You better get out of here," Robert says to the cameraman. "You and the rest."

"Can't leave you here."

"I'll be fine. Grab your camera, join the others. Now!"

The activist hesitates, looking for an opening between the bodies and bats.

"Leave him," Robert says, pointing with the club at the man under his foot. "Or your friend never gets up again."

Bodies part, and Robert watches the activist scramble up the hill toward the others. The woman at the top is taking pictures.

Seven of them now surround Robert. The shortest of the lot, a bearded man in a red T-shirt with a faded white soccer-ball print, takes a step forward.

"Man, you in trouble. Big trouble."

"Am I? That's funny. So's your friend. He's going to suffocate in thirty seconds if you and your friends don't back the hell off."

Robert increases pressure on the man's neck and watches his eyeballs bulge. The bearded man hesitates. Robert apparently picked the right captive.

"Make that twenty seconds."

The man takes a half-step back. "Let him go, and we won't kill you."

"That's very generous." Robert lifts his foot enough for the man to gasp for breath. "I don't want any trouble. I've got no dispute with any of you."

Then he steps off. The man lies there coughing.

"I'm leaving now," Robert says. "Peacefully."

"I don't think so." The bearded man smiles and displays a knife covered in blood, most likely the blood of seals. Human or animal, it all looks alike, and the thought enrages Robert. He wastes no time meeting the man halfway, leg to groin and both hands on his arm, twisting until the knife is on the ground, then spinning around with the man's head in a vise grip. Robert, on one knee, fumbles and then finds the knife.

"Back up. All of you!" He holds the knife under the man's jaw, tight enough so he won't dare open that mouth of his.

"Back up!"

Robert stands, pulling the bearded man along, and takes a step forward. He feels a wave of confidence he hasn't felt in a long time, realizing that he doesn't need a handgun. Any old knife will do. And he isn't afraid of them, isn't afraid of anyone, the adrenaline giving him the courage he thought had drained away.

The men shuffle out of his way, and he continues ahead, dragging the bearded man along by his sweaty neck. Robert feels almost disappointed. He wanted to fight them all right now, live or die, on this beach. That's what Noa would have done, and she would have loved him now, if she were watching.

Halfway up the hill, a safe distance from the others, he turns and pushes the bearded man to the ground.

Robert walks quickly up the hill, then stops and glances back. The man is still watching him, while the others have gotten back to work, dragging seal carcasses, clubbing the ones still moving. Robert looks down at his knife, covered in the blood of the murdered seals, now also mixed with the blood of one of their murderers.

3.

In the distance, Robert watches the van cough exhaust as it wakes itself. A sliding door slams shut, and it lurches away. He looks back toward the beach. The men have returned to their gruesome task, and he feels his anger rising. He takes a step toward the beach, then another. Maybe this is how he is meant to go—one final fight, witnessed by no one, on behalf of no one. A crazy, futile fight.

Then he thinks of Noa. He never got a good look at the woman, and now she's in the van and about to get away. He jogs to his car, and in a few minutes the dust cloud of the van is in his sights. It is headed south, slowly, over the pockmarked dirt road. He keeps a safe distance, needing only to follow the swirling dust. The road veers inland to a gravel road, and the temperature climbs. Robert follows the van as it continues south through a desert of some name—Namibia has so many it's difficult to keep track.

One hour turns to two, gravel to pavement. There are few signs of human civilization apart from occasional trucks and tour caravans of Land Rovers. The van slows as it approaches the closest thing to a town, and when it pulls over at a petrol station Robert continues on for another few hundred yards before parking behind a small warehouse. He gets out and watches around from the corner as the occupants stretch. He hopes for another look at the female, but she remains in the van. He tries to remind himself that this woman looked nothing like Noa, but the dust and the heat has turned his mind against itself. Perhaps Noa has grown an inch, bleached out her hair. He can imagine anything right about now.

The van has South African plates, and he has to stop himself from memorizing the numbers. Old habit. What's the good of memorizing a license plate when you can't run it through a computer? He is no longer a man with access to databases and websites that few others will ever see. He is a civilian now, living in the center of society instead of lurking about in the shadows. He must play by its rules, abide by its natural laws. And remind himself every morning that he is not so special after all.

He watches the activists get back into the van as two boys approach him, kicking a half-inflated soccer ball. They stop and watch him. He considers for the briefest moment a pick-up game. Down here in the dirt and scrub, using steel drums as goalposts and laughing as the boys play keep-away with the ball and not thinking about anything but the game at hand. If only he could let the van go and everything else along with it. Instead, he only nods to them before returning to his car.

After another hour of heading south, it dawns on him that this van is not headed for a beach but rather the border. Headed back to wherever it came from.

It is night when they reach the Vioolsdrift border crossing—two lanes funneling past fencing and a gate and, beyond that, a two-lane bridge over the Orange River into South Africa. The bright lights illuminating the checkpoint make Robert feel as though he's approaching Las Vegas at night.

Three cars back, Robert watches the van empty and sees uniformed men rummage through bags, looking for drugs or hoping for a bribe. His hopes rise as the guards line the passengers up against the van, the woman at the far end.

She is attractive—but she is definitely not Noa. Her face is long and angular, and her shoulders slump as if from irritation or exhaustion. She's in her late twenties perhaps; Noa would be a good ten years older. And this woman has skinny legs and a narrow waist. Noa had curves.

Robert hears himself sigh. Now what? He could turn around and head north again. Find another beach. Another group of activists. Or he could keep following this van. Perhaps there will be others at its destination. Perhaps even Noa.

The cameraman Robert had saved—an Aussie, he guesses—is arguing with the uniforms. The other two activists, both younger—one skinny and the other pot-bellied and bearded—keep their backs stiffly against the van. As an FBI agent, Robert would have dismissed this motley crew as amateurs or hobbyists. Certainly not ecoterrorists. Yet that is what they are, by this country's standards—by most countries' really.

When it is his turn in the queue, Robert knows he will have little trouble, as the guards had exhausted themselves on the others. Robert gets out of the car and watches the men poke at the seats with their rifles.

"Did you enjoy your time in our country?" a uniform asks. Robert studies his blank face to find any hint of cynicism.

"Not particularly," Robert replies.

As Robert is waved across the bridge, he can't help feeling sorry for its resident captives. So poor and yet so close to this relatively wealthy southern neighbor. How hard it must be to keep your pride when you struggle to earn in one year what a South African makes in a month. And how easy it is to cling to traditions, no matter how vile, when those rich relations slum it up here on vacation and start lecturing you on how to run your country, how to treat your people, your animals.

Across the river the road surface evens out, and the van accelerates. It heads south for another hour and then turns right, toward the ocean. After another hour, the van passes the welcome sign of Port Nolloth and slows as it approaches a town with few lights or buildings but a bay just beyond. Robert can smell the sea again.

The van turns down a narrow street lined on both sides by one-story, windowless warehouses. Robert hesitates before turning to follow and smiles when the van pulls over to one side. He continues straight and pulls over a block away.

He walks back and peeks around the corner of one of the warehouses as the van's occupants carry duffel bags and coolers through an open door. The ocean is maybe three blocks away, yet the area stinks like a fish processing plant.

After the activists disappear into the building, Robert drives by and, squinting through the darkness, makes out a tiny sign on the front door: SEAL RESCUE OP SA.

He finds a backpacker hostel a half mile away and books the weekly rate. In the darkness of a shared room he crawls into a lower bunk. He wishes he had alcohol as he stares at the springs above, listening to the sounds of snoring, trying and failing to picture her face.

He abandons the idea of sleep and sets out again, in search of a bar. He finds one two blocks away, with a multi-colored, cheery-looking façade that inside is low-ceilinged and dimly lit, with dark wood and a Windhoek Lager sign on the wall. Two couples circle a pool table, drunk and singing into the wide ends of their pool cues. He takes an empty stool at the end of the bar, swaying on its uneven legs, and orders a whiskey.

After the first sip, he closes his eyes. He wants simply to shut out the crooked wooden bar and the faces glancing his way—but instead he is transported, unbidden, back to the hotel bar near LAX. After the animal rights conference had ended, after he'd failed to make inroads with Aeneas or his Cetacean Defense Alliance, he sat staring blankly at the television above the bright, noisy bar, composing in his head the report he would be sending to Gordon the next day, explaining he'd failed.

Then he heard a familiar voice. "Where's your bracelet?"

He looked over to see the woman he'd bumped into yesterday, or who'd bumped into him. She was wearing a white T-shirt and a wraparound skirt, a small pack slung over one shoulder.

"I must have lost it," he said.

"I'll bet you did."

"I only recently became vegan." He hadn't known the first thing about veganism until he showed up at the conference.

He remembers they'd talked about the baseball game on the television, ordered a few more rounds of drinks. Then she said, "It's a good thing you're a vegan, Jake."

"Why's that?"

"I don't sleep with carnivores."

The next morning, as he listened to the sounds of her in the shower, his eyes wandered from the Tibetan prayer flag she'd strung across the TV down to her backpack on the floor. Something told him that it contained most of what she owned, and he felt intoxicated—not only by Noa but by her lifestyle. Just then he wanted nothing more than to leave Jake behind—but more than that, he wanted to relinquish Robert, too, before he got completely lost in bureaucracy and undercover assignments, before he lived so many lives as other people that he would no longer be able to tell the difference. Noa was authentic—this, he suddenly realized, was what drew him to her.

Noa entered the room, towel hanging from her breasts. She told him she was catching a boat to Norway, and, still under her spell, he asked without thinking if he could come along.

"We'd have to share a bed," she said. "And you'll work for your passage." Her towel dropped as she walked toward him. "We all work for our passage."

"We?"

"The Cetacean Defense Alliance. CDA. Ever heard of us?"

4.

The next morning, Robert sits up in his bunk at the hostel, a slight hangover pushing against the inside of his head. He crawls out of his bunk and makes his way out to the car, then heads back to the seal rescue building. The narrow street, dark and lifeless the night before, is now busy with trucks lumbering through to the neighboring warehouses.

He approaches the steel door, takes a deep breath, and knocks. After a few seconds with no answer, he knocks again. He leans forward, pressing his ear against the door, but can hear nothing stirring inside. He waits a few seconds longer and turns away. The van is no longer parked out front; perhaps everyone is gone again. It would be just his luck to have let them get away.

"Yes?"

He turns back to see a young woman standing at the open door—the woman from the beach. She is barefoot, and her hair, no longer in a ponytail, covers half her face. She's wearing a white tank top that reveals something tattooed in Sanskrit on her left shoulder.

He wonders if she recognizes him from yesterday, but he sees only irritation in her eyes, making him feel like a door-to-door salesman who rings during dinner.

"I'm here to volunteer," he says.

"To do what exactly?" Her accent sounds British.

"Help the seals."

She turns her head to one side to shake the straggly hair from her eyes. Her face wears a weary expression that Robert suspects is a permanent feature. How could he have mistaken this woman for Noa?

"If you really want to help the seals, we take donations, preferably in cash."

"I'm broke."

"So are we."

The door closes with a metallic clang, followed by the sound of a deadbolt locking into place. Robert holds up a fist to knock again, then takes a breath. He hears Noa's voice in his head. *Animal activists fear outsiders. They'll take your money, of course, but they won't trust you. They can't afford to trust you.* Noa, who'd said this to Robert-as-Jake, was more right than she knew.

He walks down the street and stops when the smell hits him, a pungent, fishy odor coming from beyond a tall chain-link fence. He can see into a concrete courtyard with large, fenced-in dog kennels along the far wall. In each kennel is a blue plastic kiddie pool.

In the middle of the courtyard, taking up most of the space, is a much larger pool half filled with water, as well as the source of the smell—two seals resting on small jogging trampolines that abut the pool like miniature diving platforms. One of the seals, his wet fur glistening black, has lifted his head and is watching him.

He glimpses a suntanned woman in her late thirties, with close-cropped ash-blond hair, seated with her back to him on a folding chair in front of one of the kennels. She's wearing a sweatshirt and cutoff jean shorts and has a bandanna around her neck, and as Robert moves closer he can see she's bottle-feeding a pup, holding it in her arms like a newborn. She doesn't look up as Robert lets himself through the gate.

"You need a hand?" Robert asks.

She looks up at him and narrows her eyes. "Who are you?"

Robert tries to place her accent. South African, he thinks. "I'm Daniel. I've come to volunteer."

"American?"

Robert nods.

"You really want to help? We accept donations."

"All I have to offer is my time."

"Then you're of no use to us."

She stands and carries the seal into a kennel, places it gently on a wooden platform abutting the kiddie pool. The seals pops up on its small flippers and watches as she closes the gate behind her.

"Afraid he's going to run away?" Robert asks.

"He's sick. Can't be around the others."

She turns her attention to a much larger seal, slowly circling the larger pool in the middle of the courtyard. The seal's eyes are locked on her, and when she reaches into a large plastic barrel and holds up a live fish, the seal yelps loudly. She tosses the writhing fish away from the seal, and in an eyeblink the seal is underwater, and the fish disappears.

"What is this one's name?" Robert asks.

"Toby."

"He's looking healthy."

"Wasn't when we found him six months ago."

She heads for a door leading back inside the building. "Close the gate behind you when you leave," she says.

"So that's it?" Robert asks, raising his voice. "Thanks but no thanks?"

She looks back at him. "I never said thanks."

"Right. Because I didn't hand over a credit card."

"What do you want me to say? We've got enough people who can toss fish to Toby here. What we need are people who can help us keep that bucket filled."

He finds himself without a response, and he can only look at her, into those eyes that squint at him irritably—or defensively, or both. Yet he does not look away, holding her eyes in his. There's something about this woman that reminds him of Noa—the slow burn of her anger, perhaps, or the air of defiance, or the way she unflinchingly stares back at him.

Robert breaks his gaze and looks down at Toby, who is watching them both like a child witnessing his parents arguing.

"Guess I'll be leaving, Toby," Robert says.

The woman watches him as he closes the gate behind him. He is halfway across the street when he hears a man's voice.

"Hey, mate!" The Aussie cameraman is standing by the parked van. His beard looks as if it's grown an inch since Robert met him on the beach. He eyes Robert warily. "You followed us?"

"I did. And now I'm leaving."

"Hold up." He jogs over and stops Robert with a hand on his shoulder. He smells of cannabis. "I owe you a pint, mate. Name's Mark."

"Daniel," Robert says.

"How'd you make it out of that bloody scrum in one piece?"

"I showed them what it feels like to get hit with one of those clubs."

Mark smiles. "So, what the hell brings you to this sorry corner of the world?"

Robert sees the woman standing behind the gate, watching them.

"I came here to volunteer, but your colleague over there says I'm not needed."

"Who? You mean Syd?"

"Stay out of this, Mark," she says. "Let him be on his way."

"C'mon, Syd. He had my back up on Dunkel."

She eyes Robert suspiciously. "What was he doing up there?"

"Saving my arse is what."

"I was just trying to help," Robert says. "Fortunately, nobody about to be beaten or killed asked for a donation first, or I wouldn't have been of much use." He smiles at her, and she opens the gate and joins them in the middle of the street.

"Syd, you should have seen him," Mark says. "He took on a dozen of the bastards."

"You followed the van all the way down here?" she asks.

"I didn't have a map."

"Jesus, Syd. I'll manage him, if that's what you're worried about."

Syd takes another step toward Robert, and he does his best to maintain eye contact. Those eyes of hers, dark and a bit large for her head, are staring hard, as if she's trying to see straight through him, to learn everything about him through her sharp gaze alone. He wonders if she could possibly know, somehow, who he really is, and he feels himself preparing for recognition, confrontation, failure.

"We're not feeding you," she says at last.

"Fine."

"Or putting you up."

"You're making me an offer I can't refuse." Robert smiles, hoping to elicit a similar reaction. But she shows no sign of emotion, and Robert can't help but admire her stoicism. She would make a fine agent—a better one than he was, in fact.

"Come on, then." Syd turns.

Mark slaps Robert on the back. "Welcome aboard, mate."

Robert follows Syd back into the courtyard. He notices that some seals, like the one she'd been feeding earlier, are kept in enclosures while others have free rein of the yard. "Why do you keep them separated?" he asks.

"Quarantine," she says. She points to one enclosure. "Betsy there. She's got an infection. We've got her on antibiotics."

Robert watches Toby hop up a ramp leading out of the pool to a wooden platform just out of reach. He pushes himself up onto his flippers like a dog awaiting a treat.

"No, Toby," she says. "You've had your fill for the day."

"Why do you use live fish?" Robert asks.

"We don't want them acquiring a taste for dead fish. Puts them at risk when they're out at sea—they'll end up following the fishing trawlers. Fishermen shoot them."

"Really?" Robert says, playing dumb.

"Seals are competition," she says. "Though if those fishermen were honest with themselves, they'd be shooting each other. They all take far more fish out of the oceans than the seals."

She holds up a large plastic pitcher filled with milk. "This is what the others eat. Multi-milk and fish oil, blended with sardines or mackerel or whatever we can afford."

The enclosures are carpeted with kitchen safety mats. She gestures for Robert to follow her into a cage inhabited by an emaciated-looking pup.

"This is Onyx," she says.

"Nice name."

"It's the name of the beach she was found on. Up north, across the border. Not sure she's going to pull through."

Robert can see her ribs, the bones of her neck. It looks as though the air had been released from her blubbery body, leaving behind a skeleton almost human.

Syd places a towel on Onyx's head and straddles her. "You watching what I'm doing?"

Robert nods.

"We need to tube-feed her. And I need you to do exactly what I'm doing. You tuck her flippers under her body like this. And you hold her head firmly."

Syd gets back up and lifts the towel. Onyx writhes around, mouth snapping feebly.

"Watch the mouth," she says.

Robert does as instructed and soon has Onyx between his knees, her body pulsing under him like a miniature mechanical bull. Her round, wet eyes look up at him with fear.

Syd holds up a clear plastic tube with a funnel at one end. She grabs Onyx's mouth and gently slides in the tube.

"Keep an eye on her breathing," she says. Robert watches the nostrils flare irregularly. Onyx makes sad little guttural noises.

"How do you know you've gone in far enough with that?" he asks.

"Years of practice." She holds up the funnel with one hand and pours in a small bit of water. They watch it descend down the tube and into Onyx's mouth. Then Syd picks up a plastic water pitcher filled with milk and begins pouring in small doses.

"Why tube feeding?" Robert asks.

"They're too young for bottle feeding. Too weak. We need to get nutrients into them to fatten them up first. When they get some of their weight back, we can move up to bottles. Then, as quickly as we can, we move them to live fish. It's important they get used to feeding themselves—and not used to us."

Robert watches the last of the milk drain from the tube, and in one smooth motion Syd extracts it. Onyx lets out a sad little gasp, and Robert sets her free. The seal pushes herself up on her flippers and eyes Syd, then Robert, defensively. Robert backs away.

"I want you to stay with her a while." Syd tosses Robert an old, matted-down stuffed otter. "This is her mother. You sit with her as she snuggles with her mom. Socialization is just as important as food."

Robert sits on the floor and feels spilled milk seeping through the bottom of his jeans. He places the stuffed animal near Onyx, and the seal responds instantly, her nose running the length of the toy as if looking for a nipple. After a minute, Onyx relaxes, lengthens, and leans into it.

Robert looks up at Syd. Her eyes are on Onyx.

"She's stronger than she looks," Robert says, hoping to cheer her up.

"Toby came in looking just like Onyx. So there's hope." But she doesn't speak with conviction. She turns away and leaves Robert in the cage. He watches her enter the building.

Robert spends another hour watching Onyx as she falls asleep. Then, as quietly as he can, he steps outside the cage and closes it behind him. Onyx wakes and looks at him.

"Don't worry," Robert says. "I'll see you again soon."

INSIDE THE BUILDING, Robert finds Mark and the rest of the group seated in a break room with an open laptop playing Bob Marley. The cinder-block walls are covered with faded concert posters from the Red Hot Chili Peppers and Midnight Oil, and a Tibetan prayer flag hangs from the ceiling, its rainbow colored squares swaying in a breeze from a nearby oscillating fan. Though these flags are as common among activists as tattoos, he wonders hopefully whether this flag could be Noa's, a sign that she was here.

Mark introduces him to the others, all of whom Robert remembers from the beach in Namibia. The girl who'd slammed the door in his face, the one he thought might've been Noa, is Andra. Jeremy is their cook, mechanic, and all-around handyman; T.J. is a young Brit with tattoos crawling up his arms and neck as if preparing to invade his pale white face. No one offers last names—which, Robert remembers, is normal among activists.

"Sorry about shutting you out," Andra says. "I thought you were a cop. Or a Mormon."

"Mormons travel in pairs," says T.J. "Plus, they wear ties."

"Yeah, but don't they have casual Fridays or something?"

The others laugh. Robert feels his face flush. He needs to fit in better, but he hadn't had the luxury of time to grow a beard or get a tattoo. And now they are looking at him as if he is one of their fathers, home early from a desk job. His mind pulls up the script he had prepared as he finished his last drink at the bar the night before.

"I guess I am a bit clean-cut for this line of work," he says. "Truth is, I'm ex military."

T.J. looks at him with alarm.

"*Ex* military," Robert repeats. "I flew helicopters for the Air Force, then left for the private sector. In Seattle. My wife died of cancer two years ago. She was passionate about the seals. That's why I came."

Robert pauses, and as they all watch him, he knows he needs to offer more. "She begged me for years to come down here so we could join the fight. She was ready to quit her job, sell everything we owned. She begged me to do the same, said we might actually find ourselves along the way. But I never took her seriously. Always had excuses, another assignment waiting. Morning traffic. Establishing shot for some new television series. I always told her we'd do it next year—and then a year later, I'd push it back again. Until the day she coughed up blood over the dining room table."

"Jesus," says Mark.

"By then it was too late for her to get on a plane," Robert continues. "She died six months later. I know it's too little, too late, me being here. Alone. But her death left me with too much damn time to think."

"You never know," Andra says after a pause. "Maybe you *will* find yourself down here."

"Andra here is still looking," Mark says.

"Fuck off," Andra says.

5.

Robert spends the next day following Syd around the courtyard. Feedings begin at 8:00 a.m. By the late afternoon he feels a degree of confidence in his ability to corral a seal. Toby watches over them as they move from enclosure to enclosure. Every few hours Syd pauses to toss Toby a few live fish from the barrel of recirculating water.

As Robert watches Toby doing backflips in the pool, he can picture Noa standing right where he is now. This is just the type of organization she would be drawn to—teetering on the edge of insolvency, up against the steepest of odds and the most corrupt of governments. And, at the heart of it all, the fate of widely unloved and utterly vulnerable creatures—the Cape fur seal. The largest of the fur seals, an animal that hauls itself out onto land every year, not to relax but to breed. During these stressful months it places itself at the mercy of predators, which for much of the seals' early existence were limited to the four-legged variety—jackals and hyenas. Some seals breed on outlying islands, but the islands are small and are preyed upon by humans with boats. And what horrible irony that the land these seals require to keep their species going is the same land that is now threatening their existence. Noa would have fought to the end to protect these animals.

So where is she?

Robert looks up when Mark calls his name, and he follows him into the dining room, where Jeremy is placing bowls of beans and rice on the center table.

"I thought you weren't supposed to feed me," Robert says.

"I won't say anything if you don't."

In keeping with the group's philosophy, the meal is free of any animal ingredients. For Robert, who has been living off of French fries and energy bars, it feels like fine dining. He squeezes in between T.J. and Andra and listens as Mark talks about the situation with kangaroos in his homeland.

"Locals shoot at them for kicks," he says. "Like fucking pests."

"In the States, it's the deer," Andra says. "Different species. Same result."

Syd enters and notices Robert. He braces himself for a hasty exit, but she turns her eyes to the food, fills a plate, and takes it with her to her office.

Mark catches Robert's eye. "Looks like you passed," he says.

"Do you get a lot of new faces each year?" Robert asks.

"Oh, yeah," Mark says. "But they never last long."

"Syd usually scares them off," T.J. says. Robert is desperate to ask who might have been working here over the past five years. Was Noa one of the volunteers Syd scared away? He doubts it. Noa was intimidated by no one. If anything, Noa and Syd would have made a formidable team.

After dinner, Syd calls everyone into her office to plan for the next day's trip back to Namibia. Sitting at her desk, she studies her laptop. "Weather tomorrow is dry and clear. You'll leave at the usual hour." Syd points to the people going. She does not point to Robert. He raises a hand.

"No," she says, as if reading his mind.

Mark laughs. "Syd, he's got one helluva left hook."

"Exactly. I don't want any casualties this time. Just content. Video content."

"I'll keep my fists to myself."

"Next year, maybe."

"And what if there isn't a next year?"

Syd shakes her head. "There's always a next year."

When Mark heads out to the street to have a smoke, Robert follows him. The sky is clear, but with no moon the street is dark, and with the neighboring warehouses closed for the day, it's eerily quiet.

"That could've gone better," Mark says. "But she's right, you know. Those bastards aren't going anywhere."

"What's her problem with me?" Robert asks.

"I wouldn't take it personal," Mark says, exhaling a cloud of smoke into the night air. "You're new, so there's that. And she's been a bit pricklier than usual, what with our budgetary woes."

"Is that why she doesn't go up there?"

"She can't. They blacklisted her."

"They?"

"Namibia. They've got a photo of her up on the wall there at the border crossing."

"Why?"

"You haven't heard?" Mark lowers his voice. "She once had to be pulled off the Minister of Fisheries."

"It shouldn't have happened." Syd is standing back by the front door, her own cigarette glowing in the darkness.

"You lost your temper, Syd," Mark says. "You only did what most people have wanted to do for years."

"Don't you have packing to do?"

Mark sighs loudly and drops his cigarette, extinguishing it under his shoe. He picks up the stub and goes back inside.

Syd blows smoke at the sky.

"Mind if I have one?" Robert asks.

"Cost you a rhino."

"What?" he asks, feigning ignorance.

"Ten rand."

Robert hands over a bill. She holds the bill up to the flame of her lighter so she can see the rhinoceros illustration in green ink. "An elephant is twenty rand. Lions are fifty. Our natural resources, monetized. Fitting, really."

"What denomination for seals?"

"Seals are worth nothing here, at least not alive."

He leans forward as she lights his cigarette.

"I knew you had money on you." Her lips curl slightly, the closest thing Robert has seen to a smile since he arrived.

"I'm staying at a hostel. If you let me stay here, I'll pay you instead."

"I'll think about it."

"Have you tried to sneak across the border?"

"What do you think? They know me too well now by now. It's practically become a game—*Catch Syd.* I tried sailing up one year, wrecked the boat against the rocks somewhere near Onyx. Gave them a good laugh."

Syd lights another cigarette, and Robert watches her face. Her mind is lost—somewhere up north, he suspects.

"I used to visit the seals, before dawn, before it all began. My first year up there, I thought if I scared them all back into the water before the men arrived I could save them. But they wouldn't budge. What a scene I made, whooping and hollering and kicking sand at nursing mothers."

"I guess stubbornness is not unique to humans."

"Namibians say the seals are stupid. It's easier to kill them if they believe the seals can't think for themselves. But they're not stupid. This is their damn beach. They were here first."

Robert glances over at Syd. Her eyes focus on the darkness at the end of the street, as if she can see all the way to the water a half mile beyond.

LATER THAT NIGHT, Robert lies in his hostel bunk nursing a bottle of whiskey, his mind unmoored. He feels no closer to Noa now than before he left the U.S.

She's not here. This much is clear. But what if she was never here?

What if she is not even alive?

For five years, the guilt of her death weighed on him like body armor. When Aeneas offered an exchange for Noa's whereabouts, Robert did not hesitate to make the deal, even though Aeneas had every reason to lie, to put an ocean between them. Even though Robert had no reason to believe Noa was still alive.

But how could he not take a chance? So what if he had sacrificed his career and his life for an illusion; he knew agents who had died for less. And what if the universe was on his side for once?

Noa used to say, *You can't control the outcome, only your response to it.* Yet he struggled with the sheer passivity of new-age wisdom. The *letting go*. The *putting it out there*. That the universe somehow will make everything right if you only let it. He lives in a different universe, one that requires human intervention. And even then, things usually turn to shit.

Perhaps this journey will end in a similar fashion. He'd come down here trying to keep Noa's philosophy in mind—*if it's meant to be, I'll find her*. He knows he can't control the outcome. Yet he's not sure he'll be able to control his response to the outcome either, especially if she's not here.

His memories are another thing he can't control. Like the fictional wife he'd told the others about, he finds his past, real and undercover, becoming a chaotic jumble in his mind. Some use memories to escape to more pleasant times; Robert uses his to self-flagellate.

Like memories of Aeneas's ship. The *Eminence*. Robert didn't tell Gordon how he managed to get on board, as Noa's new boyfriend, only that he was one step closer to finding Darwin.

Midwestern bred, Robert had not grown up dreaming of oceans or sailing. The seas were always something other people enjoyed, people with extended families and second homes. People who spoke of Hawaii and Aruba as his family spoke of Lake of the Ozarks. During that first week on the boat with Noa, somewhere in the North Atlantic, Robert spent most days on his knees at the toilet. His body heaved with convulsions, as if trying to repel some strain of virus, in vain. Noa took pity on him, wiped his forehead, cleaned his face. In the dark, she was a soothing voice, a warm hand on his back.

When he finally found his sea legs, he began to hope that Darwin was not on board. He already had compiled a mental list of suspects. Tommy, the explosives expert, was at the top, followed closely by

Aeneas. But if Darwin were revealed, Robert would have to make the arrest, turn the boat around—and Noa would exit his life as quickly as she'd entered. And she would hate him forever.

Aeneas attacked whaling ships and, when none could be found, attacked fishing trawlers. Robert, as Jake, took part, sometimes by Zodiac, sometimes by helicopter. And at some point north of Svalbard, Robert resolved that he would never find Darwin, not even if Aeneas confessed.

What Robert did not expect was a confession from Noa.

One day on the ship's deck she told him about the fires that she had set, the mink she had freed, the alias she had used. Noa was Darwin. And Robert saw in front of him a woman just like him, living a double life.

If Aeneas had simply avoided cutting the lines of a fishing trawler, Robert might still be with Noa. But when one of the fishermen boarded the ship and held the crew at gunpoint, Robert drew his own gun—and in killing them, he also killed Jake. Before he could explain himself to Noa, swear that he would never harm her, tell her he would give everything up for her, she escaped in a Zodiac into the blinding white fog of the polar ice cap.

Robert, along with Aeneas, pursued by helicopter. But when he found her standing on unstable ice next to the upended Zodiac, he couldn't land anywhere near without the risk of shredding the ice she was stranded on. So he landed far away, and by the time he located her Zodiac again, his helicopter had sunk, and she was gone. His only salvation was her abandoned boat.

Returning to civilization alone, in silent mourning, was his purgatory, a fitting punishment for deceiving so many people, including himself. These people have different priorities, putting animals ahead of humans. That's what Gordon had said: *These people.* As if they were another species altogether. Which maybe they were. Robert had tried to become one of them—and he'd succeeded, for a time. Just not long enough. And now he is trying again. Placing animals ahead of people, placing Noa ahead of everything, to become, with a lot of persistence and a little luck, one of these people.

6.

Robert arrives at the sanctuary at 8:15 a.m. with another dull headache. The van is gone. Syd is waiting for him in Betsy's enclosure with an impatient expression. Betsy is squirming in her arms, as if trying to make a run for an ocean that isn't there.

"Sorry I'm late," Robert says.

"Come here," she says. "Take her."

"Why?"

"She's hungry, that's why. We need to feed the little ones every four hours until midnight. And we start at eight sharp, in case you'd forgotten."

Robert gets down on the concrete floor. Syd lifts Betsy by her fins and places her on Robert's lap.

The smell, even though he's growing more comfortable with it, still overwhelms. He instinctively wants to turn his head, but he can't bring himself to look away from Betsy's eyes, staring up at him, so helpless and searching. She weighs no more than an infant, relaxed in his arms, the suede-soft fur warm against his skin. Robert takes hold of the bottle, and when he nudges the nipple toward her mouth, Betsy locks onto it without hesitation, a persistent tug-of-war.

"Keep your fingers away," she says. "Her teeth may be small, but they hurt."

"Am I doing this right?" he asks over the sucking noise. Milk drips onto his lap.

Syd nods. "You sure you don't have any children?"

"The fact that I'm here should be evidence enough."

"And why *are* you here?" she asks. "Don't give me that bullshit story about the dead wife."

He glances up at her and feigns surprise as best he can. "Excuse me?"

"Why are you here?" She is staring down at him with a blank expression, and for a moment he can't help but admire her tactics—this enclosure her makeshift interrogation room, the seal pup on his lap keeping him in his place.

"What do you want me to say?" he asks, trying to buy time.

"The truth would be a good start."

"The truth?" Robert shakes his head, his mind racing. Had Noa told her about him? Or is she bluffing? "The truth is," he says, "I'm not even sure why I'm here."

"That makes two of us."

"I'm trying to help. Isn't that enough for you?"

"No."

"Fine. You can take over here and I'll—" He feels a sudden, searing pain and looks down to see Betsy's mouth clamped on his right thumb, the bottle bouncing off the floor.

"Hold still," Syd says. She reaches over and slowly pulls Betsy's jaw open. Robert can see she was right; the teeth are small but razor sharp. Robert pulls his hand back, blood dripping on Betsy's fur.

"I told you to keep your fingers away," Syd says irritably.

"It feels like she's ready for fish now."

"Give her to me." Syd pulls Betsy up into her arms. "Go wash that out inside. There's rubbing alcohol and bandages in my office."

Robert makes his way to Syd's office. Through the small window overlooking the courtyard, he can see Syd with Betsy, oblivious to him. Robert glances at the desk: a slew of papers, a laptop computer, a scattering of spare change. He opens a file cabinet, then another. Blood is dripping on the linoleum floor, and he pulls up his T-shirt to press down on the bite wound.

Then he sees her.

Noa. Staring back at him from a photo on the wall, a bulletin-board mosaic of photographs and news articles. In the photo, she is standing in the courtyard cradling a small seal in her arms, smiling like a new mother. Her dreadlocks are gone, her hair short and even darker than he remembered.

He reaches out and touches the photo, leaving a blood-red smudge, his fingers trembling, adrenaline surging. He backs into the desk, knocking papers onto the floor, then leans over to pick them up.

"What are you doing?" Syd is standing at the doorway.

"I couldn't find the—" He glances around the room.

She pushes past him and opens a desk drawer, pulls out a box. "You okay? You're all pale."

"Maybe it's the blood loss." He resists the urge to turn around, to meet Noa's eyes again through the photograph.

"Please. That's nothing," she says. "Take a look at this." She holds up her left hand and displays a row of scar tissue—teeth marks running across the palm of her hand like life lines. "You need to clean out that thumb."

Robert takes the box to the bathroom. With the water running over his aching thumb, Robert considers coming right out and asking Syd about Noa. What's the harm at this point? Syd already distrusts him; she already suspects he has an ulterior motive. Perhaps if he confirmed her suspicions she would tell him what he needed to know, if only to get him out of her way.

Then again, she's more likely to kick Robert out onto the street without telling him a thing. And then he would be just as lost as before, worse even, because now he knows Noa is alive. But where? In Cape Town, working to protect the African penguin? Or maybe she moved inland to defend elephants or rhinos.

He opens the box to find antibiotic ointment and bandages. Better to wait and to work, he thinks as he wraps a bandage around his wound. He'll continue to change light bulbs, clean toilets, scrape the ever-accumulating rust from the bars of the animal enclosures.

Besides, in quarantining Robert from the others Syd will, eventually, become comfortable around him. Maybe she'll even learn to trust him.

FOUR HOURS LATER, THE COURTYARD erupts in a symphony of pups begging for their food, bleating like sheep. Robert and Syd attend to each of them, repeating their morning ritual, the seals as hungry as if they hadn't eaten at all that day. Robert wants to let Syd feed Betsy, but she insists he go back in. He does, this time keeping a close eye on her mouth as she sucks down the milk. He even talks to her, telling her he was certain she meant him no harm. Betsy rewards his forgiveness by peeing in his lap.

And once everyone is fed and quiet, with the other team members still gone, the courtyard takes on a monastic feel. Robert scrubs out one of the kiddie pools while Syd walks from kennel to kennel, offering treats and the occasional soothing word. Robert feels a comfort in Syd's near-silence. Syd requires nothing of him other than to follow her orders, and this is something he's eager to do, with every chore getting him a step closer to the information he needs.

But there is more to it than that. With the pups splashing water all over the courtyard, he feels almost as though they are the parents of an unruly household. It's a comforting feeling—one he'd never known, having never been married, having never been a father. For the first time he can see the appeal of it, of the shared bond parents must have. When Betsy had peed on him, he'd looked up and caught Syd's knowing eye, a parent's eye, and he received, for the first time, a real smile.

He pauses while mopping a seal pen and sees Syd on the other side of the yard, cradling one of the younger pups. She talks to the pup in a voice Robert can't decipher, a voice that belies her hardened exterior. She is far more compassionate than she allows Robert to see, even if it's reserved for the non-human animals.

He continues to study Syd as she places the pup back in his kennel and stands up, wincing a bit as she straightens her back. She looks a few years older than Robert, and her face is worn around the edges, but her eyes are dark blue, her body and arms strong and forceful, and he finds it hard to look away from her. He's drawn to strong women in a way he can't articulate. His mother wasn't strong, and maybe that's why. His father ignored her, belittled her, and occasionally hit her, and Robert resented her weakness.

Is it any wonder he fell for Noa, a woman who he always knew would not hesitate to leave him behind? Before Noa, he was the one who did the leaving, a routine he had perfected through practice. It wasn't until Noa that he realized it hurts far less to leave than to be left behind.

He's intrigued by how similar Syd and Noa are. And, despite himself, he enjoys spending time around this seemingly cold-hearted woman, whose compassion he knows runs deeper than she shows. But she reserves it all for the animals, with nothing left for people—not even herself. She wears used T-shirts with stretched-out necks, and if she owns a bra Robert hasn't seen it. Somehow her bedraggled look has a certain allure. Or maybe it's that she reminds him so much of Noa.

Later that day, as he finishes mopping the floor, he catches her watching him from behind the live-fish container. Toby and Betsy are balanced on the edge of the pool, their heads bobbing up and down in silent begging. He approaches.

"Can I feed them this time?"

She nods. "Don't make it easy for them. If they can't catch fish here, they'll never make it when they return to sea."

"And when will that be?"

"Soon," she says. "I need you to fetch more supplies."

"For them or for us?" Robert asks.

"Both."

He follows Syd's directions to the local supermarket, and when he enters, he feels as if he stepped through a time machine: worn linoleum floors and narrow aisles, antique grocery carts. He feels cold steel in his hands as he navigates the squeaky cart through the aisles, tossing in cans of beans, bags of rice, onions, garlic, olive oil. Syd told him to get as many of the largest containers of fish oil he could buy with the money she gave him. But she hadn't given him nearly enough to cover what was in the cart. So he adds a dozen containers of fish oil, used to feed the seal pups, and charges everything to his credit card.

After leaving the supermarket, he heads to the city pier, where he pays a man named Martin 500 rand for two buckets of sardines. Back at the seal rescue, he pours the fish into the live-fish barrel.

In Syd's office he places the money she gave him on the desk. Syd glances up from her laptop but says nothing.

"I thought that might make you happy," Robert says.

"Get an extension on our utilities and we'll talk."

WHEN HE FINISHES spraying down the concrete floor, he spools the hose and then sits down on an overturned bucket and watches over his rubbery little charges. Now that Betsy has been promoted to the free-feeding pool, she has worn herself out wrestling with Toby. Now they lounge together on their diving platform, and they look so relaxed that Robert begins to feel as if he is an attendant at a country club.

"The water warm enough for you?" he asks.

Betsy eyes him curiously.

"Can I bring you anything? Mai tais, perhaps?"

Toby lifts his head to give him the same strange look as Betsy. Robert glances over at Onyx. She's still prostrate where he left her two hours ago. Syd won't admit it, but even Robert's unskilled eyes can see that Onyx is getting weaker by the minute.

He enters Onyx's enclosure. Though her body remains still, her eyes open slightly. He kneels, feeling the urge to stroke her neck, though Syd says he shouldn't. The less human contact the better—only what's absolutely necessary, she says. He has come to believe that this is her approach to her fellow humans as well.

He places his hand on Onyx's neck and feels the bones of her spine. He expects her to tense and push up, but she stays motionless and watches him as he pets her. He feels his eyes welling because he's petting her like a dog—the only response he knows—yet this is not a dog. This is a creature of the ocean, and he's powerless to read her mind. Then again, he hasn't had any luck with Syd either, so maybe the problem is his alone.

THAT EVENING, HE RETURNS to the courtyard on his way out for the day. In the twilight, Toby and Betsy, motionless, watch him. The only light comes from Syd's window. He can see her inside, typing on her computer. He could have left a half hour ago, but he's not ready to face the hostel again.

He goes back inside and pops his head into her office. "You want to go grab a drink or something?"

"I already have a drink." She holds up a whiskey bottle.

"How many rhinos will that cost me?"

She nods him over and pours him a glass.

"When's the last time you left this place?" Robert asks.

"What place?"

"This sanctuary. This town."

She looks up at the wall, at a calendar from the previous year. "Eight months."

"Where'd you go?"

"Cape Town."

"Vacation?"

"Funeral. My mother."

"I'm sorry."

"Why? She wasn't your mother."

Robert watches her drain her glass and pour another. "I think we should talk about Onyx," he says.

"There's nothing to talk about." Syd shakes her head dismissively.

"She's not doing well."

"No shit."

"You really hate me, don't you?"

"I don't hate you," she says. "I just don't trust you."

"Still?"

"You're not here for the seals."

"What makes you so certain?"

"You're in your mid-thirties, right?"

Robert nods.

"How many men in your particular demographic—clean-cut, professional manner—traipse halfway around the world with the sole intention of cleaning up seal *kak*?"

"I came here to fight the sealers."

"Right." She looks at him. "So you're not going to tell me, are you?"

"I told you already."

"Yes. Your wife. May she rest in peace."

Robert puts down the glass and heads for the door.

"Hold on a second."

He stops.

Syd sighs and looks down at her laptop. "Look, we're about to get our water shut off again."

"Yeah? So?"

"What are you paying at that hostel?"

"Twenty a night." He takes a step forward, waiting for her to look up. "Are you actually inviting me to stay here?"

"I'm out of options."

"What a charming offer. It's a mystery why you have trouble fundraising."

When she looks up at him, eyes narrowed, he smiles, mostly to show he means well but also because he's enjoying the moment. For once, he feels in control of what's happening here, even if only briefly. And, by staying here, he may be able to get one step closer to Noa.

"Well?" Syd says.

"Okay," Robert says. "Where do I sleep?"

"There's a cot in the utility closet." She extends a hand. "Prepayment required."

THE CLOSET IS CRAMPED and cluttered, and Robert has to keep the door propped open for air. In the middle of the night, he gets up to pee, and when he returns to the closet, in the darkness he trips over a broom, breaking it in two.

Syd is asleep in her office, and Robert sits down in the hallway on the floor, staring at the shrapnel, waiting, almost hoping she has heard and will emerge to investigate. But after ten minutes, with no sound coming from her office, he returns to his cot and to the stale, dusty air of the tiny room.

7.

EARLY THE NEXT MORNING ROBERT enters the courtyard to find Syd standing outside Onyx's enclosure. He looks down at Onyx. She isn't moving, her eyes closed.

"Syd?"

"She's dead," Syd says, not looking up.

"Syd?" Robert asks again, hoping to catch her eyes.

"Better now than later," she continues. "We have two pups getting dropped off this evening, and we need the enclosure."

Robert stares at Syd. Despite his time with her, he's taken

aback by her seeming indifference to this dead newborn on the concrete between them.

"What should I do with her?"

"Get the carrier and load up Toby," Syd says, heading for the street.

"Wait. Why?"

"It's time for Toby to go."

"Where?"

"Where do you think? The bloody ocean."

"This feels sudden."

"It's been six months. We don't have unlimited resources. Now go on. Get him loaded."

Robert maneuvers Toby into a large dog carrier. A few minutes later, Syd pulls up to the gate in a rusting red Toyota pickup. She barks out instructions to him as he helps her move the carrier into the back of the truck.

He stays silent as she drives them outside the town center, then onto a dirt road and around the bay, to the outer reaches of the port. He wants to talk to her about Onyx, as much for her as for himself. The apparent ease with which she distanced herself from this dead creature makes him wonder if he is going soft.

The concrete sidewalks and gravel parking lots give way to brown grass, strewn with large rocks and beer cans. A place where kids come to drink. A place where a young seal can slip easily into deep water.

As he exits the truck, Robert feels a drop of rain and looks up at the gray sky. Darker clouds approach. On Syd's instructions, he positions the carrier fifteen feet from the water's edge and then opens the gate. Syd stands next to the carrier as Toby peers out, looking up at the woman who has been his mother for past six months. He doesn't move.

"This must be difficult," Robert says.

"It's impossible to know what a seal is thinking."

"I was talking about you."

Robert catches her eyes for a brief moment before they both turn back to the carrier. Toby stays focused on Syd's face, waiting for those furtive eyes to return to his.

"As hard as it is for us, it's worse for him," she says. "He's all alone in that dark world. If he's lucky, he'll find his way back to his colony, maybe even find his mother. If he's not, he'll get snared by a fishing trawler or taken by a shark."

"Do you ever see them again?"

"Sometimes. We can tell by the tags. Franklin, a pup we rescued five years ago, turned up a week ago, just south of here."

"How'd you find him?"

"A fisherman had shot him in the head. Our phone number is on the tag. A beachcomber found him and called."

Toby continues to watch Syd from the safety of his carrier.

"Lift the back of the carrier," Syd says.

Robert does as he's told, and still Toby resists eviction. Robert holds up the back end of the carrier and waits patiently. He thinks back to the time his father dumped him off at kindergarten on his first day of school, two full blocks away because traffic was bad in front of the school and he was running late for work, leaving Robert to navigate the sea of parents and their more fortunate children, walking hand in hand as he tried to find his way to his classroom.

"We don't have all day," Syd says.

Robert steps away as she takes hold of the carrier. She begins to shake it aggressively as Toby struggles to wriggle his way back inside.

"Easy, Syd," Robert says.

But she doesn't stop until Toby tumbles out, landing hard on the ground. He pushes himself back up on his fins and climbs up to the highest rock, his enormous eyes staring at them.

"C'mon," Syd says, voice raised. "Off you go."

She nudges Toby along with her left foot, firmly, until Toby begins lobbing toward the water's edge.

"Easy," Robert says again, though he's not sure why.

"He's begging for food," Syd says as if reading Robert's mind. "But he's weaned. It's time he learns to fish on his own."

"Will he?"

"Some do. Some don't. The flipper tags on the carcasses that wash ashore tell us who died but not always why."

Toby turns his head and looks back at them from his tenuous perch above the water.

"Go on now," Syd says. She waves a hand, and Toby slips into the water without disturbing it. A few seconds later, ten feet away, Toby's nose breaks the surface.

"Go on!" she shouts.

Robert is surprised by the tone of Syd's voice, a tone he hasn't heard since the day she told him to leave. He looks back at her accusingly.

"You can't get attached to them," she says. "They don't belong to us."

"Doesn't mean you have to yell at them."

"You want them to be comfortable around humans? So the next time they haul themselves ashore and they see a man walking toward them carrying a bat, they offer themselves right up?"

"No, I—"

"If he pokes his head out of the water begging for fish from one of these trawlers, he's dead. People are the enemy. He needs to remember that if he's going to stand a chance."

Her eyes reflect the water, dark and moody, and he can feel her staring him down, as if he is the source of the world's misery.

She walks past him to the water's edge. "Years ago, when we lost our first pup, I didn't know what to do with the body. Do you bury it? Where do you bury it? Do you take it to the water to feed the sharks? This guy shows up one day saying he'll cremate the bodies and do it for free. I was naive and overwhelmed and didn't realize until a year later that he was selling the skins. Forty rand a body. The thing is, we could really use that money right about now. Onyx is dead, and that money would help keep others alive. But I can't do it. I just can't."

She turns to him, her face red. He wants to go to her, put a hand on her shoulder at the very least, but he knows she doesn't want that.

"I'll bury her," he says instead.

"Yeah?"

"Yeah. I'll do it after dark tonight. Not like there's not enough land around here."

She looks relieved, but a moment later she turns back to the water.

"Is Toby gone?" he asks, scanning the water.

"Yes."

Robert watches her walk back to the truck. He wonders how many times Syd has performed this sad ritual, bringing rescued orphans back to life and then kicking them out again.

Robert turns back to the water and waits another minute to see if Toby might surface again. Syd honks at him from the car, and he reluctantly gets in. Before he can fasten his seat belt, she is pulling away.

8.

That afternoon, when Robert returns from the pier lugging two coolers full of live sardines, he sees that the others have returned. The van is parked out front, with its doors open, luggage scattered about, and graffiti spray-painted all over it in neon-yellow—misspelled curse words and gang-like hieroglyphics.

Robert stops to inspect the graffiti, and Mark approaches, beaming. "Like what we've done with her?"

"I'll bet you made the border-crossing newsletter."

"It was worse, if you can believe it. Somebody threw shit all over the windshield. Happened at night when we were camping. It was windy as hell so we couldn't hear them. They dragged a seal carcass into the middle of the camp. Andra stepped on it in the dark when she went out for a squirt. Quite an alarm clock, she was."

"You know who did it?"

"Have a good idea. Like the kid with the cricket bat spray-painted the same color. And your old friend, the one who wanted your head. He's the ringleader. Guy with the beard—name's Bernard. He was unusually talkative when we ran into him the next day. Inquired about our new paint job."

"Did you get good footage, at least?"

"Plenty. They must have felt guilty for all the abuse because they gave us a wide berth." Mark lowers his voice. "Bernard was looking for you, mate. It's a bloody good thing you weren't up there."

"Don't tell Syd."

"Speaking of, how'd it go with Toby today?"

"Syd gave me orders, and I followed them. The usual."

Mark shakes his head. "She's got a lot on her mind these days, balancing the books. Or what's left of them. Heavy hangs the head that wears the crown."

THAT EVENING, AS THEY CROWD AROUND the kitchen table for dinner, Robert listens as they share their war stories. T.J. shows off the bruises he collected on their first day, when he got caught between a small pod of seals and a dozen men with bats and clubs. Andra talks about the tourists who signed up for their newsletter, at the same time providing a hundred dollars in donations. "Namibian dollars," she adds. "Which means it's like six bucks."

Robert glances down the hall. Syd had once again taken a plate and then retreated back to her office, where she's now reviewing the video footage from Namibia. Robert can see her through the half-open door, leaning toward her computer, her face unmoved.

After dinner, Robert invites them all out to a pub with the

promise of free beer. He hopes to stir Syd from her office, but only T.J. and Mark take him up on the offer.

At the pub, Robert learns that Mark is one of the elders of the group, that he'd learned of Syd from an interview he read online. He'd been wasting his life backpacking across South Africa at the time, so he decided to swing up north and lend a hand.

"I thought I'd be here for a few weeks at the topmost," he says. "That was four years ago."

T.J. has been here only a few months. As a renowned tattoo artist, he tells Robert, he can travel pretty much anywhere and make a good living. Mark peels up his shirt sleeve to reveal a tattoo of a seal on his upper left forearm with Latin script underneath.

"T.J.'s a Matisse with the irons."

"What does the text say?"

"'Make it a desert and call it peace,'" Mark says.

"Tacitus," T.J. chimes in.

Robert nods. He had heard the phrase before—many times, in fact. Noa used to quote it in her darker hours.

Around midnight, T.J. heads back to the sanctuary, but Robert coaxes Mark into staying for another round, which isn't hard to do. When Mark is on his sixth beer, Robert takes a chance.

"So, who's Noa?"

"Noa?"

Robert waits, letting the silence sink in. He can see that Mark is surprised to hear the name, but he can't read anything else from his face.

"How do you know her?" Mark asks finally.

"I don't. I heard her name."

"From who?"

"Syd. Did Noa used to work here or something?"

Mark nods, then drains his beer.

"Why'd she leave?"

"Why do you care?"

"I'm just curious. Where does someone go when they've left this part of the world?"

"Where?" Mark considers the question. "Noa used to say this place was the sixth circle of hell. Maybe she moved on to the seventh."

ROBERT IS AWAKENED BY A FLASHLIGHT in his eyes. Blinking through the glare, he sits up to find Syd hovering over him.

"Get up!"

He feels a jab in his ribs, and then another, realizing it is her shoe.

"Get the hell out of here," she says.

"What?"

"C'mon, move it. Out!"

"Wait!" Robert struggles off the cot, still dodging the swift kicks from Syd's feet, and the next thing he knows he's standing in the hall in his boxers dodging pieces of clothing, a tube of toothpaste, one of his shoes. "What did I do?"

"You know damn well what you did."

"What, Syd? What the hell did I do?"

"You lied to me." She smells of whiskey, and her body sways.

"Lied?" Robert's mind spins. Mark must have told her about his questions about Noa.

"Just get your clothes on and get out of here, you fucking cop, or spy, or whatever." She throws his pants at him. "I knew you were full of *kak* the day I saw you. You had the stench of government. The way you walked, all full of yourself, your tucked-in shirt."

"I can explain."

"Another fairy tale about dead wives and lost causes?"

"I'm not a spy."

"Get out."

He starts getting dressed, stalling for time. He puts one leg through his pants and trips on the second, falling into the wall. "Syd, you have to listen to me. I'm not a cop. Not anymore."

"I don't care what you are."

"My name is Robert Porter." He manages to put his pants all the way on.

"I said I don't fucking care."

"I'm looking for Noa."

She laughs. "Noa? Oh, that's rich. What are you? FBI?"

"Ex-FBI. I resigned a month ago."

Syd squints at him. "Ex-boyfriend, too, am I right?"

Robert says nothing.

"She told me about you," Syd says. "I thought you'd be older."

"What did she say?"

"It doesn't matter. You wasted your time. She's not here."

"Where is she?"

"As if I'd tell you that."

"Tell me, and I'll leave right now."

"You're leaving anyway."

She reaches over and yanks on his arm, dragging him toward the door. He pulls back, and she falls to the floor. He reaches down to help her, and she pushes him away.

"Get off me!"

Robert steps back while Syd scrambles to her feet.

"I'm sorry," he says. "But you wouldn't have let me in here if I told you the truth."

"So you used us in order to stalk some long-lost girlfriend? What a fucking farce. Said you wanted to make a difference. Was that another one of your bullshit lines?"

"No. I admit I lied to you. I lied to everyone. But for the record, I worked my ass off here. I did want to help the seals. I still do."

She doesn't respond, and for a moment he thinks he may have gotten through to her. They stand face-to-face in the hallway, and the silence between them is broken only by their breathing.

Syd fumbles through her shirt pocket for a cigarette. "I still want you to go."

He finds his backpack in the closet and starts stuffing everything he can grab into it. She remains in the hallway, and he can hear her lighting the cigarette.

"So what now?" she asks. "You going to keep on chasing after her like some lovesick schoolboy?"

"There's more to it."

"Just keep telling yourself that, Daniel. I mean, Robert. Whatever the hell your name is."

"Robert."

"You're pathetic, you know that?"

"Yes, I do." Robert reaches down and picks up a shirt from the floor. "I thought she was dead. I thought I killed her."

Syd pauses. "Well. Apparently you didn't. Not yet, at least."

"Please. Just tell me. Where did she go?"

"It doesn't matter where she went. She got over you. Trust me on that one."

"What do you mean?"

"What do you think I mean?"

She gives him a knowing look and he realizes there'd been someone else after him.

"Mark," he says, remembering the way Mark had looked in the pub when they talked about Noa. Of course.

Syd nods and returns to her office, leaving him in the dark. He can see now how right she is—he is pathetic, standing there in unbuttoned jeans, no shirt, head hanging at the realization that Noa had been here with Mark the whole time Robert was chasing a memory.

Robert finishes packing his bag and finds Syd sitting in her chair in a dark office, the glow of a cigarette illuminating the glass of whiskey in her other hand.

"Were they serious?" he asks from the doorway.

"I doubt very much *she* was serious. But she sure as hell broke his heart when she skipped out of here."

Robert steps into the room and leans against the file cabinet. He glances at the bulletin board, the bloodstained photograph of Noa still there.

"This one's on the house." Syd extends a cigarette. Robert takes it and leans over as she lights it.

"So why'd you take her in?"

"She arrived with an impeccable reference."

"Aeneas?"

"That and a sizable donation. Money and a new volunteer. It seemed too good to be true. Sort of like you, in fact. When will I learn?"

"You didn't like her."

"It's not a question of like. That one was wound too tight from the beginning."

"She didn't do the chores you assigned her?"

"She never complained."

"So why the resentment?"

"I'm not resentful."

"Now who's lying?"

"Fine," she says. "You want to know the truth? She's the reason I'm stuck on this side of the border for the rest of my years."

"What do you mean?"

"She tried to assassinate the Minister of Fisheries."

"Assassinate?"

"As in stab to death. The Honorable Immanuel Robert Lohamba."

Robert is stunned. "I don't understand."

Syd gets up out of her chair and faces the window. "I had arranged a sit-down with the minister. Took me more than a year, a dozen or so letters. I intended to go alone, but our pro-bono lawyer suggested we bring a group and that we dress up all nice and pretty. I even bought a suit for the occasion. Would have returned it had it not been for the torn sleeve."

"Why did he bother to meet with you in the first place?"

"PR, mostly. Some movie star, I forget who, had done an interview, and it got traction. I guess the president is a fan, and we had a window of opportunity, an actual window. Our goal was—is—to create a protected nature reserve. I got financial backing to buy out the sealers, for good. I believed we had a shot."

She lights another cigarette. "Noa begged to go along. I thought it might help. She was going through something. Wouldn't tell anyone. Now it makes sense—she was upset about you. At the time, I didn't know anything, but I thought a trip would get her mind off whatever it was she was obsessing over. So we go up north. She's on good behavior, smiling even. Then, about halfway through the meeting, I can sense her fidgeting next to me, and I glance over. She's leaning over, like she's tying her shoe. Only she's wearing heels. So I look down, and she's removing a knife from her trouser leg. She sits up with it concealed under her arm. And I'm just staring at her. The minister is going on about quotas, and I want to respond but I can't focus on anything else but this person beside me with these martyr's eyes. I had no choice."

"No choice?"

"I jumped onto the table and grabbed the minister by the collar, and I pushed him onto the floor. I figured if I attacked him, she couldn't. It was all a blur. I was handcuffed, dragged away, locked up."

"And what about Noa?"

"As far as I know, she walked right out of that room."

"I don't get it. Why would she want to kill him if he might've helped you?"

"Because she snapped, lost her mind?" Syd says. "I don't have a damn clue. All I know is she was convinced the minister was using us. That he just wanted some photos for his website, something to prove that he was working with the greens. She told me the week before that nothing would change without us doing something drastic. I didn't take her seriously." Syd takes a long drag off her cigarette. "I should have."

"What did she say afterwards?"

"She was gone before I was released."

"Who else knows?"

"About the knife? Nobody. They all think *I'm* the loose cannon."

"You, a loose cannon?" Robert says, eliciting the slightest of grins.

Then Syd sighs. "The tragic part of it all is that when word got out, we lost our sponsors. After that fateful meeting, I was supposed to go see a donor who would have funded us for a year. She's old and doesn't use the Internet, and I had to see her in person. But I never got the chance. The grants dried up. Nobody wants to fund a *terrorist* group."

"How bad is it?"

"Why do you think I had you purchase the sundries?"

She pauses and stubs out her cigarette on the floor, staring out toward the courtyard. "We've got a month's worth of cash for food. For the seals, I mean—the rest of us will have to scrounge."

She turns and looks at him. "Did you know that five years ago, this place was a dog rescue? I wanted something closer to the water, but there was nothing we could afford. When I saw this place and the enclosures, I thought it just might work. And we very nearly did pull it off. But we'll just be another failed nonprofit in the end."

"Do the others know?"

"I've been paying half salary for the past two months. I'd say the secret's out by now. The problem is that the locals keep bringing us emaciated pups. How am I supposed to turn them away? I could say let nature take its course. But nature didn't put these seals in this position. Human nature did." She picks up the whiskey bottle. "Isn't that so typical of humans? We only want nature to take its course after *we've* driven it off-course."

She prepares to pour some whiskey into a glass, then brings the bottle to her lips instead. "I should've started turning them away months ago. But I can't do that. I won't."

Robert watches her eyes go moist around the edges. She turns away from him, and Robert again feels an urge to comfort her. But what comfort can he be? He's yet another person who will leave her in the end.

"I can get you over there," he says.

She turns her head in his direction. "Where?"

"Over the border. Into Namibia."

"You and what army?"

"I'm serious." He leans forward, trying to catch her eyes. She only squints at him uncertainly.

"As if I'd trust you now," she says.

"I can get you a passport, Syd. What good is being ex-FBI if you can't still lean on your old sources?"

"What's in it for you?" she asks. "Oh, wait. Noa."

"You tell me where she is, and I'll get you over and back again."

"I'm needed here."

"Let the others take care of the pups for a bit. You think that donor still wants to meet with you?"

He sees her eyes perk up, but then her nose wrinkles. "She probably heard everything and changed her mind."

"She's not on the Internet, right? And what if she doesn't care? How much money does she have?"

"Lots," Syd admits.

"While we're there, you can look up some of your old friends along the beach. Maybe we'll even see Toby."

The mention of Toby brings a glint to her watery eyes. And though he doubts Syd will tell him anything about Noa no matter how far away from this place he takes her, he wants to get her back to that beach. To do something good. He's waited this long for Noa; he can wait a little longer. Maybe forever.

It takes him nine hours to drive to Milnerton, a suburb north of Cape Town. He is surprised by how easily he finds the house. How little has changed in this high-walled and lonely neighborhood.

When it comes to keeping people away from your home, Southern California has nothing on South Africa. Even here, a firmly middle-class neighborhood of ranch houses and postcard-sized lawns, few driveways or porches lie exposed to passersby.

He drives around the block three times, studying the cars parked on the street and the handful of dog walkers, looking for anything unusual in this unusually quiet neighborhood.

The house is a yellow, stucco one-story with a neck-high iron gate. He punches in a key code and then lets himself through the gate. At the front door, he knocks twice and waits for a voice, to which he responds with the code word. The voice responds with an affirmative code. Robert then drops an envelope containing the passport and five hundred U.S. dollars into the mail slot. Then he walks away and gets back into the car.

He knows about this operation from his days posing as a drug dealer; when he was in need of a new identity, the gang he was working with sent him here. The Bureau should have tipped off the South Africans to shut this operation down, but it had become such a lucrative watering hole for crooks and terrorists that it was more valuable left open than closed.

Robert drives away, then checks into the same motel he used to stay in and has always hated. He leaves again for the local pub, where he orders a whiskey and stares at a soccer match on TV. Everything looks the same as it was when he last visited. The only thing that has changed are the beers on tap.

He tries to focus on the television, to avoid thinking of the obvious question rattling around in his mind: Why is he doing this? For a woman who doesn't even like him and another woman who has so far succeeded in hiding from him. He's no longer undercover, but he is still dangling between two worlds, neither of which he fully occupies, nor will ever occupy.

The next morning he returns to the house. On the porch, he lifts up the seat of a wicker couch to find a manila envelope.

9.

Syd takes forever to get out of the sanctuary. It's already noon, and from the car, Robert watches her giving instructions to Mark like a young mom leaving her kids with a babysitter for the first time. He resists the urge to tap the horn.

"Okay," she says, getting in the car. "Let's go."

"Did you leave our number on the fridge?"

She gives him a look, and he hands her the fake passport, then starts driving.

"I'm Jennifer?"

"You don't like the name?"

"I don't know. This doesn't feel right."

"I even made you a few years younger."

"I can see that. And what happens when I get arrested?"

"You won't."

Robert takes the N7 north, and within two hours they are approaching the Vioolsdrift border post. As he continues across the bridge over the Orange River, he glances at Syd. She is frozen in place, eyes glued on the Namibian checkpoint a half mile ahead.

"Relax," Robert says. "You don't have to do anything." They pass a Welcome to Namibia sign, and Robert reads aloud the words of another sign: We hope you will find our officials courteous.

"Why do they call this the Orange River?" he asks, hoping to distract her.

"Turn the car around. This is a horrible idea. I changed my mind."

"Syd, trust me."

"I'm serious. They'll throw me in prison."

"I will get you across the border. I promise."

At the checkpoint, Robert gets out of the car before the three uniforms arrive at his car. He opens his passport and holds it up, two $100 bills covering his photo. He shares a knowing look with the man out front, who leads him into a glassed booth. He squeezes in with the two men as they murmur to one another, too low for Robert to hear. Robert hands over Syd's passport. He can't be sure that his bribe will still work or whether he has kept current with rates. Judging by the lack of cars behind his, it is a slow day, and this will work in his favor, at least.

One of the men stands and hands back the passports. Robert returns to the car, telling Syd, "We're good." As they drive through the checkpoint, he waves at the guards, while she keeps one hand on the dash and another on the door handle, as if she's bracing herself for a crash. She lets out a sigh as they continue past the checkpoint.

"Now that wasn't so hard, was it?" he says.

"How much did you pay them?"

"Better you not know."

"Probably right. It might have purchased quite a few pounds of seal food."

"Forget about the money. For now, at least," Robert says. "After you meet with this donor of yours, you won't have to worry about money."

"Why are you doing this?"

"Doing what?"

"All of this."

"I want to know where Noa is."

"And what if I don't know?"

"I think you do know, or at least have a pretty good idea. Maybe this trip will jog your memory."

She rolls down her window, leans her seat back, and lights a cigarette.

"It's jogging my memory, all right, but I've done all I can to forget that woman. If you were smart, you'd do the same."

The donor lives in Lüderitz, and Robert considers inviting Syd to an evening at Kappy's while they're there, challenging her to a game of pool, something to distract her from the burdens of the world outside. Their destination is about four hours northwest of the border crossing. But before they get there they will make a detour west to Atlas Bay, one of the largest seal colonies in Southern Namibia. She and Robert will camp along the beach until Mark and the rest of the group join them.

After two hours of bone-jarring, sun-warped roadway they stop for gas at a gleaming white-and-blue Engen petrol station, looking bizarrely out of place among the neighboring tin shacks. Robert walks to the far reaches of the lot to stretch his legs as a smiling attendant fills the tank and Syd uses the restroom. Two young men are loitering around a dumpster, one swinging a stick at the ground, kicking up dust, the other in a faded blue Los Angeles Dodgers T-shirt. They stop in front of him and ask for money. Robert shakes his head and watches them move on, the stick lashing out at small stones and plastic soda bottles. He can imagine their future—trading the stick for a club, a seal at the end of it.

"Namibia has twenty-three percent unemployment." Syd, who has returned and is watching from behind him, seems to be thinking the same thing.

"Which makes seal culling a desirable job," he says, continuing the thought.

"In this country, any job is a desirable job," she says. "That's what we're up against. It's not enough to help the animals—you have to help the humans, too. Animal rights and human rights are two sides of the same damn coin."

Robert tips the attendant before getting into the car. Back on the road, Syd lights another cigarette.

"It's not just about the money," she continues. "It's about the government sending a message to the fishermen—the people you saw stumbling around drunk all over Port Nolloth. The fishing stocks have collapsed up and down the coast, and they blame the seals."

"Instead of blaming themselves."

"There's plenty of blame to go around," Syd says. "It's not just Namibian fishermen. It's South Africans. Asians. Plenty of poaching vessels out there from halfway around the world. And now there are fishermen in South Africa who are pressing the government for permission to kill seals. They used to allow it, years ago."

"I didn't realize that."

"The tragedy of it all is the waste." Syd blows out a lungful of smoke with a loud sigh. "Lives spent doing work that no man or boy should ever do. Animals being killed only for their pelts and their penises."

"Penises?"

"They slice them off right there on the beach. Why bother carrying the rest of the carcass when the penis is the only thing of value? To thousands of Chinese men, that is, with more money than self-confidence. Six thousand bulls killed each year."

"Jesus," Robert says.

"And you know all about the pelts. The pups—they have the best fur. You've felt it. Waterproof. Warm. Unbelievably soft. Nature's protective blanket. The skin gets ripped off of eighty thousand pups a year to supply the luxury fur market. A slaughter of the innocents."

Syd goes silent and stares out the side window. Robert looks straight ahead, over the horizon, flat and faded, with not a car or person to be seen among the scrub. Despite the topic of the conversation, despite Syd's dark mood, he enjoys the wide open nothingness, the lack of any people to remind them both of the cruelty that exists in this part of the world.

He hears another loud sigh, followed by a small, mirthless laugh. He glances over at her. "What's on your mind?" he asks.

"I spent most of my life wanting to escape this land. And I've just used a fake passport to get back to it. My father would have a heart attack if he could see me now. Broke. Breaking international law. As he used to say, I'm a colossal waste of an expensive education."

"I wouldn't say that."

More talkative than he's ever seen her, Syd tells him about her upper-class upbringing in the Oranjezicht suburb of Cape Town. The disappointment from parents when they learned she was giving up human medicine for animal medicine. The first time she visited Namibia, at age twelve, on vacation.

"We were headed north to the dunes," she says. "We stopped along the way and had lunch next to the car. And when I saw those seals—the sheer number of them—I was captivated. I felt as if I were visiting some foreign city, and I just stood there absorbing everything. How they interacted, the power struggles, the parenting, the subtle comedy. My father practically had to drag me back into the car. Of course, I had no idea at the time that we had arrived after the killing, that those dark patches in the sand were blood and not water. Not that I could have processed it, had I known. All I did know was that I wanted to be closer to them. I've spent the rest of my life doing just that. I sometimes regret that trip."

"Why?"

"Look at me," she says. "I've seen my former classmates online, and they're working as proper veterinarians, married, living comfortably in their gated homes with their German sedans. I envy them—but not for all that. I envy their ignorance. When they visit the seal colonies with their children, they only visit during park hours, after the slaughter is done, just like I did. I wish I could be that innocent—or ignorant—again. If for only a day."

"At least there's alcohol," Robert says.

"So that's how you cope, too."

"When I joined the Bureau, when I met my boss for the first time, he shook my hand and said, *Welcome to the dead zone.* I thought he was making a reference to the wireless network. It didn't take long for me to see what he meant. After seeing so many crime-scene photos—videos of throat cutting, beheadings, the overwhelming meanness of the world—a part of you goes numb. They call it cognitive dissonance, a mental toughening up, and you don't talk about it. It just happens."

Robert looks over to his left. In the distance, he can see a blue sliver of ocean. "When I was undercover and witnessed a Norwegian whale hunt, I thought it wouldn't bother me as much as all the rest. I thought they were 'only' animals and after all, I'd already seen humans die in front of me. But that's all crap. Suffering is suffering. Death is death. And we're all animals in the end. It's not that a part of you goes numb—a part of you dies."

"So it wasn't your wife who died," Syd says. "It was you."

Robert feels the urge to argue with her, to say something to set her straight. But it occurs to him that she is right.

ROBERT DRIVES PAST THE ROAD FOR ATLAS BAY because it's not a road, just a thin layer of gravel over brown dirt. After a half hour of listening to the angry drumbeat of rocks ricocheting off the underside of their car, the gravel fades into craggy dirt ruts formed by years of truck tires and flash floods.

"You sure this is the right way?" Robert shouts over the rattling of metal and plastic.

Syd leans over. "Keeps the tourists away. Sadly, not the sealers. You should try this road in the van. I made Mark stock vomit bags."

They arrive at Atlas Bay with about an hour to spare before dark. Before Robert can put the car in park, Syd has opened the door and is running across a dirt parking lot, over a stone wall, past the two small KEEP OFF signs stuck in the sand.

He loses sight of her over the ridge.

He gets out, and the smell hits him hard, the wind shifting over land. He wonders if the sealers use the smell as a way to work themselves up, make them angry, make the killing easier. The sooner you kill the small ones, the sooner the large ones will leave, the sooner the smell will blow away.

When Robert catches up to Syd, she is walking among the seals, as casually as if she were strolling through a crowded village. The air is filled with the deep-throttled noise of bulls barking at one another, declaring their territory. Pups yelp out to their mothers in a range of voices that sounds as if they are dry heaving. There's so much chaos all around him, and yet he knows there is an order to it all, on a level he cannot see. The bulls' guttural sounds are likely warning others of these human interlopers, or perhaps they're announcing a lost pup in search of its mother. Though Robert will never know what is being said, he has learned during his brief apprenticeship that these creatures are far more intelligent than people give them credit for. As Syd had told him on his first day, *The more we study animals, the smarter they get.*

While most of the seals don't bother moving as Syd approaches, a few rear up onto their front flippers, noses lifted to the sun, looking sideways at her and Robert, who is now close behind. She stops and kneels next to the rear flipper of one seal, lying asleep on the sand. There is a green plastic tag affixed, and she squints at the number.

"I know him," she says. "One nine four four. It's Scooter, I think."

"You named him?"

"We name all of them," she says, standing. "But we can only fit numbers on the tags."

Syd continues on. At times Robert passes so closely to the seals standing at attention that he is tempted to reach out and pat them on their upturned noses, the way he used to pet Molly, one of the dogs he grew up with, who died while he was away at college. He'd always meant to adopt a dog one day, but with his job keeping him on the road all these years, he never got around to having a companion at home—canine or otherwise.

The seals are not panicking or fleeing, as they had at Dunkel Beach. How do the seals know that Syd and Robert are not here to hurt them? Perhaps if Robert were carrying a hakapik he would witness an entirely different reaction. Even though he knows they're watching him, he's grateful they pretend to ignore him, as if they are equals on this narrow beach. Perhaps this is the ultimate compliment a wild animal can offer.

Up ahead, Syd has stopped and is kneeling over a lone pup. It's not moving, and when Robert gets closer he can see a dark red gash running lengthwise along its belly. Its eyes glisten as it looks up at Syd.

"This one must have escaped from them to the ocean, just barely," she says. "And now he's back, but he's not going to make it."

Robert catches himself reaching behind his back again. His gun would come in handy now, to put this poor creature out of its misery.

"What do we do?" he asks.

"There's nothing we can do."

The pup is looking at Robert now, eyes expectant.

"I could get a rock."

"No."

"He's suffering."

"You don't think I know that?" Her voice rises; her shoulders tense. She stands and glares at him. "I've seen those eyes more times than you'll ever know. And I'm not just talking about the seals. Five years as a vet in Cape Town euthanizing dogs and cats. Not because they were dying or sick. No, because we needed the fucking room."

"Look, I'm sorry I suggested it."

She blinks at him as if she's trying to clear something from her eyes. Then she turns to the ocean. "It's not your fault. I'm just—I don't know."

She kneels again next to the pup, then lowers herself onto the sand until she is sitting next to it. She rests her hand on its head, caressing its mangy-looking fur. "I'd pass the dog cages every night at the animal shelter, and those eyes would look up at me. I'd feel this compulsion to do something, anything, to ease that longing they all had. Nobody was going to adopt these animals. All I could do was give them a treat and walk them a bit, let them sniff the world outside. And then I'd have to take them into the euth room and put them up on a cold steel table. They knew, I think, in that moment. My tech would hold them as I gave the shot."

She shifts in the sand, moving a little closer to the seal. "The cats I could do myself, so it was a little better. I would put them on my lap. We'd sit there for a half hour, sometimes an hour. It took them a few minutes before they'd purr, before they'd trust me enough to relax. And while they were purring I'd give them the shot." Still stroking the seal, she looks up at Robert. "You know the worst part of it all?"

Robert kneels next to her. "What?"

"There was a point when the killing became a relief. A relief from the accumulating stress of too many animals and not enough cages. You begin telling yourself that death is the right thing to do. But would I have told myself that if they were little boys and girls? The day I realized that was the day that I quit."

Syd stands abruptly and continues walking. Robert turns his attention to the pup. He wants to ask Syd whether this pup has a mother looking for it. How many of the sounds around him are the wails of childless mothers?

When he looks up, he sees Syd about twenty yards away, kneeling down, eye to eye with a large seal. The tide is coming in; Robert can feel the mist from the waves. But Syd is oblivious to the inevitable, so focused on the seal in front of her that Robert can picture her swimming away with it. What a shame it is that she has no fins; how many thousands she could have saved simply by leading them through the water, across the invisible national border a few hundred miles to South African beaches? Where seal killing is not legal, not for the time being.

When Robert approaches, he hears Syd talking to the seal, the sun's light bouncing off the tears collecting just under her eyes.

"This is Eleanor," she says to him, without looking up. "I found her three years ago, tangled up in fishing line—see the scars on her belly? She remembers me."

"Eleanor?" Robert asks. "Interesting name for a seal."

"My mother's name. I found her on the beach the same day that I found out my mother was diagnosed with cancer."

He wishes he hadn't said anything and begins to back away, to give Syd a little privacy. But she stands up and meets his eyes.

"Stay here."

Then she smiles at him, in a way he's never seen before. Her tears weren't sadness after all. "This one," she says. "She got me through it—the phone calls, the helplessness. Knowing that I saved a life on the day another received a death sentence. This Eleanor kept me talking, moving, breathing."

"I'm sure your mom would be proud," Robert says. As he's been tempted to so many times, he reaches out and puts a hand on her shoulder

To his surprise, Syd doesn't shrug him off. "I never thought I'd see her again." She leans in and wraps her arms around him in a hug. "Thank you," she whispers in his ear.

How long they stay like that he isn't sure—only that when she pulls out of the hug she doesn't step away from him, and Robert brushes her face with his hand, in a gesture meant to wipe away the tears there, and he's surprised when her eyes lock onto his, expectantly. When her hands touch his own face. When their lips meet—and when, a moment later, she pushes him away. He murmurs an apology, though he honestly doesn't know who made the first move, and at the same time he wants to pull her back toward him, to feel that brief connection again. But she has turned away and is looking out toward the ocean.

10.

SHARING AN OLD ARMY SURPLUS TENT on a bluff overlooking the north end of the beach, Robert and Syd spend the evening oblivious to the chorus of seals below and the wind above shaking their tent flaps like sails. In the darkness, his lips on her back, her body smells of sunburnt skin and sand, and because they are a tangle of limbs and heat and wet open mouths, Robert can imagine he is here with Noa, that he's found her at last.

It isn't fair, he reflects later, as she dozes against his shoulder, but he knows Syd is no great romantic, that she simply needed the same thing he did, that she herself may have been thinking of someone else. That it was animal instinct, more than anything else, that brought them together in this cramped, overheated space.

He drifts off to sleep, and when he awakens he is alone, the entrance to the tent open. He crawls out and walks to the stone wall overlooking the water. He sees Syd at the north end of the beach, seated on a pile of wave-blasted stones, watching the seals.

She looks up as he makes his way across the sand. "The sealers took today off," she says.

"That's good news," Robert says.

She points at a seal with a green tag on its flipper. "That's Reggie. He's about five years old. See those scars on his back? Normally I'd assume they were from a shark or a ship's propeller. But my guess is he's survived a few close calls on this beach."

"Does he remember you?"

"I'd like to think so. He's not frightened."

"When are Mark and the others getting here?" Robert asks.

"Tomorrow," she says. "We'll need them."

"Is there ever an off-season for the culling?"

"After the pups are weaned. But off-season only means no clubbing, at least not in large numbers. Men still wander over to grab pups every few days, the way someone might take to a fishing hole on the day off work."

She takes out a small camera and snaps photos. Robert looks at a pup lounging next to its mother. The mother watches Robert warily.

"I miss the dark sand here," Syd says. "The way the seals blend in when the sun is rising."

She looks at him and holds his eyes, and in that moment Robert imagines a life here, the way he used to imagine a life with Noa. Easing the pain of a few creatures, reminding the world of the horrors, helping each other get out of bed in the morning to face another day. Maybe this is what he dreamed of even more than Noa herself—making a difference.

"You should stick around a while longer," Syd says, as if reading his mind.

He looks at her, surprised. "What makes you think I won't?"

She stares back at him long enough for him to see her loneliness. He leans forward and kisses her forehead. He can smell seals on her, a scent more familiar to him every day.

THAT NIGHT, THE WIND IS LESS WILD, BUT SYD IS NOT. It's as if she takes all her anguish about the seals, about her life—all her anger over Noa, he can't help but think—and puts it into this one act, the one thing, he guesses, that offers her release from the day-to-day chaos of her life as a rescuer. Robert brings out his nearly empty bottle of whiskey, which he'd stashed in the trunk of the car, and they take sips as they lie spent on top of their sleeping bags.

Suddenly, she takes the bottle and exits the tent. He waits for her to return and, when she doesn't, follows. She is seated on the hood of the car, cross-legged, facing the water. She holds out the bottle without looking at him.

"Hear them?" she says.

Robert listens. When the wind shifts, he can make out the gentle grunts of mothers and pups.

He watches her face. Her eyes are closed. Oblivious to him, to having walked out on him. It seems as though whatever had recently opened up between them has closed again. With a sigh, and with the whiskey bottle, he returns to the tent. The thin green walls throb above him in the wind, and he wishes he hadn't come here, hadn't slept with her. Maybe he feels guilty about Noa, about what he will say to her when he finds her, assuming he does find her. Assuming she wants to be found. So many damn assumptions—and no more whiskey in the bottle.

He hears the sound of the tent's zipper, and when he opens his eyes she is settling in next to him, and she rests her head on his shoulder, just like the night before.

Harsh light awakens him, the sun shining through the open flap. Syd is dressed and on her knees, her back to him, looking outside. She's probably looking for the others, due any minute from the sanctuary, to try to get to the beach before the seal cullers arrive.

"I could stay," he says. "Once we go back to the sanctuary. I don't have to leave."

She turns to him. "You will."

"What makes you so sure?"

"You have that look in your eyes, like a feral cat. I know that look—I used to trap them, get them fixed, release them. They were unadoptable, so that was the best we could do. We'd clip their left ears so if we trapped them again, we'd know they'd been fixed. You may as well have a clipped ear. I can see it all over you. You'll never stay anywhere for long."

"The last I checked my ears were fine."

"So you don't like the cat analogy. How about a wandering

albatross? It's all the same. That's why you'll leave. And we'll both know it has nothing to do with finding Noa."

"I haven't left yet."

"The albatross goes to great effort to take off. But once he's aloft, he tends to stay there, months at a time."

Robert says nothing. He hears a helicopter in the distance, coming closer. He looks at Syd, her eyes wide, listening. Then Robert realizes the noise is not a helicopter but multiple diesel engines—large trucks—heading their way.

Syd slips out of the tent, and Robert pokes out his head in time to see a caravan of pickup trucks and trailers pass by. Syd stands dangerously close to the road, glaring at the men blithely making their way to the water.

Robert rushes his clothes on, and by the time he's outside the trucks are out of sight with Syd pacing by the tent like a caged animal.

"They're starting," she says. "Where the hell is everyone?"

Robert looks back but sees no signs of the sanctuary's van. They may have been held up at the border crossing, or perhaps they're just running late. If that's the case, there will be hell to pay later, with Syd.

"We have to wait for them," he says.

"I can't."

She starts toward the beach, and he grabs her arm. He releases her the minute he sees the searing look she gives him.

"Please," he says. "Wait."

"You wait. Send the others when they get here."

Syd jogs toward the beach and over the ridgeline. The wind has picked up off the water, and Robert can hear the cries of the seals—so human. He turns, relieved to see the van approaching, and he waves it toward him as he runs, full speed, over the ridge.

Syd is in a standoff between a mother and pup—the pup still attached to her, milk drooling—and two men. One of the men shoves Syd down to the sand, and the other grabs the pup and begins to club it with the hakapik. Syd leaps onto the back of the man and as he straightens up, he grabs her by the hair.

Robert hits him in the nose so hard he thinks he has killed the man, whose body drops, motionless, before it begins writhing in pain. Robert grabs the hakapik and greets the other man with it by taking him down by his legs.

"Come on!" Robert grabs Syd's arm and tries to pull her away from the fatally injured pup, but she won't move, kneeling over it like a child.

"Syd!"

She gathers the pup in her arms. The mother is on her fins, head arching back, emitting a skin-crawling groan.

T.J. and Mark have joined them, with Mark filming. Another sealer, a large man in ragged khakis, approaches them, pointing with his hakapik.

"Beach closed. Leave. Now."

"You first," T.J. says.

"What we do is legal. What you do is not." The man uses the bloody end of his hakapik to prod T.J. backwards. Robert holds his ground, and when the man points the club at him, Robert grabs it in one motion and yanks it away.

The man lunges at Robert, but he is ready and swings the hakapik around and sticks the sharp end into the man's shoulder. His scream cuts through the wind, and Robert looks up to see two other men looking their way. Robert pulls the hakapik back as the man rolls on the ground, his blood staining the sand.

"What are you doing?" T.J. shouts at Robert. "You're going to get us arrested."

Robert is shaking with rage, ready to take them all on.

Syd appears at his side. "What happened?"

Robert looks past her and sees that Syd has surrendered the injured pup to its mother, who is hovering over its motionless body.

"You know the rules," Syd reminds him. "No contact."

"Jesus, Syd, they don't play by rules," T.J. breaks in.

"We do."

Now there are five men approaching them, spaced evenly apart, in a semicircle. Each carries a hakapik, and they move slowly, as if the four of them are seals about to make a dash for the water.

Robert looks to his right and sees a familiar bearded face—Bernard, the ringleader, the one who wants him dead. Bernard carries his hakapik on his shoulder and stands in front of the others, swinging distance from Robert.

"You again," Bernard says. He shakes his head, and Robert looks behind him to see another half-dozen sealers approaching.

Robert drops the hakapik and raises his hands. "We'll leave, okay?"

"Did I say you could leave?"

"He's with us," Syd says, now standing shoulder to shoulder with Robert.

"You want a beatdown, too?"

Keeping his eyes on Bernard, Robert leans in to Syd. "Get out of here," he whispers.

"Not without you."

"I'll be fine." Robert raises his voice. "Now get the hell out of here!"

Syd steps back. The men behind them make an opening wide enough for Syd and the others to pass through. Robert looks down at the hakapik at his feet. Bernard shakes his head.

"Big mistake putting that down."

"You drop yours, too, and let's settle this," Robert says, hoping that talking will keep the rest of them from going on the attack.

Bernard laughs. "We don't drop our weapons."

Robert hears a car up on the ridge and turns to see Syd waving at him from the passenger side of the van. Robert shakes his head and waves them away. A rock hits the side window, cracking it, and the van lurches out of sight. Robert turns back to see that the mob has grown to more than two dozen. Bernard wears a smug look.

"Some friends," he says. "Leaving you behind."

"I work alone," Robert says.

"You die alone, you mean." Bernard takes a step forward, holding the hakapik with both hands, waving it back and forth.

"If I die, I'm taking you with me."

Two of the others step forward, and Robert slides left to encourage one man to commit to a swing. Then he ducks, picks up his hakapik, and sticks the man in his leg. He then dives right, causing the other man to hit the sand with his club. Robert jumps up and sticks him in the rear. As he struggles to get the hook out of the man's ass, he feels a sharp stab to his right bicep.

A rock hits him on the forehead, and even as he hides his face, he can tell he is surrounded. He glimpses a man on his right and dives toward him, hoping to take at least one of them down.

But then it's he who is pinned down, and rocks pummel him from all directions. Some of them attack from close range; Robert feels his shirt being ripped off, the sharp pain of torn skin on his forehead, sweat and blood pooling into his eyes. He tries to fight them off, but there are simply too many, a blur of angry faces filling his fading vision.

He lets his body go limp, and moments later the blows cease. He opens his eyes to see Bernard looking down on him.

"This is how we kill them," Bernard says, then raises his club.

Just as the weapon reaches its apex, Robert hears a gunshot. Sudden darkness as a body falls on him. And in the brief silence he feels his mind wandering, dreamlike, floating.

Then he snaps back, and he pushes the deadweight, bleeding body off him. He looks at Bernard's face, a crisp hole where his temple once was.

"Party's over, gentlemen."

The voice is distantly familiar. Robert wipes the blood from his forehead, watching feet back away from his head. He's still holding the hakapik, by instinct.

"Go home. All of you." The voice again.

Robert rolls onto his elbows and raises his blood-blurred eyes to the voice, a man in his late forties, pointing a handgun at the sealers.

David Spencer. In their years together as agents, Robert had always called him Spence.

"Hello, Robert," Spence says. "Fancy meeting you here."

11.

Spence looks down at Bernard's body, as if to admire his marksmanship. He keeps the handgun, nose down, at his side. He is dressed in a Panama hat, seersucker blazer, jeans, and hiking shoes.

"You're looking dapper," Robert says. In the days they worked together, David Spencer fashioned himself an American James Bond, always a step above business casual, linen bespoke suits and a rotating collection of hats handmade in Quito.

"You approve?" Spence looks down at his blazer. "I picked this up in London a month ago. Unfortunately, it's a dust magnet."

"Did you have to kill him?" Robert asks.

"You'd have preferred I let him kill you?" Spence raises his eyebrows.

The sealers, at a distance now, continue to circle the crime scene, in twos and threes, some with phones to their ears.

Spence removes a checkered handkerchief from his breast pocket and hands it to Robert. "Your forehead." Robert takes the cloth and feels it soaking up warm blood from a wound he cannot see. "You need stitches."

"I'll be fine," Robert says.

"How long before the police arrive?"

"How would I know?"

Spence surveys the horizon. "I'm going to guess fifteen minutes."

"What are you doing here, Spence?"

"I heard you'd gone native. I had to come see for myself."

"A phone call would have sufficed." Robert slowly and painfully rises to his feet, taking stock of his injuries. "What do you really want?"

"A moment of your time, my friend."

"I suggest you make it fast."

"You want this?" Spence holds out his gun. "I've got another in the car."

Robert shakes his head, and the pain that blasts through his brain makes him wish he hadn't. "You're with CounterBalance now?" he asks weakly.

Robert is only guessing, but due to the intelligence company's popularity with former agents, it's a safe bet. They call CounterBalance "the country club" because you have to be invited in, and, once you get in, you're a member for life. Not that you wanted to leave, with all the perks, like company cars and phones, expense accounts and personal assistants. And no bureaucracy, just work. For agents ground down by years of government rules and slow-motion meetings, going to CounterBalance was like being reborn.

"Two years next month," Spence says. "When I joined, there were less than twenty of us. Now we've got more than sixty."

"Terrorism has been good to you."

"I've missed that dark humor of yours. You know, I asked Gordon why you quit, why you decided to martyr yourself to a bunch of seals. He wouldn't say."

"It's confidential."

Spence smiles. "Don't prevaricate a prevaricator."

"I just needed a break."

"Is that right?" Spence looks out over the crime scene of a beach. "Not exactly the North Shore of Maui, but it has its charms, I suppose."

"You still haven't told me why *you're* here."

"I'm staffing up a new division," Spence says, removing his hat and wiping his brow. "Environmental counter-terrorism."

"Then you just shot the wrong person."

He smiles. "I'm here to offer you a job, Robert. You'll pull down three times what you were making at the Bureau. Performance bonuses. Stock options. A few years with us, and you'll have that beach house in Hawaii. Or here, if you prefer."

"What if I'm not motivated by money?"

"Then you truly have gone native, and there's no conceivable hope for you. But I think you miss the action. In fact, judging by this little contretemps, I'd say you're positively itching for it."

A blue Toyota pickup passes on its way inland, seal carcasses piled high. A dead human on the ground has done little to slow down the more important business at hand. He thinks of Syd, relieved that she didn't have to witness one more killing today. He wonders how he will explain his actions to her, if she'll forgive him.

"I'll pass," he says to Spence.

"Just like that? Don't you want to know what the job is?"

"I've got to get out of here, Spence. We both do." Robert turns and starts limping away. Nothing is broken, but every part of him is badly bruised.

"I'm looking for Neil Cameron. Remember him?"

Robert stops. His head pounding, for a moment he isn't sure he heard right. But then, it's the one thing that could explain Spence's presence here.

Spence was leading the mission in which Robert had arrested Neil Cameron Jr. He was given orders, he followed orders, and he put Neil in prison, not questioning whether Neil deserved it or not. It was a strange twist of fate that Robert had also been undercover in the North Atlantic working for Neil's father—the infamous Aeneas.

"I thought Neil was in prison," Robert says.

"He's out. And back to his old ways."

"What's he done?"

"He hacked a client of ours. Stole a few files."

"Who's the client?"

"That is confidential. Until you sign on."

"Isn't this a job for the Bureau?"

"It would be if they had told the Bureau. Our client values discretion."

"Where's Neil now?"

"New Zealand. We're not sure where he's headed. That's where you come in. Remember that girl you turned witness back when we worked together? Tracy something?"

"Tracy Morris."

"She's back in Iowa City."

"She's not going to talk to me. Not after what I did to her."

"She will if she wants to see Neil again. And something tells me she does."

"And her ex? Ray Hudson—is he out of prison, too?"

"He is. But he's not involved."

"How do you know that?" Robert says. "Those two were joined at the hip when we arrested them."

"People change, my friend. Look at yourself. Risking your life not for God or country but for what—seals?"

"Doesn't make it any less of a war."

"True. But not all wars come with cash advances." Spence tosses him a thick envelope. "That's thirty grand. I want you to go to Iowa City and have a chat with your friend Tracy." Spence turns his eyes to a dust cloud in the distance, growing larger. He raises his handgun and waves two men back. "Her address is in the envelope."

"I haven't said yes."

"I thought you had a soft spot for these people. Especially Neil's old man. Aeneas, is it? You told Gordon he drowned."

"Who told you that?"

"Please, Robert. CounterBalance knows as much or more than

the Bureau. Of course, it doesn't hurt that Aeneas boarded his ship again two weeks ago."

Robert is quickly remembering just how good Spence is at getting his way. Like now—leading with money but trying to close the deal with intimidation. And now Spence has knowledge Robert thought nobody would ever have. Robert thought Aeneas would stay dead to the world forever. But if Spence knows he's alive, what else does he know—and how is he going to use it?

"Tell me this," Robert says. "What will you do when you find Neil?"

"Just talk to him."

"Don't prevaricate a prevaricator."

Spencer laughs. "We're going to get the files back, Robert. That's what we're being paid to do."

"Are you going to hurt him?"

"We're a for-profit. All about efficiency. No bad press, no collateral damage. No stray bullets."

"What about Bernard here?"

"That wasn't a stray bullet."

Robert looks down at the lifeless body. Flies have already begun to collect on the gaping wound on his face. Will the sealers cover up this blood just like they cover up the blood of the seals?

"Your ride is here," Spencer says.

Robert looks up to see that the source of the dust cloud is now in view—the sanctuary van, with Mark at the wheel and Syd on the passenger's side. They skid into the lot, but, noticing the body, they remain in the car. Syd turns to look out over the beach, probably knowing it will be her last time here. Robert feels a swell of guilt that is stronger than the pain in his battered body. What good was bringing her back if what happened here will destroy all that she's worked for?

"I've really fucked this up," Robert says.

"Indeed you have." Spence takes a step toward him. "But I still have a few connections in these parts. I could make all this go away. But I need your answer first."

Now Robert knows why Spence waited to make himself known, to extend this baited offer. He was waiting for Robert's temper to put him in this situation, to give him the leverage he needed.

Robert looks over at Syd, surprised to find her looking right back at him. Her face is blank, unemotional, as if Robert were a stranger or, worse, one of the sealers still lingering on the beach. The van lurches into gear, and Robert watches the van speed away, spewing dust in its wake.

"Looks like I'm going to need a ride after all."

Spence pats Robert on the back. "I'll take that as a yes."

12.

Robert sits in Spence's rental car as the police talk with Spence, who's shaking hands and telling jokes as if he is one of them. Robert notices the color of bills changing hands. Spence points at Bernard, reenacting an encounter that never happened. The two police officers write in their notebooks and record the scene with a handheld camera. A half hour later, a van arrives, and Bernard's body is loaded inside.

Finally, Spence climbs into the car and looks over at Robert. "Your patience is appreciated."

"So who do the police think killed Bernard?"

"A rival gang, it appears. Namibia's finest will be looking into it. Of course, Bernard's people didn't contest that theory because they'd love to see their rivals imprisoned."

Robert is ready for a change of subject. "So, who is your client?"

"Biosant."

Robert recognizes the name—one of the largest producers of

genetically modified seeds, fertilizers, pesticides. A longtime target of environmentalists and one with the resources to fight them to the end.

"They're based in St. Louis."

"Yes, but I don't think Neil physically entered the offices. This was all done remotely."

"What did he steal?"

"Even I don't know that."

"Don't bullshit me, Spence."

"I'm serious, my friend. Between you and me, it's better that way. If Biosant gave up some competitor hit list, I'd rather not be privy to that."

"But if you don't know what he stole, you don't know what Neil's going to do with it."

"What I do know is that Biosant is terrified he'll publish it. But if he were going to do that, he'd have done it already. Unless he's waiting for the right moment. Or hasn't had the time to actually read what he's stolen. Or maybe he's planning to sell it."

"To whom?"

"Biosant will pay plenty."

"For its information or for Neil?"

"Does it matter?"

Robert falls silent, and Spence begins to chat about his ex-wife and a few former agents they used to work with. And all the while Robert is half-listening, wondering how he can justify working for David Spencer and this elite group of mercenaries. Becoming Jake had changed everything, though it wasn't just the role that changed him; it was Robert, after all, who fell for Noa. And, through Noa, Robert had come to empathize with the activists—to see the world and all its suffering animals through their eyes, a darker world than any agent could imagine, for agents limited their empathy to the human animal.

Perhaps returning to the old world would be a relief of sorts, though this is just wishful thinking. Robert feels destined to straddle both worlds, like a time traveler, darting back and forth in search of someone he worries he will never find. If he takes this job with Spence, he has to give up his search for Noa, and if he loses the trail now, he may never get it back. But maybe he's not meant to find Noa. Maybe joining Spence is a step in the right direction. After all, Neil is Aeneas's son, and he's in danger. With a company like Biosant and a handful of ex-FBI agents chasing him all over the planet, Neil will never be able to stop running. Which means, like Noa, he may never resurface again. If Robert were at CounterBalance, on the inside, maybe he'd have the opportunity to do some good. He'd be going undercover again, this time as an activist posing as an ex-agent.

The thought of it makes his still-throbbing head ache even more. And he knows he has no choice. He'd just let Spence clean up the mess he'd left on the beach, and he has to follow through, or Syd and the seal rescue will be the ones who suffer.

As they approach the sanctuary, Spence tells him that Tracy is going to be the place for him to start. "She's still living in Iowa City," he says. "And she's still obsessed with Neil. Not sure what they had going on between them, but there was something there. Use that."

"How's she doing?" Robert asks, not sure he wants to know the answer.

"She might be using again," Spencer says. "You can work with that, too."

Robert feels a new heaviness in his bones, an ache more burdensome than the beating he'd taken earlier on the beach. It seems that whenever he looks back, he sees a string of broken lives in his wake.

It's dark when Spence drops Robert off at the sanctuary. "We'll be in touch," he promises, and Robert nods. He watches the car turn the corner. As he walks inside, he sees light leaking out from under the door to Syd's office. He walks past the office to his closet, where he sits on his cot and begins gathering his clothes. A few moments later, he hears footsteps and looks up to see Syd standing at the door.

Robert stands. "Syd—"

"I can see now why Noa liked you. For the longest time I couldn't figure it out. You were too quiet for her, too straight and clean-cut. But now I see it."

"See what?"

"You're just like her. Hot-tempered. Short-sighted. Misguided."

"I'm sorry—"

"We left a dead man on the beach. That was not part of the plan."

"You are not going to be involved."

"Tell that to the police. We'll be lucky if we ever make it across the border again."

"You will. I promise."

"*I promise.* Famous fucking last words."

"The man who killed Bernard is taking care of it. There will be nothing in the press. Not unless your people talk to them."

"What about Bernard's friends? Family? What are they going to believe?"

"Based on my brief interactions with Bernard, I'd say he was equally hot-tempered. So I can't imagine this outcome will come as any surprise to them."

"What happened out there? Who was that man?"

"I was in trouble. He was only protecting me."

"I had the bloody van. That would have been protection enough."

"Bernard was a half-second away from goring me with a hakapik. One of us was going to die."

She stares at Robert. He can see the frustration in her eyes, her disappointment in him. It's a look he has seen before in a woman's eyes—a look he is becoming too familiar with.

"That man," Syd says. "FBI?"

"He was. Once."

"Once? Don't tell me this is where FBI agents come to retire."

"He was looking for me."

"Naturally."

"He wants me to help him find someone."

"Noa?"

Robert shakes his head. "I have to go."

She nods, as if she has been waiting for him to say it. And now that he has, she turns away from him, staring out at the pens.

"It's better for everyone," Robert says.

"Everyone? What about those of us who have to keep the lights on, the seals fed? Thanks to you, I didn't get a chance to see that donor who could've saved this place. You stormed through here and left an awful mess." She lets out a short, unhappy laugh. "But that's what I do—clean up other people's messes. Why should you be any different?"

He looks at her and wishes they could go back to being who they were back in Namibia, on the beach, in the tent. The connection they'd had, while brief, had still felt real, and now he's severed it for good. He picks up his duffel.

"You never were one of us," she says. "No matter how much you pretended to be."

"I wasn't pretending."

"Then you were lying. To me. To yourself."

"I'm done lying."

Robert pulls the stuffed envelope that Spence gave him out of his pocket. As he walks past Syd, he presses it into her hands.

"What's this?"

"Anonymous donation."

He exits to the courtyard. The seals are alert, heads up, watching him. He gets into his car, imagining Syd's face when she opens that envelope. He's not sure how much she'd have gotten from her Namibian donor, but he's just given her enough cash to keep the place running for another two years. Enough to keep her here and, maybe, long enough for him to return.

Tracy

13.

She is scrubbing Bruce Renschen's legs when she notices his wife standing at the door. Tracy says nothing, returning her eyes to Bruce's hairy calves. So many curling black strands spiral up from his skin, refusing to stop growing, ignorant to the fact that the terrain on which they live will soon go fallow. Bruce's arms are bent at the elbows, as if frozen in a moment of pre-ecstatic cheer. His eyes, currently preoccupied with a ceiling tile, are the only part of his body that still move.

His wife, Helen, stands at the entrance of the room, watching Tracy work. Though she let her hair go gray, and her clothes look like something out of *Good Housekeeping*, Helen is fitter and more alert than most of the significant others that Tracy encounters. Helen shows up every day and sometimes reads, sometimes watches movies on her iPad. But today Helen looks irritated, and Tracy wonders if she has overlooked cleaning one of Bruce's body parts.

"He was dead the minute that stroke hit him," Helen says. "Now it's just the waiting."

"I'll be out of your way soon."

"Don't hurry on my account," Helen says, taking her usual seat at the foot of Bruce's bed. "It's not like Bruce and I have much to chat about."

"I'm almost finished, Mrs. Renschen." Tracy feels the urge to call her Helen. Surely they've become familiar enough over the past two weeks to use first names. But hospice is big on protocol. First names are for family only, and Tracy will never be family.

Other than Helen, though, few members of Bruce's family have bothered to make an appearance. An older brother arrived four days ago from Orlando, dressed in workout clothes, as if he were on his way to the gym. He said nothing to Tracy—he stayed ten minutes and never returned, and Helen only learned about his visit after Tracy told her.

One slow night, Helen told Tracy that Bruce had been too hard on the kids and that they'd never forgiven him. The eldest called a few times. The youngest sent cards and a flower arrangement.

"They're waiting on the funeral," Helen said. "Not worth making two trips, I suppose."

Bruce is fifty-nine years old, a number that no longer sounds so distant to Tracy, even though she herself is almost thirty years younger. But now that she's working in hospice, she finds it tragic to meet patients under retirement age. To be so near the finish line—all those years of stashing away money, delaying cruises and RVs and other indulgences that would have felt extravagant at the time—only to end up here, with a few weeks or months left to live, and precious little time left to think about what could have been.

Bruce had promised he would retire early, Helen told Tracy once. He was a partner in a law firm; they had more than enough money. Partner, Bruce had assured Helen years earlier, when he was still aspiring toward this goal, was when he would scale back, take trips with the family, take up carpentry. Every time he purchased another power tool for those rare Saturdays at home, Helen would get her hopes up. But partner came and went without a change in schedule. She had to threaten to divorce him to get him to join her on a two-week cruise along the Dalmatian Coast.

"He just couldn't let himself relax," Helen said that night. "I think he was scared to stop moving. Ironic, I suppose."

Now, Tracy straightens the sheets across Bruce's chest and prepares to leave. But she can't, not yet. Helen is one of the nice ones—she doesn't micromanage, doesn't complain about the temperature in the room. Tracy wonders why Bruce avoided this sweet, quiet woman for so many years.

"He said it again," Tracy says. "Last night."

"Daisy?"

Tracy nods. "At least I think that's what he said. It's hard to tell."

Helen sighs. "That was the name of our cat."

"He must have really liked her."

"Bruce hated Daisy. Hollered at me for how I doted on her. And maybe I did, but she'd come from the shelter, and I wanted to give her a good life. He used to complain about the litter on the carpet, the claw marks on the drapes. He never once lifted a finger to change her litter. But I got up late one night for a drink of water, and I caught him in the living room watching sports highlights, Daisy perched on his lap." Helen shakes her head at the memory. "When Daisy died she was twelve years old—feline leukemia. He said nothing. Just went back to work while I cried for five days straight."

Helen pulls a packet of tissues out of her purse. "I see it now. I'm already a widow. I've spent more time with him these past two weeks than all of last year. And he's said about as much. I was a widow from the day he joined that damn law firm."

Tracy keeps her eyes focused on Bruce as Helen blows her nose. Tracy has been here at the Iowa City Sisters Hospice Clinic for six months. A nurse with her experience can work anywhere, and Tracy has drifted from job to job, starting in Oregon and making it as far as the Midwest. She's done time in hospitals, outpatient surgery centers, and now here. As nursing jobs go, this is one of the easier ones. Most nurses don't like to be so close to death on a daily basis. Nor, for that matter, do visitors. Tracy observes family members and friends as they stand warily in the patient rooms, refusing to sit, to get comfortable, as if by doing so they'll become that much closer to their own demise, as if dying is some virus they might catch.

Yet Tracy feels unusually comfortable here. It's not that she relishes death, but she has come to accept it, even welcome it. In hospice, death is not just another colleague; death is the only nurse always on call, all too eager to sweep away the pain. Tracy can sense her at times, a cold draft in a sterile overlit hallway, rubbing against her shoulder on her way to another room. As colleagues go, Tracy gets along with death better than most others. But the crying, the release of emotions and nasal fluids and saltwater—she still isn't fully anesthetized to death's more common side effects.

She can hear Helen wiping her nose and wants to escape the room. Keeping her eyes down, she squeezes in front of Helen only to find herself caught up in a suffocating embrace as this convulsing, almost-widow smears Tracy's neck with tears and makeup. Tracy feels Helen's chest heaving, and she tries to picture something else, something relaxing. She thinks of the sleeping pills that Helen picked up for herself earlier and how they're in her purse right now and how easy it would be to steal them if she waited for Helen to go the bathroom to fix her makeup. She could down five or six right on the spot, and the anxiety coursing through her veins would soon fade, replaced by warmth and the slow, steady sound of her beating heart.

And then she thinks of Neil and what he would say if he knew. About the pills. About all the horrible, dark things she's done. To her body and his.

14.

After her shift ends, Tracy picks up a container of southern-fried tofu at the co-op and heads home to her apartment. It's a low-rent student building, and while she could afford to live better, she prefers to be around students because they make her feel younger than her thirty years, which she reached without ceremony last month. Her brother sent her an e-mail, which for him was a generous gesture, though she suspects it's because the date is on his digital calendar and he just copies and pastes e-mails from years prior; the messages are exactly the same. Still, she'll take it. Her parents both died in car crashes in her twenties, and her brother is the only family she has left. Her dad died in a grisly accident on Interstate 5, going over the Siskiyou Pass at the California–Oregon border; he had a heart attack at the wheel, and it took two days for climbers to reach the body. Her mom died a few months later, using her husband's death as an excuse to give up on any hope of self-improvement. She, too, drove off the road, in a single-car wreck after a long night at the local bar. The upside, if there was one, was that they both avoided hospice.

Tracy lives in a studio at the corner of South Governor Street and Iowa, in one of the few brick buildings in the neighborhood. Once an upper-middle-class area, it's now a student slum of large homes chopped up into rentals, consumed by fraternities, or replaced entirely with infill apartment buildings. Her furnishings, which haven't changed since college, consist of a twin mattress, a desk lamp, a folding chair, and a laptop. When she's here, which is rare, she'll lie in bed and watch a movie or TV show on her phone or computer. Or she'll lean over and read a book by the light of the lamp, which she found next to the dumpster when she moved in.

She watches a rerun of *Frasier* on her laptop, keeping an eye on the time. At nine she changes into dark clothes, grabs her duffel bag, and returns to her car. She takes her time driving across town, windows open, breathing in the icy-sharp chill of winter and the smoke from wood-burning fireplaces.

She drives by his apartment building and glances up to see the light on in his window. She parks on the far side of the street. Far enough away that he would never notice the car but close enough to offer an unobstructed view.

She grabs binoculars from her bag and looks up. He is home. She can tell by the shadows on the ceiling that he is moving around. Cooking something? Talking on his phone? The few times she has seen his face were when he stood by the window, when he used to smoke. He gave up cigarettes a month ago. Judging by the lights on the ceiling, he is now watching television. Shades of green and white.

Even from this distance, she feels close to him. She knows him by his patterns, by lights and shadows and things thrown away. Judging by his recycling bin, he puts down a six-pack a night, but at least that number hasn't gone up since she's been observing him.

He spends his days working IT at the University of Iowa. Low-level technical support for the many computer labs scattered across campus. He has a college degree in engineering, and if he had stuck with school he would probably be a professor at the university, or another privileged computer geek in California. But considering his criminal record, he's lucky to have this job.

She likes to think he's happy, or at least headed in that direction. She adjusts her seat back as far as it will go. She feels her eyelids falling, her breathing growing heavy.

Her mind drifts back to Bruce, her body now at a similar angle to his when she'd left him earlier that evening. What was he thinking when he said Daisy's name? Was it just another word, like bad song lyrics that ricochet around one's head until they are the only thing left? Or does that word signify, as she suspects, that the brain harbors secrets that even its owner is unaware of?

Will she be the one to have witnessed the last word spoken by this man? Helen is no doubt around so often because she hopes that she will be the keeper of her husband's last word. But Tracy thinks that Bruce won't be any more generous with his wife in death than he was in life. Tracy will hear his last word, if she hasn't already.

Now, she can't stop her mind from wondering: What will her last word be? Will it be *Neil*? And if it is, will Neil be around to hear it?

15.

TRACY IS JUST FINISHING BRUCE'S DAILY BATH when Helen enters the room, and she looks up to see Helen's face brighten. Helen holds up a dinner plate covered in plastic wrap.

"Pork chops," Helen says. "I had extra."

"I can't take that, Mrs. Renschen."

"I know you have all sorts of rules here, but really—I want you to have it."

"It's not that," Tracy says. "I don't eat meat."

"Oh." Her eyes widen. "You're a vegetarian?"

"Well, vegan, actually."

Helen takes a seat, the plate resting on her lap. "Does that mean you don't eat cheese either?"

"Among other things."

"No wonder you're so tiny, kiddo. You hardly eat."

"I do just fine," Tracy says, propping a pillow behind Bruce's head.

"Are you gluten-free, too?"

"No." Tracy knows she should let this awkward conversation atrophy on its own, but she can't. "It's not about diet."

"Is it because of your religion?"

"It's not that either. I just don't believe in eating anything that has a parent." Tracy turns back to Bruce and wipes the saliva from one side of his chin.

"How long have you been this way?"

"About eight years."

Helen moves the plate to the table next to her. "I guess I learn something new about you every day."

"It's a healthy way to live, too," Tracy adds. "Better for your heart. Body."

"Brain?"

"I would imagine so." Tracy glances over at Helen, who is staring at Bruce.

"If he knew he was being cared for by a vegan … " Helen shakes her head. "Our oldest, Bruce Junior, gave up meat in college. Bruce took it personally. Many of his clients are in the ag industry. His largest was Biosant, and that was a whole other war. GMOs and pesticides and God knows what else—the crap that company churns out. Bruce Junior came home from college his sophomore year and showed me books and articles and anything else he could find about the evils that company had perpetrated. He got me buying all organic, and when Bruce Senior finally got wind of it … " She shakes her head again, lost in the past.

"Don't worry. I don't judge."

"We all judge, particularly this man." Helen nods toward Bruce's motionless body. "He said his son made him feel like a sinner just because he liked chicken wings."

"Vegans can be sinners like anyone else." Tracy turns to Helen. "I speak from experience."

Tracy leaves Helen and Bruce and continues her rounds, regretting everything she said. It's not Helen's fault for assuming a plate of food would be met with gratitude instead of a lecture. And it's not Tracy's fault that food comes up so often in daily conversation. Her once-closest friend, Gina, a lesbian, told her years ago that it was easier to be gay than vegan. She said: *You can be gay and still not fuck up your family's Thanksgiving dinner.*

Tracy had stopped eating meat her senior year at Southern

Oregon University, and she never told her parents, not that they would have cared all that much. For every dollar her father brought home from his job as a long-haul trucker, her mother spent two on online self-help courses she never completed. Growing up, Tracy had cared for her mom as best she could, which largely meant keeping her away from the car when she was drunk and sponge-mopping vomit out of the carpet. She went for her nursing degree because becoming a veterinarian was too many student loans out of reach. Nursing, she came to believe, was a natural evolution for her; she'd grown up taking care of her parents, so why not get paid for it? More important, it ensured that after graduation, she could move far away from Oregon and still cover her student loans.

She found her university experience both eye-opening and depressing. When she was admitted to SOU, she felt she had won the lottery, the first in her family to attend college. But when she arrived, it dawned on her how many students had won the lottery at birth. Tracy was fewer than twenty miles away from her hometown, but it was an entirely different world. Many of her fellow students drove late-model cars and planned for study-abroad tours in Cologne and Beijing as casually as Tracy planned her Sunday off-campus dinner.

She lived in the dorms and made casual friends, but never truly found her niche. The library was the closest thing she could find, and she spent evenings at a table on the third floor between the tallest stacks.

Then, one evening during her last year, she skipped the library to attend a university job fair in the student union. She wandered among the tables, slowing at each but not stopping. The hospitals and clinics were mobbed by her classmates, and she didn't feel the urge to join them. All the soon-to-be graduates had such a nervousness about them, the men in suits, the women in work outfits that ranged from skirts to pantsuits to runway-caliber dresses. Tracy, wearing the dark skirt and red blouse she'd found on sale at Target, wondered why she couldn't just wear scrubs since that's all she'd be wearing the rest of her life.

She found herself standing near the bathrooms in front of a table with the banner CETACEAN DEFENSE ALLIANCE. Behind it stood a girl with her hair in dreadlocks, a tattoo on her wrist, wearing a black MEAT IS MURDER T-shirt.

"You looking to change the world?" the woman asked.

"Sure," Tracy said, trying to read the brochure on the table.

"We protect whales," the woman said, and handed over a brochure. "And dolphins and seals."

"I didn't realize this was a career."

"As careers go, this one doesn't pay much. Actually, it doesn't pay anything, not at first. We're new, and run mostly by volunteers. What's your career of choice?"

"Nursing," Tracy said. "Not nearly as exciting."

"But it does pay."

"Do you go around the country doing this?"

"Nah. I'm from Ashland. Happened to be in town and figured I might recruit a few more members." The woman extended a hand. "I'm Noa."

Despite knowing she should join her classmates at the nursing section of the hall, Tracy couldn't bring herself to leave Noa's table. At first, she believed she was keeping Noa company, as the only students who paused at the table were those on their way to the bathroom. But as the hours passed Tracy realized it was the other way around, that Noa was keeping *her* company. After four years of college, feeling like an outsider in class, in the dorms, walking across campus, she didn't know she could ever feel like she belonged. But Noa lived her life on the outside, too, on the outer reaches of the planet and society, traveling from Svalbard to the Southern Ocean for no other reason than there were animals out there that needed protection. Tracy was fascinated, not only by Noa's travels to places she'd never heard of but the way Noa made it sound: noble—heroic, even, all of CDA's volunteers bonded together by a shared passion. It never occurred to Tracy that one could live on passion alone. And here was Noa—defiant proof of just that.

She spent the rest of the evening standing at Noa's table, even going so far as to explain CDA to another student who passed by on her way to the restroom while Noa was out looking for water. When Noa returned to find the student signing up for their e-mail newsletter, she laughed.

"You're a natural," Noa said.

"I'm just filling in," Tracy said.

"Famous last words. I think I said the same thing when I manned my first table. In the end, we're all just filling in."

Tracy did not notice that the fair had ended around her until Noa began packing up the booth. Tracy stepped in to help, gathering up brochures and adding them to Noa's box of supplies.

"You hungry?" Noa asked. "There's a raw-food place on Siskiyou that doesn't suck."

Tracy had heard of "raw food," but only in the context of celebrity diets. She followed Noa across campus to the main boulevard, where they crossed the street and entered a small, crowded café.

"I don't really care whether my food is cooked or not," Noa said as they ordered salads and collard-green wraps stuffed with guacamole, black beans, and green onions. "But this is the only place in town without dead animals on the menu."

As they ate, Tracy listened as Noa talked about how the CDA crew put themselves between whales and Japanese whaling ships, even ramming the ships if necessary. She spoke in mythical terms about a leader called Aeneas and the arrest warrants he'd accumulated, from Japan to Iceland, none of which have yet been exercised. After dinner, Noa invited her over for a drink, and Tracy followed her to a small cottage in the Railroad District. "It's my aunt's house, but she's never here," Noa said. "I usually crash here for a few days before I head up to Seattle to catch our ship."

Noa sliced a lime and poured Don Julio tequila into tiny glasses, and they sat outside on the porch, a cool spring breeze washing over them.

"We ship out in two days," Noa said. "Hawaii this time. Fuckers have been attacking the monk seals, so we're going out there to do patrols."

"That sounds dangerous."

"Not really," Noa said with a shrug. "I mean, some of the poachers will shoot at you, but mostly just warning shots. They might want to get rid of us, but they don't want any more bad publicity, believe me."

Noa downed her tequila and poured them each another shot. "Now, in Antarctica—that's another story. The Japanese don't give a shit about bad PR," she said. "They'll sink your ship, aim right at your head. But what they don't realize is that we're never going to give up. Never."

"I wish I could come along," Tracy said.

"Why don't you?"

Tracy laughed until she realized that Noa was serious. "I've never even been on a boat."

"You'll get your sea legs fast enough. Besides, we could use a nurse. You'd be amazed by the weird fucking shit that happens out there. Mostly little things—cuts and bruises, stomach bugs—but every once in awhile something random happens, like the time our second mate impaled herself on a grappling hook."

"Did she survive?"

Noa nods. "Aeneas yanked the hook out of her thigh and poured whiskey on the wound all while yelling at her for wasting perfectly good liquor. That's when it became apparent that we could use a professional."

"If only I didn't have so many student loans."

"Creditors can't catch you out at sea."

"It's just that—I'll be the first in my family to get a degree," Tracy said. "I need to see this through."

"Fair enough."

"I'd feel like I was running away," Tracy added, feeling as though she had to explain herself. In truth, there was nothing she wanted more than to follow this person to any point unknown.

"We're all running from something," Noa said with a shrug. "But not all of us know it."

16.

At half past midnight, Tracy reclines in her car, allowing herself to focus only briefly on the fact that her life comprises little more than looking down on the dying and looking up at Neil's window. How quickly her life has devolved from direct action to indirect inaction. Solitary and sober, an observer of other people's moments.

She watches the shadows on Neil's ceiling as if they were stars in the sky. When she hears the sound of a van approaching, she raises her head to see it pass—a green utility van with Missouri plates. It continues past Neil's apartment building for about fifty yards before coming to a stop. She strains to see the driver, who appears to be a man, but he's still looking straight ahead, and she can't see his face.

She glances up at Neil's apartment to see the lights go out. A few moments later Neil emerges from the front door, dressed in black, carrying a backpack. When Neil opens the door to the van and the driver turns toward him, in the flash of the car's interior light, Tracy sees who it is, and hears herself saying his name, a name she thought she would never hear again.

Ray and Neil, together again. She doesn't know what is going on, only that it can't be good. As Neil gets into the van, Tracy shakes off her shock and starts her own car, keeping the headlights off, and follows the van as it meanders through town and finds the highway.

The van is headed south. Tracy glances down at her phone. It's now nearly 1:00 a.m., and she begins to consider how far she'll follow before turning around, as if she has a choice in the matter. Years ago she tried to turn around, tried to leave them behind, but the drugs only left blank spots where her life should have been. And if she turns back now she learns nothing—leaving more blank spots, more moments of regret. Now that she's sober, she wants to know everything, as if to make up for all that lost time.

During those years of lost time, she would have been a passenger of that van instead of following it.

She met Ray four years ago at her vegan Meetup group in Iowa City. Once a month Tracy and Gina joined the group at a local vegan restaurant, Trumpet Blossom, for a general bitch session. It wasn't easy to be looked down upon, stereotyped, made the punch line of Super Bowl commercials, and getting together with fellow vegans made her feel less alone, though she knew her loneliness wasn't really about what she ate. There was a hunger in her for something that no diet could ever sate.

That night about a dozen of them had gathered at the restaurant, mostly women, and so when Ray entered and introduced himself, he had their undivided attention. He reminded Tracy of Keanu Reaves, with longer hair and tattoos on his arms—a snake slithered down his left arm and a tree stretched up the right. Though he was new in town and to the group, he carried himself as if he'd known them all along.

"I'm looking for volunteers," he said, as if this request were the sole purpose of their meeting, as if he'd brought them together rather than crashed their dinner. "I'm looking for a few brave souls to join me in a protest next week over at Midwest Poultry."

Lisa—the one whom all new male members gravitated toward—was the first to volunteer. She was blond, with a body built for Instagram and the assertiveness of a real-estate agent, and when she offered up her spare couch (because Ray was living out of his van), Tracy pushed any hopes of getting to know Ray out of her mind.

Tracy knew her body looked better under scrubs, which she basically lived in. Barely five two, she was rounder than most women with a size A cup, one of the rare instances when that letter is not a such a perfect score. She had let her dyed red hair fade over the past couple of months into a marbled mix of red and brown. She rarely wore makeup, and her clothes outside of work were a mash-up of purple scrubs and Salvation Army flannel shirts.

She tried to resist looking over at him during their meal—he had, not surprisingly, taken a seat next to Lisa—but it was difficult. He was doing all the talking.

He was telling a story about working undercover at a slaughterhouse, and as she listened Tracy learned that he'd worked at several slaughterhouses, all throughout Arkansas, and he spoke like a soldier who'd just returned from the front lines. If he suffered any PTSD from his experience, it came out in the form of anger and indignation—and a persistent desire to recruit others to his cause.

"This war is in our backyards," he said. "Iowa's thick with slaughterhouses. Not only Midwest Poultry, but Tarcher Processing is only fifteen miles from here."

Lisa was leaning toward Ray, her chin resting in her hand, and Tracy looked down at her plate, where she'd been pushing soba noodles around without eating them. When she looked over again, she was surprised to find Ray's eyes resting on hers, as if they had been there for a long time. When their eyes met, a barely perceptible smile emerged above his scruffy jaw. It felt to Tracy as if he were memorizing her for a sketch, but not in a way that made her uncomfortable. And when his eyes turned to Lisa, she felt the slow burn of jealousy.

After dinner, when Ray, with Lisa at his side, suggested that they all hit a bar, Tracy declined, even when Gina tried to drag her along. She walked home alone, stopping for a bottle of cheap wine at a convenience store, reminding herself that this was the natural order of things—blond girls going home with dark-haired boys and everyone else remaining on the outside looking in. That, even among these people who were looked down upon and stereotyped by everyone else, she was never going to fit in, no matter how hard she tried.

The van ahead of her now has its right-turn blinker on.

She has spent the last hour picturing Ray at the wheel, Neil riding shotgun. And in the back? She wonders if there is another version of her sitting there, a woman more devoted to their cause than she could ever hope to be. She feels the urge to pull ahead, to catch up with the van, to reveal herself, and to confront Neil at last. To step out of the shadows and beg for his forgiveness.

Instead, she follows the van off the highway, onto an exit ramp into darkness. She can see no gas stations or fast-food restaurants—nothing but a lightless road aimed crosswise, and she has no choice but to turn left after they turn right to avoid being detected. She pulls over and waits, watching the taillights as they arc a modest hill and fade out of sight.

As she's about to get back on the highway, she notices another car take the same exit—a dark-colored sedan. Undercover cop? Another carload of activists? She can't tell in the darkness. She watches it turn in the direction of the van, until it, too, is gone.

17.

Back at her apartment, Tracy spends two anxious hours kneeling in front of her window. She isn't sure why she's so paranoid—keeping an eye out for cop cars or government sedans—and it takes her a while before she can convince herself that she was not the one being followed, that the dark sedan that disappeared over the hill behind Ray and Neil had probably not even noticed her.

Finally, at nearly five in the morning, she collapses onto her mattress and stares at the ceiling. She feels tears in her eyes when she thinks about the fact that she will be at work in only three hours. A pill would have gotten her through the night. Or two. It's been so many months, and still her body aches for those tiny palliatives, the way they soothed her muscles, softened her dour daily reality. Since Neil went to prison more than two years ago she has not taken a pill, downed a drink, smoked anything firsthand—he in his prison, she in hers.

Despite all these months of being clean, she doesn't feel clean, not after the damage she has inflicted on her body. Her skin stings at times, like she's sleeping on gravel, and at least once a week, she'll suffer a headache so severe her eyes well up. Sometimes she feels shrunken, her skin falling heavy against her sides like a uniform she can never shed.

And now Neil is out of prison, while she remains trapped within hers.

She remembers something Ray told her—about how cows are slaughtered at a rate of one every sixteen seconds. "Any time we can disrupt those killing camps," he told her. "Even for one minute. Whatever the cost, I'll gladly pay it."

And she wonders what Ray has gotten Neil into this time.

THE WEEK AFTER THAT FIRST MEETUP where Ray had shown up, Tracy had chosen not to go to his protest at Midwest Poultry. She'd made the last-minute decision the night before, after having let everyone believe she'd be there. When Gina had stopped by to pick her up, Tracy looked at the signs piled up in the back of Gina's car and was tempted—but instead she told Gina she'd been called in to work. In truth, she didn't want to see Lisa and Ray together—a silly reason and a cop-out—but she was tired. Tired of always feeling overshadowed, both by better-looking blond women as well as by the very people they were trying to reach through these protests. She just wanted a day off from all of it.

As it turned out, the protest itself was overshadowed—both in the news and within their Meetup group—by bigger animal news.

The day after the protest, Tracy was in the employee break room at the hospital when Greg, the MRI tech, walked in and said he'd nearly died that morning.

"I was this close to a mountain lion," he said, with arms outstretched. "I was headed to my car and I see it passing like some neighborhood cat. It was fucking huge, and it stopped and gave me this look like I was on the menu."

"What happened?" Tracy asked.

"A neighbor was walking his dog nearby, and the cat got wind of the dog and climbed up a tree."

"Did you call animal rescue?"

"I called 911," Greg said.

Tracy's stomach froze. "What happened?"

"What do you think? The cop shot it."

"Why?" She looked at Greg, hoping she'd heard wrong. "They could have relocated it."

"It's a public safety issue." Greg shrugged. "That cop's a hero."

That night, Tracy met Gina in a local restaurant after work, where they sat at the bar and watched the local news on the screen above them. A shaky, handheld video of a large brown cat crouched on a tree limb looking down with bottomless black eyes. The screen cut to the cop, with the shaved head and resolute jaw of one who did not acknowledge ambiguities. He told the TV reporter that there wasn't enough time to risk the animal attacking someone.

"Can you believe this shit?" Tracy said.

"Unbelievable." Gina shook her head and motioned the bartender for another round.

"If they had just left him alone, he would have found his way down during the night and disappeared," Tracy said. "People don't realize that we're surrounded by these animals. Coyotes and lions, and none of them want to hurt us."

Tracy thought the beers would relax her, but after three rounds she was just as wound up, and when they left the bar and parted ways to walk to their respective apartments, Tracy felt startlingly alone, even as the anger within her simmered. She was sure Gina felt the same way, but hanging out together wouldn't help. Even their combined outrage only seemed to exacerbate their shared helplessness.

The next day Tracy worked an evening shift, and when she left late that night, the hospital quiet, she took a vase of flowers from the room of a man who hadn't made it back from surgery that evening. She drove to the neighborhood where the lion had been shot and placed the flowers at the base of the tree where he'd died. The lion's death had already drawn a makeshift memorial of flowers and candles, a purple plush stuffed animal. A sign on neon-green paper read REST IN PEACE, BENTON; the lion had been named for the street on which he'd died.

At the next Meetup, that weekend, Benton was the topic of conversation.

"We should picket outside that goddamn cop's house," Tracy said.

"Why bother?" Gina said. "The lion's not going to be any less dead, and you'll only get yourself arrested."

"If we can protest a poultry plant, why not a cop?"

"It's not the same thing."

As she argued with Gina, Tracy noticed that Ray, seated at the other end of the table next to Lisa, was watching her. It wasn't her style to be so stubborn, especially with Gina, whom she always respected for being rational when Tracy herself was emotional. Maybe it was guilt over skipping the poultry plant protest, or just another layer of exhaustion over yet another senseless death. Or maybe that helpless creature had awakened something deeper in her; in that brief video, she saw not just a terrified animal, solitary, surrounded by strangers, growling at a world it could not understand—in that lion's dark eyes, she saw herself.

The argument circled the table, until Lisa changed the topic to Avocitos, the new vegan taco truck that had opened over on College Street, and as the conversation eagerly turned to food, Tracy put money on the table, said she had a headache and needed to get home. On her way home, she drove by Benton's memorial. She thought of how alone he must have felt up in that tree, looking down on the humans and dogs and flashing lights. How alien this world must have appeared to him. If he had been a different species of cat, the outcome would have been different—a fireman perched on a ladder, reaching out, cradling him on their way to the ground.

When she got home, she responded to Gina's concerned texts with *I'm fine, just need some sleep*, and then turned on the television, mindlessly watching one mirthless show after another while waiting for sleep to wipe away the day.

When she heard a knock at her door, Tracy opened it, expecting to see Gina. She was surprised to find it was Ray, standing there alone with a six-pack.

She leaned against the doorjamb, not sure whether to let him in. "What are you doing here? And how'd you know where I live?"

"I asked Gina," he said, taking a step forward. But Tracy didn't move aside to let him in.

"Where's Lisa? Shouldn't you two be at Avocitos?"

"Lisa? We're not together."

"Oh, really? Since when?"

Ray shrugged. "She's not my type."

"I'm not sure you have a type."

"Oh, I do. But my type doesn't seem to like me very much." Ray eyed her with that enigmatic grin of his.

"You still haven't told me why you're here."

"I thought you might be up for a little direct action."

"No, thanks," she said. "Gina was right. Better to stay out jail."

"We won't get caught."

"You might not, but I'm not like you."

"I disagree. I was impressed with you at the Meetup. You're one hard-core, badass activist, Trace; you just don't know it yet." He leaned in and whispered, "Don't you want to do something on behalf of Benton? And I'm not talking about flowers."

How did he know about the flowers? She felt an electric charge go through her body, his face close enough to kiss. She was both frightened and intrigued by the notion of him following her, by the inherent drama of joining forces with him to plan some clandestine action. The last time she'd felt this spark was when Noa had tried to recruit her to *the dark side*, as she'd called it. Back then, of course, Tracy had resisted; she had loans to pay and a future of playing it safe.

But when she thought again about what happened to Benton, she knew she was done playing it safe. She opened the door wider and let Ray in. He opened two beers, handed her one, and told her his plan. She listened and drank two more beers before agreeing to help.

At three that morning, she found herself standing with Ray behind a tree, staring across a residential street at the cop's house, the windows dark, his police car in the driveway. Even though it was a warm summer night, Tracy felt herself shivering. She and Ray were dressed in black and carried ski masks, spray paint, and nothing else. Cell phones, Ray told her, were too easily traced. He was smiling as if this were a field trip, and all she could think was that she was about to get sick to her stomach.

Ray handed her a can of paint. "I'll let you do the honors."

She looked at the can, her unsteady hand rattling the mixing ball inside. "I'm not sure I can do this."

"Trust me, you'll get the hang of it. Just be sure to go slow, so everything's spelled correctly. First time I did this, I rushed so much I spelled *fuck* with a P, as in *pucker*. Neil still gives me shit about it."

"Who's Neil?"

Ray put his hands on her shoulders and leaned in so close she could feel her lips tingling in anticipation. "You're a badass, Trace. A fucking badass." He spun her around until she was facing the car and nudged her forward.

She pulled the ski mask over her face and tiptoed up the driveway. Kneeling down next to the Iowa City Police Department decal on the door, she raised the can and pressed down on the nozzle. The paint seemed to explode from the can, so loud she expected to see porch lights blaze all around her—but nothing happened. She wrote quickly, moving around the car, penning *cat killer* and *coward,* watching the dark paint drip down the side of the car like blood, adrenaline surging through her body.

When she got safely back behind the tree, Ray pulled her close and whispered, "You have the best fucking handwriting." And then he was kissing her and she was kissing him back, her body trembling in a whole different way now, and she didn't know if it was from the crime she just committed, or Ray, or both, and she no longer cared. Whatever that feeling was, she was hooked.

Ray took her hand, and they ran together, fifteen blocks to where he parked his car, and he took side streets all the way back to her place. Once there, Tracy led him to her apartment, and inside she pushed him backward onto her narrow mattress, positioned in the middle of the room like a boxing ring. As he lay there, she tugged off his socks, jeans, briefs; he assisted with his shirt. Seeing him spread out below her, alert and waiting, she descended on him, his eyes watching her. She was in total control, dictating rhythm, her legs around him. She was not about to let him go, not now, not after having waited. He was hers now.

The next day, the vandalism made the news. They watched it on television from Tracy's mattress, both of them covered in perspiration from their most recent encounter. She blissfully forgot about her job until her cell phone came to life—her boss, wondering where she was.

"I have to go to work," she told him finally, pushing herself to her feet.

"Fine," he said, looking away from her, watching the weather girl forecasting rain. His voice sounded foreign.

"I'm serious. I'm already late."

He looked up at her. "You don't mind if I stay, do you? I'm sort of in between apartments right now."

In between women was more like it, Tracy thought, but she didn't care. He was here now, not with Lisa, and she wanted to keep it that way. "Stay as long as you like," she said.

"Cool." He looked back to the television, and she showered and dressed in silence. When she said good-bye, he echoed the word with barely a glance in her direction.

She told herself that it was no surprise that Ray was moody; everyone in the animal rights movement had issues, some inherited long before they found the cause. Already Ray reminded her of her mother, whom she tiptoed around in her darker moods. Was it going to be like that? If she closed the fridge too loudly, would she get an earful?

She'd grown up hearing how much her mother had sacrificed to *raise her miserable ass,* as she put it. All so Tracy could attend college, as if her mom had anything to do with it. So she'd been the first to college, first to a degree—but these firsts haven't stuck with her nearly as much as the lasts. The last time her mother yelled at her for burning toast while she was hungover. The last time she slept on the front porch because her friends got her home after curfew and she'd rather have frozen outside than faced her mother. All the firsts in the world wouldn't eliminate the lasts.

And so over the next couple of months, she learned to look past Ray's slights and occasional outbursts because at least she understood him, and she thought that he understood her. With Ray she felt rescued, like the hen he smuggled out of a farm in Covington, Kentucky, which he told her about one night in bed. He'd been working undercover, filming the battery cages and filth the animals lived in. He encountered a three-year-old hen who was no longer laying eggs, about to be killed, and he hid her under his jacket until he was past security. "How she stayed quiet I will never know," Ray said. "But when I got her to my car I lifted up my jacket and she looked up at me with those tiny black eyes, her red jowls shaking. She sat right there in my lap as I took her out of town."

And Ray was often just as sweet and protective of her at times, especially when they were doing actions, which she found exciting at first but increasingly distressing. One night, they drove fifty miles to release pheasants from a farm. It was raining, and her clothes were covered in mud and shit as they opened hutches and gates and shooed the birds free. In the darkness and in their haste, she felt something under her foot and heard a piercing cry, and she looked down to see she'd accidentally trampled one of the birds, breaking its wing. *Leave it,* Ray had said, but she couldn't; she picked her up and carried her with her to the car. Ray agreed to take the bird to a vet in Iowa City, but she died in Tracy's arms. Something happened in her mind then, and the last thing she remembered was the shower running, the sound of water in her ears, finally drowning out the sounds of frightened birds, screaming like little children in the dark. The sound of water, like waves, took her away, until all she saw was darkness, and she didn't learn until Ray told her the next morning that he'd turned the water off and picked her up off the shower floor, that he'd dried her off and put her into bed. That was when she told Ray that she couldn't do this anymore. He listened but said nothing.

She didn't tell him that it may have already been too late; whenever she closed her eyes, she saw animals—cows packed together in stifling barns, chickens in cages too small to fathom, their beaks cut short, struggling to peck at the imaginary seeds at their feet, acting out their natural lives as best they could.

And so, too, was she.

She went to work four days a week at the hospital, where she could focus on lives much more easily saved. But Ray wanted her to quit; he said she shouldn't be associated with hospitals, with drug companies, the way they test on animals. She didn't argue with him because she knew he was right—but she also knew Ray wasn't living in the real world. The jobs he held, when he held them, ranged from night cashier to part-time mover. After a week or two, he was fired or he quit. Sometimes a boss or coworker would make fun of his meat-free meals and would end up on the receiving end of Ray's angry fist.

After every shift of her own, Tracy returned home wondering if it was this version of Ray—the violent, short-tempered Ray—who would be waiting for her. She could tell by looking up at the clouds when tornadoes were likely, but Ray could be whistling a Frank Sinatra tune one minute and then calling her dead weight a second later. Despite the fact that her job provided the roof over his head, he would go on and on about medical testing and vivisection, despite her insistence that she never participated in anything like that. "Just because I wear scrubs doesn't mean I slice open rabbits," she told him.

She sometimes wondered how someone so fiercely protective of animals could be so hostile to her—but in a way, she understood; his fury toward those who exploited animals extended to all humans. She wished she could talk to Gina about it, but Ray insisted that their actions remain secret, and she knew he was right. The couple of times she and Gina had talked about Ray, when Gina asked how things were going, Tracy was vague, unsure how to explain his behavior without also explaining everything else. Gina, she knew, would tell her to kick him out—but that would be based on only half the story.

And in truth, she had no desire to leave Ray; he tapped into some angry part of herself that she desperately needed to release. She didn't know where it came from—a source buried deep, but, once tapped, it felt limitless, frightening in its immensity. And as the pressure within her built she found she could no longer sleep. She wanted to help the animals but also wanted to stop doing all the actions, which she worried would make her crazy, but Ray kept inventing new and more dangerous missions.

One night after she'd insisted she couldn't join him anymore—that at the very least, she needed a break—he rummaged in his bag and handed her a white pill. "Take this," he said. "It'll help you relax."

She looked at the pill, with the letters OP imprinted on one side, the number 10 on the other. "Really?" she asked. "The guy who doesn't want me working as a nurse because he hates pharmaceuticals is giving me OxyContin?"

"Look, Trace. Even revolutionaries need to chill out once in a while. The way I see it, if a little medicine keeps you going, it'll do far more good for the animals than if you quit."

"Jesus, Ray," she said. "They could test me at work any time. I could get fired."

"Welcome to the club."

"I was just suggesting a break. That's all."

"A break? So more animals can die? How's that going to weigh on your conscience?"

"I don't know. It's just that—"

Ray cut her off. "You're either committed, or you're not."

"I am committed," she said. "I just can't sleep. Don't you worry about someone breaking in our door and hauling you away?"

"You're worried about *me* getting arrested?"

"Of course."

"But not me leaving?" He looked at her with those dark eyes, infuriatingly opaque. "Because I can't stay here, with you, if you're not on board with what we're doing."

Ray must have known that he was presenting her with a lose-lose proposition. If she stopped accompanying Ray on his late-night actions he would leave her, but if she continued she would lose him to prison or someplace worse. She had seen too many outlaw movies to imagine any other outcome. Ray used to joke that they were the modern incarnation of Bonnie and Clyde, except instead of robbing banks they were robbing factory farms. All Tracy remembered about that movie was Warren Beatty and Faye Dunaway covered in blood.

Or maybe she was worried about losing Ray because she had seen too many romantic movies, which accounted for most of her experience in matters of the heart; there were so few other men—short-term boyfriends and one-night stands—and no one like Ray. Despite the distance between them—or maybe because of it—she felt as though he'd become so much of part of her that she couldn't imagine life without him. With all his restlessness and anger and moods, he was a mirror image of herself, and to lose him now would feel like losing a part of her.

She rolled the pill around in her hand. And even though she knew better, knew it could ruin her career, she took it between her lips, let it rest on her tongue until the bitter taste began to seep in, then swallowed, draining the glass of water on the floor nearby. When Ray smiled at her, she felt it in her whole body, as if the drug were already taking effect, and she pulled him onto the mattress and began to take off his clothes.

Afterward, fully anesthetized, she ran her hands along his hips, tracing his bones and twirling his hair, feeling, for once, nothing but a vague and hazy joy.

It didn't last; she woke up groggy and went to work in a daze, and when she got home, Ray was on her laptop, muttering about an animal testing lab at the university. She sat behind him on the floor and tried to rub his shoulders, to relax him, but instead of relieving his tension, it transferred from his shoulders to her hands, up her arms, into her neck. And, as she peered at the screen, she saw images of rats with computer chips fastened to their heads, their white fur matted with blood.

She pulled away from Ray, and moments later, without a word, she took the pill he handed her, swallowing it without even pausing to look at it. She had followed Ray into a new world, a darker world, one where people did not look away from violence and the blood that followed. She felt reborn into thicker skin, duller senses, and a growing belief, with each additional pill, that she would never return to the world she left behind.

Day after day, Ray dispensed the pills—and so, when he handed her a ski mask and a can of paint two weeks later, she took them both and followed him without asking where or why. It didn't matter; it was work that had to be done. As they sprayed the windows of an animal testing lab that misty night, she marveled at how calm she was this time, hands steady, as if she'd done this a hundred times before and would do it a hundred times again.

The drugs made her feel this way all the time—competent, calm, in control—and she began to chase the feeling. Ray supplied whatever she needed; bottles appeared in the bathroom cabinet, and they were filled again as soon as she emptied them. Their relationship had changed, too; he no longer threatened to leave or questioned her commitment, and she no longer feared losing him. He could ask her to firebomb a daycare center, and she'd agree. Agreeing was so easy when she was high.

But she didn't use at work, and during those hours of withdrawal, her body chemistry run amok, she hated herself; she worried she was becoming the very woman she'd run from when she left her childhood behind. She so looked forward to getting home, not so much to Ray but to that bottle, that sometimes she wished she'd get tagged for a random drug test—to finally, mercifully, be excused from the real world.

One night, she returned to the apartment, going straight to the bathroom cabinet as usual. It was empty of everything but toothpaste and a box of tampons.

Ray, at her computer, ignored her when she stood over him. "I'm all out," he said, without looking up.

"Don't fuck with me, Ray," she heard herself say, her stomach in knots.

"I'm serious, Trace. I'm all out. My source got clipped." He looked at her. "You're resourceful," he said. "If there's anything you need, I'm sure you know how to get it."

She felt the urge to claw him with her fingernails. She knew he was holding back—the only thing she didn't know was why.

She told him to leave, and to her surprise, he quietly obeyed. Alone in the apartment for the first time in months, she told herself she didn't need anything from him, least of all more drugs.

But that night, she couldn't sleep, and by the next morning, the shaking of her hands had metastasized across her whole body. She tried to eat breakfast but couldn't keep food down. Her mind wouldn't sit still long enough to focus on anything but a scrolling display of the many pharmacological wonders that were so out of reach.

She called in sick and spent hours online looking for a former coworker she'd fallen out of touch with. She knew Lucy would have what she needed.

Unlike her, Lucy had been caught. She was no longer a hospital employee, but, as Tracy discovered when she finally found her e-mail, Lucy was still an addict. They met for coffee and worked out a system: Tracy would get Lucy's prescriptions signed, and Lucy would cut her in for half. Tracy's boss, Cheryl, was going through a divorce that year and gave Tracy a wide rein.

As it turned out, it was even wider than she'd imagined—wide enough for an endless stream of Oxy and Percocet and Vicodin. Over the next month, Tracy kept her and Lucy in supply even as she told herself she didn't *need* to take the pills; she just preferred to use them when sleep didn't come easily. And because she wasn't doing any more direct actions, she would wean herself off them eventually.

Ray had shown up again a few days after she'd kicked him out—she didn't know where he went; he didn't say, and she didn't ask—and by the time he knocked on her door, she was comfortably high, feeling that loose feeling that let her forgive him and that confident feeling that enabled her to say: *No more actions.* And he agreed.

He was still vandalizing labs and farms, which he recounted in detail every morning as if to tempt her to change her mind. But she was more relieved than envious and believed that they had achieved a new stage in their relationship, one of respect for each other's needs. All the while, she kept the drugs hidden away, buried in the back of her closet and in the backpack she used for work. She didn't know if Ray realized she was still using, but it didn't matter, as every day she planned to take her last pill. A relationship based on honesty would have to wait.

One night, as she and Ray sat at the bar at the Airliner with a pitcher and a mission to finish it, she remembered her vow that morning—to get through the day without a pill. But the beer wasn't doing much for her, so she decided today wasn't the day after all. She went to the bathroom and chewed up her last three tablets, feeling the bitterness coat her tongue, the effect immediate. She splashed some water on her face and then made her slow return to Ray, passing the jukebox playing Modest Mouse, the college kids in a circle doing shots. She felt the room begin to sway, her body bending into a smile.

She stopped when she saw a man sitting on her barstool, Ray's hand on one shoulder. She watched as they clinked shot glasses and downed them, then she approached and stood behind them.

"Hey, Trace," Ray said. "This is Neil. Cameron." Ray pulled Tracy to him. She let herself sink into Ray's grip as she looked at Neil.

"I've heard about you," she said.

"Just the highlights," Ray said. She was still studying Neil's face, in so many ways the opposite of Ray's: light hair, tanned skin, evasive blue eyes.

"We're about to step it up, Trace," Ray said. "The brains of the operation has arrived. They better watch the fuck out!"

Ray proceeded to dive back into a conversation he and Neil had already started. Through the pleasant fog drifting through her brain, she heard Ray plotting as usual, planning their takedown of corporate America, one slaughterhouse and fast-food joint at a time. She noticed that Neil didn't speak much, and later, in bed, she asked Ray, "Why's Neil so quiet?"

"Still waters," Ray said.

Over the following weeks, she learned little else about Neil, not where he lived or even if he had an apartment. She wouldn't see him for days at a time, until he'd suddenly appear in their dark corner booth at the Airliner. Perhaps because of Ray's incessant and angry chatter, Tracy found Neil's silence alluring. He was an introvert, like her, content to sit back and let others talk. She liked the way his ragged, wheat-colored hair always snuck out from under his baseball cap, the way he wore jeans and a black T-shirt or sweatshirt with little variation.

"Where do you keep yourself when you're not here?" she asked Neil one night.

Before Neil could answer, Ray interjected, "The less you know, the better. It's for your own good, not just his. Neil's pulled far more dangerous shit than you and I ever have."

"Like what?"

"Like hacking into big-ass corporations. We lift a hen or two and call it a day. My boy here steals Social Security numbers of CEOs, before breakfast."

"Ray." Neil spoke up. "What happened to *the less she knows the better*?"

Ray laughed and went for another round of beers.

"How long have you and Ray been doing direct action?" Tracy asked Neil.

"I'm more about creative action," he said, leaning back in the booth. "Undercover videos were creative at one point, but now the ag-gag laws put anyone who films inside a slaughterhouse at risk of imprisonment. So we have to find new approaches."

Ray returned with the beers, and Tracy realized then why she enjoyed having Neil around—having him in town relieved the pressure on her to be an activist, and having him sitting with them eased the pressure between her and Ray. Everything, suddenly, seemed so much better with Neil around.

18.

Tracy is standing over Bruce's naked torso when she hears footsteps stop at the door. She looks up to see Helen in the doorway, her eyes wide.

"Is he gone?"

"No, Mrs. Renschen. It's okay. Bruce has a urinary infection. It happens sometimes with the catheters. The doctor has him on antibiotics."

"Is he in pain?" Helen asks, taking an unsteady step forward.

"No. Not at all."

Helen looks down at her husband's hairy chest, the skin sagging off the sides. "I hate to sound rude, but why all the fuss? He's going to die anyway."

"It's protocol. We have to do it." She looks up at Helen. "And I have to replace the catheter now."

"You want me to leave?"

"It's not that," Tracy says. "Some people don't like to watch."

"Well, I do." Helen puts her hands on the railings alongside Bruce's bed, as if bracing herself.

Tracy pulls the sheet down toward Bruce's feet, then takes hold of the thin silicone tube extending from the end of his wrinkled penis like a straw. Explaining everything to Helen as she watches, Tracy attaches a syringe and slowly extracts the air that resides in a small balloon within his bladder, which holds the tube in place. After Tracy has disinfected the area and unwrapped the fresh Foley catheter, she glances up at Helen, whose eyes are on Bruce's genitals. Tracy takes the penis and holds it vertical, then begins inserting the fresh tube. "He doesn't feel anything right now," she says.

"I know that, kiddo," Helen says. "He hardly felt anything when I did that to him while he was awake."

Tracy looks up.

"I'm kidding. Just trying to make light of an awkward moment."

Helen pauses, then says, "You know, Bruce was cheating on me."

"He was?"

"Janet Lee Carlson. A junior partner. In her late forties. Three kids. Husband's a professor. Bruce thought I didn't know, but I dropped in on him one day about six months ago when she was in his office. I stood outside the glass as they were talking, and when she looked out at me I could tell. The way her eyes dropped to the floor, like some puppy who just peed on the carpet."

"I'm sorry."

"I never confronted him about it. I was saving it for the right time—on my way out the door, a moving truck idling at the curb, empty goddamned fridge and not a toilet paper roll to be found. I was so close."

As Tracy covers Bruce's body with the bedsheet, she wonders whether Helen would have ever left him, whether it was just a fantasy that she told herself in order to live with the truth. This is the scenario that makes sense to Tracy. She, too, has always been attracted to men whose hearts lie elsewhere.

"I'M CALLING IT OPERATION TEMP," Neil said.

When Ray picked her up at work an hour earlier, he didn't head to the Airliner but to a country-western bar on the south side of town. Ray told her Neil wanted to meet there, somewhere different. They were both being unusually secretive; she had to lean in to hear Neil's voice, nearly drowning under a Waylon Jennings song.

"Who's the target?" Tracy asked. She'd snorted up two Percocet off a bathroom sink before leaving the hospital. It could be stressful hanging out with Ray and Neil, always hearing about their grand plans, and she needed something to take the edge off.

"Tarcher Processing," Ray said. "The largest cattle slaughterhouse in Iowa."

"For this to work," Neil said, "we need to get someone inside the corporate office. Fortunately, I figured out what temp agency they use, and there's an opening for an assistant to the sales director. Answering phones. Data entry. Spreadsheets."

"Ray's getting a temp job?" Tracy laughed. "I'd like to see him work an Excel sheet."

Neil turned to her. "It wasn't Ray I had in mind."

Tracy felt the weight of their eyes on her. At first, she felt betrayed. Ray and Neil had obviously talked about this already; they knew that if they sat here together, she'd be unable to say no—with Ray's hand on her thigh, Neil watching her with those expectant blue eyes.

Then she felt a wave of camaraderie toward them—something about the way they looked at her. She liked that they needed her, depended on her to do this. That she could be their hero—and maybe she needed to do something heroic. Something drastic.

"Would I have to quit my job?" she asked.

"Yes," Neil said.

"It's about time," Ray said. "Fucking healthcare system."

She thought about the close calls she'd had recently. A nurse named Robin had walked in on her one day in the locker room as she licked powdered Vicodin from her fingers; she'd neglected to lock the door. And the week before, Cheryl had begun to question her about a prescription when she was called away. Maybe it was best that Tracy left before getting caught. She could do this action, flush the drugs out of her system, then find a new job. Maybe this was, as Ray insisted, the perfect plan.

The next day, she didn't bother putting on her scrubs. She walked directly into Cheryl's office and handed over her resignation letter, which cited personal reasons.

"I don't understand," said Cheryl. "No reason. No advance notice? Nothing?" Cheryl removed her glasses, and Tracy wondered if she suspected anything about the drugs. "I hope you don't expect a reference."

"I don't."

And that was it. She was surprised she felt so little remorse as she left Cheryl's office. As she walked down the hall on her way out, she saw Robin carrying a tray of meds.

"Robin," Tracy called, and Robin stopped. "Cheryl needs to see you. It's urgent."

Robin hesitated. "I just have to—"

"I'll take it. What room?"

"B2."

When Robin turned the corner, Tracy set down the tray and pocketed the pills on her way out the door.

There was little downtime between jobs; Tracy signed up with the temp agency the next day and sat through three interviews until Tarcher Processing invited her in. As Neil predicted, Tracy had no trouble getting hired.

Her new boss, James, was a loud, rotund man who smelled of Doritos. As Tracy sat in his office, his booming voice filled the room, a side effect, she later learned, of a half-decade spent supervising the killing floor. She noticed, as his eyes roamed down the front of her blouse, a family photo of a woman and four young children, with James in the middle, his bulging arms around two of the kids.

When Neil heard Tracy's description of James, he recommended she wear low-cut blouses to work. Sure enough, whenever he needed to talk with her, James would stand close to her desk so he could get a good look down, despite the fact that there wasn't much to see.

The work was easy: James had her order lunches, set up conference calls, even call his wife when he was running late. It was so banal she could forget that her desk was on the other side of a football field–sized killing floor. The Xanax she was now buying from Lucy helped, too.

What turned out to be more difficult was Gina; she couldn't tell Gina she'd quit her job to infiltrate a processing plant, and so whenever they talked or met for drinks, Tracy had to make up stories about her day at the hospital, or pretend she'd just gotten off a shift.

It made her glad she had so few friends to lie to, though she suspected Gina could tell something was going on, even as Tracy blamed her anxiety and lack of focus on too many evening shifts and not enough sleep.

After the first week at the plant, she learned James's schedule well enough to plan exactly when she could spend time in his office alone. She only had to go through two of his children's names before discovering his password. Whenever she could, she logged in and gathered information on the other executives—home addresses, phone numbers. She printed out e-mails between James and the others, not bothering to read beyond the subject lines. She filed the papers in her backpack and delivered them to Neil at the end of each workday. Ray wanted her to wear a wire or plant a bug, but Neil assured him that they'd get what they needed. Tracy was just glad she never had to visit the floor. She'd do as much information gathering as they wanted, as long as she could stay on the other side, away from the killing.

Then one day, while James was out, the president, Gerry Reynolds, came pounding through the office and handed her an envelope. "Give this to Edward," he said.

"Edward works on the floor," she said.

"That's right."

"I've never been down there," she said.

"First time for everything, sweetheart. Move along."

She took the envelope and made a quick stop in the ladies' room, where she chewed six Xanax, rolling the grainy bitterness around on her tongue until she felt herself begin to relax. It would not be enough, but it was all she had. She'd been allowing herself no more than ten pills a day at work. It helped her get through, knowing she still had a full bottle of two-milligram pills in the drawer in the closet to come home to. Such is the life of the drug addict. She measures her life in milligrams.

She left the restroom and went to the receptionist downstairs, who, when Tracy asked for Edward, pointed to the door behind her, a shortcut. Having never been, Tracy knew the killing floor only in the abstract, but she knew the reality, too—that on the other side of this door was an assembly line of cutters and carvers and cleaners stretching nearly a mile across white-tiled and blood-slicked floor. The term *disassembly line* was more accurate. She knew what happened, but she had never seen it. And even as she opened the door, she hoped she'd never have to.

She looked for Edward, hoping he would be standing nearby, waiting for her. He wasn't.

She followed a hallway that led to a metal door with a RESTRICTED AREA sign on it. She pulled open the door and froze—the smell hit her so hard she thought she'd vomit right there. The thick, sweaty odor of animals and humans and feces and raw meat all combined into something her mind couldn't process. She held her nose with one hand, the envelope in the other.

The noise was so loud, the metallic clanging of steel chains and rollers and hydraulic pumps and, beyond, the sounds of cows, not so much moos as cries. People walked around in white overcoats, with plastic coverings and blood-covered limbs. Tracy tried to approach a couple of them, then backed away when she saw how frantic and focused they were.

She looked in vain for someone she could hand this damn envelope to. A Mexican woman waved her over.

"It's for Edward!" Tracy called, holding up the envelope.

The woman pointed to the far end of the room, to a raised platform on the second level. Tracy's eyes followed the assembly line backwards, and cow pieces became cow heads and legs and bodies until she was staring at the platform, on which a cow, still intact, spilled out of a chamber, lifeless, blood pouring from a hole in his forehead.

Men greeted the body by chaining the back legs and hanging the animal upside down, blood pooling on the concrete floor.

Tracy noticed a heavyset man in a tie with rubber boots on the platform descending the stairs. As she met him at the bottom, the sounds of a pop like a firecracker blasted from above—the sound of the airgun, she knew from Ray's stories, being used to kill the next cow in line.

She heard a noise and glanced over and saw what she should not have seen—something no one should have to see but that somehow, these people witnessed every day of their working lives.

A man's heavy hand landed on her shoulder, and as she jumped, she slipped, falling to the floor, the cow's warm blood soaking through her dress. She slid around, trying desperately to stand. The man reached down for her, and high above hovered the sad black eyes of a dying animal.

She didn't remember how she got hold of Neil, or why she'd called him instead of Ray. She only remembered the looks of those in the office when she returned, dripping with blood, and took her purse from the desk. When Neil's car pulled into the parking lot, she climbed into the backseat without a word. He covered her in a blanket, and she cried until they reached his apartment, the first time she had stepped inside. Neil led her to the shower, and when she finally emerged, skin hot and red from scrubbing under scalding water, she saw he'd left her a T-shirt and a pair of sweatpants. They were far too big for her but felt warm and soft against her irritated skin.

Ray was in the living room with Neil when she walked in, and she felt her stomach tighten.

"I'm not going back," she said.

"You have to," Ray said. "How the hell are we supposed to get intel on this company if you don't keep the job long enough to collect any?"

"You don't understand, Ray," she said. "What I saw."

"I know exactly what you saw. I used to work undercover at these places. It's awful and it stinks like death and you can't stand it. I get that. But if we can't stomach a little nastiness from time to time, we're not going to put these fuckers out of business."

"I don't think I'm cut out for this," she said.

"No shit."

"Easy, Ray," Neil said.

"I was wrong about you, Tracy." Ray looked at her with a calm chill that made her stomach clench even more. "I thought you were one of us."

"I am one of you. Just not the same as you." She held up a key card. "This belongs to my boss. He kept an extra in his desk, so he won't know it's missing. Now you can walk right in and have your way. You don't need me anymore."

She threw the card at him and left Neil's apartment. She thought of the Xanax she had at home and decided it would never be enough, not tonight. So she headed for the park, barefoot and swimming in Neil's clothes, focused on just one thing, a cure for what was ailing her, what had always been ailing her.

19.

BRUCE DIED AT 3:47 IN THE MORNING. Tracy sees it on the whiteboard when she comes in, prior to doing her rounds. Often she is around when they die, but this time she is relieved to have missed the passing, if only by a couple of hours.

Tracy goes to Bruce's room to make sure it's ready for the next patient. She finds Helen seated there, staring at the empty bed. She's wearing her winter coat, purse on her lap, as if she's been ready to go for a while.

"Mrs. Renschen?"

Helen looks up with wandering eyes. Tracy recognizes the expression. Her anchor gone, Helen is now drifting from shore. Like so many others, Helen had spent so much time waiting for death that when it finally arrived, she didn't know what to do with it.

"I was awake for it, not sure why," Helen says. "He didn't speak. Didn't even close his eyes. I suppose *Daisy* was his final word."

"I'm sorry," Tracy says.

"You were good to him," she says. "To me. I wanted to invite you over for dinner tonight."

"Mrs. Renschen—"

"Don't worry, kiddo. I won't cook anything with meat or cheese or whatever else you can't eat. I bought a vegan cookbook. The pictures don't look half bad."

"Mrs.—"

"Call me Helen, for crying out loud." She stands. "It's time we dropped the formalities. I'm no longer a client. Bruce is dead."

Tracy watches Helen's legs tremble. Helen opens her purse and hands Tracy a piece of paper.

"My address. Please come tonight."

"Mrs.—Helen."

"You need a break from this place, kiddo."

"I'm well aware."

"It's depressing here. Fluorescent lights. Stale air."

"I'm used to it."

"That should concern you. Nobody should get used to this place." She starts past Tracy down the empty hallway.

"Helen?"

"Yes?"

"Thank you for the invitation. That was nice of you. Very nice. But I'm working tonight." The lie, like the platitudes she offers to the patients, slips from her tongue easily.

"Some other time then?"

"Yes. Some other time." Tracy wants to say she is sorry, to give Helen a hug. Or maybe she should take her up on the offer, follow her to the address on the slip of paper, to the nicer side of town.

It's too late now. As Helen turns the corner, Tracy glances at the paperwork she forgot she was holding. Frances Bennett, seventy-nine years old. Failing heart.

Tonight, she has decided, there will be no hesitation. She will knock on his door, and at last Neil will know the truth about how she ruined his life. No more hiding in cars, watching shadows on ceilings. She will tell him about the letters, how badly she wanted to be close to him, to help him through those endless months. And afterward, if he has not thrown her out by then, she will invite him out for a drink—a beer for him, club soda for her.

As she approaches Neil's building, she notices a car in her usual parking spot, a late-model sedan that looks vaguely familiar. In front of the building are two other newish cars with out-of-state plates. Standing on the corner is a woman she doesn't recognize with a dog on a leash, just standing there, both of them.

Tracy stops and looks up at Neil's apartment. It's brighter than usual, and multiple shadows move across the ceiling, as if Neil is throwing a party. But she knows instinctively that this is no party.

She continues around the block, barely drawing a glance from the woman with the dog. She parks at her own apartment building, then heads back to Neil's on foot. It's not very far, and perhaps she should have been doing this all along instead of risking having her car draw attention. But there's never an easy way to spy on someone; a woman standing alone on the street draws just as much attention, if not more, than an unfamiliar vehicle.

The woman with the dog is no exception, standing alone on the quiet street, and her dog's focused attention, as if waiting for a cue, makes it all the more obvious that she's not walking her dog.

Tracy skirts down an alley to the back door, which is propped open with a brick, and she enters and turns right, up the stairs. On the third floor she comes around the corner to Neil's door, wide open.

She hears voices and slows, quietly taking the final few steps until she is standing in the hall watching them—three men in jeans and plain black sweatshirts. Taking pictures. Filling plastic bags with CDs and books.

She turns and slips back down the rear stairway, followed by the crackled voices of walkie-talkies. She bursts out the rear door and into the dark alley, then takes a narrow pathway behind a row of bushes, a path that she has taken before, when she first began watching him. She hears the crackling radio sounds grow faint as she runs through alleys and backyards, up driveways to the downtown blocks where she can blend in with the hordes of drunk students, letting the darkness keep her hidden. Once there, she slows and begins to walk, grateful for the darkness. She glances behind her a few times until she is satisfied she hasn't been followed. She continues walking, in and out of streetlights, wishing she could linger in the darkness forever. It's the only place she feels completely safe, but, like so many of the people in her life, it's never around for long enough.

20.

Back at her apartment, Tracy waits in the shadows across the street. Still worried about having been followed, she looks for anything unusual—a car passing too slowly, pedestrians who look out of place—just in case the woman with the dog glimpsed her license plate and decided to run it.

After a half hour, convinced that all is quiet, she goes upstairs. She looks for signs of intrusion but finds nothing. Her laptop would not still be on the floor if they had connected her with Neil.

She picks up her laptop, then hesitates. If they do know about her and she goes online, they could track her virtual movements. But it's too late for her to go to library and she's too desperate to know what happened.

When had Neil been caught—and how? More important, what he had done?

After that awful, bloody day at Tarcher Processing, which was, as she'd promised, her last, Ray didn't return to Tracy's apartment. She noticed his things were gone, and she wondered when he'd packed them up, or whether he'd never had things at all. The drugs were distorting her memories until she couldn't remember him ever really settling in with her. She waited for two days before texting him, asking where he was. Within seconds he texted back: *At Lisa's.*

Tracy snapped her cell phone off, added her last two pills to the dose she'd just taken, and walked to the Airliner, where she sat at the bar staring up at a college football game. She told herself that she should feel relieved to be free. But she felt unmoored, alone. She had no job. No boyfriend. She wanted to call Gina, but she'd blown off so many of her friend's calls by then she wasn't sure Gina would answer.

Tracy's mind flashed back to that day at Tarcher, when she'd looked up at the cows as their bodies were dumped from the area she later learned was the knocking box to the men waiting just outside to begin the process of carving these once-living creatures into a thousand disparate parts.

In just the minute she'd been there she'd seen three lifeless bodies emerge and would have survived that day less traumatized had she not seen the cow that was to follow. Still alive, the hole in his head squirting blood, the animal was moaning, crying out as his body landed hard on the floor—and then he looked right at her, his legs moving as if he were trying to run to her, and she felt herself moving toward him until that man's hand fell on her shoulder and spun her around and backwards into the blood.

From the floor she watched the animal next to her trying to

stand, learning herself that it was impossible to stand straight on all that blood. The men, knives in hand, descended upon the cow's neck and plunged in their knives until the animal stopped moving, eyes still open, on the floor. Tracy scrambled away, feeling as if the cow were still staring at her.

She slid off her barstool, trying to shake off the memory. She went to the restroom, feeling as though she were going to be sick. She splashed cold water on her face, and then she dialed Lucy's number, getting only voice mail and hanging up in frustration.

Tracy was terrified of a night without anything to calm her body and mind. Back at the bar, even though she knew alcohol would do little, she downed three shots of vodka and two beers, then called Lucy again. When she heard Lucy's voice mail, she left a shrill message, which she regretted the moment she hung up. Lucy had told her never to leave a message.

She took the long route home through College Green Park, where there was always a dealer or two on one of the corners. She found a man, a kid really, wearing baggy jeans and his baseball cap backwards. She asked about Oxy but he shook his head. Instead, he offered her a few packs of the powder she had for so long resisted. Pills were for pain, she told herself. Heroin was for addicts. But it was late, her hands were shaking, and she couldn't hold out on principle any longer. The kid offered a needle and she took it, realizing that she couldn't just grab a handful from work, as she was no longer a nurse.

At home, lying on her mattress, she felt the warmth roll over her, wave after wave. When she heard the knock on her door she thought she was dreaming, that Ray had let himself in with the key he never returned.

But the knocking continued, and she sat up, uneasily tossed a pillow over the spent syringe, and, with great effort, made her way to the door. Neil was on the other side.

"Is it too late?" he asked when she cracked open the door. "I just wanted to come over and see how you were doing."

She widened the door and returned to her mattress. Neil closed the door behind him and took the plastic folding chair. She gazed up at him, still floating on the receding tide of her waning high. Neil's quiet stillness reminded her that not all men were Ray and made her consider that maybe she deserved something better. Someone better. She turned on her side and patted on the floor next to the mattress.

"Come here," she said. "I don't bite."

He sat next to her and eyed her curiously. "You feeling okay?"

"A little drunk. A little tired." She closed her eyes.

"I'm sorry about Ray," he said.

"How do you stand him?"

"We share a common enemy."

"You're not upset that I quit?"

"I'm not Ray."

"No, you're not." She felt relaxed around him, unafraid to express herself. But she didn't want to talk; she wanted to listen. In all the time she'd known Neil, it had been all business, all direct action, nothing personal. She wanted to know who he really was, the man behind the silence. She reached over until her right hand was on his shoulder. "Talk to me," she said. "Tell me a story to help me sleep."

"A story?"

"Where are you from?"

He began talking, in his quiet way, and his voice drifted in and out of her consciousness as he told her about his childhood. About Seattle. About his father, a guy everyone came to call Aeneas. How Aeneas was never around, how Neil had resented his father all the time but he now thought it was time to let go of the anger, make amends. Neil told her about Lorne, a seaside town in the Australian state of Victoria, where his father had taken him when he was a boy. The rainbow lorikeets sprinting from to tree. The endless, empty beaches. The high surf.

"I'm going to meet him there someday," he said. "I'd love for you to see this particular spot on the beach. Looking over the horizon knowing the only thing between you and Antarctica is this wild, bone-chilling body of water."

It was the most she had ever heard Neil talk, and she didn't want his soothing voice to stop. She felt her mind drift, far away, to the beach stretching alongside Lorne, walking with Neil on the sand, hearing nothing but the waves.

She opened her eyes and sat up, feeling optimistic for once. She leaned over so she could see his eyes and he could see hers. When he looked at her, she felt the urge to kiss him. "Let's get away," she said. "To that beach. Does Ray know about it?"

Neil shook his head. "You're the only one I've told."

"Then let's do it. You and me. Tomorrow."

Neil pulled away from her and returned to the folding chair. "I know Ray's got problems and he should have treated you better, but that doesn't mean I can just—"

"Ray is going to end up in prison."

"I know," Neil said. "He's going to use that key card you gave him to break into Tarcher's office."

"I figured."

"He's going to do more than steal documents. He's planning to torch the entire place when he's done."

Tracy felt a sharp pain inside her forehead, and she wished, just for a moment, she was alone with her needle so she could make it all go away. "When?"

"Tomorrow night. He wants me to play lookout."

"Will you?"

Neil walked over to the window and stared out. "I'm not an arsonist."

She was glad to hear him say it, though she could tell Neil was conflicted. "Ray will never stop pushing," she said. "Eventually you either give up or you get caught."

Neil turned to her. "Maybe it is time I got out of this town and went down under. Take my old man up on his offer to join him on his ship."

"Would you take a plus one?" she asked.

Neil smiled and opened his mouth as if to answer but was interrupted by his phone. "It's Ray." He silenced the phone and looked up at her, a vulnerability in his eyes that reflected the way she was feeling now. "I think it's time he flew solo."

Inside her apartment, her laptop under her arm, Tracy goes to the window one last time, scanning the street to make sure no one had followed her from Neil's. All is quiet. For how long it will last, she doesn't know.

But she has to know what happened to Neil, when he vanished. She sits down on the floor next to the window and opens her laptop. On the website of the *Press Citizen* she finds the usual garbage about corn prices and the football team, nothing about a van or an attack on a slaughterhouse or anything that might tell her what exactly happened, and when.

She hears a creak outside her door. She peeks through the peephole but sees nothing. How quickly a settling foundation turns into a raiding SWAT team in her mind.

She shoves her laptop, a few changes of clothes, and her toothbrush into her backpack. She takes another look out the front window. Then she exits her apartment and slips down the back stairs.

Minutes later, she enters the Airliner and squints at the crowd. At this late hour, the place is jammed with college kids, shouting over the music and eyeing one another. She squeezes through bodies to the bar. She hasn't had a drink in two years. She's still just a toddler in sobriety years. Too young to walk on her own, not old enough to see the road ahead, and not too old to fall down on her face.

She catches her reflection on the back bar mirror, a pale face with sunken eyes staring back. How did she become so homely, so strung out? Two years of monastic living and nothing to show for it, not even Neil. So what about the face? she assures herself. There's a nice body hiding underneath this jacket. An energy hiding underneath the skin. Energy that made her great in bed those times with Ray, even when he admitted she was only the second-best lay he had ever had. *Number two,* she snorted. *What am I, Avis Rental Car? It's a compliment,* Ray insisted with that shitty grin of his. *It means you try harder.*

And now she will try to get numb.

She asks the bartender to bring her a pint and a shot of vodka. She downs the shot without ceremony and picks up the beer, hesitating to sip, savoring the burn of vodka in her throat. She knows these first drinks will hit her hard—but not hard enough to satisfy her epidural craving.

She slips off the barstool, grabs her jacket, and squeezes her way into the middle of the room, safely surrounded by bodies. *Two hundred of my closest strangers.* That's what Neil had said one night when they entered a bar that was too crowded to breathe. She lifts her pint and swallows until she has drained the glass.

A college kid with the beginnings of a beard is talking to her. She nods along through the music, drunk now and too tired to care what he is saying. They dance. He's holding her hand. Then he's buying her shots and she's dancing to ABBA and his mouth is on hers.

And then she is in his apartment, the couch squeaking under her, her mind somewhere else. Pleasure? Is this what pleasure, natural pleasure, is supposed to feel like? A lot of movement and moisture, new smells and sounds?

Later—she has no idea how much later, only that it is still night—she dresses in the dark and feels her way to the door. Her head spins as she walks the silent streets of the north side. She can feel her hands shaking and grips her fists to warm them.

She takes a shortcut across campus and finds herself standing in front of the animal sciences building. She can still see the outlines of the sandblasting used to erase the graffiti she and Ray sprayed there nearly four years ago. Back when she thought she could make a difference.

She struggles to remember what they wrote: *Animals Tortured Within*, she thinks. The words, like her, are faded and nearly invisible.

She continues on to College Green Park, her tree-lined drugstore, temptation growing, like an urge to bite a nail or pick a scab. If Neil is gone, what's the point of staying clean?

The kid she used to buy from isn't here, but there are others, and when they look at her, they perk up. Even though she's been clean for two years, they can see it in her eyes. Only addicts make eye contact with dealers. They offer her heroin and meth and pills, so many pills, a bazaar of her past life. She lowers her eyes and keeps on walking, until she finds herself standing on a bridge overlooking the Iowa River.

She leans over the railing, feeling the blood rush to her head, still drunk yet desperate for something stronger. How easy it would be right now to let her body fall into the water, to let the current take her far away from here. But that would be too easy, a cop-out. Until she knows Neil is dead, she must keep living.

She stands upright and feels her legs shivering in the cold air. She can tell by the incipient light in the sky that it's almost dawn. She turns back toward town, but when she reaches her building she's still afraid to go inside. Instead, she gets into her car, now her only home. She reaches into her pockets to warm her hands and finds a piece of paper, folded in four. Helen's address.

21.

When Tracy pulls up in front of Helen's house, the sun is just beginning to make its way over the horizon, casting shadows among the trees of Helen's leafy neighborhood. Tracy is so tired she contemplates pushing her seat back so she can sleep. She still feels drunk and doesn't want to admit to having driven here.

Yet the neighborhood is quiet and free of other cars, the homes spaced far enough apart to land a plane between; with the sun coming up, she won't be able to sleep long before someone calls the police.

Almost as if summoned by her thoughts, a police car passes, slowly, and she freezes. As the patrol car pauses at the end of the street, Tracy gets out of the car and walks with purpose to Helen's front door.

She hesitates only a moment before knocking; it's early, but she senses that Helen's invitation was open, even to a visit at this hour. Sure enough, within a minute, Helen is standing at the door in a robe. In the open doorway, Tracy can feel the warmth of the house, and the smell of fresh coffee fills the air.

"Look what we have here," Helen says, her eyes widening with surprise.

Tracy follows Helen through a living room that looks untouched by humans, between straight vacuum lines across thick carpet, and into the kitchen.

"Take a seat," Helen says. "Coffee?"

"Thanks," Tracy says. "And maybe some water?"

Helen turns to the sink, and Tracy, still standing, looks back into the living room. Over the fireplace mantle, she sees a painting, and she walks over to take a closer look. It's a portrait of Bruce and Helen and three children, their forced smiles and fake poses arranged around a red velvet couch.

"That was Bruce's idea," Helen says, handing Tracy a glass of water. "You don't like it?"

"The only good to come of that painting will be the frame when

I tear it apart."

"I'm sorry for bothering you."

"Do I look bothered? Come on, take a seat." Helen indicates the couch, and as she returns to the kitchen, Tracy sits. Helen comes back with two mugs of coffee and sits down next to her. "How have you been doing, kiddo?"

"I've been better."

"You've looked better. A vacation is what you need. Is it a man?"

"In a way."

"What do you mean?"

"That's just it. I don't know. I was in love—and now he's disappeared, and I—I can't find him."

Helen is absentmindedly tapping the base of her mug with her wedding ring. Tracy looks at it. Helen notices and stops.

"I don't think I'll ever take this off. My neighbor is trying to get me onto some dating website." She shakes her head. "Is that how you two met?"

"No," Tracy says. "I think he's in trouble. But I can't help if I can't find him."

"Where do you think he went?"

"I'd like to think he's still in town, lying low." Tracy covers her face with her hand. "I would probably be a lot less dramatic about this if I could just sleep. I'm so damned tired."

Helen turns away and reaches for her purse, which is on a side table nearby. She fishes out a prescription pill bottle, and then another, then another. She puts them on the coffee table in front of Tracy.

Tracy can't see the labels, but she wants to snatch a bottle, any bottle, open it up and pour the contents down her throat. She forces a disinterested voice as she asks, "What's all this?"

"Xanax," Helen says. "My doctor prescribed it when Bruce got sick, but I never take it. Mail order keeps them coming, and every time I call to cancel the next order I end up on hold and then give up. I had these in my purse to drop them off at a pharmacy. But they're yours if you want them. They're supposed to help you sleep."

Tracy hesitates. Each bottle looks as though it contains at least thirty pills. "I don't think so," she says. "Thanks anyway."

She forces her eyes back to Helen's face. She tries to listen as Helen talks about the emptiness of the house, her neighbor's invitation to dinner, how she's trying to keep herself busy. Tracy nods, but in her peripheral vision all she can see are the bottles on the table.

She stands. "I should go."

"You're exhausted. I won't hear of it." Helen stands up and herds her to the stairs. "I have three extra rooms. Pick one. Stay as long as you want."

"I can't."

"I'm not offering. I'm ordering."

They go upstairs, and Helen stops in front of a room. "This was my son Jackson's room."

Tracy enters and puts her bag down. Helen pulls the shades until the room is dark.

"Sleep it off, kiddo," Helen says. "Everything looks different once you've had some rest."

In Jackson's bed, she pictures Neil's face close to hers. They were going to be together—if only Ray had been out of the picture. It was Ray who got her hooked, who broke her confidence, broke her career, broke everything that could be broken. And Neil was the one putting her back together.

After three hours of staring at the empty pillow next to her, she gets out of bed, listening for Helen. She hears nothing but the sound of rain starting to fall on the roof. She gets dressed and packs her bag.

On her way out, she glimpses the bottles on the table. For two years she's been free of these little devils. Two years of abstinence in the hope that Neil would see how much she'd grown, how far she'd come. But what good is a clean life when life is no longer worth living? She scoops the bottles into her bag, then slips out the front door.

That had been her last evening with Neil—sitting on the floor of her apartment, listening to him talk about Australia, imagining being by his side. Later, so many times. she would play this scene again and again in her mind—right up until that moment Neil lifted the pillow on the floor, finding the needle.

"I'm a nurse," she told him. "It's not what you think."

"I know what an addict looks like," he said.

"It's purely recreational," she told him, feeling the floor sloping away from him, her sliding on the mattress, his voice fading.

"I can't do this," he said, before standing and walking out the door.

She wanted to run after him, speak the truth even though it was anything but the truth, but she was still too fuzzy in the head, and he was gone. Instead of pushing herself to her feet and pursuing the man she was prepared to run to the far ends of the earth with, she leaned over to the other side of the bed and pulled out another needle.

Voluntary euthanasia—an occupational phrase for those with terminal illnesses, those who wish to take control of their lives, which means to take control of their deaths.

To put oneself to sleep.

Despite the dose, she couldn't sleep. She lay on the mattress staring at the ceiling and the dead light bulb she never got around to replacing and thought about how much work goes into the simple act of living. The three meals, the countless inhales and exhales, the millions of fleeting thoughts flowing river-like to the ocean without anyone to appreciate them, not even her. Later that night, she left the apartment with the last of the drugs, the last needle, and found her way to the park bench, not far from the kid, knowing she would need more. As she waited in the darkness, she found a vein, faintly proud of her skills—the skills of a nurse attending to an illness she can no longer escape.

Her body flat on the cold wooden slats, she stared at the underbelly of an approaching storm, the clouds reflecting back the city lights. She imagined her head on Neil's lap once again, listening to him telling her about the Edicts of Ashoka, how 2,000 years ago the Indian emperor Ashoka converted to Buddhism and, in doing so, decided there would be no more killing of animals. He erected thirty-three pillars across his empire extolling these virtues, pillars that still stand today. *Our king killed very few animals.*

Her head was whirring with thoughts of heroes and martyrs and how little divides the two—mixing with thoughts of her own life, a series of heroic acts poorly executed. Another person might have achieved greatness in her shoes.

She pictured the beach that Neil described. He'd said that everything in life was waves. Light. Sound. Even gravity. "What about people?" she asked. He said that people were the most violent waves of all.

She saw him on the ocean, floating above it, swimming, as she stood at the shore, wanting to join him but afraid of all the creatures lurking underneath, afraid of losing control over her body to something so much more powerful. In her mind, Neil stopped swimming and floated there, his head just above the surface, rising and falling as he looked back at her.

She opened her eyes into the sun, multi-colored, welcoming her. It took her a few moments to realize it wasn't the sun she was looking into—it was something else, lights pulsing in whites and blues and reds, like waves, cascading over her body.

When she became fully conscious again, she was in a hospital bed, a man in a suit standing next to her. Her stomach lurched.

"You nearly died," the man said. "They had to shock your heart."

"Are you a doctor?"

He shook his head. "Get some rest."

When she woke again, she tried to rub her eyes, but her left wrist wouldn't move, handcuffed to the bed.

The same man stood at the doorway. "Are you well enough to talk?"

"Talk?"

"About Ray."

She vomited all over her hospital gown.

The man walked out, and moments later a nurse came in with a security guard. The guard released her from the handcuffs while the nurse cleaned her up and got her into a clean gown.

After they both left, Tracy tried to close her eyes again, but she felt someone standing over her. She opened her eyes and looked up at the man who wanted to talk about Ray.

"My name is Robert Porter," he said. "I work for the FBI. I'm not here to get you into trouble. I just need to know about Ray."

"I don't know anything about him," she said.

"Ray's gotten other women hooked on drugs," Robert said. "Did you know that?"

Tracy was silent, her body crying out for a fix.

"Did you know your dealer friend Lucy is in custody, too?"

Tracy felt as if the life were deserting her body. "Lucy has a child," she said. "You can't do that to her."

"You mean *you* can't do that to her," he said. "All you have to do is work with us, and Lucy will have her life back. You'll have your life back."

"What do you want?"

"I know all about your job at Tarcher," he said. "You're not the one we want, but if you don't cooperate, you'll be the one going to prison instead of Ray. Lucy, too."

Tracy lay there sweating, shaking, knowing her symptoms would only go from bad to worse; she'd seen it so many times before, never imagining she'd be here herself one day. Robert Porter seemed to know what she did—that soon her symptoms would worsen and she'd be unable or unwilling to talk.

She was not a rat, not one to give up a fellow activist. But she wasn't who she used to be—she was someone different now, something less.

Instead of caring for the sick, she was the one prostrate in a hospital bed, her body contorted. It wasn't just physical; she was swarmed with regret, and a seething anger toward the man who'd led her down this path. What right did Ray have to hurt her and so many others, only to walk away unscathed? How many others came before, and how many would follow? Robert presented an outlet for all that anger, one that Tracy would never have considered, one that a lesser person would gladly take.

She told Robert that Ray would be at Tarcher that night. She told him what Ray was planning to do. She signed the paperwork he put in front of her, feeling nauseous, knowing that Ray would soon be in a place far worse than a hospital room, and then she felt sicker still because a part of her relished the thought that he'd finally begin to taste the pain she'd been suffering all this time.

She was released from the hospital three days later, with a scheduled appointment at an outpatient program. But, for a change, drugs were the furthest thing from her mind. She wanted to see Neil.

She went to Neil's apartment, but he wasn't home. He didn't answer his phone. Next she went to Ray's, thinking maybe Neil had crashed there instead—but no one was there, either.

Then she realized she never learned what happened at Tarcher, so she got online and scoured the news, finally finding a short bit on it from a local station. Neil Cameron and Ray Hudson, arrested at Tarcher Processing for breaking and entering with the intent to commit arson.

Tracy felt heat burn through her body. *I think it's time he flew solo,* Neil had said. He wasn't supposed to be there.

She dug out the business card Robert had given her. "You made a mistake," she said when she reached him on his cell. "You were only supposed to arrest Ray."

"We arrested everyone who was there to commit a crime."

"It was supposed to be just Ray," she repeated. "You have to do something."

"You're off the hook. That's all I promised."

"But—"

"I'll recommend they go easy on Neil. It's his first arrest, so it won't be long."

"Long?"

"In prison. He's pleading guilty. This is good news, Tracy. You won't need to testify."

"What if I want to testify?" she asked. "To tell the truth."

"The truth? That you flipped on your friends?"

As she let the phone slip from her hand, she felt the need to face Neil and Ray so they would know who turned on them. So she could tell them and the court how weak she was and is, how drinking and drugs dulled her ability to say no, not only to herself but to others.

Neil, poor Neil. He did not deserve this. And here she was, facing no punishment at all. But this didn't mean she would not suffer. The drugs. This would be her penance—getting clean and staying clean, no matter how long Neil remained behind bars.

She began her sentence, as he did, the day he was arrested. She blew off her appointment and the treatment centers and did it alone, day by nauseous day, the cravings bringing her to her knees, pain spreading from the forehead to the toes, until her entire body was pounding at her from the inside.

After two weeks, when her hunger returned and she could stand straight in the shower, she dressed as nicely as she could, walked back to the clinic, entered Cheryl's office, and asked for her job back. She was lucky; one of the other nurses had just gone on maternity leave, and Cheryl gave her a temporary position.

The next fences to be mended were with friends. It had been so long since she'd talked with Gina she couldn't even remember when it was, and she hadn't attended a Meetup in months.

But when she went to the next Meetup, she sat down at a table full of hostile eyes. Lisa, who had visited Ray behind bars, blamed Tracy for his arrest, even though there was no way Ray could have known what she'd done. When Gina came to her defense, Tracy remained quiet; she didn't know how to defend herself, or whether she should. When Gina stood up and said, with a withering look toward Lisa, "Come on, Tracy, let's get out of here," Tracy put her hand on Gina's shoulder and guided her back down. Then she stood and left the restaurant on her own.

She attended Neil's sentencing. Neil stood at the front of the room, and when he looked back, he saw her. She smiled and felt the urge to call out, to let him know she loved him and always would. But he only turned back toward the front of the courtroom.

She wanted to believe he still didn't know. And maybe he didn't. Ray had never been the most credible source, after all.

After Neil was sentenced to eighteen months in prison, she watched him being led out of the courtroom, hoping he might look at her once more, but he did not.

When Neil was transferred to a federal prison outside Salt Lake City, Tracy began writing him letters under the name Kristina. Every week she drove across the state line to mail the letters from Illinois.

Tracy still could not bring herself to face Neil; she had no words to apologize for what she'd done. She knew from activist websites that others were writing to Neil with their support. She also knew that they were ready to ostracize whoever had leaked information about the raid on Tarcher; eventually, she would be discovered. And even if Neil responded to her before he found out, surely he wouldn't afterward. And so it was best to write as someone else.

Kristina wrote about how brave he was, how admired. Kristina sent him books with short notes enclosed. Kristina told him she hoped he was doing okay.

And after two months of letters and books, Kristina received a reply. Neil thanked her for her support and for all the books. He wrote: *Taking it day by day. Hour by hour. Me and two hundred of my closest strangers.* The familiar phrase brought tears to Tracy's eyes.

Kristina began to write longer letters. She wrote about current events, knowing he had no access to news; about movies she hadn't seen; about celebrities who had gone vegan. Neil replied: *Vegan movie stars don't help the movement because they are actors and nothing for them is real. "Vegan" is just another costume, one that they will tire of before long.* Then he asked about her. What she did for a living. What got her through the days.

While Tracy was still working at the hospital, Kristina worked in Moline, Illinois, as receptionist for a web hosting company. She told Neil that she wished there were more vegan options in town. She told him she'd moved from Chicago after a love affair had gone bad, which explained why she had so much free time to be sending letters every day. *Do you have a girlfriend?* she asked.

He replied: *There was someone once, but she broke my heart.*

22.

TRACY PARKS OUTSIDE HER APARTMENT and gets out of the car, Helen's pills rattling in their bottles in her backpack. She stares up at her windows, thinking of Neil. If only she'd acted sooner—knocked on his door, visited him in the computer lab, bumped into him at the damn market—maybe things would be different.

A light goes on, and for a moment Tracy believes she is looking at the wrong apartment window. Movement dancing across the ceiling. But it is her apartment.

She looks up and down the street. Where are the official-looking cars she saw in front of Neil's? The dog walker?

The only activity is a young kid skateboarding on the sidewalk across the street. She looks up, and the light is still on, though there are no more shadows on the ceiling. Whoever it is has either left or has stopped moving. Or she had imagined it. She shakes her head, telling herself she's being paranoid—stuck in old habits. She'd simply left a light on and forgotten, thinking she'd seen it go on.

She crosses the street, enters her building, and heads up the stairs, then turns to see her door closed, light escaping underneath.

She stands in front of the door and listens. No signs of movement. She opens the door.

When she sees the man standing in front of her, she feels her body freeze. Not because he's an intruder but because she recognizes him.

It's Robert Porter. The FBI agent. He looks so much older, as if far more than two years had passed, but she'd know him anywhere. Even with that freshly bandaged cut above his left eye.

"Hello Tracy," he says. "I hope you don't mind. I let myself in."

Of course, you did, she wants to tell him. *You and your kind are always going where you're not welcome. And people like me will always be running from people like you. Until we can no longer run.*

Amy

23.

She wonders if he is someone famous, traveling incognito. The aviator glasses. The dirty blue baseball cap pulled low over his shaggy blond hair. A celebrity sighting is just what her blog needs right about now.

She checked the stats last night in the hostel in Fiji and saw that the only regular visitors to her blog were someone from Chicago (who was searching on *cheap Fiji hotels*) and someone from Fiji (herself). No visits over the past week from publishers in New York scouting out the next great travel writer. No visits from Los Angeles from studios or agents looking for another great travel rom-com. And no visits from St. Louis; Chad, evidently, has better things to do with his time.

Her confidence—what's left of it after this long, fruitless journey of self-discovery—is quickly slipping away.

New Zealand will be different, she tells herself as she exits the plane, though her experience so far has done little to confirm this. The Auckland airport is just like any other airport: endless hallways and bland decor. And this hostel van pulling up to the curb is just like all the other vans that ferry aimless, yawning backpackers shuffling out of customs toward a bunk bed and a shower.

She resigns herself to experiencing this country as she did Hong Kong, Thailand, Indonesia, Australia, and Fiji—alone. Which was the whole idea when she left home, before she knew just how few backpackers travel alone. Just how difficult it is to strike up a conversation when you're off by yourself and you're more than a decade older than all the twentysomethings. Everywhere she landed and slept, she was surrounded by young college dropouts or recent grads, all bitching about student loans and using Snapchat while she sat around feeling like the lone chaperone at a high school dance.

The night before, she lay in her bunk bed wondering how long she'd have to stay away from Chad to prove that she had found herself. Three months should be sufficient, she decided. Which leaves her with eight long weeks left to go.

Would it be so awful if she cut the trip short? She already had the requisite tan, something her coworkers would envy in the early days of winter. A photo of herself caught in a jubilant jump in the air in front of the Sydney Opera House. She had collected pictures of coral-blue water and white sands, the distant spout of an unidentified whale, a sulphur-crested cockatoo poking along the grounds of Hyde Park. Photos she could print out and post on her cubicle wall, enough visual stimulation to get her through a few more years of work.

But where were the *stories* she'd expected to collect like passport stamps? Stories of men with sleek surfers' bodies and exotic accents, stories of bungee-cord jumps and drinking at midnight on the beach. All she has are the actual passport stamps and the knowledge that her tan will soon begin peeling like old wallpaper.

As she climbs into the hostel van, her mind flashes back to junior high. The eyes upon her, the other kids secretly judging her. Now, the eyes glance upward as she walks down the aisle of the van. She's only thirty-four years old, yet among them she feels ancient. What do they make of her? A midlife crisis? A failed marriage? A lost soul?

She squeezes into a back-row window seat. And that's when she notices him, seated across from her at the other window seat. Alone. That's the first unusual thing about him.

The other unusual thing is that he looks closer to her age than most backpackers she encounters, though she wonders if it's the wariness about him that makes him seem older. His face is angled toward the window. Arms tan, biceps toned—but not overly so. Strong but not showy. A faded black T-shirt. Baseball cap. Khaki shorts frayed around the edges and running shoes that tilt to one side. And she wonders: A midlife crisis? A failed marriage? A lost soul?

She turns to look out her own window at the low-hanging clouds. Everything is green, as if a rainstorm has just blown through. It's hot and humid, but there is no air-conditioning in the van. She begins to sweat under the jeans and long-sleeved shirt she wore for the flight. She stares down at her phone, feeling the urge to call someone, take a picture. To do something, like all the others in the van who are chatting, taking selfies, pointing out the windows.

Instead, she returns her gaze to the mystery man.

Everyone else has the requisite nylon backpacks, new hiking boots, and iPads, but this guy looks as if he's from a different era—Indiana Jones in a baseball cap. His backpack is half the size of her monstrosity, with a pair of black boxers squirming out of a pocket. Maybe it's a generational thing; the two younger women in the seat in front of her have backpacks that could double as body bags.

He turns to her. Blond eyebrows match the shaggy hair covering his forehead. She recognizes the logo on his cap—a cardinal perched on a baseball bat. Could he be, like her, from St. Louis? She smiles expectantly, but his eyes are already looking past her. She returns her gaze to the window.

So much for the shared bond between backpackers and wayward travelers, fellow St. Louisans. Maybe he doesn't live there anymore but still roots for his hometown team. And what would she say if he asked her anything about baseball? She can't keep track of the time change, let alone whether it's baseball season yet, or when it might begin. Chad would know.

She glances back. There's a tattoo on his right bicep. She makes out the letters "OR" and longs to know the rest. A voice in her head tells her to settle down. Focus on the journey. Focus on the blog.

The hostel is worse than she expected. In the course of wrapping the rented bedsheets over the stained mattress, she sidesteps two cockroaches running for cover. It is a sad place, with more empty bunks than people. She wonders if the others on the bus had taken one look at the place and returned to the airport. Maybe this will make for a good blog post. She snaps a few pictures of the dorm with her phone, secures her backpack in the locker, and returns to the lounge.

Two Brits sprawl on an old couch in front of a blaring television with tall beer cans in their hands, eyeing her as she passes through the lounge and back outside, in search of a place to eat.

The hostel is in a residential neighborhood of run-down homes that remind her more of a college town than a provincial English-inspired colony. The homes run right up to the street, some with yards the size of kiddie pools, others since converted to driveways. She walks a block, then another. What she would give for a fast-food restaurant within eyesight—a relatively clean table where she can sit and write, with food she can trust.

She passes a fish-and-chips shop, with backpackers on their phones huddled over its plastic tables. A meat-pie vendor farther down the street does little to entice her. A transit bus passes, and she wonders if there's an app with bus schedules she can download, so she can find a city center, better food, maybe a waterfront. But she's too jet-lagged to bother with another vehicle today. She makes her way back to the hostel and fetches one of her remaining protein bars from the locker.

When she goes back outside to sit at the hostel's picnic table, she sees Indiana Jones seated at one end, studying a map. She is tempted to take a picture. Who carries maps anymore?

She sits at the other end of the table, across from him. He doesn't look up. She stares at her phone, pretending to be texting someone when she's actually checking the weather, again. Then she opens Instagram, turns off the phone's volume, and holds the phone so that Indiana Jones is centered in the camera frame. *Remember when people used maps?* she writes, posting this with his photo with the hashtags #auckland #backpacking #cutemenofnewzealand. She publishes the image and waits to see if any of her 23 followers like it. How pathetic. She's in a foreign city on the other side of the world and the first thing she does is obsess over who likes her photos.

She glances back at Indiana Jones, still engrossed in his map, and she hears that voice in her head again. *If you don't speak up, you'll never be heard.*

She puts her phone down. "Hello," she says. When she gets no response, she tries again, louder this time. "You heading to the South Island?"

He looks up at her. "Are you talking to me?"

"You're the only one here, so, yes."

"Why do you want to know?"

"I'm just curious." She goes silent, waiting for him to fill the excruciating silence, but he just stares at her through his sunglasses. She stands. "Look, forget it."

"I haven't decided," he says.

"Decided?"

"Whether to head south." He takes his sunglasses off, and his eyes offer an apology of sorts. "Still trying to make sense of this map."

"I'm impressed by your old-school approach to travel," she says. "I didn't know they still made those. The printed kind." He studies her, and she feels oddly self-conscious. "I'm addicted to my phone now. It's sad. You know, I read online that people sometimes hitchhike down to Wellington."

"You don't have enough for a bus fare?"

"I do. But I thought it might be fun. Only it's safer to go with a partner." He doesn't take the bait. Is he slow? she wonders. Or just ignoring her hint? "You could join me," she adds.

He eyes her as though she'd just asked for money. "Join you?"

"Hitchhiking. To Wellington. It would be fun."

"Fun?" His face relaxes. "You clearly haven't hitched before."

"You have?"

"Occasionally. Not by choice."

"Maybe it's time you did it for fun instead. Have yourself a little adventure."

He begins folding the map. "A little adventure?"

"Yes."

"Hitching with a total stranger is a good start."

"You're not a total stranger," she says.

"How so?" He raises his eyes to her again, green specks around blue, like the beach in Thailand, like so many of the world's wonders she has visited on this trip, alone. Always alone.

"We share a baseball team," she says. "Your hat. The Cardinals. You from St. Louis?"

He pulls the hat off his head and looks at it as if he'd just realized it was there.

"A friend gave this to me."

She studies his face, wondering if he's putting her on. "Where'd this friend go to high school?"

"Excuse me?"

Judging by his puzzled expression, she knows immediately he is not from her hometown. "It's an inside joke," she says. "When you meet someone from St. Louis, they always ask where you went to high school. It's hard to explain. It's a—a St. Louis thing."

He slides the hat back on his head, and she wonders why he bothers to hide that beautiful hair and whether she should bail on this lost cause before it gets any more uncomfortable. She stands again.

"So why is high school such a big deal?" he asks.

"I'm not sure. I didn't think about it growing up. Once you do leave, you realize it's an odd little obsession. But most people never leave St. Louis, so it's not all that odd to them."

"You left."

"True. But I'm heading back. This is my last stop."

"You don't look too excited."

"Would you be excited to be going back to the wintry Midwest after this?"

"You have a point."

"That's why I'm trying to delay the inevitable as long as possible. I'm Amy, by the way."

He hesitates. "Brad."

"Have you eaten dinner?"

He shakes his head.

"There's one of those meat-pie vendors down the street. If you want to join me."

"I don't eat meat."

"Okay. Well, maybe some other place?"

He stands, as if he's suddenly realized he's late for a meeting. "I'm sorry, I have to—"

"No problem. It was nice meeting you."

She watches him walk away and then begins second-guessing everything she'd said. Perhaps there was an orientation course she missed, the one where she'd learn how to make small talk at hostels, plan last-minute hitchhiking trips with good-looking men. The course where she'd learn how to experience some of this adventure that has so far eluded her. In her head, she begins composing her next blog post, title: *New Country. New Zealand. Same Old Story.*

24.

In the dream she is dressed in white, only not a wedding dress but a suit befitting a space-age flight attendant. It fits her perfectly, and she can feel eyes upon her and she's holding blue flowers she doesn't recognize. Ahead, far away, stands a man. She blinks to focus, but either he is blurry or his back is to her—she can't be sure. Chad? She is walking and picking up the pace but her ankles are beginning to give out on the six-inch heels, also white, and she feels her upper body beginning to wobble until she is falling, until she opens her eyes.

A hand is on her shoulder. She looks up to see a pen light directed onto a face, the outline of a baseball cap. As she shakes off the dream, she sees Brad's eyes catch the light, and he whispers, "You still want to go on that adventure?"

She wonders what time it is and what he is doing here and whether he can smell her breath. Mouth closed, she nods.

She meets him outside in the darkness by the picnic table.

"What took you so long?" he says.

"It's not easy to pack in the dark."

"Let's go." He turns and starts walking.

"Wait." She stops. "It's five in the morning."

"I'm aware of that."

"Who's going to pick us up at this hour?"

"Nobody. We need to get out of city limits first. Focus on cars traveling to Wellington, not just across town. Can we get started?"

"I don't even know your last name."

"It's Cameron."

"Brad Cameron," she whispers to herself. She waits for him to ask her last name, but he has turned his back to her, and she remembers the Lifetime television shows her mom used to watch on rotation, the stupid women and their cheating, deceiving, violent men. Her mom shouting at the women who climbed into strangers' cars or let them into their homes late at night or followed them down dark and empty roads. She can hear her mom shouting at her right now, and her mouth says something as her mind reels with television dramas, and Brad stares at her, eyes wide. "What did you just say?"

"Did I say something?"

"You just compared me to Ted Bundy."

"Did I?"

"You're worried that I'm a serial killer?"

"Of course not. From what I've read, Ted Bundy had excellent social skills."

"For the record, you asked *me* to hitchhike."

"Not at five in the morning."

"Then go back to bed, and I'll be on my way."

She stops and watches him walk off. This is absurd, starting this early. But maybe he knows something she doesn't. And maybe she is getting a small kick out of the madness of it all. The darkness. No other backpackers eyeing you competitively, asking you where you've been and where you're going. And don't all great adventures begin at ungodly early hours?

She begins to follow him, thinking of what she'll tell Chad when she gets home. He was hardly supportive when she told him she wanted an adventure, and back then her adventure didn't include hitchhiking in the dark with strange men.

"Go to East St. Louis," Chad told her. "That's an adventure."

He didn't understand her need to get away—far away. Why would anyone go to the Southern Hemisphere when Florida's only a three-hour flight away?

A sabbatical. That's what she proposed to her boss, Andrea, even though nobody in her PR office ever took sabbaticals. She's been at the same company seven years. But it was this or nothing, as she tried to explain to Andrea.

Andrea called it burnout. Or early onset midlife crisis. But Amy knew it was neither. It was something deeper, a sadness for something lost, or something she'd never had.

"What about Chad?" Andrea asked. "I thought you two were planning a wedding?"

"We still are," Amy said. "After I return."

"Assuming you do return."

"Nobody leaves St. Louis for good, do they?"

"Jill did, remember? When her husband got transferred."

"That's not the same thing," Amy said. "I want to know that when I do come back here, it's because I *want* to be here."

"With Chad?"

Amy said nothing, and Andrea seemed to understand. "A woman can go crazy doubting herself over matters of the heart," she said.

And regret—this sharp-edged word that Amy could not bring herself to stop touching. She didn't want to look back on her life and see that word stamped across an empty passport.

Chad wasn't one to think about such things. "You keep saying that word, Amy. But do you want to regret losing me?"

That's what she got for sharing her feelings with Chad. He apparently never felt regret. And he didn't like taking risks. In St. Louis, it's easy to feel comfortable when you're making a good salary. Housing bubbles don't inflate as they do on the coasts. And Chad, not one to bother himself over the many racial or political struggles of St. Louis, lives in Clayton, surrounded by his own people, from high school, college, and law school. He'll probably never leave. Why would he, what with season tickets to the Cardinals? The only thing he would ever "regret" was his team missing the playoffs.

Amy confided in her girlfriends, the ones with kids and husbands, at one of those parties that couples throw for one another and invite single friends in a pretentious effort to manufacture even more couples. That was how Amy met Chad, two years before. And that was how they celebrated their engagement, eighteen months later.

And at yet another gathering, as Amy rolled her engagement ring around on her finger and told Kim and Dee in the kitchen that she was leaving to travel around the world, they went silent, as if they didn't hear her correctly. So she repeated herself.

"What about Chad?" Kim asked. "Is he going?"

"No, it's just me."

"What about the wedding?"

"We'll set a date when I get back."

"I don't understand," said Dee.

Amy did her best to explain, though it felt like talking into the fridge. It wasn't as if they weren't listening or didn't care about her—it was just that they were somewhere else. They had husbands and homes and a sense of purpose, a weight they carried. Happily? Amy wasn't sure, and when she would press them, separately, after long days with their children and a few glasses of wine, they'd confess to darker thoughts: exhaustion, tedium, too little help and too little sex. But these confessions were erased by Monday mornings and coffee and children. What Amy couldn't tell them was that it hurt to be around them. To be viewed, as a still-single woman, as broken or, worse, not entirely whole. To be told that her marriage would, finally, be what made her complete. She suspected that at some level they envied her lack of children, as if she were getting away with something—that they were eagerly waiting for her to enter their world at last. But how could any marriage survive long-term over the diversions of two or three little humans fighting over remote controls and iPads? Amy couldn't understand them, and they could not understand her—and yet she was about to join them. This was why she knew she had to leave, to figure out once and for all whether she could ever fit in.

"You're crazy, girl," Kim said. "You need to seal the deal before getting on that plane."

Yet what Amy wanted more than a wedding was an experience. She was tired of watching other people's experiences happening in stop motion, blog post by blog post, on her computer screen at work, between conference calls and meetings. The so-called travel bloggers who sold everything to backpack in India or Chile and who were always smiling, drinking, sleeping with tanned bodies, and taking so many excruciatingly enticing pictures of it all.

She was torturing herself, following these women online. She didn't know them. She knew only that she wanted to be them. And why? They were, some of them at least, running away from something. A relationship gone bad. A layoff. A too-ordinary life.

By most standards, Amy's life was hardly ordinary; it had moments of something close to glamour. Expensive suits and high heels. Managing the media. Coaching executives on how to talk to cameras. The occasional trip to LA or New York or Vegas for a conference or a client.

But deep down she knew her life in public relations had been a life spent on the sidelines. Amy had always been the one managing the drama, real or contrived, and she herself was left with none. She wanted to be the one people read about, the one posing for the camera in front of an exotic backdrop.

When she first began her travels, she was worried that Chad would read everything she posted online and think differently about her. But once she realized that he didn't follow her blog or her Instagram and Twitter accounts, she found herself forgetting about him entirely when she posted a note or a photo. With no fiancé checking in, following her adventure, she feels as if she is single again—and she hasn't yet decided whether she likes it or not.

Now, as she follows Brad along the dim road, she rubs her pinkie against the side of her engagement ring, the diamonds poking her skin like nettles. She wears it to keep away unwanted men, she tells herself, though she not sure now whether she wants it on or off. Brad is still twenty yards ahead of her. A fast walker. She feels her legs warming up.

She'll call him Indiana Jones in her blog. If Chad should ever actually read one of her posts, they'll have a lively conversation when she gets home. But maybe a little jealousy isn't such a bad thing once in a while. She got plenty jealous about his "work spouse," Kristi, until she realized that Kristi was married and not at all interested in Chad.

Amy actually enjoyed dishing on Chad with Kristi at office parties. The way he would read his e-mails aloud in a mumbled monotone that he assumed nobody else could hear. How he was always forgetting something at home or at the office and even when he tried keeping umbrellas at both locations he would still end up with two umbrellas at the wrong location at the wrong time. He was most attractive in his least-aware moments; if only he had more of those. There were no glaring red flags when it came to marrying Chad, which made him simultaneously the most eligible and most dangerous man she could be with. Dangerous because she wanted a red flag or two and was not entirely sure why. Maybe *she* was the red flag.

She didn't expect to feel great joy daily; she knew better by now. But she wanted to know their marriage would wear well, loosen up, soften with age. A notion that Chad would ridicule, telling her that relationships were not clothing.

When Chad took her on a boat ride in Forest Park six months ago, below Art Hill, paddling them into the middle of the pond on a surprisingly cool August day and pulling a ring sparkling with diamonds from his pocket as he knelt in the boat, she'd been stunned. She said yes because she had no reason to say no. Yet over the next several months, overwhelmed with bridal catalogs and e-mails as her mother and friends started pressing about the wedding date, she began trading wedding websites for travel blogs. Whenever she mentioned to Chad that perhaps they could travel a bit before settling down, he dismissed her; he wasn't interested in traveling, other than a weeklong honeymoon somewhere with a beach and a golf course, and he didn't understand that this wasn't the kind of traveling she was talking about. And then she realized that to do this kind of travel she had to be alone anyway. So finally she booked airline tickets for a single passenger and presented him with her itinerary. She recognized the look on his face immediately—Chad looked as stunned as she had felt when he proposed.

And here she is now, following a man she just met through a neighborhood she cannot name on the outskirts of Auckland as daybreak foreshadows a cloudy horizon. Even if all this amounts to is a few hours of hitching, an aimless day or two of stop-and-go travel, from this day forward her life will no longer be ordinary. A great opening for her next blog post.

25.

THEY'VE BEEN WALKING FOR THREE straight hours, with Amy glancing at her phone every half hour. The sparkle of sun lighting up the dew on the grass and bushes turns to a steady glow, warming her up as they take the side streets that run parallel to Highway 1, the road that will ultimately take them to Wellington. If they are lucky enough to find a car going all the way, they might make it there before dark.

But right now Amy is thinking only of breakfast, or the lack thereof. Brad refuses to stop walking—or she suspects he would, if she asked him to stop. But he hasn't said one word to her, or vice versa.

"You hungry?" she calls ahead. He's still walking a few paces ahead of her, as if he's angry, as if they're a couple in the middle of a fight.

He shakes his head.

He's testing her, she tells herself. That's what's going on here. But why? Is there some hitchhikers' rule against eating?

And what does it matter if she fails this stupid test? As long as they stop. Sit. Eat. Talk. It's not as if they're running late for something. Or maybe he is.

Another half hour passes, and the sun dials from warm to hot. "I need to put on some sunscreen," she calls out.

"Okay," he replies without looking back.

"I can't do it walking!" She stops and releases her backpack, letting it fall to the pavement. She squirms out of her nylon pullover to reveal her white SURF FIJI tank top, soaked through. She pulls at the front of the shirt, sucking in cool air. She feels eyes upon her and looks up to see him stopped ahead, watching her. She isn't sure if he's impatient with her or checking her out, the damp tank top revealing more than she'd like.

She removes a tube of sunscreen from her bag and offers it. "You want some?"

"No."

"Suit yourself. It's your sunburn."

He returns to her, slowly. "On second thought." He extends an open palm.

She squirts a small mound onto his fingers, then looks up at him, his eyes on her. "Is that enough?"

He nods. "Thank you."

She watches him rub the lotion up and down his arms, giving her a peek at that tattoo on his right bicep, the letters "O R E" stacked vertically. The final letters of SINGAPORE? Maybe he taught English there. Built houses for some nonprofit. Then again, maybe it says HARDCORE and he's a drug dealer and she his unsuspecting mule. She reminds herself that this is part of the adventure. The not knowing. Not knowing exactly where they're headed or how they'll get there or if this man has a girlfriend.

Around his neck is a stainless steel chain holding a rectangular pendant the size of a pack of chewing gum with a whale fin carved onto it. When he turns around, she sees the back of his neck, the streaks of sunscreen not rubbed in, and, though a voice in her head scolds her, she reaches over to smooth it into his skin. She feels him flinch at her touch. His skin is warm and she feels suddenly self-conscious. She finishes rubbing in the sunscreen before stepping away.

"You hungry now?" she asks.

"Nope."

Before grunting up into her backpack again, she pulls out the Cadbury chocolate bar she picked up at the airport.

He is stopped up ahead, pack at his feet. When she reaches him she can see down the on-ramp to a divided six-lane highway. "The Southern Motorway," he says.

"Highway 1?"

He nods. "You first."

"Why should I go first?"

"Hitchhiking was your idea, as I recall."

"Don't we need a sign? Something that says *Wellington*?"

"Ideally. But do you see any cardboard lying around? When they pull over, you just tell them. Okay?"

"Okay." She slides out of her pack and visualizes herself from a driver's perspective. The last time she got a good look at her face she noticed only creases and pores. And her hair must be a mess. She tries pulling it back, then realizes her bands are in the pack. She begins searching for one. Brad looks confused.

"What are you doing?"

"I want to look nice. Isn't that relevant to catching a ride?" She applies lip gloss.

"Show them a little leg."

"Figures you'd say that." She stands and faces the oncoming cars.

"You need to stand closer."

"How close?"

"Close enough so they'll see you, but not so close they hit you. I'll be back here. And don't waste our time with the short hops. We need to make progress."

Amy feels oddly disoriented trying to make eye contact with drivers who are seated on the wrong sides of the cars. She has to keep stopping herself from looking at passengers or empty seats. But by the tenth car she has adjusted. She makes eye contact with a man in a suit driving a Mercedes. A woman with a kid in the back of a Honda. A teenager with music blaring and every window open in a rusted-out VW bug.

Okay, she tells herself. Here goes nothing. She raises two fingers in the form of a peace sign held backwards, a hitchhiking tip she'd gotten from the two women at her hostel.

A car approaches, and the driver, a woman, scowls at her and honks as she passes.

"Same to you!" Amy shouts after.

Brad steps forward and puts his hand on her arm.

"What's her problem?" Amy demands. "I thought drivers were friendlier to hikers down here."

"What the hell are you doing?" Brad points to her fingers.

"The Brits at the hostel said this works better than the thumb."

"They were putting you on. Do you have any idea what this really means?"

"I assumed it meant *need a ride.*"

"It means more like *up yours.*"

"Oh." She feels heat flush her cheeks.

Brad shakes his head. "From now on, stick with the thumb."

She turns back to the cars, contemplates stepping out in front of one. Perhaps this will be another blog post, she thinks, though it might be too embarrassing. Not everything needs to be shared with the world.

The cars pass her in silence, which is, at this point in her journey, a step in the right direction.

26.

Gravity is winning the battle against her outstretched arm, and beads of sweat collect on her upper lip. She never imagined how humiliating this carefree, footloose lifestyle could be, how personally she would take it when every car passes her by.

The hot-looking dude in a BMW sizes her up before zipping by. The single woman in a large sedan says something to her that she can't hear, though she can imagine. Lowlife. Bum. Or whatever slang they use down here for lowlifes and bums.

She looks back at Brad. He's seated on the ground against a utility box, head down, as if he's nodding off. She's relieved not to have him watching. Though she'd love to know what ratio of cars to rides is a good ratio. Her arm now seems to weigh more than her backpack, and she begins propping it up with her other hand.

It takes a moment to realize that the pickup truck pulled over up ahead is for her. It honks. She runs.

A large man in a green polo shirt and John Deere baseball cap eyes her. "Where you headed?"

"Wellington," she says.

"Not going nearly that far."

"That's okay!" Even though Brad told her not to waste time with short trips, she figures he must've relaxed his rule by now, this being the first car to pull over. She waves to Brad, then hops in and slides over, noticing the smell of cigar. She can tell the man isn't happy to have Brad joining them, though her arm, now grazing his hairy one, has to be some consolation. Brad shakes the man's hand.

"Wellington, eh?" asks the man, who says his name is Reggie. "Going to the South Island?"

"That's the plan," she says.

"I've never been down that far," he says.

"Really? I thought most New Zealanders would have made the trip," she says.

"Nah. We go to Australia. Or Los Angeles. You from there?"

"No, St. Louis."

"Where's that?"

"In Missouri," she says.

He gives her a blank look.

"South of Chicago?" she says.

"Al Capone, right?" Reggie says.

"That's right. So why haven't you gone to the South Island?"

"Keep meaning. I'm a plumber. This island keeps me busy enough. That and my lady. You two married?"

"No," she says. She is about to say "we're friends" but holds her tongue. How can she be friends with Brad? She isn't sure anyone can be friends with Brad.

Brad looks over at Reggie. "So what's taking you to Wellington?" he asks.

"I'm not going to Wellington," Reggie says. "Like I was telling your friend here. I can only take you to Manukau."

"How far is that?" Brad asks.

"We should be there any minute."

"Any minute?"

Amy feels Brad glaring at her, and she keeps her eyes straight ahead. "Every bit helps," she says.

"Nice ride," Brad says as he watches the plumber pull away. He'd dropped them off a few blocks away from the highway, in between a strip mall and a petrol station. "If I squint I can see where we started."

"I'd like to see you do better."

"It's not my turn."

"You said we alternate rides."

"That assumes we actually got a ride. Reggie doesn't count. That was more like one of those moving walkways."

She starts walking. Mostly to get away from Brad. To clear her head. To understand why in the world he is so intense about a stupid ride. She wants to confront him, but she's tired of arguing. Ahead she sees a diner, like an oasis in the middle of an expansive parking lot. A row of large trucks are parked at the far end. She starts across the lot and stops at the entrance. She waits for Brad to catch up, bracing herself for another argument.

"What are you waiting for?" he asks.

"You mean, you're actually hungry?"

"I could eat."

"It's about time." She goes in and finds a booth. Brad follows a few moments later, as if pacing himself. She watches him as he looks for her, and she resists the urge to raise a hand, to help him in any way. It's beginning to dawn on her that despite his good looks, there is a growing list of reasons he's traveling solo.

The waitress approaches. Amy orders a hamburger with fries. Brad is shaking his head as he looks at his menu.

"Brad?" Amy asks. "You ready?"

"I'll just have the fries," he says, holding up the menu.

"Would you like that with a side of burger?" the waitress asks, flirting with him, but he doesn't take the bait.

"Fries will do."

Amy catches the waitress rolling her eyes before heading back to the kitchen.

"I thought you were hungry," she says. "If you don't have any money—"

"I told you already, I don't eat animals," he says. "There's nothing else to eat here."

"I had no idea you were so hard-core."

Brad gives her a look. "What do you mean by that?"

"Nothing. If you like subsisting on French fries."

He turns to the window and seems lost in thought. She wants to ask what's going on under that Cardinals cap but isn't confident he'll tell her what she wants to hear. And what *does* she want to hear? That he's single? Mourning a recent breakup? After a lengthy silence, Amy takes out her laptop and searches for a Wi-Fi signal.

"What are you doing?" he asks.

"Well, since you've gone mute on me, I figured I'd work on my blog."

He groans. "Don't tell me you're a travel blogger," he says.

"What's wrong with that?"

"If I had a dollar for every travel blogger I've met, I wouldn't have to hitchhike with a travel blogger. I could charter a jet."

"Don't knock it. We inspire people."

"To do what? Sell their homes, piss away their life savings on airfare and hotels, backpacks and ziplining?"

"I haven't ziplined."

"But you want to, right?" he says. "That's why you're headed to the South Island."

"If I happen to end up there, yeah, why not? It would be fun."

"Which is the motto of the travel blogger, isn't it? Just have fun."

"No. That's not it at all. Traveling is about self-discovery, self-empowerment."

"Self-absorption?"

"Cute," she says. "I might have to blog about that."

"What's with that?" He's looking at her engagement ring. "You married?"

"It's fake," she says, without thinking. "To keep away the jerks."

"The real jerks are the ones it will attract."

Their plates arrive, and Brad becomes occupied with his fries. Amy thinks back to Teo, the green-eyed Spaniard she met in Fiji the night before her flight to Auckland. He noticed her ring and said he was married when he bought her a mai tai and joined her at the bar. In his charming broken English, he said they were taking a break and now his heart was in need of healing. He took the pink umbrella from her drink and leaned over to pin it above her ear. "It matches your swimming suit," he said. It wasn't her swimsuit he was referring to but her bra strap, and after the third umbrella he had his hand on her knee and she was entertaining the idea of a fling, something impulsive and stupid that would be her secret forever, something nobody would ever know—and besides, it wasn't technically cheating if she and Chad weren't married yet. Then Teo leaned over, slipped off his barstool, and fractured his right forearm. The evening ended with ambulance lights instead of fireworks.

"What's the name of your blog?" Brad asks.

"I'm not telling you if you're going to make fun of it."

"I won't. I promise. And if I do, I'll give you the rest of my fries." She looks at his blue eyes. In the light coming through the window, a stray blond hair catches the sun.

"I already have fries."

"Then maybe you can give me some of yours." He grabs a handful off her plate, and she feels the tension between them easing. He's finally acting more like a normal guy, talkative, his mouth full of food.

"Okay. It's called *Midwestern Girl Gone Global*."

He ponders it. "Not bad."

"You're just saying that."

"I'm serious. And believe me, I've known my share of blogs. At least yours isn't all fluffy and new agey like *The Spirit Backpack* or *My Passport Muse*."

"How do you know *My Passport Muse*?"

He groans.

"What is it? Do you know her?" Amy asks.

"Our paths may have crossed."

"You met her?"

"You could say that."

Which means he slept with her. "But she's traveling with her husband," Amy says.

"Not when I met her."

"I can't believe that."

"Not everything you read on a blog is true," he says. "It's like a reality show. Nothing's real. Even the photographs are staged." He leans back and looks out the window. "I don't mean to sound harsh." His voice drifts off, as if he's stopped himself from saying more.

"What?"

"It's just that people have this tendency to confuse travel with growth. I meet so many, and they're all alike. 'Finding themselves.' Like they'll turn the corner in Hong Kong or Christchurch and see their better selves standing there, waiting to be discovered, waiting for that moment when they can return home saying they've grown."

"You do sound harsh."

He looks at her.

"Maybe people just want to blow off steam, run away for a while," she says. "What's so wrong with that?"

"Nothing. But at least be honest about it. Don't wrap it up into some holy fucking vision quest."

"So you're saying people who travel the world don't actually grow?"

"They move. But I rarely see much evidence of growth."

"Well, I have."

"You've experienced things, I don't doubt that. You've lived a heightened sense of awareness, which is in itself valuable. But are you more self-confident today than on the day you left St. Louis?"

She pauses to consider the question, the distance she's traveled. Yet the bravest thing she's done so far on this trip was ask Brad to hitchhike with her, and there is no way she can tell him that. "There's still time," she says.

"Fair enough," he says, grabbing another handful of fries off her plate. He slides out of the booth and empties some New Zealand bills from his pocket. "Come on, *Eat Pray Love.* Time to put that thumb of yours back to use."

"I'm not done yet," she says.

He rolls his eyes. "I guess when you're a travel blogger, the news just can't wait."

"Piss off," she says.

He smiles, and she watches him exit the restaurant. She tries to write another sentence but finds herself looking out at the parking lot. He is seated on his backpack reading his map as if it's the Sunday paper.

If there's an upside to this man, it is this—he will make an interesting blog post. Carefully, she lifts her phone to the glass and snaps his profile. She waits until he is looking back in her direction and she takes another. She posts the photos to her blog and Instagram with the hashtags #travelbuddy #newzealand #hitchhiking. She is tempted to add #asshole but leaves that one out. For now.

27.

As she leaves the diner and approaches Brad, he folds his map, and they walk the short distance to the highway on-ramp. "You ready?" he asks.

"It's your turn, big guy."

"You're never going to get any good at this if you don't practice."

"Maybe I need to learn by example. You're the expert. Show me how it's done."

"Very well."

She backs off the shoulder and watches as he positions himself. "And don't be afraid to show a little leg," she says.

He raises two fingers at her in a gesture now familiar.

"You're supposed to use your thumb."

Finally, a smile crosses his face. Then he turns, extends his thumb, and in less than a minute a passing minivan slows and pulls over to the side of the road.

He turns and winks at her.

When Amy catches up to Brad, he is talking to the driver through the open sliding door. A chubby woman with auburn hair introduces her two daughters, seated in the middle seats—Samantha and Tabitha, ages twelve and eight.

"I'm Marjorie," the driver says. "But call me Marj."

Amy follows Brad into the back row and introduces herself and Brad, who is occupied with the scenery.

"Growing up, everyone used to hitch," Marj says. "But not as much now. It's good you're a pair. Creepy blokes out there."

"Tell me about it," Amy says, looking over at Brad, hoping for a reaction. But his eyes are drawn to the passing cars.

"Headed to the South Island?" Marj asks.

"That's right," Amy says. "Have you been?"

"Twice," Marj says. "Though not since the little women came along. But we're planning a family adventure next summer."

"We're not camping, are we?" Samantha asks.

"That's the best way to see it," Marj says, then speaks to Amy. "I keep telling the girls that snakes are not native to New Zealand. Australia, now they have all sorts of nasty creatures. And I'm not just talking about the insects." Marj laughs loudly and the girls giggle in response. "You should know that we may be close neighbors with that country, but we don't particularly get along."

"Why's that?"

"The Aussies look down on us, even though they're the ones with all the crime and pollution. Did you know that New Zealand is nuclear-free? We don't even allow the Americans to dock their nuclear submarines or aircraft carriers. But the Australians are all too happy to bend over backwards."

Amy is not surprised to learn that Marj is a schoolteacher, and she treats the ride like a school field trip, with her narrating every few minutes.

"They filmed a scene from *The Lord of the Rings* over there," Marj says. "The second film."

Marj talks and points, and Amy follows along. She glances over at Brad, his eyes closed, face turned toward her. She lets her eyes wander across his face. She notices a scar below the left eye. He seems a bit sad, but then maybe everyone appears sad when they sleep. Except Chad. Whenever she watches him sleep, he looks tense, as if irritated that his body makes him close his eyes at all. Brad's face does not look anxious or rushed. The tanned, smooth skin, so perfect in so many ways, looks weary. When she's sure he's asleep, she lets her own head fall back on the seat, the sound of Marj's voice soothing in its rambling.

A tap on the shoulder wakes her. They are pulling off the highway and onto a road bordered by large bushes. Brad is alert, looking back and forth uneasily. "Where are we going?" he asks.

"This is Huka Falls," Marj says. "You can't visit New Zealand and not see the falls."

"We're on a bit of schedule," Brad says.

"We are?" Amy asks. "Since when?"

Brad, looking flustered, stares out the back window. Marj pulls the car into a large parking lot full of cars and campers and, at the far end of the lot, large tour buses.

Amy slides open the door, and the two girls hop out and chase each other to the crowds of people massing near an overlook. Amy can hear the thunder of water in the distance, like an ocean, never pausing to take a breath. Brad climbs out behind her and surveys the other cars.

"What's the matter?" she asks.

He is looking over her shoulder, as if waiting for someone. "Nothing," he says. "You go ahead. I'll stay here."

"Don't you want to see the falls?"

"Not particularly."

"Have it your way."

She catches up with Marj, who is waiting for her. "Trouble in paradise?" Marj asks.

"What? Oh, we're not. Paradise." She feels the words fall out.

Marj is looking at Brad, standing with his back to them at the van, still scrutinizing the cars. "He does have a rather nice … "

"Yes, he does." Amy finally takes a good long look, as if permission has been granted. His body. Lean in the midsection, those biceps. And the way he walks, not afraid to take up space.

Marjorie looks at her. "So you two aren't together?"

Amy shakes her head. "We just met yesterday," she says.

"I'd quite fancy him, if I were you."

That's when it dawns on Amy: Not only did Marj stop specifically for Brad, she'd probably prefer if Amy weren't around at all.

Brad is standing beside the van when Amy returns, a tense look on his face.

"What took so long?" he says.

"The girls wanted to get under the spray; we had to wait for the crowds to thin so we could get close. What's the big rush?"

Brad slides the door open as the two girls come skipping up and in, laughing, their hair dripping. Marj lumbers up, breathing heavily. "You missed a lovely view," Marj says. "Sure you don't want to go see?"

"No need." Brad climbs into the van, and Amy exchanges a look with Marj.

Back on the highway, the girls are alive with chatter about Dwarves riding barrels down waterfalls, with Marj chiming in about movie animation and geothermal power. But Amy is thinking about Brad, seated with his back to her, looking out the rear window.

The highway has narrowed to two lanes, and the only signs of civilization are the utility poles running parallel to the road. The road takes them through grass-covered hills, reminding Amy of driving through the western half of Kansas when she and her high-school classmates went on a ski trip to Steamboat Springs. They had spent the year raising money through bake sales and a bachelor auction with the football team. While the other girls were engrossed in gossip on their chartered bus, Amy kept her eyes out the window, her body tingling at the idea that she would be sleeping somewhere different that night. Though she loved her mother, after her father died the house had shrunk in size, and Amy felt tense around her, as if her mother was always watching her, waiting for something to happen to her, too. When Amy saw the Rocky Mountains rising up as they crossed into Colorado, she told herself that this trip was only the beginning. That someday she would travel the world. All those images she had saved on her home computer—Machu Picchu, Mont Saint-Michel, the Sydney Opera House … she would visit every last one.

She realizes Marj is talking to her and turns her attention to the front of the car. "The what blacks?" Amy asks.

"The All Blacks," Marj says. "You don't know about our rugby team?"

Samantha chants something indecipherable. Tabitha follows with deep-throated grunts.

"Very good, sweeties. They're singing the pre-match chant; it's Māori. Called the haka."

"Does Brad know it?" Samantha asks.

In the back, Brad is oblivious to all of this. Amy puts a hand on his shoulder. "What?" he asks.

"Samantha asked you a question," Amy says.

"She wants to know if you can sing the All Blacks fight song," Marj says.

"A little. But I can't sing."

"Please!" The girls have twisted their bodies around, their eager blond heads peeking over the seats.

"C'mon, Brad," Amy says. "The girls are waiting."

Brad takes off his baseball cap and wrinkles his nose, then

squints and straightens his back, then slaps his chest with both palms and chants something unintelligible. The girls are nodding along as he continues chanting, gesticulating like a bodybuilder suffering a seizure, arms flexing, hands slapping forearms, his voice growing louder and louder in a language Amy doesn't recognize but the girls clearly do until he gives one final grunt, which is followed by cheering.

"Well done, Brad," Marj says. "Now we have to get you into a uniform. A pair of those tight black shorts they wear."

"I had no idea you were such a fan," Amy says to him.

"My old man is. He taught me the song years ago."

"Is he from New Zealand?"

"No. He's American. But he passes through every so often."

"What does he do?"

"He's a … " Brad pauses. "A sailor."

"Where is he now?"

"Beats me."

He glances back outside and suddenly ducks his head, sliding down in his seat.

"What's wrong?" Amy asks. "Paparazzi?"

"Something like that," he says. He inches up again and looks back at a sedan that is close behind them. "Marj, can you do me a favor and slow down a bit?"

"I'm not speeding, am I?"

"No. I just—I want to let this car pass. It seems to be following a bit close."

Amy watches Brad peek at the car as it passes on their right. Two men are seated in front, looking up at them.

"Who are they?" Amy asks.

"Nobody." Brad's eyes are still darting back and forth.

Amy leans in and whispers, "What's the matter with you?"

"Nothing."

"Then why are you scoping out every car on the road? Or are you just counting mile markers?"

"It's kilometers," he says.

"You know what I'm talking about."

Brad looks at her, and in that moment she sees something on his face she's never seen. Worry? Fear? He turns to the front seat. "Marj, do you mind pulling the car over? Anywhere will do."

"Is everything okay?" Marj asks, pulling onto the shoulder.

"I need a pit stop," he says. "Right up here is good."

"What the hell are you doing?" Amy whispers.

Ignoring her, Brad slides open the door and hops out, his pack in one hand.

"There are bushes up on the hill," Marj says. The girls are giggling.

"Actually, Marj. I'm going to continue on my own. I'm sorry for the trouble."

"If you have to poo, we don't mind waiting."

Now the girls are laughing hysterically. Amy is trying to catch Brad's eyes and failing.

"Thanks for the ride."

"Wait!" Amy hops out of the van. "What the hell are you doing?"

"Leaving."

"Leaving *me*, you mean."

"That's not it. I just need to be on my own from here on."

"Did I do something?" she asks, searching his eyes. "Say something?"

"I just think it's better if you stay with Marj. You'll be safer."

"Safer? I didn't realize I was in danger. Are you telling me I was right to compare you to Ted Bundy after all?"

"What if I am? Will you get back in the van?"

"I don't know." She's not sure what to believe. She can't imagine Brad harming anyone, but he looks different all of a sudden, and she's not sure how to interpret his sudden change in mood.

He takes a step toward her, his face serious. "I hacked up a woman two days ago, with a table knife. Just north of Auckland."

"Oh, really?" She is tempted to laugh but can't be sure he's joking.

"And what did you do with the body?"

"I ate it."

Amy hears a gasp, and her pack lands on the ground near her feet just before the car door slides shut. Marj, eyes wide, swerves past her on her way back onto the highway, gravel spitting under the tires. Amy watches the minivan as it disappears behind the bend. The road goes silent except for the sounds of sheep on the surrounding hills.

28.

BRAD HAS HIS BACK TO HER as he watches the minivan disappear around the bend in the road. A truck passes, kicking up dust, and Amy backs away from the shoulder to the high grass bordering the road. She nearly bumps into a barbed-wire fence; on the other side, puffy white sheep are scattered like confetti across the rolling green hills.

Brad turns back to her, wrinkles showing on his forehead. He takes off his baseball cap and wipes his forehead with his shirt, exposing an abdomen with another tattoo that she can't quite see.

"You were joking, right?" she asks. "About being a serial killer?"

"Of course," he says.

"Good. I knew that."

"You should have stayed with Marj," he says.

"Well, it's too late for that. Now what?"

She feels a drop of rain and looks up at swollen, low-hanging clouds. Brad turns and starts walking. "Where are we headed?" she shouts.

"There's a town a few miles from here."

"You mean kilometers?" she asks hopefully.

"I mean miles."

The steadily increasing rain is making visibility difficult. Amy pulls back her wet hair and thinks of the hair bands in her backpack, but opening her pack would soak everything that's not already getting wet.

The rain is heavy and cold. Her pants cling to her like leggings, her backpack getting heavier as it absorbs water. Soon there's nothing left dry on her body, and probably not much in her bag either. The rain mocks her with its intensity. She's not sure what impulse made her get out of the warm, dry minivan to join Brad—all she knows is that instead of feeling relief when he stepped outside the van, she'd felt a unexplainable emptiness. The sort of feeling she'd expected to feel at the airport, saying good-bye to Chad, and hadn't. She remembers waving at Chad from the security checkpoint, her engagement ring flashing under the bright airport lights. But he was already looking down at his phone, checking his e-mail. On the plane, she'd slipped the ring off her finger and stowed it deep inside her travel pack, next to her passport. She told herself it was because showing off such an expensive ring would leave her vulnerable to thieves and other lowlifes—and of course she knew this was true—but a part of her looked down at her newly naked hand and felt a tiny thrill, a new sense of freedom.

SHE GLIMPSES A SIGN UP AHEAD and tries to read it through the rain. *Welcome to Taihape.* Brad is a few yards ahead of her, his baseball cap pulled low. The wind has died somewhat, giving Amy a respite from the angular rain.

By the time they reach the main strip of downtown, what little sun that was backlighting the clouds has dipped below the hills. A streetlight illuminates the one intersection that she can see ahead. They pass a post office, bank, and feed shop, all closed.

And despite having every reason to feel miserable, she feels quite the opposite. Every sense is on high alert. She hears the sound of the gravel under her wet shoes. She inhales the damp air, the smell of grass and trees and places too remote for intention. She knows she will never be in this town again, never be in this exact situation again, and she wants to memorize it all. The mad, drenched, uncharted feeling of it all.

She sees a neon sign for *Taihape Inn* two blocks ahead and begins to pray that there is a vacancy, then nearly runs into Brad. He's stopped in front of a bar, the door open and music wafting out.

"Shouldn't we find a place to dry off first?" she asks.

"I'm more thirsty than wet," he says.

She follows him inside. The bar is not unlike a St. Louis dive bar: a pool table with guys playing a game, loud music on a jukebox, and sports on the televisions above the bar, only the sport of choice down here appears to be rugby. She feels eyes on her as her feet squish their way to the barstool, squirting out water with every step.

Brad takes a seat at the bar and she sits next to him, propping her dripping pack between their stools. The guys at the pool table are watching them.

The bartender, a large-bellied man in a black shirt, is eyeing her wet, clinging T-shirt. "Really pissing out there, eh?"

"You could say that," she says.

"What can I get you?"

"Two beers," Brad says. "Whatever's cheapest."

When the pints arrive she pauses with her glass, expecting a toast, but Brad downs half of his glass in one gulp. She takes a drink and lets the cool liquid soothe her throat.

"So, you going to tell me?" she asks.

"What?"

"Why you've been acting so weird?"

Brad glances around, his eyes still on edge, always moving, and she wishes they would settle on her for more than a second so she could have a better idea of what is going on in his head.

"Maybe I didn't like Marj."

"Oh, yeah, she was a real ogre. Giving us a ride to the ferry and all."

"If I wanted to visit a waterfall, I would've taken a tour bus."

"Well, we got our own waterfall in the end," she says, wringing out a corner of her shirt. "Now tell me the real reason."

Instead of answering her, he drains his beer and orders another round, and she downs hers, too, just like him, and his eyes finally relax on hers. And by the end of their second round, her questions don't matter; they become lost in a haze of light and rugby and music and the spinning in her head.

29.

When Amy and Brad finally tumble out of the bar, she wonders whether she's holding him up, or vice versa.

"Where are we going to stay tonight?" she asks.

He laughs. "I can always sleep under an overpass. Nobody appreciates an overpass until it starts to rain."

"I prefer a hotel. It'll be on me."

She follows him down the street to a Liquorland, where he buys a large bottle of Coopers, and then they cross the street to the *Taihape Inn*. In the lobby, when the woman behind the desk asks one bed or two, there is an awkward pause.

"Two," he says.

Amy puts down her credit card.

They're still leaning on each other when they open the door to the room, and before they get the door closed, their lips have met, and Amy's hands have found their way under his still-damp shirt. They sprawl across one of the room's two beds, and Amy begins to pull her own shirt over her head.

"Wait," he says. "I need to tell you something."

"Later," she says, the shirt up around her face.

"Now."

She lowers her shirt back down over her chest and looks at him.

"I'm being followed. Chased is more like it."

"Oh, right, because you're a serial killer?" She laughs and waits for a sign on his face that he's joking. "What are you talking about?"

"I stole something."

"What?"

"I can't say."

"Why not?"

Brad stands, opens the beer, and takes a long drink from the bottle. "I'm sorry. I shouldn't have said anything."

"Well, you did. So talk to me."

He sits next to her. "I didn't mean to leave you like that, with Marj. I saw this car behind us, and I panicked. There I was with these two little girls sitting in front of me and you next to me, and I couldn't live with myself if anything had happened."

"What would have happened?"

"I don't know. I just know that I move faster on my own."

"You stand out more on your own," she says. "Isn't that why you asked me along in the first place?"

"That was a mistake," he says. "I shouldn't have done that to you. I shouldn't have lied."

"You didn't lie. You just omitted a few critical details."

"No. I lied." He stands abruptly and takes another long drink, his body swaying. "My name isn't Brad," he says. "It's Neil. Neil Cameron."

"Oh. Now, that is a lie. Should I check your passport?"

"You might as well take it, for all I care." He strips off his wet shirt and steps out of his shorts, without a hint of self consciousness. The word *Herbivore* is tattooed on his right bicep, the mystery solved. On the right side of his abdomen, a whale swims halfway around to his back, and she feels the urge to reach out and touch it.

"They're going find me soon enough," he says, and she stares at him, trying to rethink all that she knows of him—that he's Neil, not Brad. That he's not just a traveler but some sort of criminal.

"Everything I've been working toward—" Neil continues, then stops. "It doesn't matter. I'm a Cameron. It was inevitable that I'd end up on the run. Practically a family tradition."

He wobbles on his feet as he fishes through his pockets for his passport, then tosses it to her.

"I told you my dad's a sailor. That was only half true. He's an anti-whaling activist. Goes by Aeneas. You've probably heard of him. Most everyone has."

Amy remembers a documentary she'd clicked past on the television a few months ago: Men and women dressed in black, pursuing Japanese harpoon ships.

"Does your father know about all of this?"

"I don't know. He's not exactly easy to find these days. Three countries have warrants out for his arrest."

"Including the U.S.?"

"No," Neil says. "I suppose I'm ahead of him in that regard."

Neil sits on the bed again and leans back. She can smell the beer on his breath, and while she knows the wise thing to do would be to grab her things and get as far away from him as she can, she has no desire to. Instead, she inches closer to him on the bed and looks down at him. "Who's after you?"

"The FBI. Or someone working for them. They have an unhealthy obsession with animal-rights activists."

That explains all the vegan stuff. It also helps her relax—a man who is this committed to animals can't possibly hurt her or leave her for dead in a hotel room. "What will happen if they catch you?" she asks.

"I'm not entirely sure they want to catch me."

"But what else would they ... " She hears her voice trail off with the realization that he isn't just being dramatic; his life really is in danger. "Why?"

"Because of what I took."

"And you won't tell me what that is?"

"It's safer if you don't know." He opens his eyes, staring at the ceiling, then exhales. "I don't get how they know I'm here. I mean, on the North Island. I was so thorough."

"That's why you don't carry a phone?"

He nods. "Anything digital can be tracked, scanned. I didn't even board a plane."

"So how did you make it all the way to New Zealand?"

"Container ships, mostly. In Seattle, I stowed away on a ship to Hong Kong. Then another to Indonesia. Then I chartered a small fishing boat to the North Island. They brought me within a few miles of the port of Opua, way up north, and I rafted the rest of the way in. I hitched down from there and was going to fly out of Auckland on a fake passport I picked up along the way. Figured it was worth the risk at that point. But when I saw these government-looking types outside the terminal, I turned around. They never saw me—that I'm certain of. But I just had this feeling in my stomach. I knew if I went into that airport I'd end up on a one-way flight back to the U.S."

"And that's when I saw you?"

He nods. "So now you know. I'm not exactly the free spirit you might have imagined. Just a fugitive."

He must feel relieved to have unburdened himself, to have let another into his lonely world. She realizes she's been living the same way. "In the interest of sharing, I haven't been completely honest with you either."

His eyes narrow. "Just don't tell me you're FBI."

"Of course not." She holds up her ring finger. "This isn't fake."

"Married?"

"Engaged."

"To who?"

"His name's Chad."

"And where is Chad now?"

"St. Louis."

"He didn't come along?"

"It's not his thing."

Neil's eyes widen. "Wow. You two sound like a hell of a match."

"Don't make fun. It's complicated."

"Makes perfect sense to me." Neil gets up and drinks another shot. "Chad's your fallback plan."

"No, he's not."

"You sure about that?"

"I only left him in St. Louis because there were things I wanted to do before settling down."

"Things? Or guys?"

"Things. You want to know why I started a blog? This is why—because I thought I could make sense of my life if I wrote about it. And maybe there'd be others out there, like me. And, yes, maybe I'd find enough readers to justify leaving my job and starting a new life. Is that so wrong?"

"No."

"What I was most hoping for," she says wistfully, "was that I'd never use my return ticket."

"So don't."

"I'm not like you," she says. "I *have* to have a fallback plan. I thought I would enjoy traveling solo. You want to know why I got out of Marj's van? I'm tired of being alone."

"So you opted to hang with me?" He sits next to her. "Sounds like you've hit a new depth of loneliness, Eat Pray Love."

She puts her arms around him, and to her surprise, he doesn't resist. "Maybe I have." She pulls him back until he is lying on the bed, his eyes closed. "Maybe I can help you," she says.

A minute later she hears his breathing slow and deepen, and she slips out from under his arm and looks down at him. She takes off her wet clothes and stands in front of him, thinking about how close she was to cheating on Chad.

Amy discovers dry underwear and a T-shirt at the bottom of her backpack and spreads her wet clothing across the chair, table, and TV to dry. She pulls off Neil's shoes and wet socks. She pulls a blanket over him, then stretches out next to him, putting her head on his shoulder.

30.

Neil sleeps like a cat, occasionally drifting off behind a twitching face, then waking suddenly as though he were never asleep. She puts her hand on his forehead, and his face relaxes; his breathing slows. She doesn't sleep much that night, thinking about all that he unloaded on her, knowing there is still much left unsaid. Maybe he's protecting her, or maybe he doesn't fully trust her. Relationship gurus say trust must be earned over time, but when will they have the luxury of time? She wants him to trust her, to tell her everything. She wants to be needed, she realizes—maybe because she's never felt needed by Chad.

She runs her hands through his soft hair, wondering what it might be like to do this when he is fully awake, fully aware of her hands. She resists the urge to wake him, as his restless eyes are in a dream state.

She slides out of bed and quietly extracts her laptop from her backpack. She finds the wireless signal and stares at her blog, thinking about all the blog posts she could write if only she didn't care about what happened to her travel partner. Arguing alongside the highway with an audience of sheep. Backpacking in the pouring rain. Drinking to excess in a town with a name she can't pronounce. And all this in the past twenty-four hours.

But she does care about her travel partner, more than she's let herself admit until now. A voice in her head reminds her that she can't compare him with Chad, that their adventure here can't be replicated anywhere else. How would Neil do back in St. Louis? In an ordinary job, an ordinary life? Is that even possible? It frightens her to think of where she could be headed if she stays with Neil, and not just geographically.

She scrolls down to the first photo she posted of him. "Indiana Jones" staring at his map, sunglasses on. Then another of him outside the diner. She realizes she should remove these right now, before anyone sees them.

"What's that?"

She turns around to see Neil—awake, sitting up, staring at her screen.

"It's nothing. I'm deleting it."

"You posted photos of me?"

"I didn't exactly know you were on the run. Maybe if you'd told me—" She frantically taps at the red trash icon on the blog. "There. It's all gone. Everything."

Neil walks over to the sink and fills a cup with water. "You have no idea what you've done."

"I posted some stupid photos on the Internet. I didn't post your name. I didn't even know your name."

He turns and looks at her. "They scan the Internet for photos. The FBI has facial recognition software."

"Even with sunglasses and a baseball cap?"

"You'd be amazed at how good those computers are. Every photo has location data. The one of me at the diner—they'll know precisely where you took that photo. Which means they know we're headed south. Which means that car I saw was most definitely them. Mystery solved."

He goes to the window and peeks out from behind the curtains.

"I'm sorry," she says. "What can I do?"

He leans his back against the wall, rubbing his forehead. "You have any aspirin?" She digs out two pills and watches as he swallows them.

"Please don't be mad at me," she says. "No one reads my stupid travel blog. I didn't—"

"Forget it," he says. "I'm not mad. I'm just—if you were smart, Amy, you'd leave. Right now. Head north and don't look back."

She looks at him, his body tense. And she knows he's right. She should let him go. This isn't a backpacking trip any longer. But she can't let go and she's not even sure why at this point. Her mind is foggy and she can't think. "Can we talk about this after I take a shower?"

"I need to get moving."

"I know. But I haven't showered since Auckland. Frankly, you could use one yourself."

He hesitates, and she adds, "I'll only be a few minutes, okay?"

He nods.

In the shower, she stands there wondering if she should have invited him to join her in a more direct way. Something to take his mind off those photos. She's been thinking about it all night, having spent so much time staring at his nearly naked body.

Save a little water? Save a little time? It would have been so simple to ask, but she wasn't confident in how he would have responded. He was hungover and anxious, and if he'd said no, how would they have been able to keep hitching together?

Maybe, if he seems calmer when she gets out, she can offer to join him during his turn in the shower. She never would have asked this of Chad; he's the one who tends to initiate sex. They shared a bathtub once when she traveled with him to a conference, an expansive granite pool with a view of Lake Michigan. She would never complain about sex with Chad, certainly not to her girlfriends, who can do almost nothing else but complain about the inattentiveness of their men—Chad would do everything she asked of him, but in a methodical way, as if he had learned it from a book. Maybe it was the chaos of sex that was missing from her life, the falling off beds and breaking chairs. Or maybe it was the simple fact that she had never slept with a man with a tattoo and she longed to run her tongue along each letter.

When she exits the shower she opens the door and calls out to him. "I have a suggestion. In the interest of time, I think I should give you a scrub down. I'm very efficient with my hands."

There's no answer.

She steps out into the room, her towel loosely hanging, water dripping, but he isn't there. His bag is gone.

She feels the air leave her body.

31.

By the time she gets dressed and out to the parking lot, she isn't hopeful of finding Neil. She sees only a row of parked cars with steering wheels on the wrong side, reminding her of how far away from home she really is.

She returns to the room and finishes packing. She hears herself cursing aloud, though she's not sure who she's more upset with—Neil for leaving, or herself for posting those damn pictures in the first place. She wants to explain to him that the woman who posted those pictures isn't her. Not anymore.

But this would have sounded absurd; people don't change that quickly. Certainly there are defining moments. A graduation. A divorce. Maybe her moment was getting out of that van. Maybe her moment is now, letting Neil go for good, turning around and heading home.

She drops her key off at the empty front desk. A TV is in the corner of the room, a news program. She waits expectantly for Neil's face to appear on the screen, but when the weatherman points at an upcoming storm system, she walks back outside.

She stands by the road, her backpack propped against her leg. The sun is burning off the fog that just a few minutes before felt like rain. Cars decelerate past her as they enter city limits. If she stands on this side of the road and raises a thumb she can find a ride back to Auckland. There would be no shame in leaving. Chad would certainly welcome her home, as would her boss. And she could tell her girlfriends about Indiana Jones, embellishing him as needed.

Then she picks up her backpack and walks across the road. "I'm going to the South Island, dammit," she says to the passing cars. She raises her left arm and sets her eyes on the next car.

She feels her determination return when the second car that passes pulls over, a late-model Ford sedan. Amy leans over the open window, feeling like a professional by now. The driver is a man in his early twenties with the uneven terrain of a travel beard. The stereo is on too loud, and he has to turn it down for her to be heard.

"You going to Wellington?" she asks.

"I am. Hop on in," he says with a British accent. "Name's Ben."

She puts her backpack in the backseat, then joins him in the front. "Amy," she says, shaking his hand.

"You're Canadian?"

"American."

"Blast."

"Is that a problem?"

"No. I like to guess. The first couple I picked up, I guessed American and they were Canadian. And I would have guessed that you were American, but I've yet to meet an American traveling alone."

"I like to keep people guessing," she says.

"So you're headed to the South Island?"

"Yes. Are you?"

"Eventually. First I plan to do a bit of touring around Wellington."

"What's in Wellington?"

"I have a mate who's working at a pub near the harbor. Promised me free pints. He wants to hike the Queen Charlotte Track. Says it's quite the adventure."

"Adventure," she repeats, the word echoing through the car like a bad joke. She can still see Neil looking down at her over his sunglasses. She thought he was such a jerk at first, and who wouldn't? And what was he was seeing when he saw her? Maybe he envied her, the freedom of being on the run from nobody but herself.

"You had much of an adventure so far?" Ben asks.

"A bit."

"Only a bit? Well, stick with me then."

Amy thinks about how Ben is the sort of travel partner she probably would have ended up with, if not for Neil. British travelers on their years abroad, thick as sheep in New Zealand and Australia. As the two Brits told her back in Auckland, they can legally work here, unlike Americans.

Amy turns to the window and looks up at the hills. In less than an hour, she'll be in Wellington and then on the ferry. After a while, they pass a hitchhiker, which makes Amy think of Neil. She looks at the poor soul, arm held up, and it isn't until he is behind them, when she turns around and sees the Cardinals cap, that she realizes it's actually him. It's Neil.

"Ben, can you please pull over?"

"What's wrong?"

"The man we just passed. Do you mind picking him up? I know him."

"How do you know him?"

"It's complicated."

"Oh." She hears disappointment in his voice. "Not much room in the back with your rucksack and all."

"It would mean a lot to me."

"Yeah, okay." She watches Ben's face go from sunny to mostly cloudy. He pulls to the side of the road and waits for an opening before turning around. He pulls up right up behind Neil, who is watching the car curiously. Then he sees her.

Amy rolls down the window. "Where you headed?" she calls out.

He gives her a look she can't quite decipher. "Where do you think?"

"Ben, this is Neil."

"Pleased to meet you," Ben says without conviction.

Neil opens the door and pushes Amy's bag over.

"Are you two, a, um couple?" Ben asks.

"No," Amy says. "I dumped him." She looks back and watches a smile flash across Neil's face.

"Ah," Ben says, perking up.

"Actually," Neil says, "it's because she's engaged. Not to me, of course. Some guy in the States."

"Engaged." Ben looks over at Amy. "That's. Lovely."

"But it could go either way," Neil says.

"Really?"

"Don't listen to him, Ben. He's just upset that I dumped him."

"You headed to the South Island, Ben?"

"Ultimately. Assuming I don't piss away the rest of my savings on Speight's Ginger Beer." Ben's big laugh brings Amy to laughter. And soon she is happy and relaxed, thinking that they are going to make it to the ferry, that everything will go smoothly from here on out.

Until she feels a tap on her shoulder. "Guess who," Neil says.

Amy looks out the rearview mirror. A black sedan is about a hundred yards back.

"Is that them?" she asks.

"That who?" Ben asks.

"Ben, do you mind stepping on the gas?" Neil asks.

"Late for a meeting?" Ben laughs again.

"In a manner of speaking, yes."

"I can't afford a ticket, mate."

"It's not the police I'm worried about," Neil says. "That black car back there. It's following us."

"Why?"

Amy leans in to Ben. "Look, Ben. We really need to get away from that car."

"You two are putting me on. Right? I've read about this. A confidence game."

"We're not putting you on," Amy says. "I swear."

Neil is pulling on his backpack. "You're going to have to let me out here, Ben."

The car is now alongside them, and as they pass, Amy sees two men in front. The car pulls ahead and brakes suddenly.

"Fuck was that?" Ben cranks the wheel hard left, leaving two wheels on gravel, barely avoiding the rear bumper as he pulls around them. "This is a bloody car hire. I didn't pay for the insurance." He slams his foot down on the gas and lurches ahead.

"You said you wanted an adventure," Amy says.

"An adventure, yeah, not a bloody accident."

In the backseat, Neil is unfolding his map. "I think we can lose them on the side streets. I'm going to give you directions, okay?"

"What choice do I have?"

"Amy, get your phone out and look up the Interislander ferry. When's the next sailing to Picton?"

Amy tries to focus on her phone as her body lurches back and forth with the motion of the car. Neil is barking out directions to Ben, and she hears the tires squealing as they take turns without slowing nearly enough and speed along the windy, narrow roads.

"Two forty-five," Amy says. "Wellington to Picton." She turns around but looks past Neil to the road behind them. There's no sign of the black sedan.

"That's it," says Neil. "What time is it now?"

Her eyes drop down to his face, then to her phone. "We've only got ten minutes."

"Ben, take a right up there, and we'll be back on Highway 1."

Amy looks at the road again and still can't see the car. "Did we lose them?"

"Bloody right we did," says Ben.

"For now," Neil adds. "But I'm sure by now they know exactly where we're headed." Neil looks at Amy. "This is your last chance to walk away."

"Stop asking."

"You're insane."

"Maybe. But I set out to see the South Island, and by God I'm going to see it."

"Are either of you going to tell me what we're running from?" Ben asks.

Neil says to Amy, "Get your backpack on. Now. We're going to have to run for it." Then he turns to Ben. "Thanks, man. Take a left here—no, here!"

As Ben slams on the brakes to make the turn, Amy is thrown hard into the door, her ears ringing. When she opens her eyes again, she sees them descending a ramp, and ahead is a large white ship at dock. Ben slams to a stop in front of the loading bay.

"Ben, I don't know how in the world I can repay you," Neil says. He claps Ben on the shoulder. "Thank you."

"Here." Amy hands Ben the last of her twenty-dollar bills. "For beer." She leans over and kisses him on the cheek. She opens her car door to discover that Neil is already running toward the ferry. She runs after him, trying to catch up. She hears a dinging noise, like last call at the theater. She follows Neil up a long ramp, and suddenly Neil stops, held back by the turnstiles. "Fuck!" He looks around as if considering jumping over them, but ferry personnel and tourists are all around them.

"Don't worry," she says. "I've got a card." She veers to one of the empty ticket windows and slides her card under. "Two tickets. One way. Please please please hold the boat for us!"

The man behind the glass shakes his head condescendingly, and her heart sinks until he slides two paper tickets and her card back under the glass. "Off you go."

32.

SHE FOLLOWS NEIL UPSTAIRS to the outside deck, thick with people crowded along the railing. Neil has his sunglasses back on, his cap pulled low. They push through until Amy finds a spot of empty railing they can squeeze into. Normally she would have bristled at being in the middle of such crowds, but now she welcomes them like a security blanket.

She looks down at the pier, grateful to see it slipping away from them. A man in jeans and a dark sweatshirt runs to the water's edge and looks up at their ship, as if scanning the faces of all the passengers.

"There's one of them," Neil says, stepping back imperceptibly, putting himself just behind one of the tourists around them. "From the car."

"Who is he?"

"I wish I knew. I wish I knew if they had others on this boat."

"Judging by the way he was running, I would doubt it," she says.

"But even if they're not here, they'll be waiting for us on the other side."

"You're quite an optimist, aren't you?"

She nudges him with her body and he puts an arm around her shoulder.

"Thank you," he says.

"For what?"

"For picking up this hitchhiker. Otherwise my next ride would've been with them."

"You should have seen Ben's face when I asked him to pull over. I think he had a different sort of adventure in mind."

Amy hears excited shouts and cheers coming from the bow, the sounds of cameras firing. She leans over the railing to get a look. "What's going on up there?"

"Dolphins, most likely."

Amy looks down just in time to see two dolphins surfing

alongside the boat, keeping pace with it, like skipping stones hardly making a dent on the water.

Neil looks over her shoulder, his warm breath on her neck, his body leaning against hers. She raises her phone, like everyone else, then stops, puts it back in her pocket. "You can't capture this," she says.

Neil smiles. "There's hope for you yet, Eat Pray Love."

Amy turns her attention to the dolphins, and Neil adds, "They say dolphins ride the wakes of the boats to save energy. But there are many instances of dolphins following ferries across the straight only to hitch a ride with the next ferry going right back. I like to think they're having fun down there."

"Looks like fun."

"I envy them," he says. "They could dart across the Tasman Sea if they chose, probably make it in a day."

"To Australia?"

He nods.

"Is that where you're headed?"

He leans in, his mouth near her left ear. "Melbourne."

"And how do you plan to get there?" she asks.

"Let's cross that body of water when we get to it." He rests his chin on her shoulder and she doesn't press, relieved to feel his body relaxing.

As Wellington shrinks away, the wind over open water picks up, and most people retreat inside. But, finally safe from watching eyes, she and Neil stay huddled together, his body warming hers. Neil seems preoccupied with the scenery.

"You think they're still following us?" Amy asks, peering at the water for small boats.

He smiles. "No. I'm looking for something different." He points. "There it is."

"What?"

He put his hands on Amy's shoulders to aim her in the correct direction. She feels the warmth of his right arm as he points.

"A humpback whale."

Then she notices a puff of spray on the horizon.

"How do know you know it's a humpback?"

"I had a good teacher," he says. "My old man, when he was around, took me out on the water a lot. He even brought me down here once, when I was about twelve. This strait is a migration route. The whalers used to have stations all along here."

"So you were raised an activist?"

"I was raised to *dislike* activists," he says. "My mom was one of his first volunteers. Used to sail with him on the ships, before she had me, before she found herself landlocked, trying to create a normal home, which she was incapable of doing. And he wasn't much help. He hated being on land. Used to say he was half pelagic. But you can't be half pelagic. You either are or you aren't. And my father is one hundred percent ocean."

"What are you?"

"I'm not sure. I feel safer out here than I've ever felt on terra firma. He divorced my mom when I was twelve, right after he brought me down here, where I met his future wife, another volunteer. He may do wonders for the whales, I'll give him that, but he's not so good with humans. I wanted to be close to him, but he didn't make it easy to like him. People kept calling him a hero—but this hero never gave my mom enough child support. He was holding fundraisers for his anti-whaling trips while we lived below the poverty line. When you take the water out of it, he was just another deadbeat dad."

"I'm sorry."

"The sad thing was that I might have joined him long ago if I hadn't resented him so damn much. Instead I tried to get as far from the water as I could, as far from what he did."

"And where did that take you?"

"I worked as a software engineer in Arizona," he says. "Nothing heroic. No drama. Just a good paycheck and a nice condo. I might still be there today if my company hadn't begun bringing in guest speakers, one of those trendy employee perks, like free soda and foosball tables. One afternoon I attended an entomologist's lecture and learned all about collapsing bee colonies and neonics and GMOs—and the next thing I know I'm helping this nonprofit launch a website so people can track bees and shoot off nasty e-mails to the companies that pump out all those chemicals. It didn't take long for my regularly scheduled work to suffer, and it wasn't long before I left the job, the money, the condo. I tried so hard to fit in to that world, but in the end I think I was destined to be an outsider. I always tried to see myself as the polar opposite of my dad but somehow better. He was out there defending the world's largest creatures—but who *doesn't* want to save whales? I was protecting the world's smallest creatures, the ones no one talks about, taking on big agriculture, some of the world's largest, most despicable companies. I wasn't out to save just one species but *all* species." Neil sighs. "It was a nice idea, but as you can see, my life has come full circle. As hard as I tried to avoid the water, here I am."

"I think he'd be proud of you, if he knew what you were doing."

"I guess we'll see."

"Is that where you're headed? To see him?"

He nods. She wants to ask where, but his eyes are elsewhere, looking far past the whales.

Later, after the whales are out of sight, they find seats downstairs overlooking the water. Even inside, Neil keeps his sunglasses on. Amy goes to the snack bar and buys them avocado, lettuce, and tomato sandwiches.

"You're eating plants now, too?" he asks. "Could I be having an effect on you?"

"I wouldn't go that far. It was hard enough to find something *you* could eat, so I ordered two." She unwraps her sandwich and takes a bite.

"What do you think?" Neil asks around a mouthful of his own sandwich.

"It's good," she says. "I think the most difficult thing about your way of life is that every meal is this whole production. Maybe I'm lazy, but I don't like to have to think so much every time I want a bite to eat."

"We are creatures of habit," he says, then smiles. "So when I'm dead and gone, you'll be back to chicken wings?"

"Don't say that." She finds herself oddly shaken by his frankness. "You're not going anywhere."

"I was only kidding."

"Don't kid about that, okay?"

"Fair enough."

Neil looks past her shoulder, and she sees the tension in his forehead, neck. Wanting to give him a break from his own thoughts, she says, "You know, I once wanted to be a veterinarian."

"Really?"

"In junior high. I volunteered at the animal shelter. I was a 'cat cuddler,' as they called us. My dad viewed it as something for my résumé, but, for me, it was magical. Every Saturday I would feed them, hold them on my lap. I didn't even mind changing their litter. To get a terrified rescue cat purring is the most amazing accomplishment. I thought I could make a career of it. But my dad would only pay for college if I selected a major he approved of—and he did not approve of me becoming a vet. He was raised on a farm somewhere in Greece and resented animals because of that. So I chose journalism."

"What does your father do?" he asks.

"He died when I was in high school."

"I'm sorry."

"It's okay. Before he died he worked for Boeing. He was an engineer; that's how he got his green card. First-generation American. He was hard on me. Probably too hard."

"What about your mom?"

"She's in St. Louis, in a condo I helped pay for. She wasn't prepared to start working when my dad died. He had life insurance, but he also had debts. So my mom went to work at the mall, and I vowed that I would always be financially independent. That I would never let a man run my life for me."

"You certainly aren't letting me run it. Or your fiancé, for that matter."

Amy chooses to ignore this. "My father wasn't all bad," she continues. "He was the last person to talk about feelings, but he had his moments. He was a Civil War nut. On weekends we used to drive around to Southern Missouri battlegrounds and various cemeteries. Some little girls played soccer on Saturdays; I visited cemeteries. He once took me to Alton, Illinois, just across the Missouri River, and he told me all about Elijah Lovejoy. Have you heard of him?"

Neil shakes his head.

"Lovejoy was a religious man and an abolitionist. He started a press in St. Louis calling for an end to slavery. One day a mob raided the press and destroyed everything. So he went across the river, to Illinois, a free state, and started another press. And one night a bunch of pro-slavery folks came across the river and set his building on fire and shot him to death."

"Jesus."

"Guess the year that occurred."

"I don't know. Eighteen sixty?"

"Eighteen thirty-seven. More than two decades before the start of the Civil War. When I learned that, I realized that the Civil War started well before Fort Sumter. That change often takes far longer than you expect it to."

"I can attest to that," Neil says. "I used to think that if every slaughterhouse had glass walls, people wouldn't eat meat. I thought if we went undercover and took videos and showed the world what was going on in there, the world would change."

"You've done that?" Amy feels her eyes widen. "Surely it's helped a little bit, at least?"

"A little. Maybe the chickens get a bit more room. The pigs don't get kicked so much. But they all end up the same way in the end. I have to remind myself that some social movements are more glacial than others." He pauses for a long moment and looks around, then asks, "Do you know a company called Biosant?"

She nods. "Of course. It's only the biggest company in St. Louis."

He leans in. "A few weeks ago, I hacked into their servers and stole some files. Files that they should have deleted long ago. Files that will prove that they know GMOs are unhealthy. They know this because they've conducted tests, with results that they don't want the public to see."

"How do they know it was you?"

"I'm not sure. Except that I've been trying to get those files for years. Ever since I became an activist."

"What will you do with them?"

"Send them to the *New York Times*. I would have done it by now but I need time to read them, to send the right ones along, and I haven't had a moment's rest since … " His voice drifts off, his eyes over her shoulder.

Suddenly his lips are on hers, and he's pulling her close, turning their bodies toward the sea as he tightens his embrace. She knows she should push back, but she doesn't—even through her surprise, she's enjoying it far more than she should, and she rides the wave until he leans back again.

She looks up at him, but his gaze is focused over her head. "I'm sorry," he says.

"I'm just as much to blame," she murmurs. "I'm the one who's engaged, after all—"

"Those two men who just walked by," he interrupts. "In suits. I didn't want them to see my face."

"Oh." She feels her face flush with heat. She stands, not sure what is more humiliating—what just happened, or the fact that she enjoyed it so much. She should've known better.

He reaches for her hand. "Sit down."

"Maybe you should find some other woman to make out with,"

she says, pulling her hand away.

"I didn't kiss you just because of those suits."

"Right."

He stands up, facing her. "Amy. There are a lot of ways I could've hidden my face. Did it occur to you that maybe I just wanted an excuse to kiss you?"

"How am I supposed to believe anything you say?"

"Come here." He takes her hand again.

"What is it—are they back?" She starts to turn around but before she does, he kisses her again, his hands on either side of her face, preventing her from turning away. Not that she wants to.

Finally he pulls back. "So," he says. "Did that feel more authentic?"

She'd never tell him that even the first kiss, the one that was all for show, felt more authentic than any affection she'd received from Chad in months. That this is the real reason she'd embarked on this trip—to answer the question of whether she was doing the right thing by getting married. By getting married to Chad.

Neil is studying her, his eyes locked on her face. "I just realized I don't know your last name."

"You don't know my first name, either."

"It's not Amy?"

"I go by Amy, but my real name, my Greek name, is Amaranta. Amaranta Bakas."

"Amaranta. What does it mean?"

"Flower that never fades."

"That's fitting," he says. For once, he's not looking around the ship but directly into her eyes, and she feels almost as though he's seeing her for the first time. "I'm glad I met you, Amaranta."

"I'm glad I met you, too, whatever your actual name is." She regards him for a moment, then asks, "So what happens when we get to Picton? Are you going to try to ditch me again?"

"Are you saying you want to stick with me on the other side?"

"I'm considering it."

"It won't be a sightseeing trip," he warns. "No ziplining, no hot air balloon rides. No blogging about where we're going … "

"I think I've had enough thrills to last me a while."

His face darkens. "I don't want you to get hurt. Too many people around me … " His voice drifts.

She doesn't ask him to elaborate; she's already decided she wants to stay with him, whatever lies ahead. "Do you think we've helped each other?" she asks.

"You've helped me," he says. "I don't really want to think about where I'd be right now if it weren't for you."

In this moment, she knows one thing, with a realization so strong it feels like an explosion in her chest—that she can't marry Chad. That fallback plans don't matter anymore. That whatever happens next, she can't go back to what she'd left.

33.

SOON THE HEAVY WAVES ARE REPLACED by the glassy stillness of the sound. Back out on the top deck, Amy and Neil are at eye level with many of the hills they are gliding between, green with trees and ferns, primeval.

"Such a change from the North Island," she says. "So untouched."

"It's as if this island is the *before* and the North Island the *after*."

While the port of Wellington was as built up as any U.S. city, the port of Picton is like a small village. Homes and small business districts huddle together at the base of the green hills, and trees hover over their ship.

"I think we need to split up."

"Not this again," Amy says.

"Just as we get off the ferry. That way you can see if I'm being followed and vice versa."

As the ferry glides into the harbor, Amy remains on the top deck and watches as the trickle of people emerging from the ship turns to a flood. A handful of buildings line the bay, with rental cars and bike rentals. People roll their bags down the final ramp toward parking lots, idling buses.

As she watches Neil make his way down the ramp, she wonders again why she is so eager to follow him—especially now that she so vividly understands the risks. With each passing mile, she becomes less companion and more accomplice, in danger of losing everything waiting for her at home. But what is waiting for her at home, really?

She's never been around someone so committed to a cause and so badly outnumbered. It's not pity she feels but passion—she connects, somehow, with the passion within him, a passion she's missed out on her whole life. She's never felt the same intensity for anything, or anyone, the way Neil does.

And now, watching him from this distance, she sees that he is just as quiet and introverted as he was the day she met him—but now she knows what's going on inside that body. He's not as cold and reserved as she'd thought; he's just as nervous and lost as she is.

She shakes away her thoughts and remembers to study the other passengers, the people standing by waiting cars. Neil makes his way to a bus stop, and Amy doesn't see anyone who looks suspicious—then again, this is a whole new world to her, and she isn't sure what she's looking for.

Then, two men in suits disembark, and Amy holds her breath. But they don't even glance in Neil's direction. They are probably just salesmen, she thinks, and she grabs her bag and begins to follow them as they climb into a waiting car, which then pulls away.

Amy descends the gangway wearing sunglasses and a sun hat she purchased onboard; Neil figured that if they'd found her blog, they would know what she looks like. As she walks along the pier, she feels oddly self-aware, as if people are watching her. She tells herself that it's her imagination at work. Neil is so focused on the worst case scenario that he didn't even consider the fact that the two men pursuing them in Wellington might be the only ones, and those two would be too far behind to be here now.

She ducks into a rental-car agency and looks out the window. She sees no one around but other passing tourists. Relieved, she goes to the counter and rents a car, continuing the plan she and Neil had hatched on the ferry.

Once she has the keys in her hand, she drives a few miles outside of Picton until she gets to the first bus stop outside of town. Nobody is there, so she pulls over and honks her horn. She looks around, but there is no sign of Neil. She feels her heart rate quicken and looks in the rearview mirror, wondering if they'd been followed after all, whether she'd just been too inexperienced to notice.

Suddenly a face appears at the driver's side window, and he walks around to the other side and climbs in. "I think we're safe for now," he says. "I haven't seen anyone following us. We should find a place to crash and head out tomorrow."

"No highway underpasses," she says.

They follow a meandering two-lane road south between tree-covered hills, some scarred bare and a dull shade of brown. She is about to ask Neil about the landscape, the scattered stumps and branches of thousands of trees, when they pass three loaded logging trucks headed in the opposite direction. She glances at Neil, but his eyes are preoccupied with the side-view mirror.

In twenty minutes, they are in the small town of Blenheim, passing a movie theater just as streetlights are blinking themselves awake in the growing dusk. Neil points out an Indian restaurant, and they pull over.

She follows Neil to a booth in the back, where he sits facing the door. With the spices in the air, Amy is suddenly starving; they order naan bread and two different dishes to share. She thinks of Chad, who hates communal meals and cringes any time she tries to take a nibble of anything off his plate. But when their food arrives and they begin eating, Neil doesn't care as she puts her fork into his dish—though she considers that maybe it's because she's the one who will be paying for the meal. Still, she enjoys the subtle intimacy of sharing food, especially the brief moment when their fingers touch as they reach for the same piece of naan.

Afterward, they drive a few blocks to the outskirts of town and check into a motel, a small room with two beds and a tea kettle and two shrink-wrapped biscuits next to a bulbous TV set.

As Amy puts her backpack on one bed, he tosses his bag right next to hers. When she looks at him, he picks the bag up and places it on his bed. She feels a sudden awkwardness between them and wonders whether he'd misinterpreted her look. She hadn't minded his presumption, but can't find the words to tell him as much.

"I need a drink," he says.

"First you need a shower," she tells him.

"I do?"

"Oh, yes."

Instead of undressing in front of her, he retreats to the bathroom. While he's in there she feels something taking over her body. She stares at herself in the mirror, as if to ask her reflection whether she's crazy to be thinking what she's thinking. She hears the water turn off and the sliding of a shower curtain. She goes to the bathroom door and opens it.

"What's wrong?" Neil asks, as he wraps a towel around his waist. She approaches him, his face confused, curious.

"What are you doing?" he asks, but she's not answering, not in words. Beads of water cascade down his chest, and her tongue catches each drop before they reach the towel below. He's standing still, not with her yet but not resisting either, and then her lips move upward, slowly, past his neck to those lips.

Then his hands draw her body close to him. She tugs loose the towel, and he pulls her T-shirt up and over her head. She raises her arms to unhook her bra, and as his mouth consumes her, she feels her body wake, as if from a thousand years of hibernation, now insatiably hungry.

In bed, she traces her fingers down the steel chain around his neck, down to the whale pattern on the pendant. "Where did you get this?"

"I had it made custom back in Iowa City."

She grasps it between her fingers. It's thick, like a silver ingot, heavy and cold. "Does it have any personal significance?"

"I suppose you could say it reminds me of what I'm fighting for." He leans over and kisses her. "This was a perfect day," he says. She is surprised by how happy he appears, that anything in his strange and terrifying world can be characterized as perfect.

"I've had five perfect days in my life," he continues.

"You keep count?"

"I used to sit outside on the curb to get away from my mom. She had mood spells that would last for weeks. And on those rare clear Seattle nights, I'd look up at the moon and I'd imagine my life far away. And I vowed that I would have all perfect days."

"When was your first?"

He rolls his eyes and looks away.

"Let me guess, a girl? What was her name?"

"Noa. The day was just another day, really, only it was a Friday and neither of us had dates and we just sat around in her apartment talking. Nothing happened. Just talking. And I distinctly remember thinking, *This is perfect.* And that's when I started counting." He turns his face toward hers. "What about you? How many perfect days have you had?"

"Beats me. I never think about it."

"Think. You'll know."

"How do you define a perfect day?"

"A day that blasts through tedium and nothingness. A day free of worry. A day of getting away with something. A day of sun. A day of snow. A day that you never forget and may not even know why, just that it sticks with you. If I have ten perfect days before I die, I will have lived a full life."

"You're halfway there." After she says this, she feels her body tense with the reminder, however brief, about his reality.

"You okay?"

"Yeah, I'm fine." She snuggles a bit closer to him. "So, what if today is my first perfect day?"

"Then you've got a lot of catching up to do."

34.

When she opens her eyes, she sees Neil's silhouette against the sun shining through a gap in the curtains.

"Is everything okay?" she asks.

"I think so."

"Do I have time for a shower?"

He turns to her. "Of course."

"Are you going to tell me where we're headed?"

He sits down next to her and runs his hand through her hair. There is a calmness about him that is a welcome surprise. Perhaps she'd helped him get his first good night's sleep in a long time. She'd certainly slept well.

"We're headed to Greymouth, on the western side of the island. Should be there in about four and a half hours."

"And what's in Greymouth?"

"If I'm lucky, boats."

Amy has been quiet since she pulled out of the motel parking lot, focused on the road ahead, her brain thinking in opposites. Staying on the opposite side of the road. Turning into the opposite lanes. Not freaking out when cars pass by her opposite shoulder. So far she's doing surprisingly well; at least, no other car has honked at her yet. She occasionally catches herself drifting into the oncoming lane and has to right herself, but Neil hasn't said anything.

As they leave the strip malls and subdivisions of outer Blenheim behind, she feels her shoulders relax, and she begins to take in the view. The two-lane road parallels a river of equal width to their right with farmland and winery estates on the left. The road rises slowly toward the low-hanging clouds, interrupted by copses of trees, and, as they climb, they pass sheep pastures, countless furry white hillocks dotting the hills on either side like boulders. On the southern horizon she sees mountains turning to snow, their peaks obscured by clouds. She glances over at Neil, the map spread out across his lap, his face turned toward the window.

A voice in her head tells her that Neil is quiet because he's distracted by every car he sees in the side-view mirror. Another voice tells her that he feels guilty for last night. That he's counting the minutes until he can make his escape. A third voice, the softest of them all, tells her to stop being so hard on herself. Maybe Neil isn't talking because he has nothing to say. Maybe he's still thinking about yesterday's perfect day.

Then Neil folds up his map. "When can I drive?" he asks.

"You're not on the rental agreement."

"You don't trust me?"

"It's not that. It's just. It's safer this way. You can duck down when needed and not risk driving us off the side of the road."

"We might be doing that anyway," he says pointedly.

Amy catches herself drifting again and jerks the wheel back. "I'm doing fine."

"You are. But just wait until your first right turn."

She tries to picture what lane she will occupy when she does turn right, her brain suddenly muddled.

"Don't worry," he says, as if reading her mind. "I'll help you through it. We aren't going to turn for a while yet."

"And then what?" she asks. "When we get to Greymouth. Do you have a boat lined up?"

"I haven't thought that far ahead yet."

"Perhaps we should start thinking about it now."

He hesitates, then says. "Maybe you should consider leaving me in Greymouth, and continuing south."

Now she knows the reason for his silence. The reason he kept his mouth shut until now, trying to find the right way to say what he just said, which doesn't feel right at all.

"So I'm supposed to just drop you off? Like some taxi service?"

"Somebody has to return the car."

"You're worried about me getting my deposit back?" She feels her anger rising. "How thoughtful of you."

"Here's the thing. I'm going to have to stow away on one of these boats. That's going to be hard enough with just one person, let alone two."

"I didn't know you were going to do that."

"It's not as if there's any ferry service. It's a solid week across, assuming the weather is halfway decent. And I'm not even sure I'll find anyone headed that way. With my luck I'll end up stowing away on a boat back to Auckland. All I know is that my options are limited at this point. I don't have the money to charter a boat."

"How much does a charter cost?"

"A couple thousand, I'm guessing."

She says nothing, rattled beyond words, unable to accept that they have to part already yet knowing what he says makes perfect sense. She tries to envision the moment she lets him out at a dock. The kiss good-bye. The empty seat next to her as she drives back to Picton. No one to catch her as she drifts into the other lane.

What bothers her most of all is that he's right. She can play fugitive in a rental car, but she can't play stowaway on a boat. She's just been living a fantasy, and he's been running for his life. Eventually reality and fantasy must part.

The hills on her left have risen up to meet the road; they are rock-strewn and covered in pale-green scrub. When the road takes them right and over a two-lane bridge across the river, she glances down at the aqua-blue tint reflected by glacial sediment and wishes she could stop and take a picture. She feels a pang of regret—all this beauty around them, just out of view, and here she is racing past it. What if she were to take a turn at the next gravel road, see where it takes them? What would Neil say? Would he resist her if she pulled the car over and reached for him?

Around the next bend she sees a flash of color ahead of them, a quick movement like a shooting star, and then she feels something knock into the car, like a baseball bouncing off the front bumper.

"What was that?" Amy asks, letting her foot off the pedal and pulling over.

Neil says nothing, gets out. She turns and watches him walking back a few yards, then kneeling down. She follows until she can see, over his shoulder, a luminescent green bird about the size of a robin, with a bright yellow forehead underlined in red. The bird is on its side, looking up at them, scared and helpless or simply in shock.

She feels her heart sinking. "What did I do?"

"It wasn't your fault," he says.

"Of course it was my fault. I was going too fast."

"We're on the run, remember? Don't be so hard on yourself."

She ignores him and kneels over the bird, and she speaks to it, the way she used to speak to the sick and dying cats in the shelter. Knowing they would be put down soon, she whispered words of love, her arms around them, listening to them purr, a comforting sound that gave her hope even if it was too late for them to be saved.

She drops to her knees and looks into the bird's eye, glistening and alive. She stares at it until it blurs before her eyes, and time disappears until she feels a hand on her shoulders. “Amaranta.” Neil lifts her into his arms and pulls her close. “We need to go.”

“What about the bird?”

Neil gently picks up the broken body and places it down the embankment at the side of the road. She watches him pause over it for a long moment before returning to her. “It’s okay,” he says. “He’s no longer suffering.”

She hands Neil the keys. “You should drive.”

He hands them back. “No.”

“I killed him.”

“It was an accident,” he says. “Think about this: Every time you ordered a chicken Caesar salad, you killed a bird. What’s the difference between this bird and the chickens that live three miserable months in a cage?”

“I don’t know. I don’t want to think about it, okay? You need to drive.” She holds out the keys again, but Neil doesn’t take them.

She takes a deep breath and looks up at the snow-capped mountains. “Fine. Let’s go.”

She pulls back onto the road, trying to control the shaking of her hands on the wheel. She’d never hit an animal before, despite years of driving, and she finds herself unprepared for the sick remorse that sinks into her stomach and settles there. What’s even worse is what Neil had said—that every time she ate chicken, she was killing birds. But he was right, and she’s been doing it all her life without a second thought.

She thinks of the bird lying in the road, and how most of the chickens she ate probably died deaths even worse than the bird she hit. Then the sick feeling is burned up by anger—a thin beam of rage she directs toward Neil, for making her out to be a criminal by the simple and innocent act of eating. She glances over at him, but he’s oblivious, looking out the window, leaning forward to see into the side-view mirror. So paranoid. So judgmental. So sure of himself and all that he stands for—as if there is only one way to live, only one way to be in the world.

Yet when she looks away from him and down at her hands, she sees that her fingers are still trembling, that she's still shaken up by what she's done, and she tries to picture her next meal, whether she'll be able to order or make a chicken dish ever again. She's been eating as Neil does out of respect for him, not any great desire to change her life. But now she wonders whether the bird flying into her bumper wasn't an accident after all but a sign of some kind.

"Shit." Neil is bent around in his seat, looking through the rear window.

"What?"

"Two cars back."

Amy looks into the rearview mirror. As she rounds the bend, she sees a black sedan with two figures in the front seat.

"It's the same guys from the North Island," Neil says.

"You sure?"

"There's only one way to find out." Neil unfolds his map. "We need to find another road. Okay, there's a left turn coming up. Turn there and drive like hell."

Amy does as she's told, feeling her body fall into Neil around the turn, then hearing the engine strain to get them up a long, steep hill leading through more pastureland.

"What do you see?"

"Damn," he says. "They turned."

"I have to get back on the main road," she says. "Hold on." She turns hard, feels gravel under the tires, and drives straight at the sedan.

"Amy, what are you doing?"

"Giving them a taste of their own medicine."

"That's not a good idea."

"Yeah, well, I'm still learning what side of the road to drive on."

Right before impact, the sedan swerves out of their way and

down a hill. Amy feels an explosive mix of desperation and anger pulsing through her body as she swerves back onto the highway. She can see slivers of blue through the trees.

"Pull over," Neil says. "Anywhere up here. Drop me off."

"No."

"They're gaining on us again."

"We're almost there."

"And then what? You want to get arrested with me? This is not going to end well."

"You're not a martyr, Neil. Not yet."

She looks in the rearview mirror and sees the sedan riding her bumper, as if eager to pass.

"At least they're not using a siren," she says. "That would have really pissed me off."

She knows what she must do, but she needs to find the right cars, the right place. Not so close to the sharp edges overlooking the Tasman Sea. The car is still right behind them; she feels men staring into their car, and she worries they have guns. Neil is talking to her, his voice frantic, but she's not listening. She sees the road ahead open up, the gentle slope to the beach and a pickup truck towing an RV.

"Hold on!"

She crosses into the truck's lane and stays there. The driver's face, mouth open, horn blaring, the truck swerving, the trailer in her lane. She swerves right onto rock, gravel, the cliff looming hard up.

Then she is through, and she speeds up. Through the mirror she sees the other car, pinned between the trailer and the cliff.

"Yes!" she shouts. "You see that?"

Neil lifts his head and looks back.

"Holy crap! Not bad, Eat Pray Love. Not bad at all."

She is on such an adrenaline high from ditching the sedan, it almost pains her to apply brakes, but she does when she sees the sign for Greymouth. She slows, keeping an eye on the mirror.

"Where's the dock?"

"Straight up ahead," he says. "Then over a bridge."

She follows the road over a river channel, turns down a residential street of small homes with small yards, then veers right onto an industrial road with warehouses on one side and a narrow wooden pier running parallel to the road for about a quarter mile. The boats are moored facing the street, one next to the other like a drive-in theater. She pulls over.

"I thought there'd be more boats," Neil says.

"Just get out there and find a charter. I'll worry about the money."

"They don't exactly take credit cards," he says.

"Let me worry about that," she tells him.

She turns the car around and heads back to the city center, about half a mile away. She makes her way down the main street, scanning the store signs left and right until she sees what's she's looking for, feeling a wave a relief. She parks the car in the alley behind a drugstore, leaves the keys inside, grabs her backpack, and hurries out to the main street.

When she sees the Cash Queen sign she pulls open the door and stops to let her eyes adjust to the dim light. From behind the counter, under dangling guitars, an older man looks up from a laptop computer. "Can I help you?"

She approaches the counter. "I have something to sell," she says before holding up her left hand, her ring finger catching the light.

Part II

35.

Robert drives through downtown Iowa City looking for a place to eat. He passes the Airliner, a bar that he and David Spencer frequented years ago. He wasn't supposed to be on the case at all, after having been undercover with Aeneas, but an agent had dropped out to be with a sick wife, and Robert arrived to fill in two months after the assignment was under way. He didn't care how late he arrived, just as long as he was working in the field. Keeping busy was the only way to keep his memories—and regrets—at bay.

He met Spence at the Heartland Motel. In the parking lot underneath a sign that advertised $49 ROOMS-CABLE-AC, Spence—dressed in a white polo shirt and navy blazer, with neatly cropped blond hair framed by Ray-Bans—reminded Robert of a European soccer star. He led Robert to a room on the second floor. The room smelled like cigarettes, and Robert left the door open. "Not the Four Seasons," Spence said. "But it's walking distance to the bars."

"Where are the other agents?" Robert asked.

"Too many agents make too much noise," Spence said. "And these people have sharp ears."

Spence showed him pictures of Ray Hudson and Neil Cameron—Ray dark-haired and tattooed, Neil blond and suntanned like a surfer, both of them with the same seasoned look of rebellion in their faces. "Ray's the leader," Spence said. "I've been tracking him off and on for two years. I believe he torched the animal testing lab up in Seattle last April. And a fur shop outside LA two months later."

"Why haven't you arrested him?"

"Never enough evidence. They're smart about fingerprints, phones. They use the computers in libraries for Internet access. Pass messages through books and on Internet message boards and YouTube comments. These guys are creative as hell. The owner of a meat processor was having an affair with the city councilor, until these guys outed him to the media with photographs and video."

Spence handed Robert a photo and an address. "This is Ray's girlfriend. Tracy Morris."

Robert looked down at the photo of a round-faced woman with reddish-brown hair and sad eyes.

"Now," Spence continues, "she's your girlfriend. You're going to get to know everything about her, photograph anyone she meets, report back daily." Spence slapped Robert on the back. "And this concludes your orientation."

One night at the Airliner, Robert asked Spence why, with his tenure, he'd chosen to work this case, which was low-profile by FBI standards. "Why activists?" Robert asked. "Instead of, say, arms dealers?"

"These guys are more interesting," Spence said. "More creative. Just when you think you know who they're going to target next, they surprise you. One week Ray sets fire to a slaughterhouse under construction in central Oregon. A week later he's shooting undercover footage at a pork processor in Texas. Not long ago they spray-painted a police car just across town because the cop had to put down a mountain lion."

"That's more like vandalism than terrorism."

"You'd rather be going after ISIS?"

"Yeah, sure."

"They all want revolution, my friend."

"But these guys aren't trying to nuke Los Angeles."

"Maybe not. But if they had their way, the world as we know it would still be history. You like fishing, hunting? Forget it. You like steaks on the grill? Forget that, too. In the big picture, these people are no less dangerous than any other terrorist cell because they place animals ahead of people. With priorities like that, you never know what a person is capable of. It's jihad under another name, that's all."

Robert nodded, which was as much as he could do. He could not tell Spence that he knew better. That he sympathized with the activists more than he could ever admit. That he wasn't entirely sure he could do this assignment, after having lived in Jake's skin for as long as he had.

ROBERT WAS IN HIS RENTAL CAR in the hospital parking lot as he watched Tracy Morris hug a nurse outside of the building where staff gathered to smoke. This would not have seemed unusual if Tracy hadn't walked two miles to the hospital to hug this nurse. Or if either Tracy or the nurse were actually still working at this hospital. She'd left the hospital for a job at Tarcher Processing, which she'd abruptly quit. Now she spent most of her time in her upstairs apartment, where she drank copious amounts of vodka and whiskey, judging by her trip to the liquor store.

If Ray had been visiting Tracy, Robert had not seen it. He knew the other guy, Neil, did visit. But not for the night.

Robert waited in the hospital parking lot with a telephoto lens, and when Tracy hugged that nurse, Robert captured a photo that showed the reason for the hug. The pill bottle that went from the nurse's hand into Tracy's jacket pocket.

"Lucy is the name of the other nurse," Robert told Spencer. "We have the leverage we need. I can pick Tracy up in a few days, at the next handoff."

"No. First arrest Lucy. Work backwards from there. Use Lucy as collateral."

And Spence had been right. They'd nabbed Tracy at a time she didn't care what happened to her—but she didn't want to hurt Lucy. Tracy agreed to give them what they wanted—Ray—if they'd let Lucy go. She didn't even make her own freedom a prerequisite.

The timing was perfect. That night, Robert, Spence, and three other agents were waiting for Ray when he entered the Tarcher building. It was a bonus—to Spence, anyway—to catch Neil Cameron at the same time. But all Robert could think of was Aeneas, and he was unable to look Neil in the eyes as he read him his rights.

Now, as he walks into the Trumpet Blossom, Robert finds it hard to believe he'd been able to fulfill that assignment at all. He finds it even harder to believe he's back in Iowa City again. When a young woman comes over to take his order, she reminds him so much of Noa, in her tank top and hemp skirt, that for a moment, he wonders whether he would choose the FBI again if he could start all over.

After dinner, with the sun casting long shadows across the quiet residential streets, Robert finds Tracy's apartment building and parks in front. There are no lights on in her apartment. He goes upstairs and knocks on the door. After a minute of silence, he tries the handle, and the door opens.

Robert takes in the mess, clothing strewn across the floor. An empty plastic storage bin sits on its side, the contents spilled out. On the wall is a *Cowspiracy* movie poster, hanging by a thumbtack. No laptop. No sign of any electronic device. Either the place was searched, or Tracy left in a hurry, or both.

He thinks about what he will say to her. She told him back then she would never forgive him for arresting Neil, but Robert knows she's as angry at herself as she was at him. He closes the door to the apartment and takes a seat.

36.

TRACY BRACES HERSELF BEFORE opening the door. Even before her hand touches the knob, she senses a presence, like a ghost or a stray animal—but it isn't until she sees him that it hits her. Robert, sitting there, waiting for her.

She spins around, flying back down the stairs and out of the building.

She runs toward College Green Park, not looking back to see if Robert is in pursuit. She blinks away the rain and, when her lungs can take her no further, she stops at the entrance to the park and sits on the edge of a bench. She leans over, staring at the sidewalk, trying to catch her breath.

It never ends, this tortured cyclical life. Two years ago, she was arrested by Robert, and now he's back—for what? To send Neil to prison yet again? To make her the witness for the prosecution? The devil himself, back for another helping of her soul, or what little is left of it.

She was supposed to free of this; that was the deal, the fucking deal she agreed to when the only thing she craved out of life was a needle in her arm.

She hears footsteps and from her upside-down point of view sees two running shoes behind the bench. She straightens up and waits for him to come around and face her. Rain drips from the brim of his Nationals baseball cap. She looks around for other agents or police, but it's only Robert.

"Is he still alive?" she asks.

"Who?"

"You know damn well who. Neil."

"I think so."

"Think? You're an FBI agent, and you don't know for sure?"

"I'm not an FBI agent," he says. "Not anymore."

The rain picks up. She feels it in her hair and can hear it echo off the roof of the gazebo in the center of the park.

"Come on," Robert says, walking toward the gazebo. "Let's get out of the rain."

She stands, her legs wobbly, and follows him a hundred yards to the circular shelter. Robert shakes the rain off his cap.

"Neil needs your help," Robert says.

"He needed my help two years ago," she says. "Where the hell were you then?"

"Neil should have gone away for five years. I got it knocked down."

"Then how come Ray got out six months ahead of him?"

Robert looks surprised. "I don't know."

"Of course you don't. If you're not FBI, what are you doing here?"

"It's not the FBI who's looking for Neil."

"What do you mean?"

"There's a company. CounterBalance. They've been hired to find him."

"You're working for them?"

Robert nods.

Tracy thinks back to the last night she saw Neil. The sedan following him in the van. "Have your people been following Neil?"

"It's possible. I just got here. Neil's gone."

"No shit. Good for him."

"I'm not here to arrest him," Robert says. "I want to protect him."

She looks at his face, his eyes on hers, and she wonders if she heard him right.

"He stole something," Robert says, "something that's put him in danger. I don't know what it is or who he stole it from, but I can't sit by this time. You're not the only one who feels guilty about what happened."

"Where is he now?"

"I think he's in New Zealand. Or was."

"How do you know?"

Robert holds up his phone with a photo from Instagram of Neil. She takes it and eyes it closely. His hair longer than she's ever seen it, flowing out from under the baseball cap he wore every once in a while in Iowa City. He's staring at a map—the same map he once showed her? The map of Australia and New Zealand, where he pointed out the beach where his dad used to take him, where he said he would return one day.

"Who took this photo?" Tracy asks, clicking on the account profile: *MidwesternGirlGoneGlobal*—a young, perky woman in a hot-pink bikini jumping in front of turquoise water. What a fucking cliché.

"Her name's Amaranta Bakas," Robert says. "You know her?"

Tracy shakes her head. "They're traveling together?"

"I doubt it. I can't imagine why anyone who's on the run would have posted this picture."

"Unless she doesn't know who he is," Tracy says. "Who he really is."

She hands the phone back to Robert. "Have you seen him since he got out of prison?" Robert asks.

"From a distance."

"You haven't talked to him about what happened?"

"What do you think?"

"I think he'd forgive you."

"Oh sure. I'll tell him it was me who got him sent away for two years, and we'll live happily ever after." She feels a cramp in her side and leans against the railing. Neil is so far away now. Again.

She turns to Robert and studies his face. He isn't smiling, doesn't have that slick sheen of power she remembers. The man standing here, dressed in jeans and a long-sleeve T-shirt, looks smaller somehow, though maybe she's just grown less fearful of people like him. And maybe he's right. If she could somehow save Neil from whatever mess he'd gotten himself into, maybe he would forgive her for the past. They could make a fresh start.

Robert talks at her some more, and in the end, Tracy follows him back to his car. Because it is dry. Because he says her apartment is bugged. Because she suspects he is telling the truth about Neil. She knows something serious and dangerous is going on, and she will only be delaying the inevitable if she continues to run from it. Without Neil as the one constant in her life, the gravitational pull that kept her grounded and relatively sober, she doesn't know where else to go but to the old dealers she frequented.

Robert drives to a Costco parking lot and turns off the engine. She watches the water streak down the windows.

"What about Ray?" Tracy asks. "You're looking for him, too, right?"

Robert pauses. "Why do you think Ray's involved?"

"Because I saw Neil in Ray's van."

Robert sighs and stares ahead as if he's looking for oncoming traffic. She wishes she hadn't mentioned Ray, not that it matters now.

Her window has fogged over, and she opens the car door, letting the cold air back in. New Zealand? If Neil is there, he must be heading to Australia to find his father. She feels her body beginning to tremble, just like those dark days of detox. But this time she is suffering a different type of withdrawal, and the pain is far more acute.

She hears her name. Robert's hand on her shoulder. "Are you using again?"

"I'm drunk. I wish to God I was using, but no. I'm not."

"I'm happy to hear that."

"Why? You ruined my life," she says.

"You were a junkie when I found you. Was that my fault, too?"

"You should have left me on that park bench."

"You would have died."

"Exactly," she says. She watches Robert as he looks away from her, clearly frustrated with her response. She stares out the window.

"He's headed to Australia," she says.

"I know. They think he's sailing across from New Zealand."

"With the girl?"

"I don't know."

"And you want me to tell you what?"

"He's trying to hook up with his old man's ship. That's the theory, at least. But I need to know a precise time and location if I'm going to have any chance at defending him."

"And how exactly are you going to defend him? With everyone else chasing him?"

"I'm going to give my superior the wrong pickup location. Then you and I will go to the right location. And if you want to join Neil on that boat, sail away from me and the rest of my lot, you can be my guest."

Tracy pictures Neil standing along the beach, waves crashing behind him, a smile breaking across his face when he sees her. He told her all about this beach, how the Zodiac would come and they would swim out to it, and how it would take them to the boat, a massive white ship with a pirate's flag flying. He told her he could only ever relax on the water. And how deeply they would sleep out there. Two runaways slightly less lost.

She eyes Robert skeptically. "So what is this?" she asks. "You're like a double agent now?"

"Something like that," he says, staring out the windshield.

She studies his face for a reaction, something to betray the pain that she sees on it. How does one know what's going on behind the face? She guessed wrong with Ray and again with Neil. The only faces she trusts are those near death. They are the only ones who no longer need to lie.

37.

"I CALL IT *THE DITCH*," CAPTAIN MILO SAYS from his perch in the rear of the boat, one hand on the wheel, the other holding a cigarette. Milo is more like a retired skateboarder than an ossified sailor, with dark-red hair curling down to his shoulders, a graying beard, and a trucker cap with the word RAD on it.

Amy and Neil sit on either side of Milo—to better balance the boat, he says—with the one large sail flapping just above their heads. The temperature has dropped ten degrees since they left land an hour ago, and even though the sun is out, Amy has changed into jeans and a sweatshirt.

"Actually, most everybody calls it *the ditch*. Think it's because not every boat that enters the ditch makes it all the way to the other side. Like the *Nina*."

"*Nina*?"

"Large sailing ship. Beautiful. Nine passengers, I think. Sailed into a storm a few years back, never sailed out."

"This boat can handle it, right?" Amy asks, looking around nervously.

"It better," he says, then laughs. "Don't you two worry yourselves. You paid me to get you across, and that I will do. She's made it through plenty of chop. I took her from Auckland to Fiji two years back. The mast got snapped clean off. I drifted for twenty-two days, gnawing on seaweed, drinking my own urine, seeing double. But they found me eventually."

"That's not the answer I was hoping for," Amy says as the South Island sinks into the horizon. She gives Neil a look, and he just shakes his head and says, "Out of the frying pan and into the ditch."

"What's that, mate?"

"Oh, nothing."

"You didn't bring any food along, did you?" Milo asks.

"No, why?" Amy asks. "Is that going to be a problem?"

Milo gazes up at his sail. "Not for me." She and Neil exchange looks again, and when Milo notices he sits up straight. "I didn't pack any meat or fish," he explains. "I'm a vegetarian. I hope you don't mind beans. It might get quite pungent around here."

Neil starts laughing, and Amy joins him.

"What's so funny?" Milo asks.

"I think we'll survive," Amy says.

Milo gives them a tour of *Starry Eyes*, which, because she's only twenty-eight feet long, does little to allay Amy's concerns. Milo points out the jib sail and winches and talks about *heaving to* and *luffs* and how to *avoid the boom* when they change directions. It's all too much for Amy to absorb, but Neil is following along. He takes hold of a hand crank and begins lowering a sail as Milo nods approvingly.

Amy makes note of the cockpit, where the steering wheel is located, and the snug, U-shaped galley at the foot of a short stairway. Clothes blanket what few places there are to sit, and the tiny sink is overfilled with bowls and glasses. Milo has to bend his head to navigate the galley. "A bit grotty. Maid didn't show up as planned."

Below deck, there is barely room for the three of them to stand. Amy returns to the cockpit and looks over the water, hoping to spy a dolphin or some other sea creature. This boat that once seemed like a godsend now feels too small, and she wonders how it's going to survive waves that appear to be growing as she watches them, spouting white-tipped beards. The boat no longer feels as if it is in harmony with the waves but beginning to skirmish with them.

Dinner is a cozy affair. Milo stands by the sink and hands dishes over to Neil and Amy, who are seated around a lunch tray–sized table.

"Now, sleeping arrangements," Milo says. "I figure since you're funding our expedition, you two should have the master suite." He points to the narrow door leading to a single bed in the bow of the boat.

"Where will you sleep?" Amy asks.

"I've got a hammock I string up over here," he says, pointing to hooks that would support a bed stretching across the galley seats, just below the open hatch. "This way I can look up and keep an eye on the mainsail."

He takes out coffee mugs and pours a shot of spiced rum into each. He holds up his mug. "To the other side."

Amy feels giddy as the liquor hits her and tells herself that this is going to be a cruise she will never forget. Just then she feels a wave pick them up—it feels like airline turbulence: up up up, and then down hard. And then there's another, heaving her into Neil, and then another in a different direction.

"You two don't get seasick, do you?"

Neil shakes his head, then turns to her; he's already swimming before her eyes. It's not long until she finds herself in the lavatory on her knees. Neil holds back her hair until the convulsions end. He tries to lift her up, but she moans out that she wants to stay put, and he sits next to her.

She falls asleep and dreams of floating on her back until waves with sharp white teeth descend upon her. When she opens her eyes, she's in bed. She rolls onto her back and sees his face, floating above her, and she reaches out and touches his cheek. He smiles at her and brushes the hair out of her eyes.

"How you doing?" he asks.

"At least Milo won't have to feed me," she says. Her stomach is spent and coiled tight. Above them, waves splash over the paperback-sized porthole. "How on earth are you still standing?" she asks.

"When I was young, my old man took me out on the water a lot. Those were the better times I had with him, actually, the only times he ever relaxed. He couldn't argue with my mom when we were out at sea. Sometimes we'd be gone a few days, sometimes longer. When we washed back up at home, my mom would scream at him, and I couldn't really blame her. I didn't realize back then that some of these multi-day odysseys were supposed to be two-hour outings. But I didn't care. I loved it out on the water. I still do."

"Just promise me I'll get used to this," she says, hearing herself breathing heavily, calculating just how quickly she can make it back to the toilet.

"You will. It might take a few days."

"Days?"

"Don't think about it. That's the first step."

"Okay, okay. Talk to me. Your dad. Tell me what happened."

"Nothing much happened. He just stopped coming home. Stopped calling, sending letters. I could only follow him via newspaper articles. And then he showed up for my twelfth birthday, out of the blue. He was leaving for Antarctica and invited me along—I never heard two people argue like my parents that day. She threw dinner plates at him. The cops were called. He went back to his ship, my mom took a bottle of gin to her room, and I snuck out, leaving her a note. There was no way I was missing out on that trip."

Amy feels a wave rising beneath them, and she pulls herself back to the lavatory, wishing Neil did not have to listen to the raw and rasping noises her body was making. Afterward, she collapses on the floor, Neil watching her from above. "Can I just sleep here tonight?" she moans.

Neil brings her a blanket and joins her on the floor, and she feels his arm on her back. She closes her eyes, and when she opens them again, the room is dark. She can hear Neil breathing next to her.

She takes stock of her body. Her stomach is still on edge, though the boat isn't tossing her back and forth with such velocity; perhaps the ocean feels sorry for her.

She closes her eyes and doesn't open them again until morning. The arm on her back is gone. She sits up, using the toilet as a backrest. She can hear voices outside, and Milo laughing.

Neil hops down the steps and smiles when he sees her. "Morning, sleepyhead."

"Are we there yet?" she asks.

"Almost," Neil says.

She perks up. "Really?"

Neil shakes his head. "Sorry. Just kidding."

"Don't torture me."

"Oh, you're going to survive. We're catching a good tailwind. We could be there in ten days."

"Ten days?" Amy feels her stomach roll. "I'm not going to make it."

"Sure you are. Look how far you've come already, Eat Pray Love."

She bites her lip against the nausea. "You really think I'll make it?"

"I think we both will."

38.

Robert is at a window seat in a coffee shop overlooking the city plaza, a basketball court–sized gathering place where a pair of Guthrie-inspired vagabonds are playing guitar and banjo for tips. Steep hills of fir trees form a lush backdrop for this small Oregon town. Robert watches the tourists as they ascend a long flight of stairs up to one of the town's famous theater buildings, a matinee about to begin.

He and Tracy had checked into a hotel two floors above the coffee shop a half hour ago, but Tracy has not returned from their suite. He doesn't trust her enough to be in her own room but agreed to give her a few minutes of privacy when she insisted on changing her clothes.

He checks his watch. They were supposed to be on a flight to Melbourne by now, and he is dreading the inevitable call from Spence. Robert has nothing new to report, and he knows Spence will tell him that he's being played by a drug addict. Which is probably true. Tracy doesn't trust him—and he doesn't blame her—so when she suggested this detour, saying she could get information on Neil from someone she knows here, he was willing to oblige.

Tracy enters the coffee shop wearing the same clothes she'd worn on the plane. "I thought you were changing," Robert says.

"No."

"So what were you doing upstairs?" he asks.

"I wasn't upstairs." She hands him a ticket. "It's for the matinee of *Hamlet*. I figured you could use some entertainment."

"You trying to ditch me?"

"If I wanted to ditch you, I would have been gone by now. I need to do this alone, and I don't want you hovering over my shoulder. Okay?"

"I never understood those plays," Robert says. "Shakespeare is in another language."

"You'll understand this one," she says. "It's about a lost soul."

"Just tell me who it is you're going to see."

She shakes her head. "For once in my life, I'm going to protect a source."

Tracy walks with him to the entrance of the theater as gray-haired couples shuffle in and packs of high school students mill around in the courtyard outside.

Robert hands his ticket to the usher and looks back at Tracy, who's still standing outside the door. "You want to follow me to my seat?"

"I trust you," she says. "Enjoy the show."

Robert continues into the lobby. He turns left and stands by one of the large picture windows, watching Tracy walk across the brick courtyard. When she disappears behind a building, he exits the theater and follows her path.

He makes it to the corner to see Tracy turn right onto Main Street. Robert stays two blocks back, safely behind the window-shopping tourists. Tracy enters an outdoor store, and Robert hangs back and waits. Ten minutes later she emerges carrying nothing more than she entered with. She studies the faces of everyone who passes her. Robert stands off the sidewalk in a doorway to an office building.

Continuing down the main boulevard, Tracy enters another store and, again, emerges with nothing to show for it. Robert admires her vigilance, the way she stops every so often and uses the store windows to see if anyone is following her. For the next thirty minutes, Robert watches her repeat this ritual a half-dozen times.

Tracy reaches the end of the shopping district and turns back. Robert retreats into a dive bar and holds his breath as she passes. When he emerges she is a block ahead, turning right onto Pioneer Street.

He follows her downhill until they are in a residential area. Though he'd never visited Ashland before, he feels he knows the place. Vintage craftsman and Victorian homes share tree-lined streets with views of the hills on either side. Noa used to talk about the small towns of Southern Oregon, how cut off they felt from the rest of the world.

Robert passes a Historic Railroad District sign and follows Tracy to the right on B Street. She is a block ahead and has stopped on the sidewalk. Robert steps sideways behind a tree. He leans over to see her approaching the front porch of a small craftsman.

He makes his way cautiously forward. When he is two houses away, he crouches down and hustles to a line of bushes separating two driveways. He hears Tracy talking but can't make out the words. He hears another voice, a woman's voice, so familiar he freezes, head cocked, trying to absorb as much as he can over the sounds of passing cars.

Cautiously, he raises his head to see her, a face he hadn't set eyes upon in years, the face he's been looking for all this time. He can only risk a quick glance before he has to duck his head again to avoid being seen.

His mind spins as he tries to reconcile the three Noas in his mind—the one he'd met five years ago, the one in the photo in Syd's office, the woman he just glimpsed on the front porch. She looks like a shadow of the two Noas, her hair not dreadlocked nor cropped but shoulder-length, its color a rich, shiny brown. Her face etched with a few new lines, from the sun or the effects of her animal-rights work or both. He draws in a breath and forces himself back to the present, to the conversation taking place.

Noa's voice is loud and sharp. He hears Tracy say, *Sorry.* Robert strains to hear anything more. Neil's name. *Australia. Help him. Ship.*

Then silence. He resists raising his head.

Then a child's voice. *Mommy.* Robert raises his head again. A little boy gazes up at Tracy, his face eager, engaged, as if he is listening to every word. Words that probably mean nothing to the boy but that Robert would've given anything to hear.

Syd never mentioned Noa was pregnant. Unless she didn't know. Unless the pregnancy was the very reason why Noa lashed out and disappeared suddenly. She never wanted children—this Robert knows. Was the identity of the father something that had changed her mind? And did this make it more or less likely that the child is his?

He hears Tracy ask the boy's name. *Cameron.*

Immediately he wishes he hadn't heard it—this, of all things, when he can hear nothing else. That name can only mean one thing. Neil Cameron.

His body tenses with anger. At Noa. At himself. At the whole damn incestuous activist community. He spent enough time undercover to know how people slept around—the result of shared passions and practicality. In a world where you can trust no one, one is far wiser to stick with those who have already proven themselves trustworthy. But he thought Noa was different—or that, for her, he was. He'd believed she would wait for him.

A phone rings—his own. Frantically he tries to mute it as he drops to the ground. He crawls into the backyard, over the fence, and into the alley, cursing himself. He runs to the theater, where, standing in the courtyard, sweat dripping, he returns Spence's call.

"What did I tell you about checking in?" Robert can tell by Spence's voice that he's upset.

"I was en route to Oregon. I was going to call this evening."

"Why are you winded?"

"Long story."

"The girl with you?"

"She's the reason we're here. Says she has a source."

"Who?"

"I'm still working on that. What's the latest on Neil?"

"He's somewhere on the Tasman Sea. We're taking bets on whether or not he actually makes it across. The smart money says he won't."

"Unless his old man rescues him."

"I thought about that. But Aeneas's ship is a few days away. I think he'll be docking in Melbourne, so I've sent a team there."

"What about Ray?" Robert asks.

"What about him?"

"It seems odd to me that Neil would have done this computer break-in all on his own."

"Ray can barely work an ATM machine. He's nothing to worry about."

"Have you at least questioned him?"

"What do you think? You just get me a time and a location, okay? Don't go creating any more suspects."

The line goes dead, and Robert stares at the phone. He touched a nerve when he mentioned Ray, though he's not sure what that means. But there is one thing he is becoming increasingly confident of: Spence has no intention of taking Neil alive.

Robert fishes the ticket stub out of his pocket and makes his way back into the theater.

39.

Tracy hasn't been back to Ashland since she stepped onstage to accept her diploma, the crowd gone mute for her, the silent intermission between more popular graduates. She could have invited her brother but didn't want to force him to make an excuse. When she stepped off the stage she vowed to leave town and never look back. She succeeded in leaving—the looking back, not so much.

Ashland attracts the lost, and it's just remote enough to fool you into thinking that you really are lost. The town has more Reiki healers per capita than any place Tracy has ever known, and a significant number of people still wear tie-dyed clothing and drive rainbow-colored VW buses. Visitors come to see the theater, to mountain bike, and to watch the deer that stroll through town.

After dropping Robert off at the theater and making sure she wasn't followed, Tracy finds her way to Noa's cottage. She knocks on the door and waits. She hears feet on wooden floors.

Noa opens the door, then tries to close it, but Tracy is ready with her foot.

The last time she saw Noa was more than five years ago. Tracy was working as an emergency room nurse in St. Louis, and Noa appeared at her apartment one August evening asking to crash on her couch. The next day Tracy tagged along to protest a fancy restaurant in Ladue that was serving foie gras. She held a sign and made small talk with the others, but she didn't feel like one of them. By the end of the day, she felt even more alone, more helpless. The restaurant did not stop serving foie gras, and customers did not stop going in, and when Noa asked her to tag along for another protest, Tracy used work as an excuse. That was the last time Noa invited her.

They stayed virtually in touch; Noa included Tracy on the occasional e-mail missives, about an anti-whaling victory in Antarctica or a successful arrest of a poacher in the Galápagos or another call for donations. Until Tracy met Ray and Neil, she had been content to live vicariously through Noa.

Tracy feels the pressure of Noa's door against her foot but doesn't move. "Please, Noa."

"You should leave."

"I can't. It's about Neil."

"What about him?"

"I'm trying to help him."

"Help him? Oh, that's rich."

"I was an addict then. I wouldn't hurt him twice. You have to believe that."

"I don't have to believe anything."

"He's headed to Australia. I think he's going to meet up with his father. But I need to know when."

"Why would I know that?"

"You used to work for Aeneas. How did he get messages to you?"

Noa shakes her head. "Why in the fucking world would I tell you, a witness for the prosecution?" A child appears below her arm, a little boy with bright green eyes and a shock of dark hair.

"Hello there," Tracy says, kneeling down to get a better look at him. "You look familiar, little man." She glances up to see Noa watching her uneasily. "What's his name?"

"Cameron."

Tracy hears a phone ring outside the window and turns to see motion in the bushes. When she turns back, Noa has pulled the child back inside.

"His father is in danger, Noa. He stole files from some company that has sent all kinds of people after him."

"What company?"

"I don't know. Whatever he stole, it's big."

"How do you know this?"

"There's this guy. He's ex-FBI."

"What's his name?"

"Robert. Porter. Why?"

Noa looks past Tracy as if she's seen a ghost. Tracy follows her eyes to nowhere. "What is it?"

"I'm not sure you should trust him."

"I don't. I'm not going to give him the information he wants. I'm going to send him and all his thugs far away from Neil. But I can't do that if I don't know where he's going."

"How can I tell you anything?"

"I know I was a lousy activist when you knew me. I was insecure and stupid. But now I know better. Give me a chance to do something right for once. Something good."

When she returns to the theater, she waits in the courtyard. She thinks back to the phone she heard, the rustle behind the bushes, and wonders whether it was Robert. Then she sees him emerge from the lobby with the hordes, blinking against the sunlight.

"So what did you think?" she asks, trying to elicit some proof that he actually sat through the entire performance.

"It was long," he says. "At one point I began to wish *I* had shuffled off that mortal coil."

She feels a wave of relief. "That's my favorite part, you know. *To be or not to be.*"

"Why am I not surprised? So what did your source say?"

"That we'd better get down to Melbourne."

40.

When Amy wakes, the first thing she notices is the distant rumbling of her stomach. The next thing she notices is that she can actually hear her stomach over the waves. Meaning there aren't any.

She pulls herself to the edge of the bed and sits up. She hears snoring. She enters the galley and passes Milo, oozing out of his hammock, mouth hanging open. She climbs the steps to the deck and squints as her eyes adjust to the sun. Neil is manning the wheel, his shirt off, a blue bandanna around his neck, as if this were his boat. "Morning," he says.

She takes in the flat azure horizon, stretching out like an infinity swimming pool in every direction. "It's so. Still."

"I know. It sucks."

"No. It's amazing. A godsend."

"It's going to add a day to our trip, at least."

"I don't care if it adds a week. I can actually walk again. How long have I been down there?"

"A week," he says.

"A week?"

He laughs. "No, no. Just a day and a half."

"I had no idea these boats were so unstable."

"Not exactly the *Queen Mary*. I hope you don't resent me for dragging you onboard."

"My stomach might resent you, but you didn't drag me here."

"I'm going to pay you back, you know. That was a lot of money."

Amy hasn't told Neil about the ring, but by the way he is staring at her left hand, he's already deduced the source of their last-minute windfall.

"I wanted to help."

"That's far beyond help."

"Okay. Then maybe I might just like you."

He smiles. She feels a breeze and looks up to see the sail expanding. Neil glances behind him, reminding Amy that they are still on the run, even out here, in slow motion.

"Do you think they'd come after us out here?" she asks.

"I don't know."

She sits next to him and leans her body into his, his skin warm. "We wouldn't have much luck outrunning them."

"Who you running from?" Milo asks, standing halfway up the stairs with a half-eaten banana in one hand.

Neil says nothing, and Amy follows his lead. Milo laughs. "For fuck's sake, peoples, you're not going to tell your ol' cap'n?"

"It's better you not know," Neil says.

"In case you've forgotten, mate, I'm breaking international law ferrying you two fugitives across these waters. And I'm already on a first-name basis with many of the mainland constabulary. So, in the interest of sharing, you should at least clue me in to what law you've broken."

"I stole something," Neil says.

"Diamonds? Platinum?" Milo's eyes are wide with anticipation.

"Files," Neil says.

"Files? Like dirty pictures?"

"Like corporate files."

"Oh." Milo's voice deflates. "This company know you stole them?"

"They do."

"They going to be waiting for you on the other side?"

"Probably."

Milo looks out over the water and runs a hand through his curls. "They'll be watching Port Phillip in Melbourne. That's where all the boats come in. What if I took you to Tassie instead?"

"Tassie?" Amy asks.

"Tasmania," Neil says. "How would we get to Melbourne from there?"

"There's a ferry. But this way they won't be looking for you on a sailboat coming in from New Zealand."

Neil looks at Amy. "What do you think?"

"You don't mind taking us there instead?" she asks Milo.

"Nah," he says, then hops up onto the top deck and begins walking to the front of the boat. "Given the winds, or lack thereof, we're headed there anyway."

Milo makes his way to the bow, whistling to himself, and Neil puts an arm around her, and she thinks about how so much of life is determined by forces above and below, wind direction and current and that feeling inside her, something so strong she now entertains the idea of a life on the run with Neil. A life of misdirections and close calls, the sound of his breathing, as deep as the ocean and just as mysterious. Could this have been the adventure she was seeking all along? For the first time, she feels needed, invaluable, with this precious cargo seated next to her and a destination unknown.

MILO AND NEIL ALTERNATE DECK DUTY every eight hours. While Neil is on deck, Amy joins him so Milo can snore away below. Sometimes she takes over the steering, reveling in the feel of the ocean, the way it tugs at her, letting her know who's in control. One windy afternoon when Neil is at the wheel the ship bucks under them.

"You've got your sea legs," Neil says.

She hadn't realized until then that she was still comfortably on her feet. "If only I could have pre-ordered them."

Neil smiles. "You know what my old man used to say about the sea?"

"What?"

"He said that if the planet is mostly water and we're mostly water, then this is where we belong. That it's been all downhill since we first dragged ourselves onto land." He pauses. "That certainly was true with him."

"Does he know you're coming?"

Neil nods. "I sent him a message from Auckland."

"That must've been tricky without a phone."

"There's a website we use, to send messages back and forth. I use Internet cafés and pay in cash."

"Is it a secret? This website?"

"Hardly. It's YouTube."

She laughs. "You send videos to each other?"

"No, no. We exchange comments on this very specific, out-of-the-way video. There are a billion videos up there, so it's relatively easy to get lost in all that noise. Like whispering in a crowded subway car. We use anonymous accounts, but there are visual clues as to who is commenting. His avatar is a whale."

"What's yours?"

"You don't want to know."

"Yes, I do. No. Let me guess."

"You'll never get it." He smiles. "It's the Pacific pocket mouse."

"A mouse?"

"The Pacific pocket mouse is a tiny creature that lives in sand dunes along the beaches of Southern California. Back when I began volunteering with environmental groups, I worked for a few months with this coastal preservation outfit in San Diego. We would cordon off sand dunes, do periodic counts and measurements."

"Did you ever hold one?"

"Oh, yes. The look they give you when you grab onto that flab behind their neck. Like cats, their bodies go limp, but their eyes take you in. Completely. I always wanted to know what they were thinking. Here this giant plucks you up and stares at you—but doesn't kill you like all those other predators you're so accustomed to hiding from. I used to wonder if they know they're on the verge of extinction. And that we were trying to help. I suspect they thought we were just more humans intruding onto their land."

"Did you save them?"

"We saved some beaches. This Marine base, Camp Pendleton, blocked off a few of their beaches, which was a huge step forward. When I think of the world's most lethal men and women making way for a mouse, it's inspiring. Granted, we had to threaten a lawsuit, but the end result was positive." Neil looks up at the clouds. "The thing about this mouse. Twenty years ago, everyone thought it was extinct. They had completely written it off, declared it extinct like an emergency room doctor calling time of death. But people weren't looking in the right places, and it turned out they were still around. Still alive." His eyes return to the water before them. "That's what I'm trying to do, in a way—to be considered extinct without actually being extinct. If I can accomplish that, I might just make it."

"And how will we do that?"

"We?"

"Yes, we." She looks at him impatiently, and his eyes relent.

"We have to convince people to look for me in all the wrong places."

She leans in and kisses him, tastes the salt of his lips. He wraps his arms around her, and she squeezes his biceps, relishing the feel of his skin and the muscles underneath. She craves him right now, right here, and she wonders if she can stay silent enough not to wake—

Milo coughs. She looks over to see Milo standing halfway up the stairs.

"Sorry to interrupt, peoples. I thought you'd appreciate this." Milo holds up a small box of hair color. "It came to me in a dream," he says.

"The dye?"

"No." Milo rolls his eyes. "My ex-girlfriend left it behind, under the sink. She didn't believe in gray hair, even if I was the only one who would ever see it. And I forgot it was there until I had this dream a minute ago that I was chucking it to you. And here I am, doing just that." Neil catches the box and Amy can see from the photo on the side that the color is a dark, rich brown.

"This might come in handy," says Neil. "Thank you."

"Yeah. I do my best thinking in that hammock."

Amy leans over and studies the label. "She was planning to color her hair on this boat?"

"That was the least of it. She wanted to bring her bloody treadmill along until I told her it wouldn't fit. She was what you might call high maintenance. She also liked to wear high heels on deck. Of course, I probably got her expectations up too high. You tell someone you have a yacht, and they think you're Bill bloody Gates."

"You told her this boat was a yacht?" Amy asks.

"You should have seen the boat I owned before this one."

That evening, Amy bids farewell to Neil's golden hair as she applies the chemicals, a thick mixture that bites her nose with its sharp and pungent smell as she covers every strand of his hair.

She ties a plastic bag around his hair to speed up the coloring process. "Do you believe in fate?" she asks him.

"No."

"Why not?"

"Because I spent nearly two years in prison, and I refuse to believe that was fate."

"What was it then?"

"Bad luck. Plain and simple."

"What happened?"

"I played lookout one night while my partner broke into a slaughterhouse. And we got caught. If it were a fast-food restaurant I might have done six months at most. But because this fell under the animal terrorism statute, the feds threw everything at us."

"So if you don't believe in fate, what do you believe in?"

"I believe in heroic acts."

"Heroes?"

"Not so much heroes because that presumes there are people who are separate from the rest of us. Anyone can act heroically once or twice in a lifetime. And that's all it takes to change the world. Not a few heroes—but a few million people acting heroically. That's how the world changes."

Amy checks her watch, then positions Neil's head over the sink in the lavatory to rinse out his hair. He closes his eyes, and she runs her hands through his wet hair, gazing down on him from above. Was it only a few days ago she was resigned to returning to St. Louis after her depressing, adventureless trip? And now she's on the high seas, sea legs and all, not knowing where she's headed and embracing every moment of the unknowing. Could letting go be this easy after all? Or was it simply a matter of finding the right person?

She squeezes the water from Neil's hair and wraps his head in a towel before helping him straighten up. "Have a look."

He stands and examines himself in the tiny mirror next to the sink. "I hardly recognize myself."

"Good," she says. "Let's hope nobody else does."

Mainsail and midships. By her fifth day, Amy no longer hears gibberish as Milo and Neil call out to one another. She now looks to her right when Neil spots a whale off starboard. And when the winds hit four on the Beaufort Scale and waves spill over the bow of the ship and into the galley, Amy stays next to Neil in the cockpit, breathing in saltwater and feeling a confidence she never knew existed within her. She still doesn't think she'll ever become "one" with the waves, but at least she feels as if she can get along with them.

As the clouds give way to sunlight, a rainbow appears off the port side, and a pod of three dolphins begins to play in their wake, Amy knows there is no way she can return to the confines of an office. Or the confines of St. Louis. In those sharp-nosed creatures she watches, she feels a freedom she hadn't known existed, not in a lawless way but in an unselfconscious way. For so much of this trip she'd been obsessed over documenting every moment for a faceless audience, as if the virtual likes would somehow make those moments special. But what she now knows is that the only moments that truly matter in life are these—the ones not captured by cameras, not shared with anyone else.

Bob Marley is playing when Amy sits next to Milo in the galley as he studies a nautical map and Neil heats up another can of beans.

"Here we are," Milo says, pointing at the axis of two lines. "About two hundred nautical miles left. As the crow flies, Tassie's not far. But crows do better with their wings than we do with sails. We'll have to tack our way there."

"Tack?"

"Oh, the wind. We're heading into it. So we can't go straight into it, you know? The sails get all luffed out. We go at angles. To starboard one day, then tack back to the port the next." Amy follows Milo's finger as it zig-zags on the map. "Sometimes tacking is the only way to get where you want to go."

"We've been doing a bit of tacking ourselves," Neil says.

"You from New Zealand?" Amy asks Milo.

He nods. "North of Auckland. I was headed down here to do a bit of skiing up on Franz Josef. I only just pulled into port when you two showed up and made me an offer I could not easily refuse."

Suddenly the boat lurches, and Milo falls to the floor. Amy's on her way down until she catches herself with her left hand on the tabletop. As she pulls herself back into the booth she sees Neil standing as upright as if nothing ever happened. "Weather's turning," he says.

"What does that mean?"

"It means I won't be sleeping tonight."

Milo sits cross-legged on the floor, picking black beans off the floor and popping them into his mouth like popcorn.

In the coming days, she and Neil share the bunk below deck whenever they are not above. Amy senses his tension as they make their way toward Tasmania, and she, too, feels tense, only for her, it's about the limits of their time together. About how soon all this will end. About what awaits her once she and Neil part ways.

She wishes she could prolong these moments, as they make love in the cramped cabin, waves against the porthole, the ship heaving them into each other, the boat doing all the physical work and leaving them nothing but the sensations of pleasure, as if everything about their bodies coming together is innate, inevitable. As they lie together afterward, squeezed close in the tiny bunk, she traces the tattoo on his bicep: She runs her fingers across each letter.

"You have to admit, you kind of enjoy this," he says, watching her.

"Of course I enjoy *this*," she says. "But keep in mind that since I met you, I've been ditched, drenched, nearly run off the road, and sick to my stomach."

"You said you wanted an adventure, Eat Pray Love."

"I was thinking more along the lines of ziplining."

"What's the adventure in that? With me, there is no safety line."

"That's not fun; that's suicidal."

He turns serious. "The truth is, without you, I wouldn't have made it this far."

"Your face wouldn't have been on the Internet either."

"That's not your fault. You didn't know."

They drift off to sleep, and at some point during the night, Amy feels the bed pushing her upright until she is almost standing, then dropping her again, hard. In the galley she hears pots and plates falling to the floor. She reaches for Neil, but he's not there. The walls are groaning, and she hears voices shouting from above.

She reaches into her backpack for her pocket flashlight. As she swings her feet over the bunk and onto the floor, she steps into a puddle. When she shines the light down, she sees that the puddle runs the length of the room and that more water is cascading down the stairs.

As she enters the galley, it flashes white, and before she registers that it's lightning, the sound of thunder sends her to the floor, as if it were so close she had to duck. Her heart stops until she hears Neil's voice again, calling over to Milo, then Milo's voice in reply.

She pokes her head above deck to see Milo wrestling with the wheel. "Where's Neil?"

Milo looks at her, his eyes huge, and, instinctively, she ducks. A loud crash of sail and boom swings over her head.

"Stay down!" Milo shouts.

"Where's Neil?"

"Dropping the sails."

Amy retreats inside and holds onto the main beam. She looks through the upper windows to see feet walking past, then hopping to another part of the boat. Waves beat against the portholes.

Twenty minutes later finally Neil joins her, his T-shirt and shorts soaked through.

"Is everything okay?"

"Yeah. It's fine. We'll ride this out."

"Don't go back up there." She makes sure he sees her eyes. "I'm serious."

"Okay."

Milo enters and closes the door. "Positively pissing!" To Amy's dismay, he looks thrilled, and he pulls the cap off a bottle of gin and takes a swig. He's breathing heavily. "I have to give up on those bloody smokes," he says.

"Are we okay?" Amy asks.

"If the mast doesn't snap off, we'll be right."

Amy listens to the creaking above—the deck, the mast—and she wonders how long it will stay strong.

41.

Tracy is asleep, her forehead resting against the airplane's window. They are seated on the right side of the plane, with Robert on the aisle, Tracy at the window, and fourteen long hours to Melbourne.

Grateful for the silence, Robert thinks about Bells Beach, the beach where Tracy said Neil will connect with his father's ship. Tracy told him she would find out a date and time when they got to

Melbourne, though she wouldn't say how she intended to acquire this information. Robert isn't confident he can believe anything she tells him, but he trusts her more than he trusts Spence. He knows she is desperate to see Neil—and if she sends Robert to the wrong location, she, too, will end up in the wrong location.

By the time they touch down, Spence will want that location. Robert stares at the map on the screen attached to the seat in front of his and taps at a button, zooming in. First toward Melbourne, then closer in and to the east, following the southern coastline until he lands on a white dot named Lorne.

Spence will be keeping an eye on Aeneas's ship. This means Robert will need to provide a location that's close enough to the real location while still being far enough away to give Neil an opportunity to board the ship safely.

Spence will also be keeping an eye on Robert—of this he is certain. Which means Robert has to give Spence information that's as close to the truth as possible while still being a lie. And what will Robert do when he finds Neil? Tell him about the child and see how he reacts? Or just stand back and do something good in his life by doing nothing?

He can't think any further right now. His mind keeps getting pulled in reverse. To the day he met Noa. The last time they made love. The age of Noa's child. Four years? Maybe older, maybe younger. Parents know ages because they keep time in days before weeks, months before years, noting every growing limb, lost tooth, new word.

He is tempted to nudge Tracy awake and ask her about Noa, even though doing so would destroy what little trust they've developed so far. And what good would it do? He already knows the boy's name. Cameron. That should be answer enough. Enough to tell him that at some point Noa slept with Neil, and her child is the reminder that Robert will never again be close to her.

He takes a deep breath and forces his eyes closed. The gravity of what he is about to do is becoming more apparent. By saving Neil, he may be saving the father of a child. And that will count for something.

Does he even love Noa anymore? When he saw Noa, he felt his pulse quicken. Was that love, or simply the adrenaline rush of feeling a destination both within and without reach?

If Syd knew what Robert was thinking, she'd roll her eyes, say something cynical about love. And she would be right. Maybe it's time to face reality. He tries to picture what Syd is doing right now. Probably smoking a few rhinos alone in the courtyard, looking up at the stars.

42.

Tracy opens her eyes to find her head resting on Robert's shoulder. She sits up, wipes the drool from her chin. "You could have pushed me back," she says.

"I thought you could use the rest," Robert says.

Tracy looks at her TV screen. Time to destination: *13 hours and 29 minutes.*

"You were dreaming," Robert says.

"How do you know?"

"You were mumbling. Sounded like you said *Daisy.*"

"I did?"

"Code word for something?"

"It's nothing. Name of a cat."

"Please don't tell me you left a cat in your apartment."

"No, no. It's just something this guy said to me before he died." She sees him eyeing her curiously. "When I worked in hospice," she explains. "After you locked up Neil."

"Oh."

"Neil was serving out his sentence. I was serving mine. Watching people die. Two hundred and forty one, to be exact."

"Why'd you keep count?"

"I don't know. They deserved that much." She looks up to see the flight attendant standing at their row. "I'll have a double whiskey."

"How about one to start?" the attendant says, placing a miniature bottle on her tray table.

Robert orders a whiskey, too, with Coke. "You can have mine," he says when the flight attendant turns away.

Tracy collects both bottles and gazes at them hungrily, then looks up at Robert suspiciously. "I'm still not telling you the name of my source."

"I didn't expect you to."

She empties a bottle into a cup of ice and skips the Coke Robert offers. She downs it in one long, satisfying pour, the liquor burning her throat. She pours the second bottle and feels her body unwinding. "I never found much value in last words," she says. "What makes the last word we say any more significant than a word we said the week before?"

"Significant for those around to hear it."

"Yeah, I guess. When their families are gathered around, they don't always talk. I hear the truth during those other moments, like when I'm changing out a catheter or saline. They tell me everything then. About office affairs and broken marriages. Some confess crimes, seeking absolution, like I have anything to offer. One woman talked about the homeless person she ran over on the way home from a party. She didn't stop, and she never got caught. And now, with a few days left to live, she's wishing she had. And there was this man who stole from his wife's bank account, then divorced her and had a doctor friend declare her unfit to raise their children. She hung herself."

"Your drug addiction is starting make more and more sense," Robert says.

She looks over at him, his eyes steady and sad. "The thing about being around death all the time is that you get comfortable with it—even the idea of your own. I've started to think of life as a river. You're born, and you set off down that river, all alone. Now, death—death is a waterfall. Most people, when they see what's coming, they fight the current, even though that damn current is moving way too fast. But some people, a few, they enjoy the ride. That's going to be me."

The meals arrive, and Tracy looks down at an unimaginative collection of rice, boiled vegetables, and bread.

Robert leans in. "I assumed you wanted a vegan meal, so I requested one while you were asleep."

"Thanks." She notices that Robert's having the same. "You, too? Man, you're really trying to get on my good side."

He looks at her. She senses a vulnerability to him that wasn't there before. His shoulders aren't so pulled back and stiff, and there's sadness in his eyes. He takes a bite of wilted asparagus, and she watches him gnaw on it.

"You know what I think about sometimes?" she says. "How right now there are thousands of babies being born, babies who will grow up in a world where eating plants isn't such a fringe way of life. And these kids will grow up thinking it's perfectly normal."

"Isn't that the point?"

"Yeah, sure. But who's going to remember the sacrifices people made to get us here? When protesting outside some animal testing lab got people jailed for years?"

"We'll remember."

She smiles at him and considers his face and how it's changed since she first knew him. That face was empty of emotion years ago, those eyes so invasive. Now, his eyes are evasive, like hers, his face more weathered, and there's a scar above his forehead that she wants to ask him about. "We are an odd couple, you and me."

"We're not a couple."

She tilts her head against his shoulder, the alcohol in her head making it heavy. "Sure we are. We're both searching for Neil. Both trying to make up for past mistakes. And we both like whiskey." She holds up her empty bottle. "Speaking of, can you flag her down again?"

Robert does, and Tracy raises the bottle to her lips, not bothering with the ice.

"Why Bells Beach?" he asks.

"Neil used to surf there with his old man."

"Is there a pier?"

"Nope. Just a small beach with a high bluff running along one side. People sit up there and watch the surfers."

"So is he going to surf out to the ship? Is that the plan?"

"Beats me."

She glances over at his face, a wrinkled forehead above graying eyebrows. He is less intense than when she first met him; he is even lost for words at times. She almost feels guilty for keeping the truth from him, though she has the nagging feeling that he's withholding far more from her.

"Where is Lorne in relation to Bells Beach?" he asks.

"Lorne? Why?" She tries to appear disinterested.

"I thought we might spend the night there. Isn't it close?"

"It's about forty minutes south. But there's nowhere decent to stay. We're better off in Melbourne."

Robert nods, seemingly satisfied with her answer, but the mention of Lorne unnerves Tracy. Could it be coincidence, or does Robert know something she doesn't? She feels her body growing warm and she forces the thoughts out of her head. There's no turning back now anyway.

"What's in this for you?" she asks.

"What do you mean?"

"I mean, let's say you save him from getting caught by these people. Then what? Won't you be out of a job?"

"I suppose I will."

He leans back and closes his eyes. She studies his face, feeling a wave of self-doubt. What if Robert is actually on her side, like he said all along? He could help Neil, maybe far better than she can. She wonders what Neil would say right about now. About all this. About Robert, who helped put him in prison.

No. Even if Robert is a changed man, Tracy can't trust him. She has trusted him one time too many already. Which is why she told Robert about Bells Beach instead of the real location.

43.

By the second full day of the weltering waves, Amy has grown numb to the cold, to standing in ankle-deep water, to periodically having her body thrown against the wall or down the stairs.

The night before, while Milo and Neil traded shifts at the wheel, Amy used a plastic bucket to bail water from below, to keep the water from rising any further. Her fingers turned a shade of blue and she had to stop periodically and clap her hands together to get any feeling back. But at least the water was still no higher than her ankles. This is what she repeated to herself every fifteen minutes, even as she wondered how much longer they could survive like this, before the water finally overtook them for good.

Now, as dawn lightens a still-stormy sky, she sinks into a seat in the galley, exhausted. A few minutes later, Neil joins her from the cockpit. He's wearing the same clothes he's worn for days.

She sees that he's shivering, and she heats water to make coffee. He turns to look out the porthole, and she follows his gaze. The sky has brightened, hinting at calmer waters.

"When I was a kid," Neil says, "I had a goldfish who died—and when I saw him floating, I wondered about all the other fishes. When people die, on land, we bury them. But in the sea they float to the top, right? I was terribly concerned about all those dead fishes, floating around, and when I told my dad, I thought he'd make fun of me."

Neil turns back toward her and offers a small smile. "But instead, he looked at me and told me that the oceans hide their dead. That the oceans bury them in their own way, in a cemetery so deep that no man can ever find them."

"Why?"

"Because anything near the surface man will take. Fishermen are like gravediggers. Even whale watchers—they only see whales when they surface. That's like seeing an eagle without ever seeing it fly." He sighs. "The oceans and everything in them were the first. And they'll be the last. And we—the land people—we're just a wave on the surface."

AMY BLINKS INTO THE RAY OF SUN shining through the porthole. Neil is asleep next to her, their clothing still damp. But the seas are calm now. She hears Milo shouting something outside. She climbs up and pokes her head above deck.

"There she is," he says, pointing. "Tassie."

From this distance, Tasmania looks like the South Island, a dry lump breaking the endless, perfectly round horizon on the water. Amy approaches the bow and leans against the railing, letting the wind dry her clothing.

She looks back and sees Neil standing next to Milo. They're speaking quietly, and she wonders what they're planning. Plans are the one thing that she and Neil have avoided discussing—but that hasn't stopped her from thinking ahead. She makes her way to the rear of the boat and sits next to him.

"Good news," Neil says. "Milo gave me a name of someone in Tasmania with a boat. He can take us north to the mainland."

She doesn't move, doesn't speak. She's made a decision, not one she wanted to make but one that she knows will be best for him. "I think we should split up."

He looks at her. "What?"

"You take that boat, and I'll take the ferry, and if anyone is watching for arrivals from the ferry, which they surely are by now, they'll follow me."

"And then what? Where will we meet?"

"We won't."

She feels cruel, watching his eyes, those natural springs of blue, go dark. "But we're almost there."

"Exactly, which is why we need to do this." She grabs his hands. "If I take the ferry, they'll follow me and be looking in all the wrong places. Just like your mouse."

She can see in his strained eyes that she's right. He stands and turns away, and she watches him look ahead to their inevitable island. "You were my lucky charm."

She goes to him and puts her arms around his waist and her chin on his shoulder, breathing in the smell of warm skin and hair dye. "I still am." She turns him around. "You're my lucky charm, too."

"Here." He reaches up to remove the chain around his neck. "I want you to have this." He places it over her neck, and she holds the silver ingot.

"I'll hold on to it until I see you again. I *will* see you again."

"Yes," he says, in an unconvincing tone.

They sit in silence as the boat gravitates toward land, the sun setting behind it. Milo has lowered the sails and walks to and fro with binoculars, looking out for the Coast Guard.

"If we get boarded," he says, "you're both Australian."

Milo pulls an inflatable life raft from below deck and tries in vain to inflate it, coughing in intervals. Neil takes over, and Amy watches as the light fades and he becomes a shadow in darkness, and she listens to the sound of his lungs.

She looks up and can no longer see stars, then realizes she is staring at a hill and, a mile or so to the right, a lighthouse scanning the night.

Neil and Milo lower the raft onto the water. "You sure you won't miss your lifeboat?" Neil asks.

"Forgot I had it," he says. "No point in keeping it now." Neil and Milo shake hands. "I hope you've enjoyed your journey on Captain Milo's vessel. Comment cards are in your luggage."

Amy leans over and hugs Milo. "Thank you," she says.

"If you need a ride back, look me up."

In the dark, Neil uses a small wooden paddle to get them a hundred yards over to a rocky shore. They are in a cove, sheltered from waves, and when they get within ten feet of land, Neil slides out of the boat, waist deep into the water, and pulls the boat to the rocks. Amy tosses their bags on shore and hops over. Neil climbs up behind her and pulls up the lifeboat until it is safely above the tide, a lucky find for someone tomorrow. She can hear Neil's teeth chattering. "Are you okay?"

"Fine. Just a tad chilly."

They make their way up a rocky bluff until they are standing within view of several lighted houses about a mile away. They find a two-lane gravel road and make their way to the second home, which, just as Milo had told Neil, has a sign announcing QUEEN ANNE'S B&B.

Neil opens the door, and a bell above their heads jingles. A man with a round belly and a long beard enters from a room behind the counter. "Yes?"

"Do you have any vacancies?" Neil asks.

"Well … " The man is looking at Neil's wet clothing.

"I got a little too close to the water during our hike," Neil says.

"I told him to stay off those rocks." Amy laughs, schoolgirl-like, trying to sound lighthearted and younger than her years. Like the other backpackers who no doubt pass through. She slips her arm through Neil's and flashes the innkeeper a bright smile, hoping they look more like clueless lovebirds than suspicious characters.

The innkeeper relents. "All right," he says. He asks them to sign in, hands them a key, and tells them that though the only meal the B&B serves is breakfast, they are welcome to help themselves to the bread, tea, and coffee in the sitting room.

Their room is small but clean, with a window overlooking the night-black shoreline. Neil cracks the window to let in fresh air, and she can hear the waves on the rocks below. He flips a switch on the wall, and a gas fireplace lights up.

"This is cozy," she says as he changes out of his wet clothes.

"I wonder if they have a computer downstairs."

"Use my phone."

"That might be dangerous for you."

"I think we passed dangerous a thousand miles ago."

She hands him her phone and watches as he uses the web browser to find the video, scrolling down to the last of the comments. He logs in and then enters a new comment: *Three days.*

"That's how long it will take me to get to Melbourne," he says. "You'll get there sooner."

Three days—Amy wishes she and Neil had that much time left. But they have only tonight.

They go downstairs, where they make toast with jam and cups of tea. Amy, never much of a drinker before, finds herself wanting to spike her tea. She glimpses a carafe of what looks like wine but, when she pours some into a glass, realizes is sherry—syrupy and sweet. She laughs. "I guess we'll have to stay sober," she says.

"Big day tomorrow," he says. "It's probably for the best."

It's for the best tonight, too, she realizes, as they return to their room and get undressed; she wants to remember everything. Amy feels time slow down as Neil runs his hands over every part of her body, as if memorizing every angle and every curve. She feels the pendant, cool against her neck, as he presses into her, as close as he can possibly get.

Afterward, unable to sleep, she sits by the window as Neil snores. She squints into the darkness, trying to find the shore where they landed, wondering when she will see him again. If she will ever see him again.

44.

ROBERT STANDS BY THE HOTEL WINDOW, a comfortable distance away from Tracy as she sits cross-legged on one of the beds, cradling her smartphone. Though by the look she's giving him, he's apparently still too close.

"I can't see your screen from over here," he reassures her.

"It's not that. What's the Wi-Fi password?"

He fetches the key card sleeve and reads it to her. She taps on the screen, then pauses to look up at him. "Don't you have to call your boss or something?"

"He's going to want to know a day and time for the pickup."

"But you won't need the *actual* day and time, right?"

"Right, but I'll need something close."

"Why?"

"Because it's likely they'll be following us. I don't want them thinking anything unusual when we set out for Bells Beach."

"How the hell are we going to protect Neil if they're two steps behind us?"

"Leave that to me."

She narrows her eyes at him, and he senses an anxiety that wasn't there on the plane, a paranoia no doubt rising with her proximity to Neil. He can't blame her. He's feeling restless himself, his brain on edge from trying to untangle the mess of overlapping and unknown agendas. And who's to say that Spence doesn't already have contacts in the Coast Guard to flag down Aeneas's ship and invalidate, in one nautical swoop, all of their efforts?

Robert's phone buzzes with a text from Spence: *Meet me in the lobby.*

Tracy looks up. "That your boss?"

"I'll be back in a few minutes. Stay here."

A glare from Tracy is all he gets in the form of acknowledgment. On the elevator down, Robert contemplates asking Spence how many people, other than Spence himself, are following him. Knowing how many others are involved would give Robert a better idea of the stakes and also help him plan out how best to throw them off his trail. But he knows Spence knows better than to tell him anything.

Entering the lobby, Robert sees Spence seated in the lounge, dressed in a black blazer and white dress shirt. Spence gestures to the seat across from him and signals for a waiter. He orders whiskeys as Robert studies his face, calm and confident. The look of a man well compensated, unburdened by doubt, unafraid of failure. A look that Robert used to believe he might one day attain.

"How was your flight?" Spence asks.

"Interminable."

"If anyone wanted to torture me into giving up secrets, they need only stick me in coach."

"Well, at least I know I won't crack."

"Join us full time, and I'll make sure you fly business on your return."

The drinks arrive, and Spence raises his glass. "To the game."

Robert swirls the whiskey but doesn't raise his glass.

"Oh, come on, Robert, drink with me."

"People who say that life's a game are usually those on the winning end."

Spence considers the statement. "You could be right, my friend. You could be right." He takes a long drink.

"Where's Neil?"

"Now that's interesting, because I'm here to ask you the very same question. His old man's ship is docked just over in Port Phillip.

I'd say that's hardly a coincidence."

"I don't know where he is," Robert says, "but I know where he will be. I have a pickup location."

Spence leans forward. When Robert tells him, Spence gives him a curious look. "Why?"

"Apparently they used to surf there."

"So he's going to surf to the ship?"

"Or swim."

"Aren't there sharks in those waters?"

"What do you think? This is Australia."

Spence's eyes are dead on his, static, masking the lights of so much activity. "When?"

"I'm working on that."

"I need to know now. Let me to talk to Tracy."

"No."

"You're too kind to these people. Sometimes they need a little negative reinforcement."

"They don't respond well to reinforcement of any kind."

He shakes his head. "I love environmental activists. They're so serious. Devoid of humor, committed to saving a world beyond saving."

"They view themselves as the canaries," Robert says.

"I know they do. But canaries die first."

"Neil doesn't get hurt. You have to promise me that."

"Robert, you do know the business we're in. No betting man would cover that bet."

"Unless he stole nuclear launch codes, I don't see the need for lethal force."

"In our client's eyes, he did still nuclear launch codes."

"And you're still not going to tell me?"

"It's better you not know. Better none of us know." Spence leans back and studies him. "If all goes according to plan, no bullets will be fired. That I can promise you." Spence returns his empty glass to the table. "You know why I left the Bureau?"

"The money."

"Of course." Spence grins. "But it wasn't just the money. You don't think I had moments of frustration? Days when I felt I wasn't so much working for the United States of America but some well-financed, bumbling bureaucracy with connections to ways-and-means committee members? I knew who signed my checks, and I had no problem cashing them. But, like you, I had my doubts. I wanted to believe I was doing good, and more often than not I wasn't doing any good. Until the day when I settled for doing good by my client and being handsomely compensated for it. Maybe I'll rot in hell for my actions. Or maybe I'm on the side of the angels. I don't know, and I don't particularly care. You want to know the best thing about being a contractor?"

"What?"

"No moral hazard."

"As if you ever had one."

Spence chuckles as he pushes himself to his feet. "I'm headed back to Port Phillip. If that ship starts moving, I'm going be talking to that drug addict of yours, whether you like it or not."

Robert says nothing. He watches Spence exit the hotel, then downs the rest of his whiskey in one long gulp, feeling it burn all the way down.

45.

AFTER ROBERT LEAVES THE HOTEL ROOM, Tracy stares at the door for a few minutes before getting up and looking out the window. Sixteen stories below, trolley tracks cut through a red-bricked pedestrian mall. On either side are cafés with people gathered around smoking, catching rays of sun through the buildings. She looks for Robert, wanting to see him walk down the street for a cup of coffee instead of imagining him in the room next door, with men in suits, listening equipment, cameras. Using her as bait to lure Neil out of hiding.

Neil used to talk about guilt, comparing it to a tick, something that sticks to you where you can't see, sucking the energy right out of you until it gets so bloated that it can no longer hold on, and then you finally see it, on the floor, a round bulbous sack of your own blood. Guilt is greedy and feeds to excess. *That's why the richest people in the world are constantly in motion,* Neil said. *They're terrified of what might land on them if they stop.*

Tracy returns to the smartphone. She goes to YouTube and searches on the song, the one she'd watched him listening to one night. She finds it and scrolls down through the comments, her fingers unsteady at the thought that there might be nothing here. Then what?

But then she sees it, the day and time, thankfully still in the future. She adds a comment of her own: *Many eyes. Be careful.*

She hears a knock on the door and sighs.

"What kind of FBI agent forgets his key card?" she mumbles irritably as she opens the door. She hears a man's voice but can't make out the words, and only when she sees an unexpected face staring back, like a ghost from another lifetime, does she realize what she's done.

"Hey, gorgeous," Ray says.

"What—what are you doing here?"

"What kind of a welcome is that for an international fugitive?"

Ray looks up and down the hallway. "Aren't you going to invite me in?"

She takes a step back and he takes two forward, putting his hands on her hips. "I could eat you up, Trace."

She backs up again, moving out of his reach as the door swings shut behind him, and she doesn't stop until she's up against the window. He stands in front of her, wearing the same cocky look he always has, even years later, even after she'd put him in prison. She is both angry and afraid and doesn't know which emotion will rise to the surface until she hears herself say, "You're an asshole."

Ray sighs, drops his shoulders, and joins her at the window. "You're right. I was a dick to you. To a lot of people. I don't blame you for talking. You deserved better than me."

"I deserved Neil."

"Where is he?"

"I don't know."

"But you're looking for him, aren't you?"

"What are you doing here, Ray?"

"What do you think? Trying to save Neil's ass."

"What happened in Iowa City?"

"You don't want to know."

"Tell me. The truth."

Ray looks at her and nods. "Okay. The truth is that Neil stole some pretty serious shit. From Biosant. Big enough to buy a few countries and have change left over."

"Is that who's chasing him?"

"Us. Chasing us, Trace. So Neil hacks in, downloads the shit, and calls me to plan the next steps. We had to go somewhere that wasn't bugged or under surveillance. So I figured some farmer's field in the middle of the night was about as safe as you could possibly get. I figured wrong. We were parked there maybe five minutes before we hear all this shouting. FBI, they said. So I open my door while Neil opens the back. And then all hell breaks loose. Neil took off in one direction, and I went the other."

"You haven't seen him since?"

"Have you?"

She shakes her head.

"They're going to kill him, Trace."

"How do you know?"

"Because that night in the field, they didn't shout out at us to hold up our hands. They just started firing."

He turns toward the window and looks down, and she notices the restless motion of his legs, the way he keeps running his hand through his hair. Nervous, twitchy. Tracy is guessing it's not just that he's on the run but that he's on something else, and she feels a pang in her abdomen, an old familiar craving, an awakening of whatever beast she hoped was dead and buried, as far away as childhood. But the beast was only hibernating, and now it's stirring within her and so, so hungry.

"How did you find me?" she asks.

"You're not the only one Neil confided in about his old man. I knew he'd be headed to Melbourne. And I knew that people would come looking to you for the pickup location. I just didn't realize you'd be so willing to work for the bad guys again."

"I'm not."

"Oh yeah? And that dick I saw leaving your room? The one who put us away?"

"He's on our side."

Ray laughs. "Is that what he told you? And you believed him?"

Tracy says nothing. She feels herself blushing, Ray making her feel like a stupid kid again.

"Isn't Robert the one who got you to confess?" Ray continues.

"He didn't get me to do anything."

"And where is he right now? Who's he meeting with?"

"It doesn't matter. He doesn't know the pickup location."

Ray leans in and whispers, as if he's now worried about the room being bugged. "What did you tell him?"

"Bells Beach."

"You lied?"

She nods. "I can lie just as well as you."

Ray smiles. "I'm impressed, Trace. Very impressed. So what's the real location?"

"Why would I tell you that?"

"So I can help him."

"I've got everything under control."

"Yeah, sure you do. You're shacking up with a goon that may or may not put a bullet through Neil's head."

Tracy tries to see past those dark eyes but is no better now at knowing what's going on behind them. Ray is committed to the cause—this she knows. And he is crazy enough to think that he can somehow rescue Neil from under the noses of an army of Roberts. But he deceived her, just like Robert had before.

Caught between two dishonest people, she could only guess her way to the truth. Or trust her gut. She's familiar with the phrase but not the execution. What does her gut know that her heart and mind do not? How can she trust it or any other part of her body?

"I'm the only one who can save him, Tracy. You think you're going to ditch this FBI guy and whoever he's working for?"

"I can do it."

"I'm sure you can. You've come this far. But I'm already invisible. Nobody's following me. Nobody even knows I'm here."

"I want to see him, Ray."

"I know you do. And you will. But let's get our boy on that boat first." He takes hold of her hand. "Remember the mountain lion?"

Benton. She can picture him, sitting on the limb of the tree, looking down at the gathering crowd, perfectly still, as if a lack of movement would somehow make him invisible to the humans. If only.

"I think of him every day."

"Neil is that mountain lion, Trace. And Robert is that cop. You know me. I can get Neil down from that tree. I can get him onto that boat. And I can get you there, too. But you have to trust me."

She hears a door close in the hallway, and they both stare at the door in silence. "I should go." He walks away from her.

"Wait," she says. "Lorne. Tomorrow at noon."

Ray takes a step toward her, and this time she doesn't back away. His lips feel so familiar and foreign, and she remembers why she loved him once.

He pulls back. "I'll take care of him, Trace."

"You better. I can't go through this again." She hears her voice quivering and props herself against the window.

He returns to her, kisses her on her forehead, and places something in her hand. She can tell what it is without looking down.

"For later," he says.

She stares at the door after he's gone. All this time she had been wondering how she would escape Robert when the time was right. She never did come up with a plan. Now she wouldn't need one.

She places a pill between her lips and mixes it with the salt water that drips from her eyes into her mouth. She stares at the ceiling, feeling the pill dissolve and dissipate and bleed through the muscled wall of her stomach into her bloodstream, expanding into her fingertips and toes, ears and cheeks, her mind free to focus, to think, to plan.

She thinks of what Robert will say when he arrives at the wrong beach at the wrong time. Will he feel as deceived as she felt when Neil was arrested for Ray's crime? What if Robert is not lying to her, if he's truly on her side? If this is so, she thinks, then the gods above have a horrible sense of humor.

She lies in bed feeling the waves lap at her toes, ankles, knees, until she is floating on her back listening to the whales singing to one another in the everlasting darkness far beneath.

46.

The first thing Amy does after boarding the *Spirit of Tasmania* is take the stairs two at a time until she is standing on the top deck. She expects a mob scene similar to that on the ferry from the North to the South Island but emerges to find herself among only a half dozen people in windbreakers braving the winds coming in off the Bass Strait, charcoal clouds hanging so low she feels the urge to duck. She scans the horizon looking for a sailboat. But Neil will be on a boat she won't recognize—and not likely standing where she can see him. She walks to starboard and looks six stories down as the ferry glides slowly past sailboats and fishing trawlers, looking like children's toys from where she stands, and she is amazed that they'd made it across the Tasman Sea. And her gut sinks when she imagines what Neil is now facing as he sails into the storm.

The clouds begin spitting, sending raindrops into her eyes. She retreats downstairs and stands near a row of vending machines. She's too anxious to sit so she focuses on scrutinizing every passenger, looking for anyone who appears to be looking for her.

She passes tables of couples assembling puzzles and young men playing video games on their phones. Nobody strikes her as governmental or James Bond–like, not that he would be wearing a suit on the ferry. She reminds herself that just because two men were chasing her across New Zealand, there could now be two women working this shift.

After a half hour of patrolling the decks, reasonably satisfied that she's not being observed, she settles in the front row of seats, assembled like pews in a church, facing a row of angled windows affording a view of teal-gray water with seagulls swinging back and forth like trapeze artists.

She thinks of that moment Neil kissed her, how he blamed it on people who may or may not have been following them. She imagines him seated to her left, his hand on her leg, the way he squeezed it when she made him laugh.

She can feel the open ocean taking hold of the boat, people around her taking their seats, some looking a familiar shade of seasick. Her own stomach remains calm.

She looks at her phone, hoping for Internet, feeling the urge to visit YouTube and find out where Neil is now, even though he warned her not to go there, to stay as far away from him as possible, not just physically but digitally. And she agreed. Give him a week to get on board the ship and then wait for him to contact her, which he swore he would do. But she'd probably be back in St. Louis by then.

Her phone picks up a signal and, with it, the animated home page of YouTube. What's the harm in a quick look? But before she can bring up another page the signal drops. She waits a second and tries again, the Internet now teasing her.

"Wi-Fi?"

She turns her head to see the source of the question, a man roughly her age, with a Nordic look to him, tall and blond, wearing a bright red fleece top.

"I'm about to give up," she says.

"I could have a look."

"It's not a big deal," she says.

"I can help. Truly." He has an arm outstretched, and she turns to face him, kneeling on the seat as she watches his fingers tap dance across the screen, scrolling, and right when she thinks she should ask for her phone back, he hands it to her.

"Five bars," he says.

She looks down at the YouTube page, the Purcell song humming softly, before she puts the phone to sleep.

"You're a miracle worker."

"An engineer, actually," he says. "Erik." He extends a hand, and she takes it.

"Amy. I'm the polar opposite of engineer. A writer."

"Right brain," he says. "I'm left brain. Together we make one." His eyes are turquoise and his cheeks the color of his jacket from too much sun.

"You give me too much credit."

"Do you mind if I join you in the front row?"

"Sure," she says. "You can't beat the view." She watches him pick up his large backpack, with a strapped-on sleeping roll and two water bottles dangling.

"I hiked Cradle Mountain," he says with pride as he settles down beside her. "Thirty kilometers in two days. What about you?"

"Oh, nothing that ambitious," she says. "I'm just. Passing through."

"American?"

"That obvious?"

"Actually, no. At first I thought you were Canadian." He leans in. "You're not so … "

"Obnoxious?"

"I was going to say vociferous, but you get the idea." He lowers his voice. "The British are just as awful. I'm Norwegian. We're much quieter than the Swedes and the Finns. Is this your first trip to Australia?"

"Second, actually," she says, surprising herself with the answer. She had left Australia little more than two weeks ago thinking she'd be heading home soon, and here she is back again.

"So you've seen the sights already? The Opera House, the black swans?"

Amy shakes her head. "I missed the swans."

"Really? That's like coming all this way and not seeing the Southern Cross. They have black swans in Melbourne as well. In the Royal Gardens. I could show you."

"That's nice of you, but I still need to find a place to stay first."

"That's simple enough. I've got a hotel reserved downtown. You can have the sofa." He pauses. "I'm sorry. I didn't mean to come across so, so … "

"American?"

He smiles sheepishly, and she marvels at the irony of the

moment. Across so much of her romantically quixotic adventure she was desperate to meet a man like this, so eager to travel with her. And now, in the course of two weeks, she's met two.

"Can I think about it?"

"By my calculations, you've got seven and a half hours to think about it."

They spend the next three hours making fun of American travelers and travel bloggers and their yoga poses and selfies. Around noon they head to the cafeteria, and she buys a veggie sandwich. He buys two beers and they toast the Tasman Sea.

Back at their seats, the front windows are streaked with rain, and the waves are now white-tipped. Around them people are subdued, many prostrate on the floor or in booths. Seasickness setting in.

But she and Erik are immune to the effects of the sea. She buys the next round of beers and stops by a wall of windows, looking for a sailboat but seeing only water and sky.

They clink plastic cups and she takes a long drink, letting the alcohol wash away the anxiety. She can't stop thinking of Neil out there on the waves somewhere, and her eyes skip from window to window.

As she and Erik trade rounds, the alcohol buoys her spirits, and she sits back and listens as Erik tells her about his round-the-world trip. About Thailand and Tonga. He shows her a map of every country he has visited on his phone, and while once she would have jealously made mental notes on how to extend her own travels, now she simply listens.

"I'm so glad I did this," he says. "Backpacking you have to do while you're young."

"I just barely made the cut," she says.

"Please. You're plenty young still."

"And the beer has nothing to do with it."

"What do you think I am, British?" He laughs, hops out of his seat, and makes for the bathroom. Amy looks at the windows, trying to distinguish ocean and sky through all that darkness. Her eyes settle on a distant glow, yellow and white lights through the fog. Melbourne?

When Erik returns he stays on his feet, following her eyes. "We're almost there. Have you made a decision yet?"

She wonders what Neil would advise. Then it occurs to her that Erik, from a distance, could look like Neil, back when he had his blond hair. And if she exits the boat with Erik, anyone looking for them might assume they're still together, all but guaranteeing that they will follow her.

"Why not," she says.

When they exit the ferry in the direction of the tram station, Erik puts his arm around her and she laughs at his joke about Vegemite. She notices a man standing near the row of taxis, watching her while talking into his phone.

When Amy follows Erik into The Langham and up to the corner suite on the twenty-second floor, she realizes that Erik is not a typical backpacker. No roughing it, for one, but she isn't about to complain as she stands in the corner of the suite's living room, next to the floor-to-ceiling windows, and looks down on the sparkling southern skyline of the city and, in the other direction, the reflections on the Yarra River.

"This beats the hostel," she says. She turns around, taking in the thick, velvety drapes, the plush furniture, the polished wood. She looks at the soft-looking sheets on the bed and feels a sudden awkwardness between them, wondering if he's expecting any reciprocity.

He stands in the middle of the room. "You must be knackered," he says.

She nods.

"Well, there are blankets in the closet, and I hope the couch will do."

"It will do perfectly."

"You sleep well." He nods to her before closing his bedroom door.

She pulls blankets from the closet and settles down on the couch, looking at the lights reflected off the sky's low-hanging clouds. She realizes she should have confirmed her airline ticket home by now, and she can hear Neil's voice in her head: *I'll breathe easier knowing you're far away from me.*

But she can't leave. Not yet. How did people survive the silence of being apart? Before computers and phones surrounded couples with reassuring beeps and bings.

Back then, you were simply alone. She thinks of the wives of the great explorers, how they often waited years for news of any kind, good or bad. How did they keep moving? She wonders if they began hearing their own special noises, the beeps and bings of their minds drifting loose.

Restless, Amy tosses off the covers and picks up her phone, tempted to visit YouTube again, to see what Neil's plan is.

Instead, she goes to the window. She watches as a delivery truck idles on the street below, trying to convince herself that it's best that she let Neil go. That it's safer this way, for both of them.

As the sky begins to lighten, she returns to the couch. Her face in the still-dim room is bathed in the azure glow of her screen as she searches for the video, the music of Purcell's *Dido and Aeneas.* A female soprano singing a song of longing and loss. When she finds it, she scrolls down to the comments section. There it is, as clear as Neil's face. A Pacific pocket mouse. And a comment. A date. Tomorrow. And a time. Noon. Amy stares at the words on the screen, wondering where he was when he typed those words. The pickup is now less than twelve hours away.

She paces the carpeted floor, on tiptoe, careful not to awaken Erik. She could honor Neil's word and pretend she saw nothing. Or she could honor something far deeper. She saved him once, didn't she? What if he needs her again?

Even though Neil is not around, she is still with him; she can't help but see the world through his eyes now. She feels as though they'd come together as fractured people, like two clay figures smashed together by circumstance, then pulled apart, unevenly, the pieces of them now mixed together, with him carrying parts of her and she parts of him. With every passing moment, she knows that being with him is the only way she'll feel whole again.

IN THE MORNING she and Erik set off for the Royal Botanic Gardens, a short walk down St. Kilda Road and across the river. The day is bright, and the storm that passed through has left the air moist and fragrant with the smell of eucalyptus trees, which stand tall ahead, along with palms, elms, and other trees she can't recognize. The bridge is dense with people, bikes, and cars; women with strollers; an Asian tour group; dog walkers. To go from the emptiness of the South Island to the middle of the Tasman Sea to this street that feels like a parade.

Amy stops midway across the bridge and turns to take a picture of their hotel. She doesn't notice anyone following and feels her chest tighten. If nobody is following them, then what good was her grand plan to protect Neil? These people could be following him instead, and she now has no way of contacting him.

Unless she breaks her promise and travels to Lorne. It's not as if she would be leading anyone to him now since nobody apparently has taken an interest in her.

She feels a hand on her shoulder. "Everything okay?"

She turns to face Erik and his confused expression. "Of course," she says. "My phone is acting up on me."

They continue walking, and when they turn into the park, Amy feels her mood lift slightly, the wide-open green lawns and sounds of birds calming her. Along the way, Erik points out rainbow-colored lorikeets jetting back and forth between trees and a pair of cacophonous cockatoos right above them.

"You've been exceedingly silent," Erik says.

"Just thinking. About—about home."

"Why don't you come with me to Perth? My shout."

"I don't know."

"You scared of flying? You prefer boats instead?"

She looks up at him, wondering where that question came from.

"I have something for you." He hands her a key card. "Just in case."

"I really should be in a hostel."

"What? There's someone else? Another guy?"

"Why do you care?" She doesn't realize how harsh her voice sounds until she hears the words out loud.

Erik turns to her. "I'm sorry for all the questions," he says. "It's just. I like you."

"Erik. I'm engaged."

"Oh. I didn't realize." He glances down at her ring finger. "You're not wearing a ring."

"I lost it in New Zealand."

"Oh. I see." He continues walking toward a large, man-made pond and doesn't stop until he reaches the water's edge. She follows a few steps behind, feeling guilty for her outburst.

"There they are," Erik says. On the far side of the pond, a pair of swans, as perfectly dark as if they'd been dipped in black ink, with bright red lipstick beaks, swim along leisurely. "For many years, anyone living north of the equator believed this bird was a myth," he says. "They had to come here to learn the truth."

"They're beautiful," she says. "Thank you for bringing me."

He looks at her with forgiving eyes, then turns back to the water. She thinks about Neil, how if there is any lesson here, it's that people are stubborn, that they must see the truth for themselves before they will believe it. That's why Neil risked so much to take those undercover videos, to steal those files. People can't believe the realities of the world unless they see for themselves what goes on behind the walls of a factory farm or a slaughterhouse or a large corporation. Neil's story is the one she should write. She thinks of the irony—that all she'd wanted was to have stories to tell—yet these are stories she can never share.

At the hotel suite, she zips up her bag and drags it to the door. Erik is watching, looking disappointed and a little anxious.

"Last chance," he says. "Just north of Perth, you can swim with the dolphins."

"I'm sorry." As she gives him a quick, awkward hug, she feels sorry for him, understanding how he feels, searching for someone to be with on the road. But for once, she doesn't want company.

She is standing at the elevator when she notices the key card in her pocket. She slips out of her backpack and hurries back to the suite. When she enters, she hears a strange, angry voice, an American's voice, coming from the bedroom. She holds the door from slamming behind her.

"I told you I fucking tried to keep her here." It's Erik's voice, devoid of his previous accent, a voice purely American, apparently speaking on the phone. "If she's headed to the beach, then you'll be there waiting right? You can deal with her and Neil together."

She feels her body go numb, frozen, until she forces herself to move. She backs up, closing the door as quietly as she can, and runs to the elevator. On her way down she looks at her empty hands, realizing that she must've dropped the key card in the room. Erik will see it. He'll know she was there.

On the street, she tries to settle down her breathing. She has to warn Neil. She starts walking just to get far away from Erik.

How could she let herself be tricked like this? She should have known better. She takes a trolley to another neighborhood, where she finds a hotel and enters the lobby, using her phone to find the YouTube page.

She scrolls down to find the comment about the pickup and sees another one: *Many eyes*. She wonders who wrote it and whether Neil has seen it. This close to the pickup he might not even be looking at a computer anymore; he might be hiding out somewhere near Lorne. She can't very well go to Lorne and wander the streets, not now that they know who she is. Yet somehow she must disappear for a day.

She looks out the lobby window and notices a tour bus loading in front of the hotel, the words *Penguin Parade* on the side. She remembers something Neil told her about Melbourne, how there's an island a couple hours outside of town where people go to watch the penguins return to their nests after sunset. He'd made fun of the bleachers they had built so people could watch these doll-sized birds return home.

This would be the perfect way to disappear. She asks the driver if she can buy a ticket, and he takes her cash. As the bus leaves the outskirts of the city, she closes her eyes against the chatter of the tourists around her, and eventually she drifts off to sleep. When she wakes, they are at Phillip Island, and she feels exhausted.

She follows the parade of people to stadium seats facing the beach. Someone dressed in a green polo with a name badge speaks in a microphone. No flashes. Inside voices. Enjoy the moment.

And as Amy's eyes adjust to the twilight, the first tiny penguin emerges from the surf, stands upright, and shakes its beak. The penguin, no more than a foot tall, stands there until others join him, and then they inch their way past the humans in a shuffling group of a dozen. As her mind slowly begins to wake again, she finds the show terribly sad, reminding her of tourism a hundred years ago in Yosemite, when the park service erected bleachers around the food dumps so tourists could watch bears emerge from the forest to eat human scraps.

Neil had told her that the tourists, the noise, and the occasional rogue camera flash is a fair trade for the protection of this shoreline and the species that relies on it. She isn't sure if she believes it. She sits there long after the others have returned to the bus. In the darkness she can see the white bellies of the penguins reflecting the moonlight.

One of the rangers comes over and tells her they're closing, asks her to return to her bus. They arrive at the hotel close to midnight, and she books a room. She's too tired to care if people find her at this point. As long as she can avoid arrest for another twelve hours, she'll have a chance at saving Neil.

She lies in darkness. She feels alone, more alone than she did when she began this trip so long ago. All that stands between her and St. Louis is a bus ride and two airplanes. So little movement on her part is required to travel halfway around the world, back in time to a world she now barely recognizes. But she's not about to go home. Not now.

47.

Robert watches Spence exit the hotel into a dark-blue sedan, then hurries back to the hotel room to find Tracy cross-legged in the middle of her bed, staring at a black TV screen. She looks over at him, her eyes glassy.

"You okay?" he asks.

"Waking up still," she mumbles. "Jet lag."

He considers asking if she's taken something, but at this point he's just relieved that she hasn't left the room. "So when is it?"

Tracy is staring at the TV again.

"Tracy?"

"What?"

"The pickup. When is Neil getting picked up?"

"Tomorrow. Noon."

"Good. We'll leave first thing."

Tracy leans back on the bed and closes her eyes. He feels his stomach growling. "You want something to eat?"

She mumbles something, then rolls over, turning her back to him. He can hear her breathing deepen and slow. At least someone is getting some sleep around here; he won't be sleeping well tonight, if at all.

"I'll be right back," he says, not waiting for a response.

HE LEANS AGAINST THE RAILING, looking down on the Yarra River, listening to the voices of the tourists and people on cell phones as they pass. He has spent the past three hours walking aimlessly, trying to make sense of a situation that at this point makes no sense.

An ornate, wrought-iron light post catches his eye, and he walks a few feet ahead and reads the Latin inscription at its base. *Vires Acquirit Eundo.*

Three years in Catholic high school before getting kicked back to public, and the one thing that stuck with him was Latin. "She gathers strength as she goes," he says aloud.

He pulls out his phone and hesitates, the third time he has backed away from dialing Spence. He's never lied to Spence before, and this phone call, attaching the right time to the wrong place, will put this lie officially in motion—only to be followed up with more lies, like telling Spence he had a flat tire and, after Neil does escape, pretending he had been duped by Tracy. *We'll never run out of criminals or bullets,* Spence once told him. *But trust will always be in short supply.* To the extent that Spence has trusted him so far, there will be nothing left this time tomorrow.

Robert dials. "Spence? It's tomorrow. Noon."

"And it's still Lorne?" Spence says.

"That's right."

"You absolutely sure about that?"

"Of course."

Spence pauses, and Robert can picture those calculating eyes on the other end, but what exactly is being calculated Robert can only guess.

"I'll see you there."

"Don't hurt him."

"Robert, I won't lay a hand on the lad."

Robert pockets his phone and turns around, his gut uneasy about everything. A face catches his eyes, a woman passing him headed in the opposite direction, walking with a man he does not recognize. Robert watches as they continue along like a pair of tourists, headed toward the National Gallery or the Royal Botanic Gardens.

He knows he's seen her before but can't place her. The man is blond and tall and looks a lot like Neil. And that's when it clicks. The girl from Instagram, the one traveling with Neil. Amaranta Bakas.

Robert jogs across the bridge until he is within shouting distance, then follows them into the gardens as he debates approaching her. She might know where Neil is right now. Then again, even if she does, she might say nothing, then frighten Neil off, ruining his only chance of escape tomorrow. Robert watches as the two stand by the water's edge, the man looking at her, eyes focused, so clearly attracted to her. Robert concludes that she has moved on, or Neil has.

On his way back to the hotel, after picking up two orders of chips along Lonsdale Street, he stops at a bottle shop.

When he enters the room, the TV is blaring and Tracy is in the shower. Sunset has given their room a pink glow. Robert mutes the TV and is sitting at the table eating fries when she emerges, wrapped in a towel, her eyes alert again. "Where have you been?"

"Getting food."

She grabs a handful of fries. "Is this all?"

"You want something else, order room service." He hands her the menu and opens up the whiskey. He grabs a glass from the bathroom and fills it.

"Oh, what a surprise," she says, studying the menu. "The only vegan thing on here is French fries." She tosses the menu across the room and retreats into the bathroom, leaving Robert yearning for the comatose version of her. She returns with another glass. He hesitates.

He pours her half a glass, and she holds it up. "To Neil."

Robert says nothing, making a silent toast to Noa, then takes a searing mouthful. Tracy raises her glass to her lips and empties it.

She goes into the bathroom and returns wearing a tank top and boxers. She sits on her bed, propping up her head on the pillows, the whiskey glass resting on the mattress next to her.

"So tell me your big plan," she says. "For how we save Neil."

"Plan?" Robert fills another glass. "My plan is to make sure my people are headed not to Bells Beach but to a different one. That should buy Neil enough time to board his boat."

"How is that going to happen if they're following us?"

"We're going to suffer a flat tire. They'll see us along the side of the road, and I'll tell them to go along without me."

"And how are you going to achieve a flat tire at the exact right moment?"

Robert shows Tracy the knife he purchased at an outdoor store while walking around earlier. She eyes him suspiciously. "They were all out of screwdrivers?"

"You still don't trust me, do you?"

"I hardly trust myself anymore." She holds out her empty glass, and Robert splashes whiskey into it again. Something is still off about her, as if they're talking to one another across satellite phones, with delays in reception and reply.

If she lied to him about the location, both he and Spence will spend the day watching surfers. At the end of it all, at least Robert will know he tried. There was a time in his life when he believed that failure was not an option, just as all young men are taught to *win or go home*. What they don't teach young men is that only one man can win. And that going home is not such a bad consolation prize.

Only Robert doesn't know where home is anymore. As for Noa,

he should content himself with the knowledge that she's safe and that she has moved on. Maybe that's all he could have hoped for.

Tracy isn't moving, her eyes closed. Robert takes the glass from her and puts it on the table, then pulls the comforter over her. She mutters something before rolling onto her side. He feels the urge to lie down next to her, put his arm around her and provide some comfort. But he knows he would be doing it less for her than for him. Instead, he sits back on the chair and finishes her drink.

He is floating on his back, feeling the waves lift him gently, with regularity, and he is watching the clouds far above. He can hear his lungs taking in the air, slowly, holding it for a second before release. Then he is spitting out water, eyes blinking, arms trying to take control over the rolling water. But it's too late; the waves are rising up, only to push him down again, under; he's coughing out salt from his throat, a voice in the back of his head telling him that he is drowning. That he should relax. Let the ocean pull him into its embrace. Life would be easier that way. Life is always easier for those not living.

Robert is on the floor when he wakes to find Tracy kneeling above him. "You were shouting," she says.

"Oh." He sits up against the chair, his heart still pounding.

"What were you dreaming about?"

"I don't know." He thinks for a moment, then he sees it. A dream he is glad to leave to the night. "I was getting pulled under. The water. Undertow."

He notices the curves of her body under her tank top, the cool glow from the moon on her skin. He can hear his breathing, the hum of the clock on the stand above his head.

"Who's the father?" he asks.

"The father?"

"Noa's child."

Tracy leans back on her toes.

"I followed you," Robert says. "In Ashland. I saw the boy."

Tracy's eyes widen. "Are you saying—you and Noa?"

He nods.

"When?"

"A few years ago."

"Neil is the father."

"Are you sure?"

"The baby's name is Cameron. Not Robert. Or Porter. Cameron."

"Right."

"Jesus. What kind of fantasy world have you been living in?"

"Forget I asked." He pauses, then asks, "When did she and Neil—"

"Does it matter?"

"I suppose not." Robert reaches over for the whiskey bottle and drains what's left into his throat.

48.

STILL HALF ASLEEP, Tracy hears the crackling of Robert's ankles as he stands. A yawn. Then the bathroom door closing. She gets out of bed, her jaw aching, a reminder that she's coming down. Last night. She closes her eyes, worried that she might have said something about Lorne.

She needs another pill. Something to soften the landing. She sees her jacket on the chair and she remembers. In addition to what Ray gave her, she still has Helen's pills. She is holding the jacket when Robert enters in boxers, one hand under his T-shirt scratching his stomach.

"Morning," she says, and he grunts something in reply. He fiddles with the coffee maker and then fetches water from the bathroom sink.

"How you feeling?"

"Like I got kicked in the head by a kangaroo." He fills the pot, then returns to the bathroom. When she hears the shower, Tracy opens his laptop and returns to YouTube. She scrolls down to her comment, the last comment on the page. Nothing new. The plan is still on.

Now that she knows Robert's true agenda—that he's out to hurt the man who he thinks stole his girlfriend—she feels a comfort in having told Ray everything. Now she won't worry about escaping from Robert at Bells Beach. Now she can stay until Neil is safely on board the ship. And she'll have to trust that Neil and Ray will find her somehow, and she will join them on that boat, and Neil will forgive her. And after so many painful years of mistakes and regrets and hangovers, she will find her final second chance at happiness.

49.

AMY BOARDS THE 6:49 A.M. TRAIN at Southern Cross Station, headed to Geelong. From there, she will catch a bus to Lorne via the Great Ocean Road. If all goes well, she will arrive a half hour before noon, just in time to see Neil.

But not all is going well. When the train stops just outside of Melbourne and a garbled voice says something about a signal malfunction, a voice in her head begins telling her this is all a mistake. That no matter how hard she tries, she can't prevent the inevitable. She pushes the voice back after the train begins moving again.

At Geelong she catches the bus to Lorne just before it pulls away. Panting, she makes her way down the aisle until she is at the very back, and she takes the window seat in an empty row.

Within minutes the bus is hugging the curves of the shoreline, and she loses herself watching the surfers and young men playing cricket in the sand. The endless ocean, through darkened glass, taking her back to *Starry Eyes*, leaning into Neil as the sails chafed in the wind, wishing for placid winds so they could be left forever floating in relative peace.

She looks for him—on the shore, on a boat—but she knows that he will be in Lorne already. When they pass a sign reading 10 KILOMETRES TO LORNE, the bus makes another stop. She grips the seat handle in front of her, silently shouting for speed, speed. She glances at her watch, and it is nearly noon, nearly too late.

And as they merge back onto the road she begins praying that Neil's father is late, even though she knows this will only torture Neil after years of missed connections and broken promises.

If she arrives in Lorne and there is nobody at the shore but families with kids on paddleboards—if there is nothing for her to see but the sights, at least she will know Neil is headed away from this country, safe, and that this means someday they will see each other again.

50.

HEADING WEST ON THE GREAT OCEAN ROAD, Robert hugs the left lane as it winds along empty beach. He glances out at the blue expanse of water, the only thing separating Australia from Antarctica, as if he might spy Aeneas's boat. But all he sees is the occasional fishing trawler and gatherings of surfers like flotsam just beyond the surfline.

Every few miles cars collect on pullouts along the left side of the road. Some people are changing into wetsuits, others snapping pictures. Tracy, on his left, is surprisingly quiet, though her foot keeps tapping at the floor as if searching for a gas pedal. They pass a sign: LORNE 40 KM. They should be at Bells Beach any minute.

Robert's phone rings, and he puts it to his ear. "Where are you?" asks Spence.

"On my way," Robert says. "You?"

"In position."

"Really?"

"Early bird catches the criminal."

Spence hangs up, and Robert glances in the rearview mirror.

"That your boss?"

Robert nods, partly relieved that Spence isn't tailing him but also unsettled as to the reason why. Robert looks at the mirror again.

"Are they following us?" Tracy asks.

"If they are, they're keeping a comfortable distance."

He follows a sign for Bells Beach, turning left into a narrow parking lot that overlooks the bay. Beyond the break, surfers are scattered like birds on telephone lines, waiting for the next set.

Robert gets out and scans the beach for Neil, then notices that Tracy hasn't left the car. He returns to the car, opens the trunk, and removes the tire jack. She gets out and watches him.

"Aren't you going to look for Neil?" Robert asks.

"We're early. Where are your comrades?"

"I don't know."

"Shouldn't they be here by now?"

Robert has the knife in his hand, hesitating to puncture the tire. Tracy's face reflects how Robert is feeling, tense and unsure.

"What if they don't show?" she asks. "Then what?"

"Then I suppose they went ahead to Lorne without me."

"Lorne?"

He looks at her, surprised by the shock on her face. "What's the matter? I told you I wasn't going to send them to Bells Beach."

Tracy leans over, hands on her knees as if she's going to get sick. "We have to go. To Lorne."

"Why?"

"This isn't the spot." She gets back into the car.

Robert tosses the knife and the tire iron in the backseat and gets in. Tracy is breathing heavily, her head in her hands.

"The real location is Lorne? Why'd you lie to me?"

"Start the car!"

Robert pulls out of the parking lot without looking and hears a car horn in his wake. His mind is reeling, backtracking. Spence is still nowhere to be seen. Did he know that Lorne was the actual location all along? How could he?

"I picked Lorne off a map, for fuck's sake," Robert says. "Why didn't you tell me the truth?"

"I'm sorry, okay? Shit, shit." She turns to him, her eyes red. "What's going to happen to Neil?"

"What do you think?"

"Ray will protect him."

"Ray?" Robert tries to keep control of the car as he speeds around the road's curves. "What does he have to do with this?"

Tracy is silent.

"Tracy, what happened?"

"Ray came to the hotel room yesterday. While you were out."

"And you told him the real place?"

Tracy doesn't answer, and Robert puts it together immediately. It happened while he was downstairs with Spence. Spence got Robert out of the room to give Ray a chance to get the real location.

"Ray wouldn't hurt Neil."

"He's working for Spencer. That's why they weren't at Bells Beach. They knew it was Lorne as soon as you told Ray."

"Ray would never work for anybody."

"He got out of prison early—how do you think that happened?"

Tracy retreats back into silence, and Robert glances over at a face in shock. "It was all one big setup. Except that Neil got away."

He can hear Tracy's ragged breathing next to him, grateful for the silence and for the lack of traffic as he uses both sides of the road to make up time. Glancing at the dashboard clock, he sees it is almost noon.

"I was just trying to do something right for once," she says.

"There's still time."

The WELCOME TO LORNE sign is a blur, and Robert nearly rear-ends a delivery truck, veering to the right onto gravel, then left to avoid a compact car, followed by car horns and tires squealing as he circles a roundabout, his eyes looking left at patches of sand between trees, and grass—and up ahead is Spence, standing where the parking lot meets the beach, dressed in a seersucker suit, holding a pair of binoculars as if bird-watching. Robert pulls over next to him and gets out.

"You're late," Spence says.

Robert follows Spence's eyes to the waterline, to Neil, his hair dyed dark, standing at the water's edge looking out across the surf toward a Zodiac, fast approaching. Beyond them is a large fishing vessel painted white. Aeneas's ship.

"Why didn't you arrest him?" Robert asks.

"Did I say I was going to arrest him?" Spence doesn't bother to look at him.

Robert glances back at Tracy. She's still in the car, window rolled down, listening. "So Ray was working for you?" Robert turns back to Spence. "All along?"

"You can never guess what will happen to a man behind bars. Some cope. Some will do absolutely anything to get out early."

"Where is he now?"

"He overdosed last night. Tragic."

Spence lowers his binoculars, and Robert follows his gaze. Neil is barefoot and removing his shorts.

"What the hell's going on, Spence?"

"I'm observing a young man about to go for a swim. You hear about the shark attack at Bells Beach last month? Terrible thing. Could happen anywhere."

That tells Robert everything he needs to know. About the men in wetsuits and scuba gear awaiting Neil in deeper waters. About a much-rumored technique the agency used to fake deaths by shark attack: Divers would lay in wait in their scuba gear, and when the target got close, one person grabbed a leg and the other cut, using a jagged-edged knife resembling sharp teeth, hitting the femoral artery. And then they let go and disappeared. Just the style of murder that Spence's group would embrace.

Spence smiles. "Robert, don't look at me like that, like I'm some amoral creature. I operate outside of the system. Life happens outside of the system."

"He's not worth it."

"So says you, a man with unhealthy sympathies. For people out to destroy a company that is trying to save this planet from starvation. How are we going to feed ten billion people, Robert? With kale smoothies and free-range chicken? There's not enough land. Not enough water. This is about the survival of a species—our species."

"You don't have to kill him."

"I don't make that decision. But I do know this much. These people multiply like weeds. If you don't extirpate fully, they'll keep coming back."

Robert watches as Neil approaches the first wave break, diving into the water. When he surfaces again, he is a good twenty yards out to sea. Robert takes a few steps toward the water, then stops when he hears the familiar click of a now-charged Glock.

"Now hold it right there, old friend." Spence has his gun raised. "I am not dressed to play lifeguard."

"I'm not going to let this happen."

"You'll die before you reach the water."

Robert watches Neil, now paddling over a steep bank of waves. Soon it will be too late. Robert pulls off his shirt and begins removing his shoes.

"Robert, all martyrs die in the end. Let him be."

Robert turns and takes off running, waiting for the pain that is sure to come. And when he hears the shot, he stumbles down into the sand and then realizes there is no pain, and he raises his head.

Spence is on the ground, a spot of blood leaching across the back of his seersucker suit. Tracy standing over him, Robert's knife in her hand. Robert gets to his feet, stunned.

She yells at him. "Hurry!"

He turns back toward the water, and within seconds he is swimming, the waves fighting him with every stroke. He looks up to see spray and another fast-falling wall of water.

Robert should have known, should have seen it coming, and he is reaching, saltwater stinging his throat, lungs on fire. He slows to lift his head, to orient himself as a wave flips him into darkness, grasping sand and spitting and kicking to get himself back up above, and now he's trying to breathe, just treading water, trying to see which way is shore and which is ocean. Another wave drops and he sees Neil's head surface, one arm flailing.

Robert dives just as the next wave crashes, and he can see movement ahead, glints of steel, like fish scales reflecting the sun. More air and he reaches for Neil, grabs an arm and pulls him over, then dives into the spreading redness. He sees the scuba kit and reaches for the mask, punching and pulling until it comes off. Arms are holding him back, and he turns over and grabs a hand, the knife, and he's slicing into the rubber suit, the chest, arms, until he is left alone to rise to the surface for more air.

Where is Neil?

Another wetsuit grabs him, and he writhes, seal-like, until he is free. Hands pull him down again. He feels piercing stings, like jellyfish.

Another wetsuit, another knife, cutting. Waves turning him, sinking him, but he knows that he will outlast the man struggling for air in his arms. He will go a third length, a fourth length, and Neil will make it to the boat.

Billows of red in the water, like smoke. A pain in his abdomen.

To hold one's breath underwater is like dreaming—it can never last. But like any dream, it's real while it lasts. There isn't just another world underwater, there is another world in himself that opens when he enters it. And in this dreamlike underwater world, his muddled mind asks: What about the boy? What will Noa tell him when he is of age?

Robert had nearly forgotten that the water's embrace is complete and suffocating. The human body is 70 percent water, and yet he is drowning in it; Neil is drowning in it. Maybe this was the original sin, Robert thinks—leaving the water behind. *A million years ago we pulled ourselves onto land, renounced fins and scales, and have spent every moment since wishing we were back here, floating, living in the world and not on it.*

51.

TRACY DROPS THE KNIFE AND WATCHES Robert dash into the water, disappearing under a collapsing wave. She can no longer see Neil. The Zodiac is now roller-coasting in circles. She hears Helen's voice in her head. *Bruce was dead the moment that stroke hit.* And Ray's. *Those cows are dead the moment they climb the ramp into that knocking box.* And now Neil.

He was dead the moment he got into Ray's van.

And what about her? If she had to choose a moment, she feels she died on that killing floor, the smells stinging her eyes and the sights making her wish she'd kept them closed.

She looks up to see the woman from Instagram, searching the water with desperate eyes. When the woman turns her way, Tracy approaches and tells her she is a friend of Neil's, a very good friend. And she tells this woman that she needs her to pass on a message. A very important message.

The woman, distracted and wide-eyed, nods in agreement. She opens her mouth as if to ask a question, then closes it again and turns back to the water.

Tracy returns to the car and removes Helen's pills from the hidden pocket in her jacket. "The world will catch up with us one day," she says to no one.

She empties the bag into her hand. Helen's pills. She adds Ray's pills. She doesn't count them, doesn't take them one by one; she takes them by the handful, chewing, swallowing them with water from a bottle in the cup holder. She hopes that, whatever the number of pills, it will be enough.

She looks up and sees the Zodiac, undulating in place. And then the men pull aboard a lifeless, half-naked body.

She closes her eyes, and she sees him climbing into the Zodiac, waving to her, and she's waving back. So much waving, so many waves, crashing over her now, pulling on her legs, her body surrendering, letting the water spin around and under, taking her down.

Maybe someday Neil will find her again, or she will find him. And all the animals that died while she was alive, the cows and the chickens, the dogs and the pigs and the mice with wires in their brains. The mountain lion, Benton. The house cat, Daisy.

She is with him—she can taste the saltwater in her mouth—she is trying to speak, but she can't, and it doesn't matter because he hears her perfectly now, every word she says.

52.

The best Amy can do now is pray that her watch is running fast because this bus is running slow. She's five minutes late, and by the time they pass by the Welcome to Lorne sign she is standing in the aisle, leaning over like a runner at the starting block. She looks ahead and squints into the sun reflecting off the water, looking for a large ship, a small ship, any ship that might be picking up Neil.

Around a large sweeping beach, the bus slows excruciatingly, and through the window she sees him on the shoreline, getting undressed. His shirt hits the sand, then his shorts; then he's high-stepping into the water and swimming away from her.

She wants to call to him, but she is trapped behind the glass of the bus. When the bus stops, she nudges forward, squeezing past the other passengers and leaping down the steps to gravel, falling on her knees. By the time she's crossed the street and reached the sand, she can no longer see Neil.

She hears a woman shout and glances to her left to see a man racing toward the water; then she follows the voice back to the woman, a knife in her hand, standing over another man's body, a well-dressed man in a suit.

Amy looks back at the water and sees Neil, swimming, thankfully, away from shore. A Zodiac is closing in, with two men on board in bright red lifejackets, one seated back by the engine and the other standing up front, a large man with a graying beard. Neil is inching closer, his arms outstretched, one after another, clawing against the water.

53.

Robert blinks to confirm he is not dreaming. Or dead. Faces above, looking down on him. Salt burning his eyes, his legs chilled and damp.

A surfer in tie-dyed board shorts is bent over him, his damp blond hair dangling inches above Robert's nose. "You okay, mate?"

Waves of pain, sharp, emanate from below his chest. Robert raises his head as far as he can before his abdomen seizes up, and he hears himself moaning. A woman is holding a T-shirt, stained red, over his stomach. He blinks and tries to focus. Her face. Why is it familiar?

"Easy now," she says. "You're cut."

Robert turns his head toward the sound of the waves. The horizon is empty. No Zodiac. No boats. He drops his head back down; what little energy he has left is gone. The surfer is now kneeling next to him.

"Where is he?"

"Who?"

"I was so. So close."

"Too right you were. Bloody shark attack," the surfer says. "You're lucky to be alive, mate."

Robert turns his head to the other side. He can see his car, and now a police car is alongside, with a woman in uniform looking over Spence's body. Sirens in the distance.

Robert pictures Tracy's face as she stuck the knife into Spence's back, that tortured expression of rage and regret, causing Spence to lose his aim just as he was firing the weapon. She saved his life—his was not the life she intended to save, but she saved him nonetheless. He can't see her and wonders where she is. He can imagine the guilt she's feeling, but she didn't know any better, couldn't have known all the reckless games people like him play for a living. For her, this was never a game.

He remembers the woman's face and looks at her again. "Amaranta Bakas?"

She nods, tears welling in her eyes, telling him all he needs to know.

THROUGH THE REAR WINDOW of the ambulance Robert watches the Great Ocean Road pass by in reverse, his body swaying with each curve, the sounds of radio chatter behind him. He looks over at Amaranta, who told him to call her Amy, as she stares out the same window.

In the hospital, as the Diprivan takes hold, he finds himself resenting the absence of pain, for it was all he could process on the road here. Now he must think about Neil, about the young woman seated next to him.

A male doctor with a Greek accent tells him he's lost a fair amount of blood but that nothing internal appears to be nicked. They have sutured him up but need to watch him overnight. Then he lowers his voice. "They tell me this was a shark attack."

Robert nods.

"Did you see the shark?"

"Yes."

"These wounds are not entirely consistent with a shark's bite," the doctor says. "I've seen my share over the years."

"I saw it." Robert stares down the doctor, hoping he'll believe the lie. Nothing good can come out of the truth at this point. Neil is gone, the divers are gone—whose lives will the truth save now?

The doctor looks at him doubtfully, then types a few sentences on a computer terminal and leaves.

Amy is staring at him with accusing eyes. "Did you really see a shark?"

Robert shakes his head.

"You tried to save him. Why?"

"I knew his father. I thought I could help."

She grabs a tissue from the counter and turns her back to him.

"Were you and Neil close?" he asks.

"How close can you get in two weeks?"

"Close enough."

Robert's mind turns to Noa; hadn't they known each other only a week before he would have sacrificed everything for her?

Amy turns to him. "This woman, the one by your car. The one with the knife?"

He remembers the way the police looked inside the rental car, just as Robert was being carted away.

"She overdosed on something."

Robert remembers Tracy looking at him with pleading eyes, the knife at her side and a limp body below her. "Her name was Tracy," Robert says.

"I know. She spoke to me. Before. She wanted me to tell you something." She pauses. "If you lived."

Tracy would have recognized Amy from the photograph that Robert showed her. Would have known that Amy would wait on that beach until the awful end.

"What is it?" Robert asks.

"She said she lied to you that night. In the hotel."

"Lied?"

"She said Cameron has your eyes." Amy looks at Robert. "What does that mean?"

Robert leans his head back and stares at the ceiling tiles. He wants to tell Amy that it means he is a father, but he can't speak—the beeping noise grows suddenly loud; the doctor rushes in, shining a light in his eyes; the taste of blood fills the back of his throat.

One surgery and five days later, Robert is released from the hospital. A surgeon removed the damaged half of his spleen, leaving behind a pain in his side that won't quit.

Amy escorts him to a waiting taxi, and they go back to the hotel. Robert is able to walk unassisted but appreciates having her there to spot him every step of the way. He can tell she stayed in Melbourne to avoid going home, that she is obsessing over him as a way to keep her mind off Neil. And, for a similar reason, he refuses to take his pain medication, letting the searing ache in his abdomen keep his mind off Noa.

That afternoon, Amy brings him a baked tofu sandwich and salad. "How are you feeling?"

"Okay. Relieved they didn't take part of my liver. Because I'll need a drink soon."

They sit in silence at the room's small table. She looks unhinged, or maybe he's just projecting.

The next day Robert leaves Amy at the hotel for one final trip. His body rigid with bandages and bruises and pain, he manages to drive the rental car back to Lorne and lets out a loud moan when he reaches into the car to grab the slate-colored urn.

It's cloudy and drizzling, and he walks the empty beach to the edge of the water. The urn is made of plastic, and he imagines Tracy asking if it's recyclable. He pries off the lid and looks inside. The urn is only half full, and he wonders whether this is typical or whether Tracy was lighter than most bodies, whether there was less to burn.

The instructions to cremate the body had come from Tracy's brother, when he was reached by local authorities, but he hadn't wanted the ashes shipped home. It made Robert sad to think she had no one—no one at all to return home to, even in this state—and at the same time a part of him was glad because he knew what she would have wanted. To be with Neil, whatever the cost.

As he stands at the shore, the water soaks through his shoes, his body sinking under unstable sand. He turns the urn sideways, and the breeze pulls the ashes into the water until he is left holding an empty container.

54.

In the lobby, Amy gives Robert her contact information. She feels a sudden bout of loneliness at the thought of him leaving, and he stands hesitantly in front of her, as if he doesn't want to leave either. He has been a good distraction this last week, and perhaps she's been one for him, too.

Impulsively, she leans into him, and he meets her halfway. By the time her head touches his shoulder, she is in tears.

"I could stay a few days longer." His voice is soothing in her ear.

She pulls away. "No. I'll be fine."

She forces a smile and walks him outside, sees him into a taxi. Then she returns to her room, where she sits on the bed and stares at the TV screen, flipping channels aimlessly, not listening but letting the sounds crowd her brain so she doesn't have to think of anything else.

She rubs her thumb along the necklace Neil gave her. She presses it with her fingers, as if it's a worry stone, and suddenly she feels something click.

When she looks at the necklace, she notices a gap in the metal that wasn't there before. She pulls until one side of the necklace comes off, like a cap. Inside, there is a USB connector.

This necklace is a flash drive.

On her laptop, she clicks on the drive, named *Mouse*.

And there are the files. Hundreds of documents. She opens one and tries to read between the legalese and scientific words. Something about *harming test subject, long-term damage*. She opens another file. An e-mail. One person asking what to do about the study. The reply: *DELETE IT ALL*.

Tests that show damage to children, women, pets. Long-term spikes in skin and stomach cancer. Water-supply contaminations. Carcinogenic outcomes.

She selects a half dozen files and e-mails them to the *New York Times* with the subject line: *A brave man died to deliver these.*

BEFORE HER PLANE TOUCHES DOWN IN LOS ANGELES, the news will have seeped across Internet news sites like spilled coffee. She sits in the terminal, waiting for her connection to St. Louis, as a talking head on the television comments on this morning's *New York Times* story. The leaked files.

THE GREATEST HEALTH CRISIS SINCE THE JUNGLE, reads one headline. Biosant has no comment. Attorneys general from three states promise investigations, hearings, litigation. And it's not even the end of the business day.

Her mind drifts back to the beach, as she'd stood on the sand, helpless, watching his lifeless body pulled into the Zodiac. Sirens were on their way, a crowd beginning to gather. Her legs gave out at some point. She remembers looking at her hands, half buried, her tears making a pattern, like stars, in the sand.

Now, she stares at her phone. The status updates. The overflowing inbox. She thinks of how Neil would see her now, what he would be thinking. *Well done, Eat Pray Love,* he'd say. *Well done.*

Chad will be upset she didn't tell him when she was landing in St. Louis. But it's better this way. He'll want to know what happened to the ring, and she doesn't want to lie to him. Not just yet. There will be time.

Besides, he will have his hands full with his client. Biosant will want to sue the *New York Times* and will try to find the insider who leaked the files.

She reaches up for the necklace. The files are still on it and will remain there, until she finds something to replace them with.

When she lands in St. Louis, she catches a cab to her apartment, dumps her mail on the counter, gets a drink of water. The living room feels so much smaller than when she left it, and quiet. Too quiet. She turns the TV on, then off again. She opens her backpack and spills the contents onto her bed, clothes she grew to loathe from wearing them day after day.

Neil's baseball cap. How it ended up in her bag she doesn't remember. She picks it up and smells it, his salt and sweat, and she can picture him seated below the sail looking at her with those eyes, no longer so elusive. When did he sneak it in there? Maybe after she dyed his hair. Maybe he figured he was too recognizable in it.

She adjusts the strap and slides the cap onto her head.

When Chad sees her that evening, he says, "Nice to see you're finally supporting the team." She forces a smile to hold back the tears.

It's after midnight, and she's at her laptop. Earlier, she broke up with Chad. He wasn't as upset as she imagined he'd be. He stared at her quietly and asked if she had met another guy.

"No," she said.

"What about Indiana Jones?"

She's surprised he knew, that he'd been following her blog all along. "It's just me now."

"I had a feeling when you left that you wouldn't come back," he said. "To me, I mean."

"I'm sorry, Chad. I didn't plan it this way."

"I know."

They'd parted with a long hug, and to her surprise, it felt good. Being with Chad had always felt like being in the past rather than looking toward the future, and now, finally, they fit—just two people who had once been in love, saying good-bye.

Now, she's doing a search on the Pacific pocket mouse. The San Diego Zoo is breeding them, using PVC pipes as homes. And one day they will be reintroduced to the beaches. "We can reverse extinction," says the director. "As long as we save the last mating pair."

She imagines Neil hibernating somewhere, under the sand or sea, waiting for the right moment to reappear and wake her from her sleep with that question, that question that she could have ignored, should have declined. But she didn't. She nodded. She dressed. She joined the stranger outside. And together they walked in the darkness.

55.

ROBERT STANDS IN THE MELBOURNE AIRPORT terminal looking up at the departure monitor. So many places he could go from here, back to Washington or South Africa, somewhere else altogether. But he knows there is only one place left for him to go.

As he drinks a whiskey and watches the digital airplane hovering over the Tasman Sea, he thinks about how this plane will take fifteen hours to arrive in LA and yet, by crossing back over the dateline, the calendar will not move forward. If only he could turn back that calendar, he might have saved more lives, might have spent the past four years raising a boy instead of chasing a ghost.

HE ARRIVES IN MEDFORD just before noon. During the twenty-minute drive to Ashland, he thinks about what Noa will say when she sees him standing on her porch. The prodigal father returned to a fatherless child. Will she let him inside so that he can kneel down and extend a hand to the little man who shares his eyes?

Ever since he left Melbourne he has replayed Amy's words in his head: *Cameron has your eyes.* Of course he does. And of course Noa would name the boy after Aeneas. Not Neil, as Robert had believed.

As he makes his way down Main Street, past the theater, he begins to appreciate this tiny town at the base of fir-carpeted hills, a snow-capped mountain in the distance. He could be happy here. Maybe Noa won't take him back, but he'll rent a place a nearby so he can be here for the boy, for soccer games and teacher's meetings, for hikes up into the hills, to help field all those questions little boys ask.

He pulls up in front of her house, half expecting to see her on the porch.

Robert climbs the steps and knocks. Then knocks again. After another minute he walks over to a window and peeks in, seeing an empty room.

He tries the handle, and the door opens. The bare walls and floors amplify his footsteps. The bedroom, kitchen, closets—all empty.

The only evidence that she was ever here is a magnet on the fridge, in the shape of a pirate's flag with the words CETACEAN DEFENSE ALLIANCE. And under this flag an old map, probably torn out of an atlas, displaying the Galápagos Islands with one island circled in blue ink. He tries to read the name of the island, but words are becoming hazy before his eyes.

Robert had sworn to follow Noa to the ends of the earth and every body of water in between. And before he returns to his car to head back to the airport, he pulls the map from under the magnet and folds it into his pocket.

Acknowledgments

This novel is dedicated to the researchers and activists who have dedicated their lives to protecting animals. To learn more, and to lend your support, please visit:

Center for Ecosystem Sentinels
www.ecosystemsentinels.org

Farm Animal Rights Movement (FARM)
www.farmusa.org

International Fund for Animal Welfare
www.ifaw.org

Our Hen House
www.ourhenhouse.org

The Sea Shepherd Society
www.seashepherd.org

About the Author

John Yunker, author of *The Tourist Trail*, writes plays, short stories, and novels about the conflicted and evolving relationships between humans and animals. He is a co-founder of Ashland Creek Press and editor of the anthologies *Among Animals*, *Among Animals 2,* and *Writing for Animals*. His plays have been produced and staged at such venues as Centre Stage New Play Festival, Oregon Contemporary Theatre, and the ATHE (Association for Theatre in Higher Education) conference. His teleplay *Sanctuary* was performed at the Compassion Arts Festival in New York, and his short stories have been published in *Phoebe*, *Qu*, *Flyway*, *Antennae*, and other journals.

Ashland Creek Press is a small, independent publisher of books for a better planet. Our mission is to publish a range of books that foster an appreciation for worlds outside our own, for nature and the animal kingdom, for the creative process, and for the ways in which we all connect. To keep up-to-date on new and forthcoming works, subscribe to our free newsletter by visiting www.AshlandCreekPress.com.

www.ingramcontent.com/pod-product-compliance
Lightning Source LLC
Chambersburg PA
CBHW020554310726
48979CB00008B/1216/J